Pr[...]

". . . who has c[...]
erotic an[...]
—Es[...] Romance

KISSING MIDNIGHT

"A dark velvet caress for the senses, *Kissing Midnight* is a powerfully seductive, decadent paranormal romance. Emma Holly's name on the cover guarantees a smoking-hot read."
—Lara Adrian

COURTING MIDNIGHT

"There is mystery, adventure, and lots of hot sex. Fans of vampire, werewolf, and shape-shifter romances can savor this one."
—*Romantic Times*

"A wonderful blend of emotional depth and explicit sensuality—it's just what I always hope for in an erotic romance. The result is a rewarding experience for any reader who prefers a high level of heat in her romance reading."
—*The Romance Reader*

"A wonderful . . . supernatural romance."
—*ParaNormal Romance Reviews*

"A torrid paranormal historical tale that will thrill fans."
—*Midwest Book Review*

continued . . .

HUNTING MIDNIGHT

"Sets the standards on erotica-meets-paranormal . . . Will have you making a wish for a man with a little wolf in him."
                                        —*Rendezvous*

"Amazing . . . Red-hot to the wall."   —*The Best Reviews*

"A roller-coaster ride of hot passion, danger, magick, and true love."   —*Historical Romance Club*

CATCHING MIDNIGHT

"A marvelously gripping mix of passion, sensuality, paranormal settings, betrayal, and triumph . . . Dazzling . . . A sensual feast."   —*Midwest Book Review*

"Holly has outdone herself in this erotic tale . . . A must read."   —*Affaire de Coeur*

"A wonderfully passionate read."   —*Escape to Romance*

ALL U CAN EAT

"Amazing! . . . A must read. There are no excuses for missing out on this book."   —*Romance Junkies*

"The sensuality level is out of this world . . . It's light-hearted, deliciously naughty, and simply perfect fun."
                                        —*All About Romance*

THE DEMON'S DAUGHTER

"A sensually erotic novel, and one of Ms. Holly's most entertaining."
—*The Best Reviews*

"Thoroughly engrossing . . . An exceptional book . . . A must-have for fans of more erotic romance." —*Booklist*

STRANGE ATTRACTIONS

"A sizzling, erotic romance . . . Readers will enjoy this wild tale."
—*The Best Reviews*

"A different kind of erotic story." —*Sensual Romance*

PERSONAL ASSETS

"For a sensual and sweeping examination of contemporary relationships, with the extra zing of some very hot erotic writing, you can't do better than *Personal Assets*."
—*Reviews by Celia*

BEYOND SEDUCTION

"Holly brings a level of sensuality to her storytelling that may shock the uninitiated . . . [A] combination of heady sexuality and intriguing characterization."
—*Publishers Weekly*

"Emma Holly once again pens an unforgettably erotic love story." —*Affaire de Coeur*

More praise for Emma Holly and her novels

"Emma Holly is a name to look out for!"   —Robin Schone

"A sensual feast."   —*Midwest Book Review*

"A wonderfully passionate read."   —*Escape to Romance*

"Fans of bolder romances will relish [Emma Holly]."
—*Publishers Weekly*

"A wonderful tale of creative genius and unbridled passion."   —*Affaire de Coeur*

"Ms. Holly is a rising star who creates tantalizing tales . . . Delicious."   —*Rendezvous*

"Steamy sex, interesting characters, and a story that offers a couple of twists . . . A page-turning read."
—*The Romance Reader*

"The love scenes were an excellent mixture of eroticism and romance, and they are some of the best ones I have read this year."   —*All About Romance*

"I was captivated . . . and fascinated . . . Powerful erotic overtones . . . that will fulfill readers' desires for Holly's signature erotic love stories."   —*Romantic Times*

"A winner in every way."   —*Romance Reviews Today*

"With an author like Emma Holly . . . a sizzling erotic novel is guaranteed."   —*A Romance Review*

Books by Emma Holly

Upyr Books

The Fitz Clare Chronicles

SAVING MIDNIGHT
BREAKING MIDNIGHT
KISSING MIDNIGHT

COURTING MIDNIGHT
HOT BLOODED
(with Christine Feehan, Maggie Shayne, and Angela Knight)
HUNTING MIDNIGHT
CATCHING MIDNIGHT
FANTASY
(with Christine Feehan, Sabrina Jeffries, and Elda Minger)

Tales of the Demon World

DEMON'S FIRE
BEYOND THE DARK
(with Angela Knight, Lora Leigh, and Diane Whiteside)
DEMON'S DELIGHT
(with MaryJanice Davidson, Vickie Taylor, and Catherine Spangler)
PRINCE OF ICE
HOT SPELL
(with Lora Leigh, Shiloh Walker, and Meljean Brook)
THE DEMON'S DAUGHTER

BEYOND SEDUCTION
BEYOND INNOCENCE

ALL U CAN EAT
FAIRYVILLE
STRANGE ATTRACTIONS
PERSONAL ASSETS

Anthologies

HEAT OF THE NIGHT
MIDNIGHT DESIRE
BEYOND DESIRE

SAVING
MIDNIGHT

EMMA HOLLY

B

BERKLEY SENSATION, NEW YORK

THE BERKLEY PUBLISHING GROUP
Published by the Penguin Group
Penguin Group (USA) Inc.
375 Hudson Street, New York, New York 10014, USA
Penguin Group (Canada), 90 Eglinton Avenue East, Suite 700, Toronto, Ontario M4P 2Y3, Canada
(a division of Pearson Penguin Canada Inc.)
Penguin Books Ltd., 80 Strand, London WC2R 0RL, England
Penguin Group Ireland, 25 St. Stephen's Green, Dublin 2, Ireland (a division of Penguin Books Ltd.)
Penguin Group (Australia), 250 Camberwell Road, Camberwell, Victoria 3124, Australia
(a division of Pearson Australia Group Pty. Ltd.)
Penguin Books India Pvt. Ltd., 11 Community Centre, Panchsheel Park, New Delhi—110 017, India
Penguin Group (NZ), 67 Apollo Drive, Rosedale, North Shore 0632, New Zealand
(a division of Pearson New Zealand Ltd.)
Penguin Books (South Africa) (Pty.) Ltd., 24 Sturdee Avenue, Rosebank, Johannesburg 2196,
South Africa

Penguin Books Ltd., Registered Offices: 80 Strand, London WC2R 0RL, England

This is a work of fiction. Names, characters, places, and incidents either are the product of the author's imagination or are used fictitiously, and any resemblance to actual persons, living or dead, business establishments, events, or locales is entirely coincidental. The publisher does not have any control over and does not assume any responsibility for author or third-party websites or their content.

SAVING MIDNIGHT

A Berkley Sensation Book / published by arrangement with the author

PRINTING HISTORY
Berkley Sensation mass-market edition / August 2009

ISBN: 978-0-425-22904-0

BERKLEY® SENSATION
Berkley Sensation Books are published by The Berkley Publishing Group,
a division of Penguin Group (USA) Inc.,
375 Hudson Street, New York, New York 10014.
BERKLEY® SENSATION and the "B" design are trademarks of Penguin Group (USA) Inc.

PRINTED IN THE UNITED STATES OF AMERICA

10 9 8 7 6 5 4 3 2 1

To Herman and Edna
who came through it all
and always remained themselves.

Chicago: April 1, 1934

❧❦❧

The vampire in the double-breasted suit and fedora strode down Michigan Avenue as if the city belonged to him. In that moment, it almost did. The hour was just past dusk—Jack didn't need to sleep as long as he once had—and on the so-called Magnificent Mile, the night was murky and thick and cool. The inescapable scent of the Union Stock Yards, that hog butchery extraordinaire, made his nostrils flare pleasantly. Through the astringent mist, the spires of skyscrapers rose. Some, like the floodlit Wrigley Building up ahead, were barely ten years old. While the boom had lasted, the frenzy of construction had excited him. Humans had died building those towers, simply slipped from the great steel girders and plummeted.

But that was done now, and there were other pleasures to be had. Times were hard in the Windy City. The Great Depression had coated the Americans' spirits like a film of soot from their factories. Hopelessness, despair, a poverty that was all the worse for having taken them by surprise, created a bouquet as sweet to the vampire's nose as the dying hogs. Why, under this very street, on the shadowed lower level that had been built to ease the city's traffic snarls, dull-eyed men waited in breadlines. Their misery made them easy pickings, nor did Jack have to worry over-much about discovery. These days, the authorities barely blinked if people died mysteriously.

Thanks to the Wall Street Crash and its ensuing social chaos, Jack was stronger than he'd ever been. Thanks to that strength, he had thralled himself both riches and a lovely penthouse on Lake Shore Drive. *Some* people always had money, and why shouldn't they hand it to him? Soon he would be an elder, a prince among vampire kind—and all before the age of two hundred.

Life had been good since Jack had broken faith with his queen a century ago.

His stride hitched at the thought of her. Ten centuries could not erase his memory of her ruthlessness, the utter lack of mercy with which she met betrayal. He reminded himself Nim Wei must have lost track of him by now. He'd been wise to run to this country, though it had been a harrowing trip at the time. His maker had never had much affinity for the Americas, preferring the cities of Europe and Asia as the base for her empire. Jack was forgotten, anonymous, gathering power day by day until he could stand toe-to-toe with any immortal—even his queen—without flinching.

He jiggled the old brass box that lay wrapped in a kerchief in his coat pocket. Hard to believe this homely item was the key to his dreams. The casket looked like nothing: a three-inch tarnished round that wouldn't have fetched two dollars at an antique shop. Its lid bore a worn engraving of a Chinese dragon, with small, clear rubies to serve as eyes. On one side, a hinge allowed the lid to flip back, revealing razor-sharp jagged edges—a tiny shark's mouth in stained metal.

When placed over a dying human's heart, that mouth would swallow their soul and transfer its strength to him.

Smiling, Jack turned left on Harrison, heading across the Chicago River toward his favorite shantytown. The Hooverville was named for America's recently unseated president, an honor that worthy gentleman likely would have forgone. Jack's footsteps made no sound as cars continued to roll by him, fewer now, worn tires whooshing on the cracked macadam. Many were black and boxy and—by human standards—years out of style. Presumably their owners were glad to have them. Jack ignored the drivers' glances at his tall, well-dressed form. Perhaps they thought him a heartless factory boss or a still-thriving

bootlegger. Few men walked with his confidence these
days.

Reminded of the need not to lose all caution, Jack
pulled his glamour closer around him to damp his glow.
Every vampire shone a bit to human sight, and drawing
more attention would be unwelcome. Though his glamour's camouflage could hide him, he did not speed up from
his human pace. Why should he, with prey so plentiful and
no fellow immortals to share it with? He, alone, hunted
this birthplace of skyscrapers. He could afford to savor the
stroll to his nightly meal.

His meal waited up ahead. The Canal Street shantytown had risen from a large empty lot beneath the shadow
of the "L"—the humans' nickname for the elevated train.
The ramshackle village didn't shelter hardened criminals,
just ordinary people down on their luck in ways they hadn't
known how to prepare for. They'd built their homes, if you
could call them that, out of whatever materials they could
scrounge: tar paper, flattened tin cans, the remnants of
broken cars. Sometimes whole families lived in the small
structures, drawing rainwater from the ditches and sleeping under "Hoover blankets" of newspaper. Tonight, fires
burned in rusted barrels, clots of men gathering around
them to warm themselves—an oddly primitive scene for
this modern world. Though Canal Street's residents came
and went, in Jack's experience, their conversations rarely
varied. Work was what these men's talk circled around:
who had heard where it might be found; how Roosevelt
was changing things.

For his own sake, Jack hoped the "New Deal" president
wouldn't succeed soon.

He slipped into the coal black shadows beyond the reach
of the fires, seeking likely targets who had strayed from
the herd. Women worked, while the men waxed wistful,
struggling to contrive a meal, to keep themselves and their
children clean. Jack admired them with the intensity of a
predator for a fawn. They were so beautiful, so vulnerable,
so blessedly unlikely to fight when he caught their tired
eyes with his.

And then he saw her: his lily of the valley of vampire death. She was seventeen or thereabouts, with long jet curls and cornflower eyes. Her skin was creamy, her lips and cheeks stained as if with wine. She was carrying an empty wooden bucket, picking her way barefoot toward the communal cistern where the cleanest water was. He'd been watching her for weeks now, waiting for his chance, but he'd never caught her apart from the protection of her family. His chest tightened with longing, and he pressed his fist to the budding ache. Such life there was in her, her spirit too young to be worn down yet.

He knew her soul would be rich.

No one else waited at the tank. She bent to the cistern, her breasts swaying forward in her cheap printed dress as she dipped the bucket in. Jack's heart thundered in his chest.

"Might I be of help?" he asked.

Startled, her gaze came up. She hadn't seen him waiting in the dark. The moment her eyes met his, she belonged to him.

"Hush," he murmured, putting his thrall in it. "You don't want to make a sound."

She was frozen, trembling, her lips parted on a gasp. Jack felt his body harden in a dizzying surge. His hand was in his pocket, gripping the brass casket. He rolled it once and then let it go. He would play with her before he killed her. He would drive his cold vampire hardness into her beautiful human fire. He stepped toward her on the rutted ground, close enough to draw the tips of his fingers down her lovely neck. Her pulse was skipping. His fangs surged as his cock had, the sharp points pushing over his lower lip.

The thought of his victim seeing them and being frightened was thrilling.

"God," she whispered, surprising him. "They didn't pay me enough for this."

Jack's mind refused to comprehend her words. Who would have paid her and for what?

Without a single twig to snap in warning, he heard the

hollow rachet of a shotgun cocking behind his head. Now Jack was the one to freeze, his muscles twitching at the suddenness of his alarm. Had his lily's family followed her? And, if so, how had they gotten the drop on him? Jack's ears could perceive the bending of a blade of grass. He cursed his lack of weapons, but a creature like himself had little need for guns. Certainly, not among mortals.

When his accoster spoke, his shock doubled.

"Hello, Jack," said a cool, German-accented voice. "Long time, no see."

A shudder rippled down Jack's spine. He'd been caught by another vampire, by Frank Hauptmann, unless his memory misled him: his queen's steel-hearted enforcer and private guard.

A female he didn't know, who must have been changed after Jack escaped Nim Wei's rule, stepped with equal silence in front of him. Dressed in trousers and a dark pea-coat, she was Oriental and delicate, many inches shorter than the victim he had culled tonight. Despite the difference in their sizes, his lily deferred to the vampiress as the female took her shoulders in a soothing hold, shushing her with a soft *there, there, everything's all right.* He saw then what he had missed in his elation at finding his prize alone: the faintest smear of *upyr* energy halfway up her throat.

"You bit her," Jack burst out. "You marked her before I could!"

Such was his outrage that his limbs tensed in preparation to defend his claim.

"I wouldn't do that if I were you," the female vampire warned. "Frank has iron rounds in that gun."

Though his kind healed most injuries, iron could kill them—no matter what power they had amassed. Jack controlled his impulse with an effort. "How did you find me?"

"There's an interesting story." The female's eyes lit with amusement, gold sparks swimming in her dark irises. "It seems the shapechanging vampires have been keeping a list of *upyr* whereabouts, a supernatural address directory of sorts. Few of Nim Wei's get are on it, but you slipped into their sights when you stole a certain trinket from a buried cache in Mongolia."

His lily shivered when her captor's fingers trailed across the bend of her arm, seeming dazed by the gentle touch. Watching her reaction, Jack felt equally hypnotized. He swallowed as his mouth watered.

"Those mountains are wolf territory," the vampiress continued, "in case you had any doubt. And wolves tend to take notice of intruders. They tracked you to a trawler heading for New York, where, apparently, the scent went cold. Luckily, my darling Frank remembered your predilections, and we simply followed the trail of pretty young disappeared girls here." She wound one of his lily's sable curls around her forefinger. "You do have a type, Jack. Very distinctive. I love when our kind do what we expect, don't you, sweets?"

Her "sweets" may have made some gesture of agreement, but Jack didn't dare take his eyes off the woman in front of him.

"We want the casket," the queen's enforcer said crisply.

"I don't have it," Jack lied, his voice as earnest as he could make it. "Someone stole it from me in New York."

Frank pushed the shotgun's double barrels into Jack's skull. "Don't waste our time, Jackie-boy. We know you have it. You reek of power you never had the stones to wield. Hand it over, or I'll blow your head off."

Jack didn't have a choice. Frank and he might be close in age, but from the moment of his change, the German had been more powerful. Frank probably would have been a master if their queen hadn't been so good at denying those she made that gift. Jack's only hope was to pray that his precious casket had given him an advantage.

He spun before Frank could shoot, his fist smashing in an arc across Frank's handsome Teutonic face. This was the last good hit Jack got in. Frank was used to fighting his own kind and, by nature and training, was as vicious as he was quick. Blood flew from Jack's nose, from his ribs, from his ears, as Frank boxed them at super speed. Jack tried to grab the gun, but his hands were slippery with gore.

A weight jumped onto his back. Jack threw himself backward as Frank's diminutive partner wrenched at his hair, practically tearing it from his scalp. He should have disabled her when his greater weight slammed her into the ground. Instead, he felt her little hand searching among his clothes.

"No!" he growled, lifting his torso so he could drive her into the dirt again.

His attention strayed from Frank, and that was no small mistake. With nothing to block it, the German's boot kicked a lightning bolt of agony straight up the center of Jack's groin.

"Got it!" his partner gasped, drawing the round brass box from Jack's coat pocket.

Jack couldn't even try to grab for it. Helpless not to, he rolled, groaning, onto his side to cradle his injured crotch. It felt like Frank had pulverized his genitals, the unbelievable pain of his shattered pelvis causing tears to squeeze from his eyes. He almost didn't notice Frank taking aim with the long shotgun.

"Wait," he managed to say as Frank braced the stock in the forward cup of his broad shoulder. Frank's trigger finger jerked but did not contract. Jack mustered a shred of hope. "We can share the casket. This city is a feast, like fruit falling in your mouth. All of us could prosper. None of us need return to our queen."

Frank's laugh was low and husky, his fangs still sharp from the fight. "What makes you think we were planning to?"

The news that Frank had slipped Nim Wei's leash turned the blood in Jack's veins to ice. Frank was close to being an elder already. Add the power of the Chinese casket to what he had, and no force on earth would keep him contained.

"You'll need instruction," he tried to bargain, knowing Frank thought he had no reason to spare his life. "Guidance on how to handle what the casket does. If you're not accustomed to it, it's a lot of energy to assimilate—especially if you start taking souls too fast."

"Oh, please. If an idiot like you can work it, how difficult could it be for me?"

"For us," his female partner corrected. She was cuddling Jack's lily again, chafing her long, bare arms—though whether to warm the human or herself was hard to say. Apparently, her hold on the girl was so compelling she had not thought to run away. Seeing this, Frank regarded his partner with a fondness Jack would never have expected.

Back when Jack knew him, Frank hadn't loved anyone but himself.

"Yes," Frank agreed. "Most certainly it will be easy for both of us." Seeming reluctant, he refocused his gaze on Jack. "We heard the same stories you did. Let me assure you, your prize will not go to waste."

Grinning now, he crooked his finger tighter on the trigger. Jack's pulse beat like a drum behind his clavicle. Still Frank didn't shoot. He was dragging out the moment, perhaps for no better reason than because he relished drinking in Jack's fear. Jack would have run if he'd been able, but his broken pelvis precluded that. Soft crackling sounds signaled that the bones were trying to knit. Too bad Frank wasn't likely to give him the long, slow minutes he'd take to heal.

"Do it then," he said, his defiance unconvincing even to himself. "Kill me if you're going to."

"Soon," Frank promised, his whisper sweet and caressing. "Any second the timing will be right."

Then Jack heard what Frank was waiting for: the distant rattle and wail of the westbound "L." The wail became a shriek as the train barreled toward them on the high, dark track, more than loud enough to drown out gunfire.

Now, Frank mouthed, and pumped both barrels of shot into him. Jack's field of vision flashed white with shock. The pain was astounding, the multiple iron pellets like ice boring through his bones. His body began convulsing, the souls he'd stolen escaping from his wounds in shining, evanescent wisps. In flocks they abandoned him, hundreds flickering like ghostly rainbows into the night.

No, he thought, but he had no power to call them back. Those souls would go to whatever fate they'd been destined for before he'd captured them. They hadn't saved him, in any case.

"Pretty," the female vampire observed. She tossed his box in the air, the tarnished metal gleaming dully as it spun back into her palm. She had Jack's lily by one elbow, the human's long black curls falling with picture-perfect grace to obscure the vampiress's deceptively gentle hold. Jack felt himself weakening by the instant, though every nerve still blazed with torment. He no longer had the breath to warn the girl of her danger.

She, by contrast, seemed unconcerned that he was dying.

"What were those lights?" she marveled. "Where were they flying to?"

The female vampire stroked her downy cheek without answering. "You're pretty, too, aren't you? And so convenient with us needing to test our new toy."

"Very," Frank concurred, stepping over Jack to draw nearer to the pair.

He was letting his glamour fall, letting the human see his true beauty. The girl's jaw dropped as his unearthly glow rose into his face.

Her awe must have been arousing. Frank's breath came quicker.

"Look at you," Jack's lily exclaimed. "I swear, you're the swellest thing!"

Jack hated hearing her admiration, hated that his killers would pluck the fragrant flower he had so desired. But there was nothing he could do to stop it. The last thing he witnessed before the world went black was Frank sinking his fangs into the human girl's soft, fair neck.

London

Pen's relationship with her father was both simple and complicated. She adored him, as he did her, but because they were equally strong-willed, they had the occasional tendency to butt heads.

Considering she was already in the doghouse for some recent actions on a friend's behalf, she decided not to butt back today.

Her father had rung her at Claridge's, where he and Pen resided while in London. When he'd asked her to his office, his tone had been brisker than usual. Alerted that something was up, she'd pulled on a new and rather modest dress. Though she was more comfortable in trousers, and her father was in many ways a progressive man, he liked seeing her "look like a lady," as he put it.

She stepped out of her cab in front of his building and hoped her fashion choice would serve. Arnold Anderson's London offices were in the City, not far from St. Paul's Cathedral. The exterior was grimly Victorian, and the interior was a warren of halls that—no matter how they were cleaned—seemed permanently begrimed by time. By contrast, to enter the Anderson corporate suite was to be slapped in the face by the modern age. From top to bottom, everything had been refurbished and refreshed. The floors were spanking-new Italian marble, the walls done in the latest colors, the furniture sleek and artistic. Paintings of contemporary London street scenes hung on the walls, a celebration of life today. Never mind the world was strain-

ing under the Depression, this place—her father's place—
was confident and bright.

Arnold Anderson never let original conditions limit
what he planned to make of them.

In the alcove outside his personal office, his new secretary—her friend Graham's replacement, as it happened—
was working late. The young man seemed efficient, but
Pen didn't know him well enough to press him for clues to
her father's mood. Certainly, his thin-lipped, pinchy mouth
didn't invite trust. He nodded when he saw her, indicating
she was welcome to go in. Pen found herself wondering—
bitchily, perhaps—if his gift for languages was as good as
Graham's.

Her father was on the 'phone as she entered, discussing
production schedules with the head of a bottling plant. He
lifted a finger in greeting, but didn't actually look at her.
Too accustomed to such behavior to take insult, Pen sat in
a streamlined leather guest chair, smoothed her dress over
her knees, and observed the stack of files piled on his desk.
Whatever he wanted to discuss, her father was interrupting
a heavy load to broach it with her.

In no hurry to be enlightened, she enjoyed the familiar
sight of him working. It was one of the earliest sights she
could remember being comforted by. Like her, her father
was tall and rangy, getting heavier with passing years,
though Pen thought he still looked fit. His dark brown
hair was touched with silver and creeping back from his
high forehead. His most striking characteristic was his
dark, bushy brows, which—when lowered over his sharp,
whiskey-colored eyes—had been known to cause shudders
in full-grown men.

Pen's eyes were the same sunlit brown, though, thankfully, the genes for bushy eyebrows had passed her by.

At last, he placed the telephone in its cradle and met her
gaze.

"Penelope," he said, which he only called her when he
was serious.

"Daddy."

He folded his hands on his desk blotter. The desk itself was huge, a glossy black rectangle like a pool of oil. His sober posture tightened her nerves.

"I'm not sure how you're going to take this," he began, "so I'll just say it straight out. One of your aunts called me this afternoon. Your mother had a stroke this morning, and now she's dead."

"*Dead.*" The word came clearly out of Pen's mouth, but in that moment it meant nothing.

"Yes," he said, and pushed a fresh glass of water across the desk.

He'd had it poured and ready, clearly meaning her to drink, but she suddenly wasn't sure her hands were up to holding it. How could her mother be dead? Livonia Peachtree Anderson had been one of the less pleasant facts of Pen's life, someone to be avoided when possible, ignored when not, but not a person she'd thought could cease to exist. Her mother's perpetual complaints about her health had never struck Pen as authentic, even as a child. They were an affectation, a pretense to make Livonia's inborn languor seem important.

"Really?" she said aloud.

"Your aunts are idiots, it's true, but I don't see how they could be mistaken about this."

"Well." Without thinking, Pen picked up the water and gulped it down. "I suppose this means there'll be a funeral."

When her father's facial muscles contracted, she knew they'd reached the crux of this meeting. He drew a determined breath.

"You're going to Charleston. It's imperative that you attend."

"Daddy, no. Mother and I barely spoke in the last few years."

"I'm sorry, Pen. There's no getting around it. Your mother and I had an understanding. I agreed not to divorce her and to continue paying her bills. In return, she'd leave the Peachtree house to you when she died. We drew up a binding contract, but I know those sisters of hers. If you aren't there to exercise your rights, they'll convince those crazy Southern lawyers to do Lord knows what."

Pen could hardly speak through the throat-constricting power of her dismay. Yes, she liked the damn plantation—almost in spite of herself—but this was not a fight she wanted to be mixed up in. "Daddy . . ."

"A deal's a deal," her father insisted. "I won't have that woman welshing on a bargain from beyond the grave."

His hostility startled her, the way he said *that woman.* Despite her father's estrangement from his wife, he'd always been careful how he spoke about her in front of Pen. Seeming to realize what he'd done, he closed his mouth.

Then a look of decision came into his expression. "Do you remember your seventh birthday, when I had to go to Europe on business, and your mother took you back to Charleston?"

"Not really," Pen said, her shoulders tensing nonetheless.

"Well, you might remember the daughter of your mother's cousin Bob getting a fancy dollhouse as a surprise gift."

"I do!" Pen exclaimed. "It was amazing. Three stories tall, and it had furniture. Felicia bragged about it so much one of her little friends bashed her in the nose. As I recall, I was annoyed I hadn't done it first."

"That was *your* dollhouse."

"What?"

"I shipped it to our house in New York, where the housekeeper—not knowing any better—sent it on to Peachtree so you wouldn't think I'd forgotten you. Your mother decided it was 'too much of a present for you to handle.' I was so furious, I nearly took the next boat back. You'd never mistreated a gift I gave you, not from the day you were four."

"Good Lord." Pen sagged in her chair. "I *do* remember thinking that dollhouse looked a lot like our brownstone."

"I special ordered it," her father said.

"But you brought me back a gift from your trip! A little Swiss watch that kept time in two countries. For years, I'd set the second dial to match wherever you'd traveled to. And that was a replacement? I swear, Daddy, it never crossed my mind that you'd forget my birthday."

"That's something at least," said her father. "But you see why you have to go."

Pen bit her lip, hating her own weakness but unable not to make the suggestion. "You could come with me."

Her father's whole face softened. "Sweetie, I wish I could, but I've got too many irons in the fire these days. I *can't* let another company go under. Too many people depend on every job I can provide. Besides which, your temper is a damn sight better than mine. I'm afraid I'd plain kill your aunts if they started on their stuff with me."

"I understand," Pen said around the lump in her throat. "I didn't mean to be selfish."

"Jesus." With a snort she couldn't interpret, her father reached across his desk to squeeze the knot she'd made of her hands. "Sweetie, you're the least selfish girl I know. If you weren't, you wouldn't have gone gallivanting across Europe after Graham Fitz Clare and his family."

"Dad . . ."

"I know. We agreed to drop that topic, and Lord knows, I'm glad you helped save Graham's father from those kidnappers. The thing is, I know you love that damn moldering wreck. I want you to have it, and I think you do, too."

Pen pulled a face and drew her hands back into her lap. "As long as I'm in the States, I *could* swing up to Chicago and see Binky afterward."

"You could," her father agreed with the faintest smile.

"And it probably wouldn't hurt if one of us made an appearance. The newspapers might get hold of it if we don't."

"They might, though I wouldn't send you on that account. What your mother owes you is what matters."

"Everything matters," Pen said, pulling more of her usual crispness into her tone. "You're the one who taught me even gossip can hurt business."

"Now you're just scaring your old man."

Pen came around the big desk to hug him. "I love you, Daddy," she murmured into his shoulder. "And I love that you insisted on this for me—even if it is going to be a pain in the ass."

"That sounds more like my daughter," her father laughed.

He embraced her as he always did: strong and unstinting. He smelled of Pear's soap and wood shavings, his habit of sharpening pencils when he was thinking imbuing the fragrance into his clothes. He wouldn't live forever, any more than Pen's mother had. Her eyes stung with gratitude that she had him now.

"Go on then," he said, pushing her back gruffly. "I'm sure you have a few dozen trunks you're planning to pack."

Pen straightened and fought a sigh. She did have packing to do. She also had someone to say goodbye to before she left London for an undetermined amount of time.

Pen drove her smart red speedster to Bedford Square, parking the Duesenberg by the fenced-in park. The Fitz Clares' narrow Georgian-style town house stood directly opposite. For a moment, she simply sat without getting out. Her heart was thudding too fast for her own comfort.

Nearly three months had passed since she and Graham had parted in the aftermath of their adventures rescuing his father in Switzerland. During those adventures, they'd been as intimate as two healthy people of the opposite gender could become. They'd had *sex*—not to put too pretty a word on it—rough, repeated, fantastically earthshaking sex, the likes of which Pen had never experienced.

And that was leaving out the fireworks that had exploded when he'd bitten her.

Pen's slim fingers tightened on the steering wheel. In his desperation to save his father from some nasty supernatural enemies, Arnold Anderson's stolid, dull dog of a secretary had turned vampire.

Pen couldn't forget how Graham's transformation had altered her response to him. To be honest, which she thought she was mature enough to do, she'd always had a teensy bit of a thing for him. Graham was a good man: reliable, intelligent, hardworking—and, if not handsome, by no means ugly. When he'd become a vampire, the unexpected increase in his masculine confidence had turned Pen's knees to jelly. Despite having captivated many men herself, she hadn't known how to resist him. Once she'd sampled his new forcefulness in bed, she hadn't really wanted to try.

This annoyed her inordinately, especially since Graham seemed perfectly content to forget her.

He hadn't rung her up once since he'd said his last polite "thank you for saving my life" in front of her hotel. He hadn't written or sent flowers or gazed up mooningly at her rooms. Pen should have been relieved. Her father had admired and trusted his secretary, at least until he quit so summarily. Graham the vampire, however, would have been a creature so alien to her father's view of the world that Pen could not imagine how she'd have accounted for dating him. Arnold Anderson was a man of reason. How would she explain Graham roasting like a lobster if he went outside when the sun was up?

"As if you're going to *need* to explain," she muttered to herself. She and Graham weren't dating. They weren't anything, as far as she could tell.

All the same, she didn't like the thought of flying to another country without telling him.

Angry with her dithering, she opened the driver's door and slammed it shut behind her. Because she wore the ladylike dress and shoes she'd donned to mollify her father, her heels clacked across the tree-shaded street. Night had fallen, the streetlamps glowing in patches among the young spring leaves. Up the front steps she went, to the shiny black painted door. She had her hand on the knocker when she realized not a single light shone behind the Fitz Clares' tall, multipaned windows.

She craned her head back to be certain, but the rooms up to the attic were dark as well.

Pen rubbed a knuckle across her chin. The hour wasn't much past dinner, and both Graham and his adoptive father, Edmund, were vampires. Oughtn't someone to be up and about?

The click of happily trotting canine toenails brought her head around. She saw at once this arrival wasn't Graham's father in his wolf form. An older woman, presumably a neighbor, was walking a miniature terrier on a leash.

"Excuse me," Pen said. "Do you know if the Fitz Clares are home?"

"Oh, they're gone, dear," the woman said, unknowingly causing Pen's gut to drop. Her dog let out a bark at having its stroll interrupted, but the woman just patted it. "There was some sort of family emergency. I heard they might be putting this place up for sale."

Pen's mouth worked as she fought to decide which of her questions were most strategic to ask next. The Fitz Clares had left? Without a word to her? And what sort of "family emergency"? Was Graham's father in trouble again? She tried to conceal her distress, lest it cause her informant to clam up. As it was, the woman was peering at her with more curiosity than was useful.

"Do you know where they went?" Pen asked.

"Not a clue," said the woman. "One day they were here and the next—" She pursed her prunelike lips on a whooshing sound. "It was odd, now that I think back. Usually they were so good about keeping up with the neighbors."

Pen imagined Graham's family had been good at "keeping up." They had too many secrets to wish to draw attention with unfriendliness. She wanted to ask if they'd *all* left together, but hesitated. The Fitz Clares' neighbor had her head cocked at her, her eyes bright and interested.

"How do you know them, dear?" she asked.

"I used to know Graham, but we hadn't been in touch lately."

"Ah." The woman's sudden grin did frightening things to her wrinkled face. "That boy was a deep one. Not as pretty as his brother, but nice and tall. When I was your age, *I* would have kept in touch with him."

"Well," said Pen, at a loss to respond to this sally. "I suppose I should let you finish your walk."

Her long legs felt stiff as she returned to her waiting

car, her pulse out of sorts as she slid sideways into the white leather seat. She took one last look at the blank, dark house. The Fitz Clares were gone, possibly never to return. An ache like an icy splinter lodged in her breastbone.

Pen wondered if she'd ever see Graham again.

Bridesmere

The Fitz Clares' hereditary castle—if you could call a property "hereditary" when the previous owners hadn't died—was built on a scarp above a river in Northumberland. Not surprisingly, considering it was owned by vampires whose energy preserved their possessions, the fortress remained much as it had been in medieval times. Four stout towers guarded each corner of the thick square keep. Though the moat was dry, the drawbridge functioned. The battlements had not crumbled, nor the curtain wall. The interior had undergone a renovation a decade back, equipping it with plumbing and electricity and other mod cons like that.

Estelle suspected she and Edmund's daughter, Sally, would have mutinied had this not been so. Ben as well, perhaps. In the time since Estelle had become Edmund's fiancée, she'd noticed Edmund's handsome human son was quite fond of showering. Ben was a married man now, so Estelle gave him credit for continuing to put his best foot forward with Sally—and never mind how irregular their union was.

No doubt they were lucky Edmund's thrall had silenced official questions, but they were adoptive brother and sister, *not* blood relations. In any event, Estelle was in no position to tell them who and where they should love. She herself had fallen for a bloodsucking professor of history.

Eccentric connections seemed to be the name of the game these days. The castle's residents had gathered for their evening powwow in the castle's two-story library. The group included the newlyweds, plus Graham, Edmund, and Percy. Percy was a direct Fitz Clare descendant and the current owner of Bridesmere. Like his forebear, he was a vampire, though a mere eighty-some years old compared to Edmund's five hundred. In the weeks since they'd moved in with him, Percy and Ben had become fast friends, Percy being as mad for aeroplanes as Ben was for motorcars. Their host was rarely seen in anything but Charles Lindbergh–style flight clothes—including an aviator helmet and goggles. Thankfully for those who wanted to converse with him without snickering, he didn't wear the latter all the time.

De-goggled for the present, he braced his forearms on the library's second-level brass railing. He must have performed some reverse preserving trick with his aura, because his bomber jacket appeared worn. As he gazed down at his guests, he dangled his headgear casually from one hand.

"I don't know why those yobbos haven't attacked me yet," he said. "Gillian swore I was on the list Frank and Li-Hua stole. We practically issued an invitation by breaching the outer wall under the guise of creating access to my aerodrome. Given that our fearless leaders have fended off *two* assaults on our kind near Rome, I'm beginning to feel insulted."

Their fearless leaders were Aimery and Gillian, Edmund's brother and sister-in-law, who more or less shared leadership of the *Upyr* Council. References to Aimery rarely failed to set Edmund's fangs on edge. Though younger than Edmund, Aimery was the brother who'd always seemed born to rule, a situation that had not changed when they became vampires. He'd turned elder almost at once, while Edmund had taken centuries. Now Edmund was seated next to Estelle at a slanted reading table. At Percy's daredevil words, Edmund dropped his face in his palms. Though his gold-coin hair fell across his hands, it did not obscure his frustration.

Estelle knew he felt responsible for the spot they were in. Frank and Li-Hua, both less powerful vampires than Edmund, had kidnapped him in an attempt to torture out his knowledge of how to change humans. Edmund's family had rescued him in time, but because Edmund hadn't been as reckless as he might have been, Frank and Li-Hua had escaped to wreak more havoc. No one knew where the pair was now, only that they'd been targeting other members of Edmund's line. Thus far, their cohorts had killed two shapechangers in Italy and seriously injured the head of a Spanish pack. The victims had been living too remotely to receive the warnings their Council sent, nor had protecting them been Edmund's job; his brother, Aimery, had that lookout. Nonetheless, Estelle knew Edmund was taking this personally. She wanted to rub his back to comfort him, but that seemed *too* supportive. Instead, she simply placed her hand between his shoulder blades.

"Maybe I guessed wrong," he said, uncovering his face as their energy joined through the light contact. He didn't look at Estelle, but she sensed he was immediately more aware of her. Tingles moved through her arms and thighs, and she had no doubt they moved through his as well. No matter their situation, the sexual component of their connection was impossible to deny. Seemingly without thinking, he dropped his hand to her knee. "Maybe they're not planning to come after Percy."

"And maybe they are," Percy countered. "It's early days."

"We left Robin alone in London," Edmund pointed out, speaking of the son he'd sired when he was human. "If Frank and Li-Hua realize we're holed up with you, he might present the more attractive target."

"They won't go after Robin," said the smooth, emotionless voice of the final member of their party. Christian Durand had taken a chair in the farthest, darkest corner of the library. Despite his professed willingness to aid their cause, the Swiss mercenary's presence filled Estelle with unease. He'd been in Frank and Li-Hua's pay not that long ago. He'd helped the couple torment Edmund.

As if he knew what Estelle was thinking—which perhaps he did—his cool black gaze slid to hers. A green-shaded banker's lamp lit up half of his lean, hard face. He did not move to let them see him better as he continued.

"Robin is a master vampire, and my former employers have a strong attachment to their hides. Percy here"—he jerked his head toward their host—"is Edmund's closest blood tie who doesn't have sufficient power to destroy them. They know Edmund isn't liable to let you or the rest of his mortal family out of his sight. If they want revenge for Edmund mucking up their plans, Percy is the one whose death is both the most achievable and the likeliest to cut. As for them discovering Edmund is here, I doubt they can. Your . . . fiancée's skill at cloaking is formidable."

Durand's lip curled just a little as he forced out the word *fiancée*. From these and other clues he'd dropped, Estelle concluded the mercenary was no fan of the human race, and certainly not of his own kind marrying them.

"Be that as it may," Edmund said, the dryness of his tone indicating that he, too, had picked up on Durand's distaste. "I don't know how much longer we ought to sit here, waiting for them to come to us."

"I think we need to be more patient," Graham put in. Like Durand, he stood apart, though unlike the mercenary, he wasn't halfway across the room from the rest of them. While the others talked, he'd been slowly spinning a Victorian globe between his large square hands. Graham was such a big man, so tall and substantial, that the painted sphere was dwarfed. This was the first time this evening he'd spoken. When Edmund looked at him, Graham's shoulders braced slightly.

"Frank and Li-Hua haven't been spotted on the other raids," he said. "I think they're leaving those attacks to underlings, because, to them, they're only distractions. I think they're here, in England, waiting for the perfect moment to jab at you."

The two men stared at each other longer than they had to. Oddly, considering he was the elder, Edmund dropped his gaze first. Ever since returning from Switzerland, tension had been building between the pair, though Estelle had yet to winkle out the cause. Perhaps it was a father-son thing, the effect of them both being supernaturally powerful now. All Estelle knew was that she wished they'd get over it. Whatever the reason for the strain between them, it was hurting them equally.

She laid her hand over Edmund's where it gripped her knee. Apparently thinking he'd squeezed too hard, he drew his own out from under it.

"You may be right, Graham," he said, his voice too carefully gentle.

"Well, I don't think so," Sally piped up with her usual candor. She was cuddled up to Ben on a red divan that would have been the height of fashion fifty years ago. Her stockinged feet were tucked under her bottom, her blonde curls firmly pressed to Ben's chest. "Those wankers abducted Daddy because they wanted to found a new vampire empire, with themselves as emperor and empress. Revenge doesn't get them any closer to achieving that. It only increases their risk of being caught and killed."

"She has a point," Durand admitted reluctantly.

"Of course I do," Sally huffed. She curled one hand over the bump in her belly, where her and Ben's child was growing. "You all should listen to me more often."

"We foiled that plot," Graham said reasonably. "And they can't return to the Nazis to help them now."

"So they'll try from another angle," Sally said. "I mean, I'm sure they'd like revenge on all of us, but whoever they try to kill, there has to be something extra in it for them."

Edmund rose and began to pace, clearly troubled by the doubts Sally raised. The agitation wasn't like him, or it didn't used to be. *Upyr* as strong as Edmund were very much in control of themselves physically. When he shoveled one hand through his wavy hair, Estelle felt real alarm tightening.

"You're the boss," Durand said from his disrespectful slouch. "You decide, and we'll follow."

Edmund stopped pacing to look at him. Except for the arch of one golden eyebrow, he had gone absolutely still. It was a quirk only a vampire could accomplish, as if he'd turned into a wax figurine: no pulse, no breath, no vibration of life at all. The elegance of his face and form shone without distraction. Estelle could stare at him as boldly as if he were a statue. In spite of the eeriness of his immobility, her breath caught at how beautiful he was.

When he filled his lungs to speak, the spell was broken.

"We'll give it another week," Edmund said. "If Frank and Li-Hua haven't attacked by then, we'll find some way to bring the fight to them."

Their debate concluded, Edmund slipped from the room too quickly for Estelle to follow, a streak of light and dark like a rocket trail. His disappearance was disconcerting, though his speed might not have been deliberate. Edmund's control over his powers wasn't as reliable as before. His weeks of captivity and torture, coupled with the exertion it had taken to search and erase the memories of the citizens of a small Swiss town, had compromised what should have been an easy recovery.

Or that was the explanation everyone subscribed to. Sometimes it seemed, a little, as if Edmund were avoiding *her* when he rushed away.

Estelle pressed a thumbnail between her two front teeth and stared forlornly down the empty stone passage outside the library. Rows of flags leaned inward from the walls, standards for kingdoms that had fallen centuries ago. Percy collected the banners, as he did aeroplanes. Their colorful silk stirred in the wake Edmund had left behind.

"Uncle Edmund must be eager to hunt," Percy commented, appearing at her side with his kind's habitual noiselessness. His grin was genial but fangy. "Might just follow his example. We can start the night's patrols that way."

He streaked off as swiftly as Edmund had. Estelle shook herself, stopped gnawing her nail, and began to walk. She'd knock together dinner for herself and Sally and Ben. Unlike Edmund and Percy, the humans couldn't turn wolf and catch a meal on the grounds. How the mercenary, Durand, had been supplying his dietary needs she didn't want to know. Durand was from a different line of *upyr*, who couldn't change into animals. Consequently, human blood was his sole repast. Chances were, the bustling town of Bridesmere had a few sore-necked young ladies who believed they'd been having dreams of tall, dark strangers.

"Estelle," Graham called from the library. "Hold up."

She scarcely needed to "hold up," since Graham was a vampire, too, but Edmund's eldest adopted son was nothing if not polite. She paused in the nearest doorway and waited. Graham caught up at a human pace, which she appreciated. In some ways, her life had been more comfortable when the handsome man she'd known as the professor had kept up a pretense of normalcy.

Though she was taller than most women, Estelle had to crane her neck at Graham. "Is something wrong?"

"No, I—" His head swiveled back, an odd, not quite human movement. A moment later, Estelle heard Ben and Sally's giggles approaching. From the sound of it, they'd be off to bouncing on their mattress soon, an activity their married state hadn't in the least put a damper on. Obviously wanting to exclude them from this conversation, Graham took Estelle's elbow and steered her into one of the castle's many sitting rooms. Estelle barely registered the click of him locking the door behind them, and sincerely doubted Ben or Sally would. Exchanging energy with Edmund hadn't only made her stronger, it had enhanced the hearing in her right ear. Luckily for their privacy, Graham was just as quiet as she was sharp-eared.

He turned to her now and shoved his hands into his trouser pockets, the gesture a holdover from his pre-vampire awkwardness. "I just wanted to ask how you thought Father was coming along. Recoverywise, you know."

The urge to prevaricate rose inside her, but this was Graham and not Sally. Unlike his little sister, he wouldn't want to be coddled.

"Honestly, Graham, I'm not certain. Your father seems strong enough to me, but possibly not as strong as a new master vampire is supposed to be. He's been . . ." Estelle trailed off. "He's been guarded since we came back from saving him."

"Is he angry with me?" Graham asked.

This question was so human, so vulnerable, Estelle simply had to lay her palm on his smooth white cheek. Before she could think what to say to soothe him, Graham's fangs jutted over his lower lip.

"Bugger," he said, slapping his hand across his mouth and spinning away. "Estelle, I swear, I didn't mean to do that."

She caught a wisp of thought from him—the other, less common effect of her preternaturally improved hearing. Graham was thinking his blasted fangs behaved like his prick had when he was fifteen, perpetually shooting out when he least wanted to betray himself.

Perhaps she shouldn't have, but Estelle couldn't help laughing. Graham was generally so serious that it was hard to resist teasing.

"This isn't funny," he said. "I should be able to control this." His voice sank. "I promise I'm not carrying a torch for you anymore."

"Maybe you're missing Pen," she suggested to his broad, tense back.

"Please don't say her name," Graham groaned.

"I'm sure she wouldn't mind if you rang her up. She really seemed to like you."

"I can't. We aren't—" He put his shoulders back stiffly. "It wouldn't be fair to contact her until this cock-up with Frank and Li-Hua is laid to rest."

"Mm," Estelle hummed, deciding she ought to stop twitting him. To her, Pen had seemed like she could take care of herself, but that wouldn't be the conclusion of a somewhat old-fashioned man like Graham—or not the willing one. "I suppose your reaction could simply be because it's your dinnertime. Perhaps Percy and Edmund would enjoy company."

"My cat doesn't like hunting with them," Graham confessed. "I have to fight like blazes to keep it from scrambling up the nearest tree."

"Oh," Estelle said, this not having occurred to her. Traditionally, shapechanging *upyr* took wolves as their familiars. For strategic reasons, Graham had joined with a big tomcat. The choice had helped during his father's rescue, but she supposed a feline wouldn't naturally interact with wolves. "Well, maybe your cat would like a jaunt to town. They must have mice there, and you could keep an eye on Durand at the same time."

Graham finally turned around, his incisors mostly returned to their normal state. "You don't trust him."

"I know he says he wants to help defeat Frank and Li-Hua, but he's just so cold. And I'm convinced he doesn't like humans."

"Do you think Durand means to betray us?"

Estelle hitched her shoulders in a shrug. "Edmund seems to trust him."

Graham held her gaze, taking in what she wasn't saying because it would have felt disloyal: that Edmund's judgment might not be up to snuff right now. Honey-colored sparks gleamed in what had once been Graham's plain brown eyes. He didn't have Edmund's ability to thrall, but the effect was still mesmerizing. For an instant, Estelle remembered him biting her on a rocking train, his moans of longing and hunger, the tightness of his hands gripping her. Gritting her teeth, she shoved the images away. That time was done. Graham wasn't newly changed anymore. He could feed without hurting ordinary humans. He didn't have to rely on her and her more than ordinary strength for sustenance.

"I can't read Durand," Graham confided. "Not even hints."

"I can't, either, not since Edmund helped me dreamwalk him in Switzerland. What I saw inside him then wasn't reassuring. He's . . . he's a violent, complicated man."

Graham broke their eye-lock to purse his mouth at a cobweb in the corner of the high ceiling. Percy maintained a small human staff, but this wasn't one of the rooms they normally went over. "Durand is strong. I'm not experienced at judging, but I think he must be close to master level now."

"He's not as powerful as Edmund."

"No," Graham agreed, just as sure of that as she was. "But he might be more ruthless."

"Which makes me even more grateful that you're here."

The change in Graham's expression was magical. He looked like an angel when he smiled at her, sunny and magnificent.

"Me, too," he said, and bent to hug her as sweetly as any harmless old chum could have.

Edmund hunted, taking down a stag with Percy in the tall, dense forest that had been preserved behind Bridesmere. The chase through the bracken had been exciting, the feast that followed rich, and still his restlessness persisted. He wished he felt more in command of himself, more the vampire he'd been before he was abducted.

Frank and Li-Hua had taught him he could die just like any man. Edmund wasn't invincible, or immune to former flaws of character. He didn't have infinite power to protect the people he loved. He didn't even have complete control over Estelle's heart.

When Percy changed back to human form beside the boulder where they'd stashed their clothes, Edmund sat on his tail and stayed as he was. He was fond of Percy, but he'd have preferred his son Robin to be with him, rather than back in London overseeing X Section. Edmund couldn't deny the secret MI5 department needed overseeing. He just didn't feel as easy counting on Percy.

Returning to Bridesmere, where he'd once ruled as lord, brought back too many memories of his mortal weaknesses.

Percy did up his last shirt button, eyeing Edmund's wolf for a moment before crouching down beside him.

"Still twitchy?" he asked sympathetically. He dug his fingers into Edmund's thick fur ruff. "Can't blame you, I guess. I'd be twitchy, too, if those bastards had done to me what they did to you."

Edmund closed his eyes, his wolf never averse to a good scratching.

"'Course, I'd work off my twitchiness with Estelle," Percy added. "That's a damned fine female you're engaged to."

To Edmund's dismay, a growl trickled out his throat. Though the primitive response embarrassed him, he felt his hackles lift as well. When Percy chuckled and rose, his annoyance swelled uncontrollably.

His wolf wanted Percy to fear him.

"Don't let her miss you too much," Percy advised, his grin too cheeky to tolerate. "It's been my experience that beautiful women need regular seeing to."

Edmund barked at him, nearly choking on his anger, at which Percy had the sense to streak away laughing. Tempting though it was, Edmund refrained from pursuing him. He *saw to* Estelle, as Percy put it—every night, in point of fact. What matter if it was only once a night, instead of the multiple couplings they'd been accustomed to? Estelle was human. Making love to her a single time was hardly tantamount to neglecting her. She knew Edmund loved her. He'd made that as plain as it could be. There simply were things inside him he wasn't comfortable baring to her now.

He became aware that he was growling to himself again. Leaping to his paws, he forced himself to start patrolling. This wasn't some carefree holiday they were on; Edmund had responsibilities.

He was well equipped to meet them. Only Percy's knowledge of Bridesmere equaled his. Edmund remembered every rise and dip of its moors, every stone of its pastures and tall, strong towers. If Edmund's former captors showed up tonight, he felt perfectly ready to rip them into pieces.

Naturally, they did not oblige him. That would have been too convenient.

Dawn was shouldering toward the horizon as he trotted back to the house, a hint of gray muting the crispness of the rural stars. Edmund judged he had half an hour before full sunrise. He could stay out longer if he kept his wolf form, but he was tired enough to have calmed. He was ready to be his rational self with Estelle, ready to treat her with the kindness and caring that she deserved.

And then he saw her tall goddess figure on the battle-

ments. The wind was up. She was leaning between the
crenelation, looking townward with her long, silver-kissed
brown hair blowing behind her. His heart stuttered at
how dear the sight of her was. She was alone and hadn't
seen him, her expression pensive—a fact eyes like his
had no trouble discerning even from the ground. Positioned as she was, she could hardly have made herself more
conspicuous.

If Edmund could identify her, so could their enemies.

His rage seared through him in a spume of fire, the
terror that had sparked it making it burn hotter. Nausea
gripped him, a sensation he hadn't experienced in so long
he barely recognized what it was. His stomach felt like it
was dissolving—and then it did dissolve, along with the
rest of him.

He knew he wasn't changing, because his body didn't
reform as human. A fog surrounded him, blank and thick—
no turf beneath him, no wall above. The heart he no longer
had tried to pound harder.

Estelle, he thought, panicked at the thought of losing
her this way.

The world racketed back to him without warning. He
landed naked on the battlements, as if he'd been dropped
there by a big raptor. He had feet and hands, but his mind
seemed more predator than man. For whatever reason, his
cock was aching and hard as stone.

"Edmund!" Estelle exclaimed, as startled by his appearance as he was. "Where did you come from?"

His throat worked, but he couldn't answer. He was
picking up a scent on her: Graham's scent, aroused and
male. His fangs erected so fast they stung. He leaped for
her before she could move, tackling her to the ground. He
cradled her head to protect it, but she still cried out, her
soft sound of alarm a spice to the wolf in him. She was
mate *and* prey, an irresistible combination. Every muscle
taut, he flipped her onto her stomach and wrenched up her
white nightgown.

He should have scolded her. What was she thinking, leaving their room dressed like this? The reprimand

refused to form. The sight of her bare pink bottom, squirming and vulnerable, robbed him of the power to organize the words. Intense sexual arousal shot from his eyes to his throbbing groin.

He was shoving into her in an instant, with a groan of pleasure like a dying man. She wasn't ready, and he could only penetrate a few inches. His head flung back with a throttled howl. Lord, he didn't want to hurt her, but he was so hard, so hungry. He had to get all the way inside her, had to claim what was his. He felt himself swelling with the need of it, his girth pressing more urgently against her soft walls.

"Edmund," she moaned, but the tenor of it was different from her previous cry.

Her wetness had begun to ease him, hot, silky cream around his hard-lodged flare. As if to tease him with the promise of engulfment, he slid half an inch farther. Groaning, he bit her nape, not breaking skin but using the grip to hold her in place while he drove his erection to its limit.

When that didn't quite succeed, he shoved her thighs wider with his own and heaved into her again.

Estelle's back arched as his tingling crown bumped the end of her passageway. He grunted with bliss, but didn't close his eyes. The last thing he wanted was to miss her reaction. Estelle looked like she was having a convulsion, her hands fisted on the stones, his name moaning from her throat.

Knowing she was the opposite of ailing, he wedged a hand beneath her writhing body, cupping the ripeness of her pubis with immense relish. His hold perfected the angle of her hips to his. Even better, his finger found her clitoris as easily as if the bursting little organ belonged to him. He pressed and circled its swell just the way she liked: firmly, from top to bottom, letting each tiny nerve enjoy his supernatural adeptness. Desperately short of patience, he squeezed manipulations that would normally last ten minutes into ten seconds.

She came screaming, her pleasure gushing and contracting her on his cock.

That delectable sensation came within a hair's breadth of triggering his own climax. Refusing to let it, he tightened his jaw's grip around her nape and growled into her vertebrae.

"Oh, God," she gasped, shivering. "Edmund, please don't stop there."

The corner of his brain that was still thinking realized Percy must have been correct. If she was begging, he hadn't been seeing to Estelle well enough. Edmund's lust rose with his anger at his own mistake. He began to shaft her, strong and deep, driving his groin into her lush, firm bottom with ever greater abandon. Flesh slapped flesh and grew sweaty, a goad he couldn't afford to succumb to if he wanted to reestablish his mastery. The flare of energy inside Estelle told him precisely which portion of her channel wanted stroking most. Despite the dizzying rise of his excitement, he kept his aim unswervingly on it.

Naturally, the wolf in him adored taking her from behind, but so did the man. He and Estelle were matched in this position, the ultrasensitive throat of his penis lining up with the tender cushion at the front of her vagina. He rewarded both of them by running over and over her there. The friction felt so good his irises took fire and lit up the air. Delighted by her helpless mewls and craving more of them, he slid his free hand down her half-bent leg. The strength of her thigh and calf muscles was a gift, the way her toes curled and her cunt contracted when he dragged his nails lightly up and down the sole of her foot.

That added stimulation was sufficient to do her in. Her next orgasm became a chain she could not stop—even had she wanted to. She was grabbing for his hip, urging him with the sounds she made to thrust into her harder. More than willing to comply, he shifted his hold on her neck slightly to the side, where his three-month-old mark of claiming glowed under her skin.

He'd put it there the night they reunited, an instinct he hadn't been able to suppress. His fangs pulsed with temptation. He'd sworn he wouldn't give in to the compulsion to deepen the sign of his possession. Estelle deserved more respect. For that matter, so did Graham. Unfortunately, cruder emotions were ruling him. He wrestled with himself, gasping and groaning as he continued to pump hungrily into her. The wet friction on his cock felt incredible.

In the end, Estelle decided him. Her right hand, the one his energy had made stronger, came up to clasp the back of his neck.

"You know what you want," she panted between the contractions of her climax. Her molars ground together as it peaked again, but she gulped for air and went on. "Stop holding back on me."

Her eagerness was too exciting. Whether she understood what she was urging him to or not, he bit the mark and his cock erupted, her blood rolling like an aphrodisiac down his throat. He was lucky she was resilient, because he couldn't prevent his weight from grinding her under him. He couldn't even be sorry. He *covered* her, in the most primal sense of the word. Both the man and wolf in him exulted until he was roaring in triumph against her neck. With every swallow, his ejaculation jetted, and with every jet, his pleasure swelled higher. White lights danced around the edges of his vision. His beloved trembled and twitched, the ecstasy of his feeding overwhelming her. As the pleasure crested blindingly, their auras and sensations intertwined so closely Edmund felt as if he were penetrating his own body.

Edmund, he heard her groaning inside his head.

Sanity slapped him back to himself. He couldn't do this, couldn't let their thoughts join until he'd conquered his demons. She'd hate him for what he was feeling about her and his own son. Hell, he hated himself.

His fangs did not retract, but at least he got them out of her vein.

Estelle didn't seem to register his turmoil. She moaned, low and throaty, going limp beneath him as he stopped feeding.

Still only human, so to speak, he jammed his cock as deep as it would go into her pussy for the last sweet spurts. Then he was collapsing, too.

"Goodness," she murmured, patting his shoulder where it hunched over hers. "That truly was something."

Careful now—and slightly sheepish—he eased off her, sitting beside her with his knees bent up. Estelle remained where she was, as if she'd been flattened by a steam-roller. Little shreds of white cotton lay around her on the hard granite. Her breath was not recovering as quickly as usual.

"I'm sorry," he said. "Was it too much?"

Estelle snorted and squeezed his ankle. "It was too much for my nightgown. It wasn't too much for me."

She rolled onto her side to look up at him. Her cheeks and brow were deeply rosy from their lovemaking, caus-ing the incredible gray of her eyes to glow. "How did you do that, Edmund? How did you suddenly appear out of nowhere?"

"I don't know. I was standing by the moat, thinking you really shouldn't be up here alone, and my body seemed to dissolve. Next thing I knew, I was on the battlements with you. I couldn't even tell you how I did it."

"Do you think it's part of your master powers?"

"It must be. I only wish I knew how to control it. It could be handy." He reached for her hair, curling a silky lock around his forefinger. He hesitated, but couldn't leave the warning unspoken. "You know you shouldn't be out here walking, not by yourself. Other vampires might not be able to materialize as I did, but they have no trouble jumping or climbing."

Estelle's gaze evaded his. "I couldn't sleep. I'm used to you being in the bed with me."

"I will be once this is over. Whenever you want me to."

She curled her hand around his, pressing it lightly against her breast. She wore her engagement ring, the dia-mond glinting like a chip of ice in the predawn light. They hadn't set a date for the wedding yet, though he suspected she'd wondered why when Ben and Sally had exchanged their vows. Edmund's heart felt close to breaking at the steady thump of her pulse. Her life was precious to him, more than he thought she could comprehend. The thick fans of her lashes still hid her eyes.

"I look forward to that," she said.

Bridesmere

Estelle didn't know what had woken her. The house was quiet, and Edmund lay in the stonelike slumber all *upyr* fell into at dawn. His oblivion separated them as surely as a wall, adding to her unease, though one would think she'd be used to it. Taking care not to disturb Edmund's nest of blankets, she squirmed out into the open.

Because there was plenty of space at Bridesmere Castle, Percy's guests had spread out. Percy's private rooms were in the west tower, Sally's and Ben's in the east, and Durand's in the north. As the youngest of the vampires, Graham had decided he was most comfortable in the windowless cellar flat. Edmund and Estelle's suite took up the southern tower, aboveground but well protected. The walls were smoothly plastered, the dark oak moldings as fine as any her grandparents might have owned. The bed wasn't huge, but it was comfortable. The windows, which had once served as arrow slits, were covered by both shutters and tapestries—though light still seeped around the edges of the good-as-new antique cloth. Quieter than she had any need to be, Estelle padded to the nearest arras and peeked out.

The window's view overlooked the bailey, which was empty and still. It was early afternoon, her hours turned upside down by Edmund's. Nothing moved in the opening Percy had bulldozed in the curtain wall. Outside it, on the smooth black tarmac, Percy's small fleet of planes sat poised in silvery splendor.

We're safe, she thought, fighting off a shiver. *Our enemies won't attack us in broad daylight.*

The words didn't reassure her, so she pulled a robe over her pajamas—Edmund's pajamas, actually. She'd gotten into the habit of wearing them when he'd been missing. That they remained a comfort was probably a sign of her wound-up nerves. Not that being nervous was unreasonable. When Frank and Li-Hua had kidnapped Edmund, they'd used drugs to travel during the day. Ben was probably keeping watch this shift, but that didn't mean no vampire could slip past him. Estelle knew how swiftly Edmund's kind could move. With fingers that had gone a little shaky, she opened the door and stepped onto the stone landing.

Her nape prickled as strongly as if an electric current were being dragged over it. Did her funny ear perceive a cry? Was that Sally's voice in the faint distance?

Not daring to wait for confirmation, she ran back to shake Edmund. Naturally, that had as much effect as shaking a rock. She cursed, then held her breath. She heard footsteps, too staccato to be human, running up a flight of stairs. Abruptly desperate, she yanked down the covers and threw a carafe of water into Edmund's face.

He came up like a shot, in full vampire mode. His fangs were daggers, his eyes ablaze with mindless blue fire. She'd never, ever seen him look at her like this. He must have taken her for an attacker. His hand slammed around her neck in a strangling grip.

"Edmund," she choked hoarsely through his hold. Her heart was racing a mile a minute, which was hardly going to shut his triggered instincts off. "Edmund, it's Estelle. Sally's in trouble. I think the raiders are here."

He blinked and shuddered and then released her throat in horror. "Estelle, I thought—"

"They're here," she repeated, not caring a damn for apologies. "I heard them running up the east tower stairs."

His eyes fired with a far more conscious but equally deadly flame.

"Stay," he barked, grabbing a blanket to wrap himself against exposure. "And bar the doors and windows behind me."

She couldn't stay, though, not when she didn't know

if either Percy or Graham was up. Edmund wouldn't stop to rouse them. He'd head straight for his daughter—and danger—without anyone to help. Estelle waited until he'd blurred away, then grabbed a sharpened iron poker from the fireplace. At least if she startled the others as badly as she had Edmund, she'd be able to defend herself.

To her dismay, she ran into Durand in the stone-flagged entry on the ground floor, where the old Fitz Clare family armor stood displayed. The metal suits were bigger than most she'd seen in museums—the Fitz Clares had been tall men for their day—but their greater stature seemed not to impress Durand.

She tried to ignore the fact that he was naked, and that his straight black hair hung to his shoulder blades. A faint raised starburst marked the skin above his breastbone. Interesting scars aside, his disgust on seeing her was justification enough not to have intended to awaken him.

"Idiots," he sneered.

She didn't get a chance to argue with his opinion, which might have been meant for everyone in the place but him. In a move too fast to counter, he flipped her over his shoulder, streaked to the nearest cupboard, and locked her in with the winter coats. She didn't remember she had the poker until it was too late.

"Be quiet!" he snapped when she banged it against the thick mahogany door. "You're going to draw the enemy straight to you."

"Damn it," she hissed, though she did lower her voice. "I'm not helpless, you arrogant Swiss bastard."

She was reaching for the lock to snap it with her strong right hand when more vampire feet pelted by. Not knowing who they belonged to, she froze and waited until they passed. Trying again, she broke the lock with a single twist, but the door still refused to budge. Apparently, the mercenary had placed an exceedingly heavy object in front of it. He'd lifted and set down whatever it was in seconds—and silently.

That said something scary about how powerful he was.

"Buggering hell," she swore, slamming her right shoulder into the barrier. To her frustration, she didn't move it an inch.

"Estelle?" said Ben's voice from right outside.

"Help me out of here," she said, relief flooding her. "Durand blocked me in."

Something wooden screeched across the stone. Ben grunted over whatever he was shoving. As soon as there was room to, Estelle squeezed out of the door.

"Get Graham," she said, taking a second to gape at the elephant-size cabinet Ben had pushed. She could see she wasn't the only one who'd been turned a bit more than human by Edmund's energy.

"I *did* get Graham." Ben was breathing heavily but not breathless. "His room was under the stairs I took from the ramparts. Are you okay? Is Durand betraying us?"

"I don't think so. I think he's just being an—"

A bloodcurdling scream from the castle's upper reaches stopped their exchange. The voice was male, and not one she recognized. A loud crash followed, the force of it sending a tremor like a tiny earthquake through the wall and floor. Ben's face went white beneath the disordered spikes of his sandy hair. He knew that noise had come from the part of the castle where he'd left Sally. Grim and tight-jawed, he pulled a pistol from the back waistband of his trousers. Like all their store of weapons, it was loaded with iron. The gun looked surprisingly at home in his two-handed grip.

Pen must have taught Ben more during their adventures than Estelle had known.

"We're going up," he said. "Try to stay behind me."

This, at least, was an order Estelle could obey. They ran in an awkward crouch through the shadowed corridors of the keep to the east stairway, with Ben ducking around the corners first to make sure they weren't ambushed. Daunted by Bridesmere's size, Estelle began to wish rather heartily for vampire speed. Her grip was slipping on the heavy poker, and Ben's hands were white-knuckled.

"Sally's all right," he muttered under his breath, a sheen of sweat glistening on his chiseled face. "I told her what to do if anything happened. I'd feel it if she were hurt."

Estelle knew it was himself Ben was reassuring. She decided not to mention the cry she'd heard earlier.

"Of course she's all right," she said. "Sally's very resourceful."

They reached the entrance to the east tower stairs. Yet another crash shook its foundations, the tremor stronger now that they were close. Estelle heard Edmund roaring, which she supposed was good news. Ben drew a chest-filling breath and yanked the door open.

"Don't get between them," he warned over his shoulder. "You know how vampires are when they fight."

Estelle did know. She'd seen two of them whirl like dervishes in the entry to Edmund's home a few months ago. Her heart was pounding sickeningly fast, and her left knee wobbled so badly she had to lean harder on the right to get up the twisting steps. The spiral stairwell was engineered to give the castle's defenders the advantage in an attack. As a result, her and Ben's approach was vulnerable.

She choked back a shriek and shrank to the wall when a severed head bounced past her and disappeared in a burst of light.

With a jolt of delayed shock, she realized the head's fangs had been gnashing before it poofed.

Ben grabbed her wrist and unfroze her.

"I'm okay," she gasped, shifting her grip to hold the poker more effectively. She'd been working with Percy and Graham on her fighting skills, not wanting to place all her reliance on the more than human strength of her right side. She knew she could kill a vampire, especially one who wasn't expecting her to be able to. She also knew Ben was liable to do better with his gun. "Go ahead. I'll follow."

They surmounted the final curve to find Graham and Percy flat on their backs on the top landing. Their eyes were open and staring, their pupils shrunk to pinpricks. The sight of his older brother drew a cry from deep in Ben's chest.

"They're not dead," Estelle said. "If they were, their bodies would have dematerialized."

Ben jerked from his horror and nodded. "Stay with

them," he said, and edged into the hurricane of sound and motion that filled the tower's upper room.

What had once been handsome furniture was kindling: barely identifiable bits of bed, chairs, and chests of drawers littering a violently disarranged silk-wool rug. The warring vampires—three or four of them, she thought—were blurs even to her enhanced vision. Ben must have told Sally to open the shutters if the bad vampires came, because bright afternoon sunshine slanted into the room. Luckily, Edmund's age would protect him from the direst of its consequences. Durand's, too, she gathered. Estelle heard the mercenary shouting at the top of his lungs.

"*Stop!*" he was saying, the sheer will he put in the word making muscles jump beneath her skin as they tried to obey. "We need to interrogate one of them!"

"Babies!" Edmund roared. "They bloody send babies after me!"

A body flew, hitting the wall so hard a chunk of plaster and underlying stone fell out. Edmund might not have meant to kill the attacker, but when the vampire dropped, its upper body toppled into a patch of sun beneath one window. It was wearing what appeared to be a hooded monk's habit. Possibly, its injuries had weakened its aura's protective abilities. As the hood fell back, the vampire's hair caught fire, the hot blue flame swallowing its head. When enough of that had burned, the whole body disappeared in a blinding flare of white light.

"Damn it!" Durand cursed, motionless at last and panting in the room's center.

Ben was panting, too, though he hadn't had a chance to shoot anything.

"Damn it," Durand repeated, softer this time.

Edmund threw his head back and howled. It was an eerie sound, as if his wolf had taken over his vocal cords. His fangs remained down like Durand's and—also like Durand—his exposed skin had suffered an extreme sunburn. Though he didn't need to breathe as much as a human, his chest bellowed in and out. Even under these circumstances, Estelle found the sight arresting. He must have lost his blanket at some point, because he was in the altogether now. His arms and legs were roped with muscle that was extra taut from battle.

Perhaps she shouldn't have noticed, but both he and Durand sported slight erections. No matter how high the stakes, their predatory nature found the fight exciting.

"Daddy?" came Sally's tentative voice from the bathroom where she must have barricaded herself. A heap of accordioned carpet blocked her exit. "Can someone open the door?"

"*Don't*," Edmund ordered so sharply Ben nearly fell over as his muscles locked.

Under no such restriction, Estelle hurried into the room to close the shutters. As she did, she found two pairs of Ben's relatively unscathed trousers in the debris. Durand accepted one with a nod that might have been a fraction less icy than usual. Then she girded her nerves and tried to act like walking over to Edmund didn't require a soupçon of bravery.

Maybe Edmund sensed her struggle. His blazing eyes tracked each step of her approach. As if he couldn't help it, or perhaps wasn't aware of what his body did, his nascent erection bounced a little higher from its nest of golden curls.

Her second guess was right. When she reached him, his first words to her weren't at all suggestive.

"Sorry," he sighed as he took the clothes. "I don't want Sally to see me like this. She and the baby have had enough scares today."

Estelle watched him pull on the trousers, then laid her hand on his bunched bicep, her thumb sweeping gently over a bulging vein. Edmund's elongated fangs weren't the only sign of frayed control. Though his sunburn was fading, angry embers burned in his eyes. To her relief, he didn't evade her gaze. Their connection snapped into place between them, not as strong as it had been, but enough to calm both of them. As it did, she sensed him ordering his muscles to unknot.

"I should have known," he murmured. "You said you

heard their feet running up the stairs. I should have known the raiders were too young to be Frank or Li-Hua."

"You wanted this to be over. Everyone does."

"What happened to Graham and Percy?" Ben thought to ask. "Couldn't they stay awake like the two of you?"

Though unable to disobey Edmund's order not to let Sally out, Ben had stepped closer. Edmund glanced at him before looking at the floor guiltily.

"Your father thralled them," Durand answered in his place. His arms were crossed, his gaze half-lidded with the scorn that was his second-favorite expression, his first being none at all. "He ordered them to stay outside. Truly, it was a marvel. I don't think I've seen one vampire bespell another with just his eyes, certainly not one who has as many decades as Percy."

"I didn't mean to thrall them *that* well. I only wanted to keep them out of the fight."

"You ordered them not to help?" Estelle exclaimed.

"There were only seven attackers. I knew I could handle them."

"And you did," Durand drawled. "You handled them right out of existence."

The air around Edmund prickled as he peeled back his lips and growled.

"Stop it," Estelle said, her pulse skipping in her throat. "Both of you."

She glared at Durand until he turned away, most likely because having a human speak to him as if he were a child was beneath his dignity. When she looked back at Edmund, he'd managed to draw his fangs fully up. He touched her cheek with the back of his fingers, then eased his upper rm from her hold. Despite their separation, she could feel the unnatural energy from the fight draining out of him.

"Let Sally out," he said wearily. "I'll see to Percy and Graham."

Sally flung herself into Ben's arms the moment she was free, and for a moment every eye—including the icy-hearted mercenary's—was drawn to them. The naked love in Ben's face as he embraced his young, pregnant wife, the worry and the care and even the amusement, was intense enough to set the air humming. The pair might squabble from time to time and have their quirks, but in all the ways that mattered they were one unit.

Estelle's throat constricted as Ben bent his head to murmur soothing phrases in Sally's ear, something he had to nose her curls aside to do. Up on her toes, Sally clutched his lean, broad shoulders.

"I did what you told me," she cried with her trademark passion. "Exactly as I promised."

Ben laughed at that, and the spell was broken—at least for the rest of them.

Edmund made an odd throat-clearing noise as Ben took Sally's face in his hands and the couple began to kiss. Edmund was crouched on the narrow landing beside Graham and Percy, both of whom lay as corpselike and glassy-eyed as before. A single furrow creased the ivory skin between Edmund's brows. His hands were resting lightly on each of the men's shoulders.

"Durand," he said, sounding uncomfortable to be addressing him. "I'm afraid I need your help with this."

Edmund was somewhat aghast to discover that, even with Durand's help, he couldn't wake his relatives. Percy stirred and made a disgruntled noise as he and Durand fed their energy into him. Graham didn't respond at all. Finally, Edmund gave up.

"They're young," Durand said, the reassurance coming out grudgingly. "And the sun is up. It's hardly a wonder that your will rolled straight over them."

It might not have been a wonder, but it was unsettling. Edmund didn't like seeing people he loved this vulnerable to his power, or imagining the harm he might have done had he put any more push behind his thrall. His care for his loved ones' safety was no excuse. He'd known he could be a menace if he was not careful.

He looked across the bodies at Durand, schooling his

face to hide his thoughts as well as he could. Ally or not, it wouldn't pay to show weakness in front of a man like him.

"Can you carry Percy to his room?" Edmund asked.

"I can," Durand said, and scooped him up as if the favor were nothing.

His alacrity—and his absence—loosened a tightness Edmund hadn't known he was harboring. He trusted Durand, as far as it went. He simply couldn't be easy around his former torturer. Durand would, ultimately, follow his own agenda.

As Edmund lifted his own burden from the floor and started down the stairs, Graham's head fell against his shoulder. Edmund didn't think he'd carried his eldest more than a handful of times. Graham had been twelve when Edmund adopted him, and already thinking of himself as a man. He'd appointed himself Sally and Ben's protector at the orphanage. He hadn't put himself in situations where he'd need carrying.

Now Edmund had to take care that Graham's huge bare feet didn't bump the walls. He was taller and heavier than Edmund—and more selfless than almost anyone he knew. He wouldn't even be a vampire had it not been for his desire to rescue Edmund from his abductors.

This was a debt Edmund had no means to repay.

Guilt and an odd species of grief washed over him as he laid his unconscious son on his bed. Though comfortable, Graham's apartment in the cellar was stygian dark and cool. Edmund switched on a lamp and pulled the coverlet over Graham. He stared down at him, trying to find in Graham's strong, carved features the too-serious boy he'd been. Edmund remembered the triumph he'd felt the first time he heard Graham laugh, the sense that maybe he hadn't been crazy to want to be a father again. Though the memory couldn't bring the human child back into Graham's face, Edmund thought he saw his eyelids flutter, a tiny butterfly movement.

He had to blink his own eyes to clear a sting.

"Leave it be," Edmund murmured to himself. He couldn't

undo any of Graham's choices. It would have to be enough that Graham didn't seem to regret them.

Sleep called to him like a drug as he trudged to his and Estelle's rooms. His legs refused to move at more than a mortal pace, but he reached them eventually. Estelle was in the bathroom when he collapsed back onto their bed. The minute it took before she came out to sit beside him seemed far too long. He couldn't contain his exhalation of relief when she stroked her gentle fingers through his outspread hair. Estelle was his heart, the peace and pleasure he'd never thought to deserve. His lashes drifted downward at her caress, though his pulse hadn't slowed the way it should in the daytime.

"Rest," she said. "I'm sure the danger is past for now."

Perversely, he rolled his head toward her voice and opened his eyes again. Smiling, she traced one fingertip across his eyebrow.

"I'm sorry for frightening you when I woke up," he said.

Her silk robe hissed with her shrug. "I knew you wouldn't truly hurt me."

"Did you?" He turned his gaze to the wooden beams of the tower's round ceiling. She knew better than he did if she knew that.

"Don't," she said. "Don't shut me out like that."

Lord knew he didn't want to. He looked at her, catching her hand and carrying it to his lips. Hurt shadowed her clear gray eyes. Her emotions were so open. Even if some of his thoughts needed guarding, surely he could give her the rest in words.

"I was thinking," he said, his voice sleepy-thick. "Trying to remember whose room this used to be. I'm reasonably certain Ben and Sally's used to be my brother's bedchamber. As I recall, he and Gillian did some damage to the walls themselves, though for more pleasant reasons than cracking an *upyr*'s skull."

His hand had gone limp, and Estelle pulled it to her breast. Her thumb was drawing a twisting pattern in the cup of his palm. Sometimes Edmund thought her touch

must be as mesmerizing as his thrall. Despite his increasing languor, a subtle buzz of feeling ran through his groin.

"What was the great Council leader like when he was
mortal?"

Edmund laughed softly. "Not all that different, to tell
the truth. He did have a terrible scar across half his face,
from the Battle of Poitiers. Gillian never minded. Nor my
wife, for that matter."

"You told me once she was in love with him."

"Everyone loved Aimery. He wasn't glib or charming.
He was . . ." Edmund let his eyes fall shut as he sighed. "He
was like Graham a bit. Quiet, but a man you couldn't help
but trust. Even I trusted him not to break faith with me.
There was no braver soul in battle. No better sword at your
back. If I'd been the younger brother and he'd been lord, I
suspect I'd have hated him."

Estelle caught a small, sharp breath—protesting his
honesty, no doubt. "You felt that way then, maybe. I know
you respect him now."

"Sometimes I wish I didn't. His standards can be hard
for ordinary people to live up to."

She hesitated just long enough for the pause to register
in his consciousness. "Do you want to call him?"

He shook his head against the pillow. "I'll ring him
tonight. It's beginning to look like Sally was right, and
these raids are merely a blind to keep us from discovering
what Frank and Li-Hua are really up to."

"I didn't mean that." Estelle's voice became even more
careful. "I meant do you want to call him about the trouble
you've been having with your powers? He's been an elder
longer. Maybe he'll know something."

Edmund's eyes snapped open, startling both of them.

"No," he said, ignoring that the refusal was a bit too
sharp. Better not to have his perfect brother poking his
nose in. He loved Aimery, but he knew the Council leader
never would have gotten himself in a fix like this. "I'll sort
it out. Auriclus dumped a lot of power on me when he died.
I need more time to adjust to it."

Estelle looked down at their joined hands, resting now

on her thigh. Her mouth was compressed in a stubborn line. "As you wish," she said.

"All will be well, love. I promise." Edmund tried to squeeze her fingers, but sleep chose then to crash over him like a wall.

"I love you, Edmund," was the last thing he heard her say.

Graham jerked awake snarling, momentarily unaware where he was. Fury had overwhelmed his heightened senses, causing his heart to slam and his skin to burn.

His father had thralled him, had forced his will into submission. Graham had been powerless to stop it, as though he were as weak as a child. The beast in him wanted to tear Edmund's throat out for the offense. His fangs stretched to do it, his clawlike fingers punching through the coverlet. Graham could almost feel the tail he didn't have twitching.

"Christ," he swore, forcing the urge away.

He shuddered a minute instead, reminding himself who and where he was.

When he'd calmed, at least somewhat, he noticed the professor's cool forest essence clung to the bedding. Edmund must have carried Graham here himself.

That idea shook Graham's balance. No matter what was wrong between them, his father cared enough to . . . well, what could he call it but tuck him in? He'd also turned on the Tiffany lamp, the soft glow illuminating the not quite familiar shapes of the bed and chairs. The walls of the cellar room were warmed by brown velvet curtains, the floor by a red and cream Oriental rug. Graham's clothes hung in the half-opened wardrobe. The inventory settled him a fraction more. He was at Bridesmere, and Edmund had thralled him to keep him out of a fight. Graham sent his mind questing through the castle, not adept at the process, but able—one by one—to ascertain that the people he cared about were alive.

His relief whooshed from him hard enough to flutter the draperies.

As he extricated his nails where they'd pierced the covers, he realized he was hungry. He groaned at that, because these days hunger meant Pen and his unbelievably vivid memories of fucking her. He always woke up partially hard; he'd often done so as a human, but the real-as-life images he was prone to as an immortal had his cock punching up the cotton placket of his sleep pants. In instants he was erect—and as thick around as a woman's wrist.

The woman the wrist belonged to went without saying.

Graham cursed the insistence of his aroused cock. Some nights he could ignore his waking erections, but this wasn't going to be one of them. His frustration over Edmund having slapped him down had changed direction too handily. For the sort of creature he now was, ignoring a hard-on this forceful was dangerous.

Inconvenient didn't begin to describe the problem. Why couldn't he forget Pen? Why was her skinny body with her warm, spiced veins the only ones he wanted to feast on? He ran his tongue around his sharpening eyeteeth, then flung himself from the bed in disgust.

He was out of control, his new vampire needs overruling his personal wishes as surely as Edmund had. Pen was a harridan, an asp with hips like a boy. Flashes of those hips riding him clenched his fists. He knew how her hip bones felt when he gripped them, knew how her nipples tightened against his tongue. Her breasts were beautiful creamy swells, her legs an endless invitation to shove between.

Lust stabbed through him, causing his prick to throb crazily. The pain of wanting her was getting worse, irrational though it was. Pen might desire him, but anything more than scratching her itches was the farthest thing from her mind.

A growl coiled in Graham's throat as sweat broke across his skin. The smell of the blood that tinged his perspiration had his balls aching. Cursing, he yanked a sheer white scarf he never should have stolen from his bedside drawer. It was Pen's scarf, with her personal perfume infused into it. Worse, it had a bit of her blood on it. She'd worn it to cover the first bite he'd given her.

Caught in a compulsion he no longer had strength to fight, Graham shoved his drawstring pants down his hips. His cock stuck out like a flagpole, jerking with eagerness. It knew what was coming and wanted it. Graham's breath gasped from him as he started wrapping it in the silk, starting at the base and winding the smooth, long length round and round his shaft. In half a minute, only his taut and shining tip was uncovered.

He was aroused enough that its immortally pallid skin had gone red.

Giving in so quickly was a mistake. Sensation bolted through his straining flesh, the rising heat of his normally cool body incredible. He tried to wrestle his reaction back, but he came from no more than the constriction of the expensive cloth, a hard, hot jet of fluid that barely took his edge off.

That little fountain wasn't going to sate him tonight.

Grunting at the inevitable, Graham faced the bed and planted his feet firm and wide. He wasn't seeing the rumpled sheets, he was seeing Pen on them. Something about standing up to do this, about standing *over her*—if only in a vision—truly got his blood pumping. She writhed in his imagination, as he'd made her do every time. No other male had shown her the pleasure he had, though she hadn't wanted to admit that. Her body admitted it just fine: her sex glistening with arousal, the muscles of her long, restless thighs drawn tight.

Too excited to wait for the next step in his increasingly obsessive ritual, Graham squeezed both fists onto his erection, screwing them in opposite directions over its wrappings. His sensation rose, better this time, more pressure behind the urgency. *Upyr* might be sex fiends, but they had the tools to wank themselves really well. The fingers of his second hand swallowed his prick's bare head, where clear fluid was leaking thick from the hole. The lubrication was as sweet as it was unnecessary. A little pain was hardly going to stop him. Graham twisted faster, tighter, the grip burning so good his neck fell back while he moaned.

Hold off, he ordered himself, feeling the twitch of immi-nence in his balls. *Hold off this time and make it good.*

He groaned because he wanted the release so badly, because his groin always felt so bloody stuffed these days. It was a peculiarity of his makeup that the pain of restrain-ing shot him that much higher. His dream-Pen, his tormen-tor, came onto her knees and bent over him. He felt her lips, her mouth, the heat and cling of wet, satiny skin. She was as fearless as she'd been when she was with him, suck-ing and licking and hollowing her cheeks until his scalp hairs all stood on end.

Use your teeth, he thought, unable to fight the urge, though experience warned this particular fantasy would drive him too far, too fast. *God, Pen, bite me.*

The scarf was strangling him as his dream-Pen com-plied, the scent it held rising as he rubbed it with insane speed. He knew exactly what he needed, what he'd feel guilty for afterward.

"Damn it," he rasped, the verge threatening. The wave was rising, impossible to hold back. His desperate hands were clever even in their fumbling. He didn't care then if this compulsion was damn near sick. He couldn't miss the moment, had to order everything as he liked. He shoved the silk to the inches that loved it best, positioning the bunched-up creases to bind the flare of his cockhead and the skin just beneath. This was where his nerves gathered thickest, where they screamed for the strongest stimula-tion they could get. Graham was going to give it to them. His molars ground together as he wound the ends of Pen's silk scarf around stiff fingers. He didn't even wince as he pulled them outward with all his strength.

The tautened cloth formed a tourniquet of pain and bliss. Only his aura kept it from ripping. He gulped for air as the coming crest rose and rose. He was hanging, shud-dering, nearly blind from the focus of his terrible need. Blood filled his mouth as his jutting fangs cut his lip. In his mind, it was Pen's blood. In his mind, she was moaning out her intense climax. He couldn't hold the pleasure, couldn't stand it . . . and then his orgasm burst from him.

The sound he made as it exploded wasn't even close to human.

It went on too long for comfort, but in its trembling wake it left emptiness.

Done now, Graham threw the scarf from him. As if to spite him, the thing flew two feet and fluttered to the floor.

"Fuck," he said, then bent to retrieve it resignedly. Self-disgust notwithstanding, he folded it carefully, his aura already smoothing the creases his crazed masturbation had put in it. He knew he'd want the thing again, probably sooner than he liked. This time, he'd waited three nights before indulging. Prior to that, it had been a week.

Sighing, he tucked the rapidly unwrinkling scarf back into his drawer.

He dragged his sole consolation to the forefront. At least, now, he could hunt for dinner without risking someone's life.

Charleston, South Carolina

Peachtree Plantation, the moldering treasure Pen had crossed the ocean to claim, rose from the moatlike surround of a rich black-water swamp six miles upriver from Charleston. Great fields of rice had waved here once, the famed Carolina Gold. Today, Peachtree's cash crop was reduced to pecans. The wildly overgrown condition of the irrigation ditches and grounds, always a danger in this climate, suggested Pen's mother hadn't been managing her family's legacy well—nor did her aunts seem likely to reverse that state of affairs. They'd never seen the point in spending money on anything but themselves, and if they could weasel out of paying, all the better. As a result, what should have been the community's financial anchor was looking more like a drain.

But Pen didn't have time to deplore the property's less than flourishing appearance. Mere hours after she arrived, the funeral for her mother was held at a nearby church, complete with reporters all the way from Boston. Pen could tell her aunts thought Livonia and not her estranged husband had been the draw. So what if Arnold Anderson's decisions affected hundreds of thousands around the world? Livonia Peachtree had been a famous beauty hereabouts, and the eldest daughter of a fine Southern family. Given that Charleston was the center of the universe, no Yankee—no matter how successful—could amount to a hill of beans by comparison.

To their way of thinking, the honor Livonia had done Pen's father by marrying him couldn't be repaid.

However annoying her aunts' assumptions, the presence
of the media made Pen grateful she'd come. Dressed in an
elegant but not overdone dark suit, she'd fielded their questions smoothly, long years in the spotlight having taught
her how to say what was expected while revealing nothing
much at all. Yes, her father was sorry not to be here, but
she knew everyone understood how crucial keeping business going was these days. Pen appreciated that her father
trusted her to pay his respects.

The reporters' lack of interest in photographing anyone
but Pen at the verdant graveside had taken her aunts aback.
Like all Charlestonians, whose egocentric view of the
world was immovable, they'd recovered quickly enough.
Northerners couldn't be expected to comprehend who was
important.

Pen had been ready to fly to London after the last
prayer, but she knew the urge was simple cowardice. She
had to stay until the will was read, even if—regardless of
its contents—the aftermath was bound to be unpleasant.
She'd clenched her teeth all through the car ride to the family lawyers' offices downtown. The lush spring warmth
and the feathery tunnels of Spanish moss failed to soothe
her. As the historic section of the city caught them in its
embrace, her aunts were aflutter, wondering how their
"dear, dear sister" might have remembered them. Pen suspected they knew exactly what Livonia's last testament
contained. For as long as she'd known them, the Peachtree
sisters had been as thick as thieves.

The young Negro driver let them out at a converted
Colonial row house a stone's throw from the Battery sea-
wall. The area was drenched with color: the bay, the sky,
the beautifully poisonous oleanders aburst with bloom.
Beneath their patina of storm and age, the houses were
rainbows, too. Pen wished she could remain outside. For
all that history had beaten down this city, it was every bit
as achingly lovely as its blinkered natives believed. Alas,
the door to their destination soon opened. However old-
fashioned Pen had felt pulling on white gloves, she was
glad for them when she shook the doddering attorney's

hand. Under the cotton, her palms were sweating as if it were high summer.

As it turned out, they had reason to. Her mother's nerve had been bolder than Pen expected. Not only had she left her sisters the house, the land, and the contents of a hefty expense account that, rightly speaking, reverted to Pen's father upon her death, she hadn't mentioned Pen's name at all. Not to say, "I know my daughter's father will take care of her, but I wish her well." Not to leave her the silver rattle she might have chomped on as a teething babe. Certainly not to express regret for the poorly veiled dislike with which she'd habitually regarded her. The only individuals who'd been treated worse were Livonia's underpaid and overworked servants.

Like Livonia's daughter, they might as well never have been born.

"Heavens!" her aunt Elizabeth exclaimed as Pen sat in cold-faced and stunned silence. The humiliation she should have known better than to feel washed over her in waves. "Who'd have thought our dear, dear sister would be this generous?"

"Not I," chimed Pen's plump aunt Mary, hand to her breast. "I declare, I'm quite overwhelmed!"

Pen's legs were shaking, but she rose anyway. She wanted to run, to say to hell with this half of her family, once and for all. The money didn't matter, and she was loved—not by Livonia, but she was. Her temper seemed a distant thing, too weak to come to her rescue. Who cared if she tucked her tail between her legs? Who but her father would even know? He, of all people, would understand.

"Yes?" said the lawyer, looking up at what must have been the very strange expression on Pen's face.

Blood surged into her cheeks a second before she spoke.

"It can't be enforced," she said quietly.

The lawyer's wispy white eyebrows rose. "Pardon?"

"The will. It can't be enforced." She pulled the papers her father had given her from her purse, waiting until the man spread and flattened them on his desk. His hands shook as he did so, but she was certain that was due to age and not nervousness. This was an old Charleston firm, built on social connections rather than brainpower. If this man knew his ass from more than a dozen statutes she'd be surprised. "Livonia had a prior agreement with my father, giving him control of those assets. She had the use of them while she lived, but with her death, the house and land pass to me. As you can see, their agreement includes settlements for my mother's sisters. As long as they don't go wild and buy out the shops on King Street, they should do fine on them."

The lawyer didn't get as far as opening his mouth.

"Oh, Penelope! Honey!" her aunt Mary cooed. "I know you can't mean to do this. Your dear mother's dying wishes should be respected."

"My dear mother left you things that weren't hers to give."

"Your father adored her!" her aunt Elizabeth objected. No doubt she thought so. Never mind Livonia had been avoiding anything resembling wifely duties for the last fifteen years. To Elizabeth, it would have been impossible for anyone not to worship her sister.

Pen turned back to the lawyer. "Those are copies," she said, snapping her purse briskly closed. "You're welcome to go over them with your associates. I should warn you, though, should my aunts contest the contract in any fashion, their settlements disappear."

"Well," said the lawyer, his lips working. "I can see we . . . have a thing or two to consider here."

"Consider all you like. Should you need a consult, I'm sure my father's firm will be in touch soon."

"Penelope!" her aunt Mary cried. "Don't be a silly goose!"

Pen stopped at the door, but couldn't quite make herself turn around. "I'm taking a taxi back to the house. You're free to return for now, but I'll expect you to make alternate arrangements relatively soon."

As she strode away, her aunts burst into protest like startled birds—dubiously innocent ones. Pen's legs moved faster, not running but near enough. Her knees almost gave out when she hit the sidewalk. The sunshine was bright enough to shock her. Afraid she might fall, she braced her hand on the palm that grew from a square of dirt across from the lawyer's door. The trunk was dry and husky, its simple strength somehow reminding her to breathe.

"All right then," she said to herself. "You did what you meant to, and you're the one with the power. Your mother's dead. Her stupid sisters can't hurt you like they did when you were little."

If they couldn't hurt her, she wouldn't have been trembling, but the reminder served its purpose. This fight was just beginning, and she would need her resolve, especially since there was no one here to lean on or take her side. The memory of Graham's honest face jabbed through her, but she pushed the image away. Spinning fantasies about him would do her no good.

Straightening once more, she tugged her smart suit jacket over her hips. Her father had been right to send her. Pen would never be free of her old shadows until she saw this through to the end.

Kansas City, Missouri

On the floor!" Frank shouted, a gangster-style machine gun braced on his hip. "This is a stickup!"

Li-Hua shivered at this display of Frank's authority. He looked gorgeous in his dark pin-striped suit, tall and strong and dangerously male. Thanks to the Chinese box they'd stolen in Chicago, with every soul they swallowed, their power drew closer to the supremacy they deserved. Though Li-Hua's lover had bitten no one yet today, the twenty-odd people in the lobby dropped readily at his order, as if their knees had been chopped. Li-Hua's own thrall was hardly less persuasive, though she wasn't taking the lead for this particular bank job.

"Don't move," Frank added sharply to the single teller. Four empty cages stretched beside him, testimony to Frank and Li-Hua's excellent timing. "Keep your hands where I can see them."

The clerk did, of course, leaving Li-Hua free to survey the street through the large plate glass front window, declared by its bright gold lettering to be the Kansas City Bank and Trust. She'd taken up her position in the corner beside the door, guarding it against anyone undesirable coming in. She was dressed like Frank in a dark man's suit, and a bright red handkerchief hid her face. A brown fedora shaded her eyes, which jittered from the drugs she and Frank had taken to stay alert while the sun was up.

Li-Hua didn't mind the odd sensation. Since they'd started robbing banks, this had become her favorite moment, when the humans first realized their safe little lives were being rent asunder, when the air turned electric with adrenaline and fear. Tingles swept strongly up her spine. The scent of their victims' sweat was almost as sweet as blood.

"Oh, my God," one of the women murmured, a touch of excitement in her quavering voice. "We're being robbed by Bonnie and Clyde."

Li-Hua snorted behind her bandana. Bonnie and Clyde's press might be more impressive, but those stupid mortals were amateurs compared to Frank and her.

"Nose to the tiles!" Frank ordered, giving the female who'd spoken a nice sharp kick. "Hands behind your head. Any of you look at us, and you die."

The woman moaned as a rib snapped, the other hostages exclaiming in sympathy and horror. This was entertaining, but the whisper of a thought tugged Li-Hua's attention away from them. She heard the teller wondering if he could reach the alarm switch before Frank saw. He didn't understand why it was so difficult to move his arm. He'd been trained for this. Fear shouldn't have paralyzed him. The sheriff was probably at the barbershop. He'd be here in minutes if the teller could summon him.

"Frank," Li-Hua said, because she was better at reading mortals than her lover.

Receiving *her* thoughts clearly, Frank punched one fist through the fancy teller's grill. The hole he'd made in the brass allowed him to grip the teller beneath the jaw. The bespectacled man's eyes went white as his feet left the floor.

The teller would have a devil of a time explaining how Frank did this, but at the moment Frank's incaution simply added to Li-Hua's thrill.

"Fill the bag with money," Frank said, handily trapping the human's gaze. "Including what's in the safe."

"We h-had a run," the teller stammered, because he hadn't been ordered to tell the truth. "The safe is empty today."

"Lie," Li-Hua said, her eyes on the street again. "The manager was worried about a panic and got an extra delivery of cash."

Cars were passing on the tree-lined avenue, but no one

seemed to have noticed a crime was in progress. They were going about their business, walking their juicy little children and carrying their groceries. Not wanting anyone outside to see, Li-Hua held her Tommy gun down by her trouser leg—no loss, since it wasn't her best weapon anyway. Behind the outlaw handkerchief, her fangs had begun to sharpen, her mouth filling with saliva. She adored what she and Frank were doing almost more than she could express.

"The safe is on a time lock," the teller tried. "I don't have the power to open it."

Frank's bandana fluttered as he laughed. "Don't you worry about that."

When Frank ripped the entire brass cage off the marble counter, Li-Hua could have clambered up his big, scrumptious body and given their human audience a show they wouldn't soon forget. Instead, she watched Frank leap nimbly over the half wall, his speed too fast to stop even if there'd been anyone brave enough to try. He barely grunted as he tore the heavy door off the thick steel vault.

The teller inhaled so hard in shock he choked. A large chunk of wall had wrenched off with Frank's efforts.

"Hah!" Frank chortled at the stacks of green bills inside. "Looks like we're going to need more bags."

Li-Hua saw the take was good, maybe seventy thousand American dollars. Frank filled two sacks in no time, then took care of the teller by smashing his skull with the machine gun butt. From the sound of it, Frank had killed him, but there were plenty more where he came from.

"You," Li-Hua said, nudging the legs of a tall young man who'd caught her eye earlier. "You're coming out with us."

"God have mercy," said the man, stumbling up shaking.

Frank tossed Li-Hua one of the bulging bags, freeing his hand to grab a weeping woman up off the floor. She was Li-Hua's physical opposite, a pretty blonde with big breasts, though not the one whose rib he'd broken. Jealousy spurted like acid through Li-Hua's veins . . . until Frank's ice blue eyes flared into her own. He was looking forward to killing this pair together, to each of them drinking up a new soul. Li-Hua's body tightened at the images of blood and sex he was sending her, the power they would celebrate by fucking each other afterward. It was *her* Frank wanted. She was the love of his life.

He chuckled as she momentarily forgot what she was doing.

"Car," he reminded. "It's time to get these hostages on the road."

"Please," the woman sobbed as they dragged her onto the pavement. One of her low-heeled shoes had fallen off somewhere, though—oddly enough—she still clutched a canvas carrying bag. Women and their attachment to their purses never ceased to mystify Li-Hua. "I have a baby. Please don't hurt me."

Frank shoved her, bag and all, into the roomy back of their stolen Ford.

"Stay," he said, looking first at the woman and then the man. "Both of you stay where you are and keep quiet."

Since the people in the bank had started screaming, Frank laid down a thick burst of fire. The front window was still shattering as he floored the gas pedal.

The shiny black V-8 careered around a corner with the wheels squealing. Her heart pumping with excitement, Li-Hua twisted to watch the humans in the backseat. They squeaked and braced themselves, but they were firmly under Frank's thrall, forbidden by his words to make more than the slightest noise. Their eyes went wide as Kansas City's flat-roofed buildings whizzed by at a reckless rate. Frank glanced at the humans in the mirror and laughed softly under his breath.

"Boo," he murmured, and Li-Hua had to laugh, too.

Determined not to miss a single reaction, she came up on her knees to face the back. A wild joy rose inside her as the Ford tipped on two wheels when it took a turn. This was so much better than bowing and scraping in the London nest. This was living for vampires.

"Here," she said, tugging down her bandana to bare her fangs. "Get a peek at the real danger."

To her delight, the humans gasped in unison and shrank

back. Fortunately, Frank never ordered their hostages to stay calm. Their terror was so delicious she simply had to run her tongue across her sharp eyeteeth.

At that, the man reached out to clutch the woman's hand, desperate for even her questionable support. "My God, what are you?"

"A devil," Li-Hua teased, curving her nails into playful claws. "And I'm going to steal your soul."

The woman moaned and hid her face in the man's shoulder. "*He's* going to steal yours," Li-Hua added to the woman with a sideways nod at Frank.

Clearly appreciating her humor, Frank took his hand off the gearshift to squeeze her thigh, high enough that the compression of her leg muscle tugged the folds of her sex. Moisture flooded from her like a dam breaking, a perfume Frank's senses were too sharp to miss.

"Lord," he said, amusement warming his husky voice. "The only thing that could make this better is if the police actually gave chase."

Li-Hua grinned, in tune with his sentiment. Though they'd be wise to keep a low profile until their new powers were established, part of her was disappointed local lawmen never seemed to scramble fast enough for pursuit. The only human who'd come close was a fellow with a cowboy hat and a Texas drawl. She and Frank weren't sure which branch of law enforcement he belonged to—perhaps the new Bureau of Investigation. He'd given them a few bad moments in Indiana, but after that he'd fallen behind. It was a shame, she thought. The spice of real opposition would have been exciting.

Looking for consolation where she could find it, she leaned to slide her fingers over and around the giant bulge rising from Frank's lap.

He kissed her even as he drove, tangling their tongues so that the kiss was deep and openmouthed. This caused the woman to squeak again in alarm. Frank broke free before they could crash and laughed.

"Hold on," he warned, spinning the wheel sharply.

He shot them down the ramp to their rented underground

garage on 18th and Vine, the infamous corner where jazz clubs and brothels had thumbed their noses at Prohibition since the day it went into effect. Kansas City might be the supposed Heart of America, but that heart had been far from dry. The Ford jounced to a halt a second before it bumped the formerly secret liquor unloading dock. Half a second after that, Frank streaked out to push the garage's rolling door over the opening.

Li-Hua doubted their victims noticed his unnatural speed. They were too busy shaking in their shoes over her.

She had them out in a twinkling, yanked from the car, tossed, and left sprawling on the bloodstained mattresses she and Frank had thrown across the cement platform. She pulled the fraying cord that turned on the one lightbulb.

It was crucial that the humans be able to see her.

"Strip," she said to the man, so hot and bothered she wasn't certain she could wait for him to comply.

Though his hands were already moving, he shook his head.

"Yes," she insisted, pushing her will straight into his eyes. "You want to be naked for me. In fact, you want me to fuck you more than you've ever wanted anything in your life."

The man's face flushed dark as his cock punched up in helpless obedience. Clearly embarrassed, he crossed his hands above the tent his instant erection made. That resistence lasted about a second. Almost as soon as he'd dropped his hands, his fingers started fumbling to remove his belt. His eagerness made him curse, or maybe it was his shock at what he was doing. Shock didn't matter as long as the rest of him went along. His heart was beating twice as fast as before, compelled to keep him as stiff and ready as he could be. Giddy with her power, Li-Hua helped him tear his shirt down his chest.

"You want me," she repeated as buttons flew. "You'll die if I don't take you."

A weight hit Li-Hua's shoulder, the woman swinging her canvas satchel. "You leave him alone! Look at his wedding ring!"

Frank caught the woman easily from behind, letting her struggle in his hold as much as she liked. Li-Hua knew he didn't regret the way her buxom breasts bounced across his arm.

"You look," he laughed, his sharp-fanged grin up against her ear. "Look and see how my beloved makes this man beg to break his vows."

The reminder of his marriage seemed to trouble their male victim.

"Sh," Li-Hua said as he opened his mouth to speak. "The only words I want to hear are how much you desire me."

The man looked at her, shuddered, and then he broke completely. He shoved his pants so desperately down his legs his shoes got caught in the cuffs. Li-Hua held him down by the waist, the only way she could prevent him from rising to embrace her.

"Jesus," he said, his hips and erection thrusting frantically up at her. She had to lick her lips at the sight of that. He wasn't as big as Frank, but his engorged prick was a deep brick red from the blood in it, positively tortured looking as it throbbed. "Jesus, lady, please take me."

Eager enough herself, Li-Hua spun off her clothes, straddled him on her knees, and sank down.

She didn't have to tell the human this was the best thing he'd ever felt. He groaned at the sensation, his neck arching hard as his eyes threatened to roll back. More *oh, Gods* and *pleases* followed, the tremor of his strong young thighs warning her he'd reached the teetering edge of coming.

If this was all the stamina he had, Li-Hua might be doing his better half a favor.

"No," she snapped, grabbing his jaw to force his gaze to hers. "No coming until I say."

His eyes were a pretty hazel, his pupils as big as dimes. His welling tears made the black shine with misery.

"Please," he begged low and rough. "Please let me have a release."

The sound of a zipper rasping said Frank was feeling the mood just as pressingly. When she looked back, he was pushing the woman's hand along his shaft's thickness. She was still weeping, so he hadn't ordered her to be willing. Li-Hua supposed she shouldn't have been surprised. Frank always relished the use of force, whether as instigator or recipient.

He blew Li-Hua a kiss as she stared.

The man was staring, too; Frank's cock *was* a bit of a prodigy. He jerked his eyes away and colored when he saw Li-Hua had noticed.

Oh, she thought, *innocents like this are too priceless.*

"I'm moving now," she warned the man whose prick twitched frenziedly inside her. "And you're going to enjoy me riding you enough to cry."

He did, of course, enjoying and enjoying until his pleasured moans turned to agony. His body shook with its thwarted need to climax, but Li-Hua had no mercy. She scaled more peaks than she could count until, at last, Frank tossed her the Chinese box.

"Finish it," he urged, his voice almost as strained as the man's. "Finish it so I can."

The man came like a geyser when she bit his neck, long, groaning jets her strongest thrall couldn't override. By that point, she didn't care. Down she drank him in great swallows, her head soon spinning with the way she gorged. She barely heard Frank roar out his orgasm. Glutted, she tore from her victim as his pulse reached the near fatal skipping point. With movements she was glad she'd practiced, considering how badly she was swaying, she flipped the box open on its hinge. Her right hand ground it down until its little brass teeth dug into the flesh above the man's breastbone. The box seemed to awaken as it tasted blood. A tiny stream of light flowed around the faint dragon engraving, bursting into a red glow when it reached the rubies that formed the eyes.

The human's fear slammed back as he sensed his life being sucked away.

"No," he said, the quiver in it music to Li-Hua's ears. "I don't want to—"

His dying rattle cut off his plea. His soul rushed into her like a surge of electricity, through her palm, up her arm, causing every cell in her immortal body to sing with power. Her heart pounded her ribs like a jackhammer—more than it did for climax, more than it did for cocaine. Li-Hua was a goddess no force on earth could oppose. Beautiful. Potent. The mistress of her own fate. London's queen was nothing compared to her. Frank's eyes burned with a fierce white fire as he watched her soar, drinking in her pleasure as he soon would drink in his own.

When his hand found hers and contracted, she knew she and Frank were destined to rule the world.

His lust jacked up from watching Li-Hua, Frank took the human female with less patience. She barely suffered before she died, but Li-Hua couldn't bring herself to mind. Stealing souls had more than one side effect. Frank took Li-Hua heartbeats later, his huge, stone-stiff cock jamming in and out like he had an engine inside his groin. They collapsed as soon as they came together, sleeping like the dead until full sunset.

Li-Hua woke first. She wrinkled her nose at the bodies they'd barely bothered to roll aside. They were cold now, their skin the unappealing color of dirty snow. One thing Li-Hua had never liked about using the dragon box was figuring out where to toss the trash afterward.

Sighing, because of course they would think of something, she tugged the woman's canvas bag out from under her. Inside, she found a teething ring, a wallet with two whole dollars, a crocheted sweater, the human's passbook for the ill-starred bank, and—last but not least—a copy of yesterday's *Kansas City Star*.

Frank mumbled and struggled to sit up as she opened the newspaper.

"Christ," he said. "I'd give my left nut for a clean toothbrush."

Li-Hua didn't answer. Heat flashed through her angry and raw as she touched a grainy photograph on the Society page. "Industrialist's Wife Passes" said the headline. The young woman in the picture wore a nicer-fitting suit than any mortal deserved to own.

"What?" Frank asked.

She passed him the article.

"Well, well." He stroked the caption beneath the photo with one finger, concentrating on the printed name. "If it isn't the bitch who dynamited our nice castle. And, look, she's here in the same country."

"It's fate," Li-Hua said, sure of it.

Frank bared his lengthening fangs in a brilliant smile. "Perhaps it is, sweets. At the very least, it's a chance for a bit of sport."

Peachtree Plantation

Having her aunts residing in the house was not conducive to sleep for Pen. Too restless to lie in bed staring at the ceiling of her childhood room, especially given the memories she had of it, she padded to the small office on the second floor. For the last hour or so she'd been going over the accounts.

That activity hadn't relaxed her, either.

Peachtree's financial situation was as she'd feared. Staff hadn't been paid in almost a year, probably on the excuse that times were tough. The argument was hard to counter, unless you knew how long Pen's mother had been overstating her expenses in order to pass "treats" from Arnold's pocket to Mary and Elizabeth. Pen could guess to the penny what her aunts had squirreled away, but servants were working in return for their room and board. Only two had given notice. The rest were too frightened to leave the only home they'd known to seek other employment. Pen couldn't blame them. Jobs that paid enough to live on were a challenge to find these days. Welcome though they were, Roosevelt's work programs simply couldn't fill all the holes.

She cursed how easy it had been for her mother and aunts to take advantage of the servants. Pen could pay them out of her pocket for a while; her father's allowance was generous. At some point, though, if she were serious about making Peachtree hers, she was going to have to turn this plantation into a going concern, one that could support itself. How in tarnation she'd do that she didn't know.

She could pray, she supposed, and hope the price of pecans shot through the roof.

That bit of gallows humor had her dropping her face into weary hands. She was tempted to call her father and consult with him, but the hour was even more ungodly in England.

Graham would be up, wherever the hell he was, probably biting some sighing maiden on her fair white neck. Pen caught herself stroking her clavicle and grimaced. She refused to remember the bliss of giving him her vein, though Graham *did* have a head for business—not as sharp as her father's, but sharp enough.

"Stop," she ordered, disgusted with herself. "You don't even have a number you can call."

That, however, wasn't strictly true. She could 'phone the university where Graham's father had been teaching. Most likely, someone there would know how he could be reached.

The mere thought of that kicked her pulse faster.

"Damn it," she snapped, pushing up from her chair in annoyance.

Rising put her in the perfect position to be tackled by the shape that burst in through the dark window. Glass rained down as Pen cried out, crashing to the floor beneath a big male weight. Countless hours of training were all that allowed her legs to snap up and shove her assailant with all her might.

The vampire—for she didn't know what else it could be—flew off his feet and into the wall. Knowing the impact wouldn't stun him long, Pen snatched up a letter opener, using it to stab him straight through the vocal cords.

When the thing just grunted and tugged it out, Pen decided to run.

Quick as lightning, the vampire grabbed her calf and upended her, with no particular effort that she could discern. Pen was glad she was wearing male-style pajamas. A nightgown would have been up around her head. As it was, her recently waved auburn hair was sweeping the floor.

"Now, now," the vampire scolded. "Is that any way to greet an old friend?"

"Crap," Pen said, realizing she recognized this blood-sucker. He was one of the pair who'd kidnapped Graham's father—Frank, she thought he was called.

Evidently, Frank remembered her.

Already dizzy from being hung upside down, she debated flailing, then concluded it would be pointless. "I can't help you," she said instead. "I honestly don't know where the Fitz Clares are."

"Aw," Frank responded insincerely. "Too bad for you I'm not interested in them—at least not for now."

"Do you want money? I think we have some silver you could sell."

Frank snorted out a laugh. "Have enough to compensate for you *blowing up our castle*?"

Because he was shaking her rather forcefully by the ankle, Pen didn't have the breath to answer. With a swift-ness that made her queasy, he zipped out of the office and down the grand curving stairs to the entryway. Twice he let her head bonk the treads, which she doubted was acciden-tal. She was reconsidering her decision about the flailing when he skidded to a halt in the front parlor.

"Sweets," he called out in dulcet tones. "I found what we were looking for."

His partner in crime streaked in a second later, looking far too dainty to be a bloodsucking fiend. When she saw Pen, she clapped her delicate white hands.

"Shake it some more!" she cried. "Its face has gone nice and red."

Its *face*, Pen thought, her temper flaring. She'd show that fangy little runt *its* face.

She swung in Frank's grip and grabbed the fireplace poker—a heavy iron one, thank the Lord. The momentum of her backswing jabbed the point deep into his thigh, forc-ing her to grunt when she yanked it out in preparation to use it again. He dropped her, taken too much by surprise to retaliate.

Li-Hua's open, screaming mouth seemed an admirable follow-up target.

As Pen wrapped both hands on the poker and prepared to charge, she spared a fraction of a second to wonder where her aunts were during this uproar. The fraction ended when the poker crunched through the other side of Li-Hua's spinal cord.

Cold, sticky blood sprayed Pen's face. Frank roared and swung at her. The clout he landed across her chest was like being hit by a locomotive. Pen hurtled across the room into a portrait of her mother, turning its frame to splinters as she slid down the wall. She shook the stars from her head, but her limbs wouldn't cooperate in helping her get up.

"You die," Frank growled, stalking toward her. Pen's heart jumped into her throat. The gouge she'd made in his thigh wasn't troubling him at all. His fangs were glinting, and his eyes looked like they were literally shooting sparks. "You die with my fist shoved up your pussy."

"Right," Pen gasped, discovering she could speak after all. "Fist up pussy. Can't wait to get it over with."

Frank's fit of paralyzing rage gave Pen a chance to notice his wounded lover crawling toward them across the threadbare carpet. Li-Hua looked bad. She was panting, and blood was running from her mouth at a speedy clip, but the poker wasn't skewering it anymore. Pen could see it lying in the foyer where the vampiress must have thrown it. Even worse, the awful rent behind her tonsils was sealing closed.

"Lordy," Pen breathed, terror sweeping icily over her. "Don't you people know how to die?"

It didn't seem she was going to get an answer. Frank seized her by the scruff of the neck, dragging her like a naughty puppy to his lover. He pushed Pen under the gory half ruin of her face.

"Drink," he said to his partner. "Her blood is yours by rights."

Li-Hua struck too fast for Pen to roll away. The sound of fangs penetrating skin was wet and disgusting. Despite her repulsion, it felt good when Li-Hua sucked—which might have been the most alarming development of all. Pen tried to be open-minded but—given a choice—she'd rather die cranky, thank you very much.

Determined to salve her pride, she fought the waves of pleasure. She fought Li-Hua, too, but had less luck there. Wounded or not, the vampiress's hold was steely. To make matters worse, she drank faster—and more—than Graham ever had. Pen thought Li-Hua should have been swelling like a tick, but she couldn't make her mouth form the words. Her struggles were growing feeble, her hands and feet tingling with numbness. Shivers had begun to wrack her by the time the vampiress let go.

Her face was clean and perfect when she sat up astride Pen's waist, a true flower of the Orient, from her high white brow to her rounded chin. The darkest sort of satisfaction turned her exotic eyes to gold. Her too-long canines were all that spoiled the curve of her scarlet mouth.

"Now," she said, her voice as thick and rich as if she'd had sex. "You stay where you are and don't move a thing."

Pen wasn't sure Li-Hua could thrall her. She thought Graham's earlier claim might have made her immune to that. Unfortunately, it didn't matter. With all the blood she'd lost, she didn't have the strength to do more than twitch.

From the depths of her front trouser pocket—tight black leather trousers, Pen observed—the vampiress pulled a small round box. It was the sort of antique bric-a-brac Pen's mother would have used to store her multitude of pills. Made of tarnished brass, it had what looked like a Chinese dragon engraved on it. Still smiling, Li-Hua flipped it open.

"Your aunts gave you up," she mentioned, as if it were by the by. "We didn't even have to thrall them. They must care about you a lot."

Pen had a moment to register the honeyed drip of sarcasm before the vampiress tore Pen's nice silk pajama top above her breasts.

Pen suspected she wasn't going to like what was coming next, but she didn't expect the box to bite into her skin as it did. Light sprang up around the worn engraving, deceptively beautiful pearly rays. Abruptly, Pen felt like she was bobbing, like the floor beneath her had been transformed into an unsteady sea. An odd, sucking sensation tugged at her heart, this one not a bit pleasant.

No, she tried to say, but her lips wouldn't move at all.

"Yes," Li-Hua mocked, her palm grinding the box down into her flesh. The drawing feeling strengthened, reaching deep into Pen's abdomen.

That's mine, Pen thought, though she wasn't certain what she was referring to. *You're not allowed to take it.*

She might as well have saved her protest. Her vision didn't fade so much as snap to black.

Pen thought she must have been shunted straight to hell. Pounding boots echoed through the cavelike dark, Lucifer's soldiers running in formation.

"Captain!" someone called. "In here!"

Pen couldn't see Li-Hua, but she could hear her. She hissed like a creature from a horror movie, her hand still grinding the box between Pen's breasts.

"God Almighty," breathed a wondering male voice. "Look at those fangs."

"Did you get it?" Frank asked, urgent and low.

"She's not dead yet," Li-Hua snapped back.

She . . . me? Pen thought, because she was pretty convinced she was.

"Shoot it," ordered another, naggingly familiar voice. "Forget takin' 'em alive. Empty your clips into both of 'em."

The roar of gunfire deafened her—as if she hadn't lost enough of her senses. She *might* have seen ammo flashing in the blackness, *might* have felt a weight lift off her just before another window crashed. Her body, if she had one, was leaden. People shouted instructions she couldn't make out, the words jumbled together by her confused mind. Feet ran this way and that. The gunfire grew distant and then stopped.

"They're gone," said a man. "Jesus, Captain, I know we hit them. I can't believe they could run that fast."

The one they were calling captain knelt by her.

"Pen," he said. "Can you hear me?"

Pressure was being applied to her neck. It hurt, but she couldn't moan.

"Get Ehrlich," the captain barked. "She needs a transfusion."

Pen knew an Ehrlich. He'd been a medic at a secret training facility. If she needed medical attention, she must not be dead. A gentle, callused hand brushed her blood-drenched hair from her brow. She wondered if her eyes were open or shut.

"Hang in there, honey," said the captain. "Help is on the way."

She faded out, coming back when something pricked her, a sharp sliver of sensation piercing the back of her hand.

"How could they just keep going?" one of the soldiers asked. "I thought silver bullets killed those bastards."

"Iron," Pen croaked in a voice like a rusty nail. Only iron bullets killed vampires.

"What, honey?" said the captain.

Shit, Pen thought, lips pressed together in dismay. That bit of information wasn't supposed to slip out.

Peachtree Plantation

When Pen regained consciousness, more or less in one piece, she was lying on a soft canopy bed in one of the good second-floor bedrooms—the ones her mother never put her in because she claimed they were for guests. Swaths of white mosquito netting, not unlike wedding veils, looped back to the rice-style carvings on the posts. The sun was shining, the huge live oak outside her window whispering in a breeze. The distinctive caw of a peacock—half cat, half human baby—floated to her from the otherwise quiet grounds. In the comfy armchair beside the bed, her agency mentor, Captain Roy Blunt, snored softly into the cowboy hat he'd slid over his face.

He wasn't a big man—five nine at the most in his battered boots, with nothing but wiry muscle to brag about. He was fifty, but could have passed for ten years older, given the seams the Texas sun had baked in his face. His eyes were his best feature, a clear, bright blue that made you want to trust him on sight.

Pen had certainly fallen for their ostensible honesty.

"You knew," she said, at which—like all good military men—Roy snorted and sat up. "You knew about the vampires."

He set his hat aside on a table doily and dragged one hand down his face. Pen suspected he was stalling.

"Of course I knew," he said. "Those yahoos from last night have been hittin' banks from here to Chicago. I've been trackin' 'em for a while now. They gave away what they were near a dozen times."

"You knew what they were before. You knew about the *upyr* before you recruited me."

Pen's voice trembled with anger. Roy had deceived her, had told her he wanted her to join his top-secret intelligence agency as a way to test what female spies could do. The organization was so stealthy it didn't have a name; all anyone ever called it was the agency. To her, this added to its glamour. Pen had been flattered down to her toes, delighted to be invited to play with boys, and more than a little gratified by the opportunity to contribute to her country. Up until then, the most use she'd been to the world was playing hostess for her father. The idea that her recruitment had nothing to do with her smarts or pluck infuriated her.

She'd let Roy play her ego like a violin.

Biting back an exclamation of discomfort, she shoved a stack of pillows behind her back so she could face Roy. As she moved, she realized her ribs were tightly wrapped in bandages. She wasn't covered in blood, and she wore fresh pajamas—probably thanks to Ehrlich, the medic. Pen didn't let that distract her, not even when Roy shot out his hand to support her arm.

Lots of things were becoming clear to her now.

"It wasn't my connection to my father that interested you. It was his connection to Graham Fitz Clare. You approached me a week after my father hired him. You knew his adoptive father was a vampire. You were hoping I'd hit it off with Graham and give you an in."

"Honey, I don't know what you're talkin' about."

"Don't," Pen said so forcefully she had to gulp for air at a stab of pain. "You know I can tell when someone is lying."

Roy sighed and tugged his ski slope nose. "I know you can," he said, his drawl as thick as barbecue sauce. "Seein' as I'm the one who taught you."

"Well?"

"You sure you want to talk about this now? You're still recuperatin'."

"Spit it out."

Roy leaned forward over his narrow, jean-clad knees. His hands were loosely clasped together, the thumb of one rubbing the simple gold signet ring he always wore on his third finger. "All right. I admit I wasn't entirely honest about why I wanted you to work for me—not that you haven't lived up to any expectation I could have had. You're every bit the pistol I'd hoped you'd be."

"But?"

"But in certain small human circles, the name and nature of Edmund Fitz Clare ain't unknown. When I started formin' my agency, I ran into one of those circles." Roy shook his head in marvel at the memory. "I'm tellin' you, Pen, learnin' what was out there changed my life. Immortal people. Amazin' powers. My head just about exploded considerin' what that would mean. These creatures could settle questions I've been ponderin' since I was a boy. I knew I'd never look at the world the same."

Roy's bright blue eyes pleaded with her to understand. And she did, to a degree. The idea of vampires had a romance no one could deny. Understanding, however, didn't mean she'd trust him again.

As for Graham and his ilk "settling questions," Pen thought Roy was barking up the wrong tree there. From what she'd seen of vampires, they didn't have any more answers than human beings.

For the moment, she kept her thoughts to herself. She smoothed the coverlet across her waist, her gaze steady on Roy's face. "Last night, I heard you talking about taking Frank and Li-Hua alive."

The tiniest flinch deepened the squint lines around Roy's eyes. "Well, I'd hoped we could study 'em. I admit I'm in over my head with this pair. But when I saw they were about to kill you . . ."

Pen believed he hadn't wanted to let her die; Roy was fond of her, and he took care of his men. She also believed he thought he'd have other chances to "study" the *upyr*. Hiding the truth about Graham and his family had cost her some guilt. Now the decision seemed justified. Roy had his Stetson in his hands again, his thumbs drawing arcs on the dusty brim as he angled his upper body over his thighs. The shoulders of his blue Western shirt were bleached almost white from the sun.

"Pen," he said, like he knew she was going to argue. "If you could put me in touch with Professor Fitz Clare, I'd be mighty grateful. I could use his advice on how to catch these things. The strategies I thought would work are lettin' me down."

"Oh, no," Pen said. "I can't vouch for you, Roy. Not anymore."

"I know all vampires ain't bad." Roy took her hands and squeezed them even as she wagged her head back and forth. "I'd never do anything to harm your friends, but I really think you have to help me. Those two are out of control. They've killed twenty people that I know of, and they seem to be gettin' more powerful and more reckless as they go along. If we don't move on 'em soon, I don't know what will stop 'em. Plus, there's the not so tiny matter of coverin' up their indiscretions. I don't want to contemplate the panic it would cause if people knew they had more to worry about than the Depression."

"Damn it, Roy."

Roy smiled, just a little, at her exasperation. He sensed he had her on his hook. "You know I'm right, honey. You saw what they could do. That Chinese gal nearly drank you dry. Whatever else I'm misinformed about, I know that ain't normal for their kind."

Pen frowned, which only broadened his grin. "I'll *see* if I can contact Graham's father. Whether he talks to you will be up to him."

Wisely, Roy let this drop. "Your aunts are all right," he said, sitting back in his chair with the appearance of laziness. "Claim they slept through the whole attack, though your aunt Elizabeth has a suspicious hand-shaped bruise circlin' her neck, and your aunt Mary seemed a tad disappointed that you'd survived."

Pen snorted. She bet her aunts were disappointed. They'd assume they were that much closer to keeping their precious Peachtree if last night's intruders had taken care of her. Then again, she was in no position to be offended.

She hadn't remembered to ask if they'd lived or died.

Roy's men remained in and around the plantation. Pen had her doubts as to what protection they could provide, surmising they had other reasons for staying . . . like keeping an eye on her. That being the case, she didn't make her call from the house, but had Thomas, the driver, take her to the Miller Grocery in town. Plenty of folks around Peachtree didn't own telephones. Ham Miller had a booth with a little stool for them in the back of his store. Since Ham was also a purveyor of illegal 'shine, just on principle he wouldn't be sharing her business with any stranger who came asking.

Thomas was settled on the grocery's rickety porch with a Coca-Cola while Pen began the lengthy process of placing a call across the ocean to England. Her two cracked ribs made sitting straight obligatory. She tried to ignore the sweat that dotted her palms. This was, after all, hardly a social call.

Reaching the university and Professor Fitz Clare's department required some patience. Pen rolled her eyes as yet another secretary asked her to hold. To her surprise, the rich male voice that came on half a minute later was pin-drop clear.

"Is this Penelope Anderson?" it asked.

Goose bumps skittered along her spine. She knew at once that she was speaking to a vampire—which explained the good connection. *Upyr* made everything they touched work better.

"It is," she said. "May I ask to whom I'm speaking?"

"Robin Fitz Clare, Edmund's son. We met briefly at the train station."

As she recalled, Edmund had clocked his son in the

nose, preventing formal introductions. "I remember you. I'm hoping to reach Professor Fitz Clare, or Graham, if that's possible. It's rather important."

A pause stretched down the crystal clarity of the line, long enough for Pen to hear the vampire inhale.

"Hell," he said, sounding genuinely appalled. "Don't tell me you've been attacked!"

Bridesmere

Graham paced the library's balcony like a caged tiger. Very well: a caged *tomcat*, but he felt sufficiently tiger-like not to quibble. His blood was hot, his skin itchy. He wanted to change into his beast shape and rip his claws down something.

Pen had been attacked by their enemies, and she was alone in America. Or not all alone. Robin's report of her call was unsatisfactory on that score. Evidently, she had an ally: a Captain Blunt who'd recruited her for some clandestine cowboy agency in the States. Blunt knew about the *upyr*, but not enough to capture the renegades.

If Pen was screwing Blunt, Graham might have to kill the man.

"Graham!" Sally snapped from the lower level, her hand tightly laced with Ben's. For a second, Graham feared his crazy homicidal urge was written on his face. "Would you stop pacing? You're making me dizzy."

He stopped, naturally. Dizziness couldn't be good for expectant mothers.

"Sorry," he muttered, then gripped the metal rail so hard his fingers left depressions. It took a conscious effort to relax his hold. Lord, what he wouldn't have given to be with Pen that instant. He'd feel better even if he were strangling her.

If his cousin Percy noticed his tension, it didn't show. Percy sprawled, ankles crossed, hands propped behind his head, on a nail-studded brocade chaise near the crackling hearth. Per usual, he wore his aviator helmet and flight togs.

"Getting you to America isn't a problem. Unlike human pilots, I can navigate at night. Luckily, I know a few aerodromes where we can refuel, places where I . . . made friends with mortals on previous trips."

His toothy grin conveyed how he'd done this. "The question is," he continued, "should we join forces with this Captain Blunt? Robin said Miss Anderson didn't sound too certain about his trustworthiness."

"We can't just abandon Pen!" Graham burst out.

"No one's suggesting that," his father soothed. Edmund sat on the red divan with Estelle's head nestled on his shoulder. His back was straight, his right ankle braced on his left knee. To human eyes, he would have looked calm. To Graham's, his energy was jumping all over. Graham knew his father hated not having anticipated Frank and Li-Hua's actions, though he didn't see how Edmund could have predicted they'd escape to America.

"You won't know whether you can trust Blunt until you meet him," Durand put in from his dark corner. "If he doesn't have immunity to our thrall, a bite should take care of that. If he does . . ." Durand shrugged, and Graham surmised the mercenary had a more permanent fix in mind.

"There's still the European attacks to protect against," Ben said. "This family owes Pen, but we can't *all* go to America."

No one got a chance to answer. A sudden flare of hair-ruffling power had all the vampires except for Edmund surging to their feet. The power smelled of forest and earth and intense wildness. It was Graham's father's scent, though at the moment it didn't comfort. Instead, it seemed to multiply his own frustrations. Graham inhaled in shock as feline claws started breaking through his fingertips. It was happening to *his* body, but he couldn't control the reaction. In truth, he hadn't known it was possible. He'd thought *upyr* shapes never overlapped. Being this helpless made him want to attack something. His heart galloped as he wrestled back the almost overwhelming instinct to fight.

Graham's moods had been ragged lately, but if this was a taste of the turmoil inside his father, Graham was thankful he wasn't him.

"Edmund," Estelle murmured warningly.

Her cautioning him didn't help. Shorted out by some conflict with Edmund's power, every electric bulb in the room exploded. Except for the fire, the room plunged to black. To Graham's relief, his urge to change subsided. When he glanced down, his fingernails were normal.

"Well," Durand said into the silence that stretched behind Sally's shriek. "I think I can guess who needs to stay here."

The curse Edmund snarled was too guttural to make out. Graham regretted his newly sharp vision. He had no trouble perceiving his father's frightening expression.

"Sh," Estelle said, stroking his cheek and guiding his gaze to hers. "Love, you know he's right."

"They're mine," Edmund growled, an odd plea underlying the violence of his words. "It was me they tortured. Me who was too stupid to avoid their trap. I have to be the one who ends them."

"Love, I understand why you want to. Everyone does. But you know Durand will enjoy it almost as much."

Durand surprised them all by bursting into a brief, sharp laugh.

"I will," he said once he'd recovered. "And I promise you, those two won't die easily."

The zealous light in his eyes caused Estelle to pause. No one could doubt the mercenary meant the assurance. Her throat bobbed as she swallowed.

"Right," she said, turning back to Edmund. "And Graham will go with him to protect Pen."

"They'll need Ben," Percy pointed out. "Daylight eyes, don't you know."

"Oh!" Sally gasped. Her arms crossed the little swell of her belly. "Really? Ben has to go?"

"It can't be Estelle," Percy said. "I think we've all

noticed she's the only one who calms your father. Sorry," he added when Edmund hissed. "But even you can't deny it's true."

Edmund didn't argue, just jumped to his feet and squeezed his temples between his hands. This time Estelle didn't try to touch him. Possibly, she felt the rising buzz of his aura, too.

Sally stared at the near wreck who was her father and gnawed her lip.

"I'm sorry, Daddy," she whispered. "I know this might upset you, but if Ben is going to America, so am I."

"*No.*" Edmund spun toward Sally so fast even Graham was taken aback. His father's finger seemed to burn from the inside as he jabbed it at her. "You are *not* putting yourself and your baby at risk for this."

"I have to." Sally wrung her hands. "It's my baby who wants me to."

Sally and Ben withdrew to their new rooms on the second floor of the castle, their previous quarters having been destroyed by the vampire raid. Sally and the baby both liked the replacement. Clearly the creation of an earlier generation of Fitz Clares, the tester bed was fit for a queen, the windows were bigger, and the walls had been covered in an exquisite watered silk that matched the blue of her eyes. Sally thought it nice of the baby to be pleased by that, though chances were her daughter would have blue eyes, too.

She didn't bother continuing to build her case until she and Ben were alone. If he supported her, the others' protests would fall away. She watched as he strode to the window and closed the drapes. He looked stiff as he jerked them shut, but that was to be expected. Ready to fight her way, Sally started undoing the pearly buttons that marched down the front of her dress. It hadn't escaped her notice that Ben found it more difficult to oppose her wishes when she was naked. Their sexual relationship had been combustible from the first, but the added tenderness inspired by her growing baby almost did make her stubborn husband putty in her hands.

"Sally," he said, turning with a sigh. "You know this situation is too serious to be making up stories."

"I'm not making up anything. I can sense the baby's feelings. I've been able to for the last two months."

"Sweetheart, the baby's nothing but a"—Ben waved his hands—"a little frog in there. It's too tiny to have preferences."

Sally shrugged her dress from her shoulders, letting it drop around her ankles so that she stood in her slip. As expected, Ben's attention fell to the more generous swell of her breasts. Looking nervously away, he rubbed the cleft in his chin.

"It might be a frog," she said, pretending she hadn't noticed. "But it's a frog with a soul, and it really, truly doesn't want me to be apart from you."

"I believe *you* really, truly don't want to be apart from me."

"Well, of course I don't. I love you to pieces. But that isn't why I'm saying this. I want our baby to be safe, too."

She shucked her slip and faced him in her bra and panties, a white, lacy set she'd bought to show off her changing curves. Her breasts thrust out like a shelf, but her legs were as slim as ever. Ben's gaze ran over both with flattering thoroughness. A second later, as if he simply couldn't control the reaction, he licked his lips.

Before he realized he'd done it, Sally stepped to him and smoothed her hands across the width of his strong shoulders. Being this close to him, touching him, couldn't help but have an effect on her. He was so handsome, so beloved, sometimes she couldn't believe he was hers. His hands came up to squeeze her waist. Despite the worry his expression held, his clear green eyes powered into her as potently as ever.

"Ben," she said, her voice already shaded with huskiness. "Do you remember how sick I was the time you spent all night flying with Percy?"

"That's normal, love. You're pregnant."

"It's not normal for me. I hadn't been sick at all before that."

"Then you should stick closer to the professor. You always say his energy soothes you."

"I can't." Sally took a breath and framed his face gently with her hands. "I didn't want to hurt Daddy's feelings, but the baby doesn't like being close to him anymore. His energy is all buzzy and irritating, and sometimes it flares too strong. It's you she wants to be close to. It's your aura that soothes her now."

"Mine." Ben pulled away and stepped back. "Why would mine do her any good?"

"I don't know," Sally said, confused by his abrupt withdrawal. "Probably because of whatever Daddy did to you back in Switzerland. You said your souls mixed together when he drank your blood. He must have left you with an extra something or other—like he did to Estelle when he saved her from that lightning bolt."

"He didn't make me a vampire."

"I know he didn't." Perplexed as to why he was stating the obvious, she moved to him again. This time he didn't tug away when she caught his hand. "Ben, why are you upset? I think it's nice that our baby needs you as much as she needs me."

"I'm not upset. I just don't think it's normal." He raked his free hand back through his spiky hair. "Babies aren't supposed to need their fathers."

"Bollocks," Sally said, because the moment seemed to warrant it. "Most might need them differently than ours does, but they do."

She brought his hand to her mouth and kissed it, startled to find it cold. She covered it with her other hand, pulling it against the warmth of her breasts. She didn't want to tell him this next bit, but she couldn't imagine him budging until she did.

"Ben," she said, rubbing his icy knuckles more fervently. "I didn't want to tell you this, but that night you went off with Percy, there was blood."

Ben actually staggered, his face draining straight to white.

"*Blood?* You mean from the *baby*?"

Sally clutched his arms to steady him. "It was only a

little spotting. Apparently, it happens sometimes, and it might not mean anything. It just . . . frightened me a bit."

"Jesus, Sally. How could you keep that from me?"

"I didn't want to worry you. In case you hadn't noticed, you can be overprotective. The cramping went away as soon as you came back."

"Christ." He pulled her to him and hugged her hard. A few tears rolled down her cheek, but that was commonplace for her now. She sensed what Ben was going to suggest before his mouth opened.

"You have to go," she said, her face buried in his shirt as she soaked up the comfort of his embrace. "Graham needs to help Pen, and you need to watch his and Durand's back. Plus, I'm certain Daddy will get better once Frank and Li-Hua are dead."

Ben's sigh was raw and low. "Sweetheart—"

"I have to go, too. Both of us do. It's the only way to make everything work out. You know you'd never forgive yourself if you stayed with me and something happened to Graham. I promise I won't take risks or try to fight. I'll hide somewhere while you men take care of things."

Ben hugged her tighter and kissed her curls. "You're the most important person in the world to me, you and the baby. If anything happened to you . . ."

"It won't." Sally tipped up her face to him.

He met her kiss with a roughened groan, instantly tortured for other reasons than anxiety. "Sally. *God*, what you do to me."

"Show me," she pleaded, needing him inside her. "Show me what I do."

He sank to his knees before her, his hands spread to either side of her belly as he pressed soft kisses to her navel. "Sally . . ."

"Now, Ben," she said, familiar with his reluctant tone. "You know our baby doesn't know what we're doing. All she can tell is that we're happy."

Ben didn't seem convinced. "Take a nap, little frog," he whispered to her abdomen.

To Sally's amusement, she felt some tiny tension inside

her ease. She wondered if Ben had gained a share of their father's thrall. She couldn't wonder long, though, because he was sliding her lacy panties slowly down her legs and turning his face back and forth across her bared skin.

"You drive me crazy," he said. "I can't stop wanting you, even when you're like this. My cock started getting hard the minute you shut the door."

Sally could hardly take offense at this. She pushed her fingers into his hair, kneading through the strands to his scalp until his eyes closed helplessly with bliss.

When they opened, the green in them seemed to burn. Watching her, he edged her thighs apart and pressed a different sort of kiss to her core. Sally let out a little exclamation, which caused the flush on Ben's cheeks to intensify. That was fun to witness, but her head fell back nonetheless. He was so good with his mouth—his beautiful, satiny, perfectly cut male mouth. He tugged and licked and sucked her to the brink of orgasm, knowing when to stop from the rising pitch of her cries.

"Ben," she groaned, clutching his shoulders as he got to his feet. The muscles of her sex pulsed as if she had jumping beans in there.

Ben ignored her protest, kissing her nose and lifting her to sit on the side of the tester bed, the platform so high she normally needed steps to climb onto it. When the feather mattress finished sinking underneath her, she was at the perfect height to wrap her thighs around his hips.

The hardness of the hump between them, the breadth and throb of his shaft, caused a rush of silky wetness to escape her. With a stifled rumble for feeling that, Ben cradled her head and covered her mouth with his.

His kiss was voracious, startling her with its eagerness and noise. He turned this way and that, claiming every inch of her mouth with his thrust and pull. When he sucked her tongue hard into his mouth, she thought she'd go up in flames from her strong hot flash.

"Ben," she gasped as he snapped open the back of her brassiere.

Then he moved to conquer her next vulnerable spot.

"Sally," he moaned, ducking to pull one nipple into his mouth. His hands surrounded her, lifted her, pushing her bosom into his face. She was already swollen, but her nipples hardened painfully at his suckling.

Unable to stop herself, she bucked against him. The ridge that pushed out his trousers arched even higher.

Ben grunted as her pussy squirmed over him. Maybe he found the pressure too stimulating. He jerked up from her breast and locked his gaze with hers.

"Open my zip," he said, harsh and husky. "Pull out my prick and put it in you."

A fiery tingle tumbled through her body. She could feel her clitoris twitching almost as if she were coming.

"Yes," she said, and a shudder wracked Ben's shoulders.

He shuddered again as she dragged the teeth of his zip carefully down him. Pulling out his shirttails was another challenge, because the cloth was tangled around his shaft. With the sense that she was freeing a dangerous beast, Sally eased it up.

She had to touch him when she had the monster out. The skin of his erect penis was always so smooth and hot, so tautly wrapped around the solidness of its core. The drawn-up weight of his balls was a pleasure for her to cup, and the drops of moisture welling from his slit certainly deserved to be rubbed around. The strong veining on his shaft was no less worthy of exploration, but Ben didn't give her long to enjoy. Impatient with her caresses, perhaps because they felt too good, he sidled closer, nudging the drum-tight crown against the heart of her sex.

The muscles of her entrance quivered uncontrollably.

"Yes," she said again, arching her hips up to meet him as he slid between her lips.

He was thick and long, but her body was too wet to present any but the slightest resistance. They groaned together as he sank into her, balls-deep. When he pressed a grunting fraction farther, Sally's nails bit into his back through his shirt. He kissed her, deeply, and then his hips began to swivel.

He was a bit too gentle as he thrust in and out, but she

loved how fighting his natural urges caused him to tremble. Obviously needing to exercise his dominance, he pushed her back into the mattress, capturing her hands and spreading her arms wide as he bent over her.

"Will this do it for you?" he asked, his voice so strained it made her tighten greedily around him. "Is this enough to push you over? I'll rub your clit if you want."

Sally's spine arched as his cock bumped something deep inside her, something that ached nearly enough to scream over. It felt so good she couldn't speak for a few seconds.

"You always push me over," she panted, once she was able to. Since her hands were trapped, her legs climbed his back and squeezed. "Now that I'm pregnant, I feel everything better than I used to. I love making love to you even more."

A mini earthquake rolled up his spine.

"Sally," he breathed, his thrusting suddenly speeding up. He was hitting that deep spot repeatedly and bang on. To her dismay, she didn't have the breath to beg him to keep it up.

Fortunately, the pressure must have felt just as good to him, because he didn't stop doing it. His hands gripped hers so tightly her fingers threatened to go numb.

"It's not too much?" he asked, pushing his chest up so he could see her eyes. Sally fought a groan of pleasure. The new position gave him even better leverage and aim, allowing him to bump her clit with each roll of his hips. "You're sure this is okay for you?"

She thrashed her head, desperate for him to continue. "Please, Ben. Oh, God, please, what you're doing feels brilliant."

He liked hearing that. Pleasure-pain flashed across his expression, veins standing out on his corded neck. His erection swelled with excitement, though it had been plenty stiff before. She could feel it stretching her even more. Using a care she knew must have cost him, he lengthened his strokes without making them more forceful. At each retraction, the flare of his cockhead tugged her but did not come out. The plunge back in was even better. For him as well, apparently. He was gulping for air as her sheath began to tighten harder around him.

"Oh, God," he bit out, the way he often did when he felt his body's needs taking over. "Sally!"

She growled at how close she was, shifting her heels to pull his rear in harder. His buttocks felt like rocks, so tightly were their muscles clenched for his thrusts. She heard his teeth grind as he struggled not to go over.

"With you," she managed to promise. "I'll come with you."

She was usually the loud one, but tonight Ben roared out his orgasm, driving into her and holding fast mere seconds before a mammoth climax unsprung for her. He'd released her hands and was clutching her close to him, his fingers like iron around her bottom—as if his life depended on keeping her exactly where she was. Just as she thought his ejaculation drew to an end, he broke out with a second, even more desperate spate of pumping. The springs of the mattress squealed at his speed.

"Ah!" he cried, his face buried by her ear, his shirttails flapping like a whip. "Jesus. Jesus."

His breath gushed hot as he came again, quite explosively. Shivering with pleasure at having brought him to this extreme pass, Sally felt his lips suck hard enough to form a seal against the tender skin of her neck. Ben groaned and groaned and then, at last, he collapsed.

Sally stroked his back while he recovered. Her body glowed all over, relaxed as melting toffee and twice as warm. If this was what pregnant sex was going to be like, she might not even mind getting fat.

"Thank you," she said, running one hand up beneath his shirt. "That was absolutely the cat's whiskers."

Her sexy husband snorted and struggled up on one elbow. His amusement faded when he saw the bruise on her throat.

"Damn it," he said. "I marked you again."

"Oh, pish-tosh. I don't mind when you do that. Besides, you know I heal fast."

"It still isn't right," he grumped, easing carefully off

her. His cock came out with a pop. "You're having a baby. I shouldn't be . . . biting you."

His beautiful lips flattened in a line, his pretty green eyes avoiding hers. Not sure why he was troubled, since *she* wasn't complaining, Sally watched him zip up his trousers and shake down his sweat-creased shirt. Even clothed, Ben was the yummiest man she had ever seen—lean and muscled with an arse so cute she didn't know how she held off from pinching it all day long.

"Tell you what," she said, hoping to make him smile. "The next time we do this, I'll bite you."

Ben's smile was more like a grimace, but he didn't say there'd be no next time. They both knew themselves too well to promise that.

Estelle realized dawn was coming when Edmund's weight pushed down the edge of the big mattress. Naked, he sat with his shoulders bowed, his hands loose and dangling between his thighs. The heathery scent of the moors clung to him, so she guessed he'd been running in his wolf form. He probably was aware that she was awake, but she turned the covers down to her waist. At the least, he'd know she welcomed him under them.

He turned his head to her, his blue eyes bright even in the dark.

"I'm not sure I can stand this," he said.

It could have been a hundred things he couldn't stand: the strange distance between them, the fact that his very power was making him weak.

"They know," she said, reaching for his hand. "Everyone knows you'd go with Graham and Durand if you could."

He nodded and closed his eyes, his fingers squeezing hers very tight. "I love you," he said.

Estelle wasn't certain why those words made her want to cry.

America

According to Percy, the best and biggest bird in his fleet was a DC-2 designed by Douglas Aircraft. The traveling party gathered around it soon after darkness fell, hesitant fledglings on the moonlit tarmac outside the castle walls. Edmund was patrolling, and Estelle was on the telephone with Robin, keeping him apprised, so they'd be seeing themselves off. A breath away from bouncing with excitement, Percy was enjoying the audience he had.

Graham's vampire cousin liked few things more than nattering about his toys.

"This plane is much better than the Boeing I tried to buy last year. The DC-2 has twin engines, low-set all-metal wings—not to mention the latest in directional radio beams. The cabin seats fourteen *and* has a lavatory, which I'm sure Ben and Sally will appreciate. Take it from me, pretty soon every airline in the world will be flying these."

"*Pretty soon?*" Graham squinted uneasily at the propellers. Were two engines really enough? All the planes Graham had ridden in were trimotors. In the best of circumstances, he disliked flying. His stomach wobbled at the thought of how far Edmund's crazy nephew would be taking them.

"She's brand-spanking-new," Percy said, fondly patting the fuselage. "You can't expect me to fly you across the ocean in some antique rattletrap."

"But you *have* flown it before?" Graham asked.

Percy laughed uproariously. Whatever Edmund's nephew

might think, the flame-blue glow of his eyes behind the buglike goggles did not inspire confidence. He walked away chuckling, running his hands over the sleek silver skin. He didn't seem to think Graham's question warranted an answer.

"He's flown it before," Ben assured him in an undertone. "Don't worry. He really is a good pilot."

"He'd better be," Graham thought he heard Durand mutter.

The mercenary's doubts made Graham feel a smidgen better about his own.

"I like your crest," Sally said, gesturing to the leaping wolf Percy had painted on the tail fin.

Percy beamed at her, then slapped Graham's brother heartily on the back. "You're up front with me, Ben. If we get caught out during daylight, you can take the stick."

"Oh, Lord," Graham sighed as Ben's face lit up. "Please promise that's not going to happen."

"He can handle it. The lad's a bally genius with anything mechanical."

Graham was well aware of his brother's gifts, and—actually—he did feel better knowing Ben would be co-pilot. For one thing, Ben wasn't bonkers. For another, he wouldn't let Percy play his daredevil tricks—not with Sally and her precious cargo tucked up in back.

Percy grinned at him sideways. "Precious cargo," he snickered, plucking the phrase out of Graham's mind. "You are a clever puss, aren't you?"

Graham stifled his next sigh, hardly liking the reminder that Percy the Nutter was an older and more powerful vampire. When Percy whipped the rolling stairs into position beside the door, Graham followed Durand up them with a sense of doom. He doubted they'd return to solid ground soon enough for him.

His only consolation was that the mercenary looked just as grim.

The salon—as Robin called the cabin—had a single seat on either side of the narrow aisle. The chairs weren't as tiny as some Graham had seen, but he knew they wouldn't be comfortable for a man his size, not for the duration of a transatlantic flight.

Predictably, Durand chose a seat in the very back, farthest from the rest of them. As much from habit as suspicion, Graham watched him stow his duffel in the overhead rack. Before he sat, he removed a small leather case from one of its zip pockets, opening it briefly to check the contents.

Graham inhaled sharply when he spied the injection kit and vials inside.

Durand looked up at him. "Cocaine," he said as cool as ever. "Seventeen percent solution. I don't know about you, but if we get caught out in daylight, I'd rather not sleep through it."

"*Seventeen* percent?" Graham repeated, realizing his shock was—at least in part—human prejudice. Human drugs affected *upyr* differently.

Durand nodded. He seemed to debate whether to let more words out of his slash of a mouth. "I'll have to increase the dosage eventually, as my tolerance goes up."

"*You* don't need cocaine," Sally said, coming up beside Graham to rub his arm. "You can turn into your cat. In fact, if you're feeling nervous, maybe you should change now. I bet you could curl up and sleep through the flight."

"I'm fine," Graham said, proud of the sharpness he *didn't* let tinge his tone.

"As you like," Sally said airily. "It was just a suggestion."

Durand ducked his chin before lowering his whip-lean fighter's body into the seat. Despite the concealing posture, Graham couldn't miss the tiny smile tugging at his lips.

Graham held his nerves together for the first leg of their journey, though their pilot displayed a diabolic fondness for turbulence. Percy seemed to go out of his way to find it, after which he'd send his energy through the plane, a feat Graham knew he was performing by the way his skin prickled. The third time Percy acted out this odd ritual, Graham stomped to the cockpit.

The sight of the starry sky outside the nose made his heart lurch uneasily. It didn't help that Percy's eyes were shut.

"Safety measure," Percy told him, quite undisturbed. "I'm trying to determine how well my energy can smooth out the ride in an emergency."

"You're going to *cause* an emergency. You're flying with your eyes closed."

Apart from the tips of his fangs peeping out, Percy's smile was saintly. "Don't get your knickers in a twist. I know what all the needles are pointing to."

"He does," Ben interjected unhelpfully. "I tested him."

"Well, this bumping about can't be good for Sally."

"Sally's sound asleep," Percy said when Ben glanced at him in alarm, still gazing peacefully at the inside of his eyelids. Graham should have known Percy would sense the state of his passengers. Of course, this also meant he'd sensed Graham's and hadn't bloody well cared if he was irked.

"This isn't a game," he said. "Save your experiments for when you're solo."

"My." Percy lifted one set of golden lashes, the blue eye beneath twinkling. "Someone's gotten cranky since he let his bit of fluff slip through his paws."

"Pen isn't my—" Graham snapped his mouth shut at the sound of Percy laughing inside his head. "Just knock it off," he said, and strode to his seat.

Despite his irritation, the mention of Pen gave him an erection he wasn't able to shake for the next two hours—or do anything about aside from squirming in his cramped seat. His mood was not improved by them touching down as lightly as a feather on a buckled tarmac in the Azores.

He was convinced Percy had finessed the landing to annoy him.

They holed up for the day in a building that was little better than a hut, though it did provide the vampires shelter against the sun. Durand made use of his hypodermic and took turns with Ben keeping guard.

"You're too young to be up around the clock," he said

to Graham when he offered to take a shift as his cat. "You need to save your strength for what we'll face in America."

Grumpily, Graham conceded to his reasoning . . . and just as grumpily woke at sunset. The moment he squeezed himself back into his seat on the DC-2, he knew he wasn't going to be able to stand a repeat of the previous night.

"Bugger it," he said, and stomped to the lavatory to peel off his clothes.

His cat form didn't fit the seat much better than he did, but—unlike him—it enjoyed the sensation of being pressed into close confines. To a feline, walls at one's back meant safety. It wasn't long after Sally reached across the aisle to pet him that Graham dozed off.

He next opened his eyes to the impression that he'd missed something. It was daylight, and warm, and his belly was draped uncomfortably over a hard shoulder. He was being carried up a long, shaded path. Unfamiliar smells assaulted him: some sweet, some briny, some simply strange. Birds cried out in the distance, causing his claws to flex pleasantly. His ears swiveled toward the calls, his whiskers twitching as he tried to figure out if this was Bermuda.

When he attempted to wriggle around for a better look on his moving perch, a human arm tightened on his spine.

"Don't you dare change," Ben ordered. "You're hard enough to carry as a cat."

Since he was the size of a cougar, Graham supposed this was true. He quieted enough to notice Durand walking beside Ben. The other vampire was bundled up like an invalid, his steps supported by a black wooden cane. The bowler hat that shaded his face was decades out of date, but luckily Graham didn't have the proper vocal cords to laugh. For some reason, Percy wasn't anywhere to be seen.

"He stayed at the airport," Durand said wearily. "And this is not Bermuda. Your kitty decided you should sleep through that stop."

That meant this must be South Carolina. Despite Graham's shock at having slept so long, his body tingled all over with interest.

"That's Pen's house," Sally said from his other side, pointing in the one direction he couldn't twist far enough to see.

This was too much for Graham *and* his cat. He let out a yowl in Ben's ear.

"Let him go," Durand advised. "He's awake now. He can walk for himself."

He could trot, as it happened, his muscles warming as he bounced ahead of the others up the crushed-shell path. The huge trees that lined the drive were magnolias, their white waxy flowers as big as his head. Unable to resist, he sharpened his claws and stretched his back on the trunk of one. He sensed an area of wildness farther out, untouched in recent memory by human hands. His throat made a funny chirping noise he realized was happy. These were good hunting grounds.

The house, by contrast, intimidated his cat. It was big and white with a deep columned veranda stretching all around. The smell of humans—quite a number of them—overlay a fading whiff of vampire. Graham bared his cat fangs as he recognized Frank and Li-Hua's scent. Spending a day chained up in their dungeon had made that fragrance hard to forget. His nose told him they were gone, but he still slunk cautiously up the steps.

Unable to proceed without causing a stir, he plunked down beside the door with his tail wrapped close around his hindquarters. Though he could have jumped for the doorbell, he judged it best to wait for the others. His heart nearly beat straight out of him while he did. Pen was here, her scent a wonderfully exciting grace note among the rest.

"Oh, dear," Sally said when they joined him. "There's simply no making him look smaller, is there?"

For the second time in a week, Graham heard Durand's bark of a laugh. Perhaps embarrassed by the lapse, Durand rubbed his forehead beneath the bowler while Ben knocked.

An older man—maybe fifty—came to the door. Despite wearing dusty jeans and a cowboy shirt, he gave the impression of being crisp—the effect of his military bearing, most likely. Graham ordered his cat not to sniff his boots or growl. To his consternation, Pen's scent was all over the man, exactly where it did *not* belong. Putting two and two together, Graham knew this had to be Captain Blunt.

"Oh," Blunt said, his sun-creased eyes making a quick trip around their group. Graham had the feeling he wasn't missing one detail. "We didn't expect you this soon. I'm Roy Blunt. I'm very pleased you could come."

He put out his hand and Ben shook it.

"I'm Ben Fitz Clare. This is Christian Durand and my wife, Sally."

Sally nodded, but Durand's sole response was a stare. The weariness he'd shown earlier was concealed, perhaps by glamour or just sheer will. Drugs notwithstanding, he'd been awake a long time. Graham's cat admired the mercenary's ability to convey cool disdain while wearing what amounted to an old lady's muffler around the lower half of his face. As for Blunt, he held Durand's gaze as if he couldn't quite look away, torn between fascination and leeriness.

"I don't believe I've heard your name before," he said.

Only a vampire would have registered the suppressed eagerness in Blunt's tone. Durand neither blinked nor answered the implied question. Quite obviously, he preferred keeping the American uninformed.

"Well," Blunt said, rubbing his hands together to fill the pause. His gaze snagged on Graham, and his eyes widened. "You must be Graham. We have heard about you."

"We're going to talk about that 'we,'" Durand said. "You and I."

Durand's voice was dark enough that Graham knew he was testing Blunt's susceptibility to his thrall. Blunt's jaw dropped half an inch before he pulled himself straighter. He'd also guessed what Durand was doing.

"No," he said quietly. "None of you have my permission to bite or thrall me."

One corner of Durand's mouth hooked up in a smile.

"I mean it," Blunt was unsettled enough to say.

Durand's quarter grin remained in place. Graham suspected it could stay there all day. Durand wasn't outright saying he didn't care a rip for the Council's rules regarding human will, but Blunt would have to be an idiot not to draw that conclusion. Whatever else Blunt was, Graham didn't think he was short on brains.

His own went haywire as another, lighter set of footsteps approached. Graham leaped to his paws before he could stop himself, his tail raised high in greeting.

"Roy," Pen said as she came into view in the entryway. "Have you—"

She stopped when she saw Ben. "Oh," she said, almost as Blunt had. She pressed one hand to the waist of her linen trousers. "You're *here*."

There was such relief in her words that Graham's chest tightened. His Pen was glad they were here—so glad it suggested she'd doubted they would come to her aid. He meowed in protest at that idea, and her hand rose to her mouth to cover a laugh.

"Heavens," she said. "I forgot just how big you are."

Her voice and scent spoke equally of pleasure, and neither could lie to him. Unable to care who was watching, he ran to her, snaking so closely around her ankles he nearly made her fall over.

"Graham," she laughed. "Be careful."

He sat then, contenting himself with curling his tail around the back of her flat-heeled shoe. He hadn't forgotten she'd called Blunt "Roy," but he let that go for now.

"Hullo, Pen," Sally said from the porch. "Nice to see you. We left our bags at the end of the drive where the taxi dropped us off. And Ben and I are married now."

"Um, congratulations," Pen said, blinking a bit at Sally's announcement. Too distracted to react beyond that, she looked behind her as if she'd misplaced something. Sensing her unsureness, Graham rubbed his cheek on her trouser leg. Her hand fell absently to caress his head. "I—I'll send someone for your bags. I suppose I need to scare up some rooms for you."

Pen didn't seem as familiar with her childhood home

as Graham expected, though he knew from working for her father that Arnold Anderson and her mother had been estranged. She led them up the impressive sweep of the double stairway with an air of hesitance. It was hard to tell from his current position in relation to the ground, but he thought they passed a lot of portraits of the same woman. He supposed there might have been a faint resemblance between her and Pen—around the chin and the sharp, proud nose.

Though he turned his head in every direction, he didn't see any pictures of Pen.

"Those are my aunts' rooms," she said, waving down a long carpeted hall. "I think . . . I think I'll just put you on the other end for privacy."

The room she gave Ben and Sally was airy and high-ceilinged, the one she offered Durand a glorified closet.

"Sorry," she said. "I know it's small, but it's the only one without windows."

Durand drew his head back out from peering in the door. "It can be barred," he said, too expressionless to tell if he was offended. "That's all I need for now."

The final room Pen opened smelled wondrously of her. Graham thought the slightly cracked ceiling from which its mosquito netting swooped had been painted blue, but sometimes his cat's eyes mistook colors. The bed itself was fluffy and white. Graham jumped into its center, kneaded the lofted covers, and settled into a satisfied sphinxlike pose. He could see all of his new territory from where he sat.

"Yes," Pen said with a hint of teasing. "This bedroom can be yours."

Now that they were alone, she plopped beside him on the mattress, her breath coming out in a tired sigh. Her hand dropped to his back and stroked him from ear to tail. Graham had no trouble interpreting her actions. Pen had missed him, and now that he was here, she felt better. Surrounded as he was by the emotional simplicity of his cat, Graham thought this a gratification beyond compare.

"Oh, Graham," she said, her fingers digging deliciously

through his fur. "I hope I didn't do wrong by calling, but I am so very glad you came."

He nipped her gently—because how could she think he wouldn't?—and allowed his throat to rumble in a purr. He'd hoped the sound would comfort her, but it had the opposite effect. A moment later, she buried her face in his ruff and let out a sob.

She pushed back as abruptly, leaving Graham to stare at her in amazement.

"Shoot," she said, swiping at her cheeks. "I didn't mean to do that. I guess you're too easy to talk to when you can't talk back."

Graham ignored the insult; Pen was always saying things like this. Instead, he narrowed his eyes at her. Pen was more than upset. She had one arm wrapped around her ribs, and she was wincing. She hadn't been moving stiffly because she felt awkward with her guests. Pen had been injured.

Graham changed forms as quick as thought, then hissed when the strong Southern sun struck him in the face.

"For goodness sakes!" Pen exclaimed, jumping up and running to the windows. "Wait until I close the drapes before you do that!"

"You're hurt," he said, not caring about the rest. "Take off your shirt and let me see."

"Graham!"

Her instant objection stung worse than the sunburn. "I'm not trying to be forward. You know I can help you heal."

Despite this very reasonable suggestion, Pen batted at his hands.

"I'm fine," she huffed as he undid the buttons to her blouse himself.

When he unwound the wrappings beneath—taking care not to hurt her more—the extent and vividness of her bruising forced him to catch his breath. The front of her rib cage looked like she'd been struck by a car, though he supposed a smack from a vampire would do the trick. He was enough of a man to notice her handful-size breasts were bare and extremely pretty, though he wasn't really thinking about that.

Even his rage couldn't drown out the sympathy he felt.

"*Pen*," he said, and laid his palm on the mottled marks. Her eyes rose unwilling to his. "They're just cracked."

"Just." He shook his head as he smiled. "I'll never understand why you have to be so stubborn."

"Maybe you bring it out in me."

"Ha. You're stubborn with everyone."

She choked out a sound of ease as he sent energy through his hand. It felt good to heal her, small a thing as it was. Though he was in human form now, his throat threatened to purr again. Such narrow ribs she had. Such delicate, porcelain skin. He began to stroke the willowy curve of her waist in spite of himself. Her skin was silk, requiring the sensitivity of immortal hands to appreciate just how fine it was. When he swept her flat belly with his thumbs, her pulse accelerated. That caused his cock to twitch like an animal waking up. He became very, *very* aware of his nakedness, and even more aware that he'd been craving Pen for months. All those nights he'd woken hard and hurting piled into his consciousness. He didn't think he could bear it if she turned away.

The tracery of blue that decorated her upper chest made his mouth water.

As if her balance were unsure, Pen gripped his arms. Graham wondered if she knew her fingers kneaded his biceps with a catlike curiosity.

"Why aren't you asleep?" she asked huskily.

At this evidence of her arousal, Graham's prick punched out, thickening up as if there truly were no limit to how big it could get. The tip was almost close enough to touch her belly, the heat of her human body radiating through her remaining clothes. He bent his head, inhaling her, rubbing his cheek in her smooth, waved hair. The contact sent intensely sweet sensations streaking to his groin. Perhaps because his cat had napped for so long, he felt more lazy than sleepy—as though he were doing this in a dream. His fangs stretched from their sockets in slow motion.

"I don't know why I'm awake," he murmured into the soft spot beneath her ear, thrilling to her small shiver. "Something must be keeping me up."

"*Something?*"

When she tipped her head back to see him, he covered her breast in his hand. He shuddered at its softness, her nipple tight as a pebble against his palm. He pinched it gently, giving her time to protest as he tugged it out, watching her pupils dilate in reaction. A heart-stopping second later, her hand reached down for his cock. She jerked at the initial contact, sending him into an agony of dread, lest she draw back. Then her slender fingers slid down him, ringing his base and pulling up again.

Pen was strong for a woman. The force she used to squeeze his erection was precisely what he'd been aching for.

As easily as that, they were on each other, kissing, nipping, tearing down Pen's trousers and ripping her underwear. They both moaned when she was naked and against him. Pen tried to climb him, but he wasn't having that. He wanted full body contact, his weight pressing down on hers. Remembering how she always liked that, Graham threw her onto the bed with a growl he could not contain.

"I hope you're ready for me," he said.

Pen was readier than any self-respecting modern woman should have to admit. Her every nerve had jolted as she hit the mattress—even the ones that weren't touching it. She was panting to have Graham, so wet she knew she must be seconds from dripping. She tried to press her trembling thighs together, but that simply made her more aware of the swollen tissues between her legs. It was just her luck that Graham was the only man who'd ever driven her to this state. Resentment, distrust, even common sense flew out the window in the face of her desire for him. Nothing mattered—nothing—except getting him into her as fast and deep as possible.

It certainly didn't help that the size of his big gray cat wasn't the only thing she'd forgotten. His cock was a fucking fence post, faintly pink beneath its marble skin and as thick around as her wrist. It should have frightened her, but instead she creamed all the more.

"Graham," she said. His name came out so breathy she could barely hear herself speaking.

Graham had no such problems. His exhalations soughed out harder as he prowled up the bed, his big body crowding hers, overwhelming hers, in the most tantalizing way. Pen's sexual predilections sat up and begged. To her dismay—or maybe it was delight—he wasn't trying to hide his fangs. They gleamed like ivory daggers between his smooth, parted lips. Pen gasped when his nostrils flared.

"You smell good enough to eat," he declared.

Wonderful. Now he could smell her. Pen tried scrambling toward the headboard, but he was too fast. He grabbed her thighs where they joined her torso. His big hands contracted on their muscles, pressing in and out, in and out, like the damn cat he'd been. As a human, she didn't have the strength to stop him. Inch by inch, he pulled her legs inexorably apart, guaranteeing her exposure. His eyes bored into hers as if searching for her soul.

Or they did until she felt one great gush of arousal overflow her control. Then his gaze dropped to her pussy and the sheen that must coat its folds. The sound that rumbled from his broad, slabbed chest was a cross between a growl and a purr. His tongue curled out to lick his lips and fangs.

"I wonder how you taste," he said.

Her legs were over his shoulders before she could do more than squeak.

Even that power was lost when he latched his mouth on her sex. He didn't bite her, but she could definitely feel the hard curve of his fangs, a pressure and a danger that did funny things to her breathing. He'd lifted her hips off the mattress, ruining her balance for any sort of defense.

Not that she wanted to defend herself. His tongue was inhumanly strong, inhumanly agile. And the suction . . . She tried not to groan too loudly as the force made her writhe. Her labia were buzzing, swelling, growing more sensitive with each sucking lick. When he began purring into her pussy while also flicking the tip of her clit, she knew she had no chance in hell of muzzling her cries.

"Graham," she panted, "anyone could walk in."

He released his delicious, pulling hold on her sex, and she really could have groaned at that. He let her settle to the bed beneath him, every inch of her skin pulsing in protest as her calves slid down his shoulders. She hadn't been able to come since he'd left her in London three months ago. He'd spoiled her, even for her own hands.

If Graham ever guessed that, she'd have to kill him.

"You're not saying 'no' to me," he said harshly. His normally brown irises were gold, their glow muted but visible in the curtained light. "Unless you do, I swear I'm not going to stop. I'm going to do exactly what I want to you."

Pen's mouth opened, but nothing came out except ragged gasps for oxygen. Graham looked very serious about this threat. Even so, her hands had found their way to his hefty shoulders, clutching his muscles with curved fingers. The fact that she'd probably break her nails before she broke his skin didn't lessen his appeal at all.

Sensing her vacillation, Graham rumbled out another purring growl.

"I want you," he said, dark as midnight and hot as coals. "I feel like I've had a hard-on for the last three months."

Her body gushed at his declaration, utterly enraptured. "Take me then. Get it over with."

His eyes darkened with annoyance. "Pen," he warned . . . and then the great wide head of his cock made contact with her drenched folds.

A small convulsion rolled up his spine, his hips dancing once—helplessly—against hers. The little motion was all it took. The pulsing curve of him notched her gate like a wine stopper. Graham shook his head as if he needed help to think straight.

"Jesus, Pen, you're wet."

Pen gave him her own growl, locking her ankles behind his back so she could pull him in. He didn't have to let her override his strength, but he did. As his cock began to slide inward, a low, resonant sound broke inside of him—as if entering her were the equivalent to a kick in the gut. The noise repeated when he gripped her hips. She feared he'd stop her attempts to take him, but—

"*More*," he demanded, shoving in harder.

He was so thick, so long, it wasn't easy going, no matter how badly she wanted all of him. Pen reached up and slapped her hands on the headboard so she could brace. Graham's gaze dipped to the jiggle of her small breasts.

"Yes," he gasped, halfway in . . . three-quarters . . .

Pen's inner walls began to flutter, her hips twisting desperately up to him. He felt so heavenly throbbing inside her all smooth and hot. Not that she had others of his kind to compare him with, but surely nothing could be silkier than vampire cock. When he ducked his head to suck her sensitive nipples between his fangs, she thought she'd combust. Her groans got louder as she thrashed, the sensation of him filling her frighteningly pleasurable.

"Don't let me scream," she begged.

Fire flashed from his golden eyes as his head came up. Clearly, he liked the idea that she might lose control this way.

"Bite me if you think you're going to," he rasped.

Her sex seemed to liquefy. She wanted to bite him, wanted him to bite her. Graham grunted as her sudden increase in lubrication shot him in all the way. His head flung back at the sensation of her surrounding him, a smoky growl trickling from his throat. The veins in his neck grew darker, their distension intensified. Pen could feel him shaking, slower than a human would but more violently. The quiver took his arms, his hips, his buttocks as they tightened to keep him shoved deep inside. His head fell toward her again with an effort, his fangs digging into his lower lip. Absolutely fascinated, Pen watched a tiny bead of red blood well up. Whatever was happening to his body, it took all his strength to fight.

After a few deep breaths, which lifted his immense chest, his crisis appeared to fade but not pass.

"Christ," he said, the curse coming out on a shaky laugh. "Looks like I might have to bite you, too."

Never mind screaming, Graham almost had a climax from penetrating her. The feel of her around him was simultaneously like coming home *and* leaping into an exciting adventure. With Pen, he never knew what would happen, but he always knew he'd want her.

To his surprise, she flung her arms around him to hug him tight. The spontaneous gesture of affection touched him more than was wise.

"I wouldn't mind if you bit me," she whispered, her cheek rubbing against his. "I know you must be hungry."

His prick gave a hot, hard throb.

"I'm saving that," he said softly. "For the end."

Her eyes held his. She didn't often meet his gaze during sex; it was too intimate, he suspected. Now he sensed her looking inside him, taking in his words, maybe imagining what waiting to bite her would do to him. He wished he could think of something to say to encourage their connection, but then she moaned, pulling her hips up his shaft with the strength of her coltish legs. Rational thought failed him. Her pussy's sleek, wet friction nearly took his head off, especially when she tightened muscles that were already snug.

"You're killing me," he growled. "I'm going to lose it in two seconds."

She stretched up to play-bite his jaw. "I know you can come more than once. I want to feel you pumping out of control."

He couldn't resist her. He met her on her next upstroke, pushing into her with a muffled groan. That thrust demanded another, and another, harder still, until he was almost going at her full out. Their efforts were stunningly in sync: truly exhilarating for two people who couldn't stop arguing. Pen braced one hand again on the headboard, the other clamping so tightly on his arse that nerves he wasn't used to noticing began to vibrate with pleasure. Added to his other stimulations, this was truly phenomenal.

"Please," she said, the elegant cords in her neck straining. "Graham, I really need to go over."

Graham ground his molars together. He wanted her to enjoy this more than she might believe. He shifted angles to bring her clitoris more directly beneath the pummeling of his strokes. She inhaled like he'd got it perfect, her death grip accidentally shifting on his rear.

"Don't move your hand," he ordered gruffly, too aroused to be shy. He shoved her fingers back to the tight, tingling creases around the hole.

"Graham," Pen gasped, blinking rapidly.

He almost said "please," but he knew that wasn't what got her blood pumping.

"Do it," he demanded. "Rub me there."

She did more than rub him. She drove her finger past the ring of muscle and detonated fireworks beneath his prick.

The pleasure was so sharp, so unexpected and delicious, that it was like he came without coming. At the same time, his craving for release jumped to a new level, one that nearly stole his sanity. His hips went wild of their own accord. He would have screamed if he'd had the breath.

"Yes," Pen moaned, now being fucked too hard and fast to do anything but accept his ferocity. Her hands held his churning rear as if it were a lifeline, the finger inside him wriggling like an eel, driving the hidden nerves delirious. "God, Graham. *Yes*."

He could feel how near she was to finally getting what she needed, the tension that had blocked her climax thinning to a thread. He should have been blasting through himself; the sensations in his cock and arse were more than good enough. Apparently, his body was determined to wait for her. He wrapped his hand where hers had been on the carved headboard, grunting as the extra leverage helped him control his strokes.

From the way she moaned, he couldn't doubt her gratitude matched his. He'd never felt so close to her, to anyone. This felt like turning the corner for both of them.

A little faster, he thought. *Just a little faster and we'll be there.*

Then, without a heartbeat's warning, the heaviness of daytime slumber seized his muscles.

"No," he slurred, his need to come ironically spiking to killing intensity. He'd missed her so much, needed her so much, and now a wall of sleep was trying to slam the back of his skull. "Fuck."

"Graham," Pen cried. "Why are you stopping?"

"Fuck . . . Sleep . . ."

Pen grabbed his ears and dragged his head to her neck. If his fangs hadn't still been partially down, he couldn't have nicked her. Luckily, the first taste roused him. He fastened onto her, moaning, bringing his thrusts back to their formerly frenzied pace. Either this or his bite did the trick for Pen. Her aura blazed as her orgasm broke, shaking her whole body. The long, tight spasms sucked his cock like a hungry mouth.

"Fuck," he moaned against her neck, the curse dragged from deep in his chest—but for different reasons than before.

He was coming at last, forcefully but slowly, each contraction of his testicles a separate burst of ecstasy. He'd never felt anything like it, not as a human or an immortal. The climax was uncannily intense, rolling back his eyes and setting his skin to pounding from scalp to toe. He heard Pen cry out his name, her mouth pressed so tightly to his shoulder she might have been biting him. She was coming again and—Lord help him—that was as sweet as coming himself. His penis jerked and jetted in sympathy, only stilling, spent, when she finished quivering.

His cock did not grow smaller. His blood seemed to have stopped moving now that daylight had caught up with him. He blacked out, then blinked awake to Pen shoving him.

"You're really heavy," she reminded him.

Groaning, he rolled off of her.

She sat up and looked down at him. Her hair was tousled, her cheeks and lips stained red by sex. He was so tired he thought he'd drop off with his eyes open. He tried to reach for her hand, wanting to kiss it, but his sleepy arm fell short.

"Well," Pen said, her lips pressed together in a thin, wry smile. "I suppose we had to get that out of the way."

Peachtree Plantation

The hurt Pen's words elicited knocked Graham from his stupor as handily as being dashed with cold water. He sat up to stare at her. He'd had the most amazing, the most welcome, the most *well-matched* sex of his life, and she was treating it like they'd brushed their teeth.

"What?" Pen said. "Am I supposed to act like you gave me flowers? Graham, you didn't even tell me you were leaving London. I had to find out by going to your old house. To tell *you* goodbye, I might add."

"Pen, I didn't want you involved in my family's problems. I was protecting you."

"Protecting me?" Pen climbed off the bed and started pulling on her scattered clothes. "For goodness sakes, Graham, sometimes you're positively prehistoric."

Prehistoric, was he? Graham forced his fangs not to slide out in anger—or in lust at the sight of her buttoning her cream silk blouse over her bare breasts. Her nipples were still tight and red from the things they'd done. "Are you telling me you haven't noticed these vampires are dangerous?"

"I can take care of myself."

"You would have died, Pen—*died*—if your old mate, Roy, hadn't shown up with the cavalry."

She paused in the act of shaking out her trousers, her perfectly plucked brows pulled together above her nose. "Why are you saying his name like that?"

"It's what you call him, isn't it: *Roy*?"

The flush in Pen's cheeks deepened, which caused his

own to feel a trifle warm. "Are you suggesting— Graham, Roy is old enough to be my father."

"Well, he's not your father, and you shouldn't be sharing my family's business with him!"

He hadn't meant to say this so forcefully. Roy Blunt was her boss, after a fashion, and naturally Pen would want to be loyal to her own country. Now that the words were out, though, he didn't see the point of taking them back.

Pen thrust her second leg into her trousers and zipped them up. "You think I told Roy about the *upyr*. You think I betrayed you." She shook her head in disbelief. "Roy knew about your kind before I met you. In fact, the only reason he was interested in me was *because* I met you, which— believe me—I find more infuriating than you possibly could. I'm good at what he taught me. I don't relish the idea that skills I took pride in learning were simply a carrot he used to reel me in."

"If you don't trust him . . ."

Pen jabbed her shirttails in. "I trust him enough, Graham. And I like him enough not to want to see him killed. Oh, and excuse me for thinking you'd want to help catch the monsters who tortured your father!"

"I never said I didn't want to do that."

Getting up from the bed, he handed her the shoes she'd been looking for. Pen accepted them, frowning.

"Stop being mad at me then," she huffed. "I've had a helluva week. I really don't have the patience to tiptoe around your feelings."

Graham would be surprised if she knew how to tiptoe. He managed—with herculean strength, he thought—to swallow the retort back. When he spoke, it was with kindness. "I'm sorry about your mother."

This wasn't what Pen expected him to say. She shrugged jerkily and looked away. "You don't have to be. We weren't close."

"I'm not sure that matters. Losing a parent tends to stir up feelings."

Pen's eyes were red-rimmed, but he could see she wasn't going to cry again. Her jaw was too tightly clenched for that. Suddenly exhausted, Graham sat on the side of her bed.

"You should rest," she said. "I'll lock the door behind myself so you won't be disturbed."

"Pen."

He probably put too much compassion into his voice. She looked at him, drawn up straight, brittle enough to crack into a million shards. "I'm indebted to you for coming. Please don't let my . . . temper make you think otherwise."

Graham swore under his breath, too weary to argue. "I'd have come for less, Pen, but I don't know how to make you believe that."

He wasn't sure he wanted to make her believe it. Graham was normally a calm person. Pen twisted him up like no one he'd ever met.

"I'll wake you for dinner," she said. "Roy will want to speak to you. You can take his measure for yourself."

Graham nodded and fell back, awake only long enough to hear her shut and lock the door quietly. The care she took struck him as oddly tender. It followed him like an echo into oblivion.

While the rest of Pen's guests were dead to the world—or napping, in Sally's case—Ben caught Pen up on what had happened in England. This included the latest twist in Sally's pregnancy. He tried to make a joke of it, saying Sally had finally succeeded in wrapping him around her finger. Despite his attempt at humor, Pen could see he was eaten up by anxiety.

They sat on the wicker glider on the back veranda, watching the Ashley River roll past a distant line of moss-draped oaks. Here and there, members of Roy's team patrolled Peachtree's weed-tangled paths. *Just out for a stroll, ma'am*, one had claimed, which Pen didn't even try to believe. Apart from Ehrlich, the medic, Pen didn't know the men. Their unfamiliarity increased her caution, though she understood her old mentor's strategy. From Roy's perspective, Pen's loyalties might be suspect. Ben didn't seem to notice the casual surveillance. He was drawing nervous patterns on the sweating side of his sweet-tea glass.

Pen hadn't seen him this tightly wound since she'd informed him the two of them were going to dynamite their enemies' Swiss castle.

"Sally's strong," Pen said, twisting on the creaking seat to face his profile.

"I know," he said, and pressed his lips together.

"It might not be as bad as she's saying."

"I'm afraid it's worse. She—" Ben stopped and cleared his throat. "She doesn't want to worry me."

"Ah." At a loss, Pen patted his leg with an open hand. "Well, I'm here. I can help you watch out for her."

Ben's gaze came around to her, his brow furrowed. "You shouldn't have to do that. Hell, you shouldn't have to comfort me. Robin told us you could have died in that attack."

Pen smiled, touched by his concern. "Guess I'm a hard dog to put down."

"This isn't funny. You keep helping us Fitz Clares, and all we bring you is more trouble."

Not just trouble. At the rate things were going, Pen seemed likely to end up with a broken heart.

"I'd rather help than sit on the sidelines," she said aloud.

Ben squinted at her as a shaft of sunlight turned his eyes to a brilliant green. "You mean you'd rather help than be helped," he said slowly.

"I did call you here."

"But not for yourself. You called us to help Blunt stop Frank and Li-Hua."

Uncomfortable with the sharpness of Ben's attention, Pen took a swallow of iced tea. The drink had enough sugar dissolved in it to support a spoon.

"Graham cares about you," Ben said. "We all could tell he missed you."

Pen could tell he missed her, too, at least physically. That, however, didn't mean his true feelings for her—his exasperation, his lack of trust—wouldn't win in the end. She rose and lightly squeezed Ben's shoulder, realizing that somehow, in all this craziness, he'd become a bit of a friend.

"I'd better see to dinner," she said to his upturned face. "Some of y'all will be hungry for food tonight."

Pen had taken charge of dinner—a task she was well equipped to handle, given her years as mistress of her father's house. Despite this, her aunts Elizabeth and Mary were still behaving as if they were Peachtree's hostesses, rather than being here on Pen's sufferance. The third time they tried to countermand a request of hers—behind her back, of course—Pen lost her hold on herself and snapped.

"I'm paying the staff now," she said in a low and, had her aunts but known it, dangerous tone. "Your dear, dear sister hadn't in a year. So, really, whose choice of wine do you think it's in their interest to serve?"

Her aunts had gaped at her, then turned their energy to fussing over the seating arrangements. Fearing an even bigger blowup, not to mention the unwanted attention it would attract, Pen removed herself to the entry hall for a few deep breaths.

She'd managed half a dozen when Graham came down the leftward curve of the stairs. He looked a good deal more sprightly than he had before, dressed in a beautifully cut dark business suit and white shirt. Thanks to his vampire powers, both looked as if they'd been freshly pressed.

"Pen," he said, slowing as he saw her. "Are you all right?"

Not wanting to discuss it, Pen waved her hand in front of her face. "I'm fine. I trust you slept well."

"Perfectly." The faintest of flushes swept up his cheeks, probably due to remembering why he'd been relaxed. "I'm sorry to have put you out of your room."

"*My* room?" Pen hadn't meant to sound startled. Graham widened his eyes.

"It *isn't* your room? Your scent was all over it."

He'd made one of his speedy vampire shifts and was standing too close to her, his palms cupping her elbows. Pen's hands were knotted at her waist, but she couldn't make them relax. She also knew she couldn't hide the acceleration of her pulse.

"I have another room," she said, brazening out her response to his touch. "I was simply laid up in the blue room temporarily."

"Oh," he said. "Well, it's very nice."

"Dinner will be served soon," she added. "Perhaps you'd like to tell the others."

"Not necessary," Durand said, gliding smoothly down the stairs. He, too, looked a different man, his shining black hair tied back, his clothes older in style than Graham's but no less pristine. "I heard Sally's stomach growling from my closet."

He and Graham nodded at each other, an edge of challenge in the acknowledgment. Pen knew Durand was older and had more power, but Graham seemed to hold his own in their staring match. Pen's nerves were the ones that weren't up to watching it.

"We're having fish," she said. "Graham, I thought I'd save a portion for your cat later. Mr. Durand, I'm afraid I wasn't sure what to do for you."

Belatedly, she wondered if she ought to ask him not to nibble on her staff, or harm the people who lived nearby. Pen didn't want to insult him, but perhaps such things needed spelling out.

The tiny twitching at the corner of Durand's mouth suggested her worries hadn't been private. She hoped he was polite enough not to rummage in her mind at will.

"Miss Anderson," he said with a small, crisp bow. "Please don't fear I'd do anything to abuse your hospitality."

His manner was unexpectedly elegant—not courtly, exactly, though she could imagine the mercenary, in some distant past, working for people who were. Pen's hand rose to her throat, her heart rate having picked up again.

When Durand's eyes cut to Graham, Pen could have

sworn the gleam in them was sly. Considering his usual icy
demeanor, that was a surprise. He bowed once more and
disappeared around the foot of the stairs.

"You be careful around him," Graham growled. "That
one doesn't play by our rules."

"I will," Pen promised, shocked to see that in the few
moments she'd spent watching the other man, Graham's
fangs had run halfway out.

Plainly, Durand wasn't done playing games. All through
dinner, he flirted with her aunts, who—predictably—had
seated themselves together at the head of the table. Mary,
in particular, was reduced to girlish giggles by Durand's
attentions. Elizabeth simply couldn't take her eyes off him,
her fork pausing halfway to her mouth more than once. Pen
couldn't blame her. With his narrow face and his ink black
eyes, the mercenary was a striking man. He must have been
swarthy as a human, because his skin was faintly olive in
the candlelight. When he smiled, his slashing mouth was
almost pretty.

"Is it my imagination?" Pen asked in an undertone to
Graham, who was, luckily, seated beside her. "Or is Durand
making himself appear more handsome?"

"He's dropped a portion of his glamour," Graham murmured. "That's how he really looks. He's thralling your
aunts, I believe. He's nearly an elder. Given sufficient
time, he can control a human without a bite. That, I have to
admit, isn't against Council rules."

Well, Pen thought, sitting back in her chair. *Learn something new every day.*

Her gaze slid to her old mentor. She suspected Roy
hadn't had many opportunities to study the *upyr* up close,
because he was watching her aunts succumb to Durand's
spell as if he were mesmerized. He'd barely touched his
meal of blackened catfish on dirty rice, an omission he
shared with more than half her guests. The red Bordeaux
was a hit at least; even Graham and Durand were drinking
it, but only Sally had responded to Pen's other choices with
gusto.

"This is *delicious*," she exclaimed now, gesturing toward her corn bread. "And the baby adored those greens."

Pen couldn't help smiling. Whatever else could be said of Sally, nothing kept her down for long. "Cook said they were good for pregnant women."

"Your cook was right!" Sally said and beamed. "Graham, I know you're going to love this fish once you, er, get around to it."

Ben kissed Sally's cheek just as Pen's aunt Mary broke into a fresh giggle.

"Oh, Sister," she said to Elizabeth, her plump cheeks as flushed as the wine Durand was sipping from Peachtree's antique crystal. "Do you remember the pecan liqueur Tooty used to make when she was cook? Heavens, but didn't we have some parties serving that? Penelope's mother was the prettiest girl in five counties, and when the men had a bit of those spirits in them, they'd all swear she was their queen."

"I'm sure she wasn't any lovelier than the pair of you," Durand purred as smoothly as if he had Graham's cat in him.

"Oh, you!" Mary pushed playfully at his marble hand. Pen was certain her aunt didn't notice Durand's flickering grimace. "Livonia was truly lovely. A lovely girl and a lovely woman. This place will miss her sorely."

"Sorely," Elizabeth seconded with a wistful sigh.

"What was that nickname she used to have for Penelope? Oh, it's on the tip of my tongue. We used to love it because it was so clever."

"Peahen," Elizabeth said firmly. "Livonia called Penelope her peahen."

Pen set down her fork with a click. Hungry as she'd been for her mother's love, she'd treasured having a nickname . . . until she'd figured out why Livonia chose it. Then she'd simply felt unbearably stupid. Her next words grated from her throat before she could stop them. "She called me peahen because they're ugly. Because she thought I was ugly compared to her."

"Oh, poppycock!" Mary said. "It was an endearment. Heavens, Penelope, you really are oversensitive."

Pen's face blazed, too many humiliating memories rushing back at once. She realized she was staring at yet another portrait of her "lovely" mother, this one hiding a water stain on the papered wall above the old sideboard. Her mother had used to do exactly what Mary was: conceal her insults in a pot of honey, while pretending Pen was being silly if she took offense. Pen wanted to scream she knew what she knew; she wasn't a child to be forced to choke on lies anymore. She couldn't scream, though, not with Graham and everyone watching. Even supposing they'd believe her, her pride couldn't bear their pity.

To her amazement, her rescue came from a highly unlikely source.

"Well, I don't know about *Southerners*," Sally said, one hand fluffing her flaxen hair. "But everyone *I* know thinks Pen is frightfully good looking. Your sister must not have realized she'd grow up to be a beauty."

She turned her sweetest smile on Pen's aunts, who—despite their facility at shoveling sugar—seemed flummoxed. No doubt they hadn't expected to meet their match in a curly-haired comfit from England.

Sally wasn't one to waste her advantage. She rose and twinkled at Pen across the table. "I am *so* full," she declared. "I don't suppose you'd be kind enough to walk with me on the porch? Not that I haven't enjoyed everyone's charming company."

"Of course," Pen said. Her knees felt stiff, but they got her onto her feet. All the men at the table rose. "Please." Pen waved them back, unwilling to face what was in their eyes. "Enjoy what's left of dinner."

Sally and she made a complete circuit of the house before Pen could think of a word to say, and that was only after Sally stopped and leaned forward on the front railing. Pen took up the post beside her, comforted by the sound of cicadas chirping in the dark. Their rhythmic song had been her lullaby during visits here as a child.

"You didn't have to do that," she said.

"Of course I did. Those aunts of yours are witches of the first water."

"But you don't even like me. When we met, you thought I was after Ben."

"Only for half a tick. Anyway, Graham likes you. That's good enough for me."

The little sigh Sally let out a moment later betrayed that this was stretching the truth. Sally still disliked her, but she was doing her best. Pen grinned to herself, her balance magically restored.

"You're a good sister," she said. "Graham is lucky to have you."

Peachtree Plantation

Christian Durand might not have had a beast inside him, but he could almost smell his life becoming more interesting. As Miss Anderson's dinner drew to a close—thankfully, a quick one now that she and Sally had withdrawn—he could feel the two old ladies falling deeper under his influence, without the least need for a blood bond. This wouldn't have been possible had Durand not been closer to achieving master status than he'd believed.

It made him wonder why Roy Blunt had resisted him.

Tucking away that question for a more convenient time, Durand pushed back in his spindly chair and rose. Like puppets, Pen's aunts stood, too. The skinny one gazed up at him with stars swimming in her eyes.

"Heavens," she sighed, "you're handsomer than Valentino in *The Sheik*."

Durand had no idea who that was.

"Honored, I'm sure," he said, and took her sharp, papery chin in his hand. "And now I have a request for you."

"Anything," both women promised, inspiring a rush of triumph within his veins. He could see how, over the years, Miss Anderson's snake of a mother had convinced these two to follow her lead. Among *upyr* or humans, the strong would always compel the weak.

"I want you to return to your rooms. You may leave them if you must, but I want you to keep out of our way for the duration of our residence. You will not reveal our presence to anyone. You may dream of me, if you wish, but when I leave, it will be as if I were never here."

"Oh, thank you," the plump one gushed, touching his arm. "We're so glad you came, what with those nasty robbers running around. We'd be happy to please you in any way, you hear?"

"Go now," he ordered, before his repulsion slipped out from his glamour.

When they left, he removed their chairs from the head of the table, placing his own there instead and sitting down in it. He truly had not liked the feel of their energy.

"Will that really work?" Ben asked, twisting around to gawk at the now closed door.

"It will work long enough for our purposes. Biting them would strengthen my hold, but Graham seems reluctant to allow me the full advantage of my powers."

Graham gave him a long, cool look that, considering his tender years, wasn't lacking in impressiveness. Durand knew he shouldn't have enjoyed twitting him; indulging any sort of humor was out of character for him. Graham was simply such an upright member of vampiredom that Durand couldn't resist the temptation to make him snarl.

Durand hid his smile, but only just.

"Since we're alone," Graham said, "perhaps Blunt could tell us in more detail what he knows about our enemies' movements."

"We should wait for Pen," Durand said, which was a tease in itself.

Graham's stare was hot this time.

"I want a firsthand account of the attack on her," Durand explained blandly. "And a better description of that soul-sucking box. I could call her, if you like." He tapped two fingers to the center of his forehead, demonstrating what he meant.

"No." Graham pushed up from the table. "I'll get her. Pen might not want you rummaging in her mind."

That was interesting. Graham used the same term for his intrusion as Miss Anderson had. Durand hadn't thought the boy capable of reading his lover's mind, but perhaps the tie between them wasn't as superficial as it appeared. Not that it mattered except as a point of curiosity. As long

as they took direction, Durand didn't care what these Fitz
Clares did with their little human-vampire romances.

Peachtree's dining room was the perfect setting for a
frightening tale, with its flickering candles and its stained
French shepherdess wallpaper. All the deep-set windows
opened onto the Southern night. Between the warm,
moist air and the alien insect choruses, the room took on
an atmosphere where the ghosts of Confederate soldiers
might indeed be believed to walk. Of course, being frightened presupposed one wasn't a monster oneself. Monster
or not, Graham had a hard time listening to Pen's account
of the attack on her. She told it all so calmly—including
the part where Li-Hua had started drawing out her soul
with the strange brass box.

"It was an extremely peculiar feeling," she said, seeming more intrigued than afraid. "As if someone were taking a Hoover to my insides. I'm not sure how I would have
defended myself if Roy hadn't shown up."

The sound of wood beginning to splinter warned Graham he was clutching the arms of his Sheraton chair too
hard.

Blunt glanced at him, then took up the narrative. Durand
was the person both he and Pen addressed, the mercenary
having claimed leadership of the proceedings without a
peep of debate. Power had its persuasions, Graham supposed, because he didn't feel inclined to argue. Not for now
at least.

"My men shot at 'em," Blunt said, his twang so thick
that understanding him demanded concentration. "They
hit 'em, too. Probably a couple dozen times. Pen suggested
silver ammo wasn't the best call." Blunt raised an eyebrow
but got no response. "Anyhow, my men chased the vampires along the river, but even wounded, those two were
too fast to keep up with. One of my men swears he saw 'em
disappear into thin air, just pop out of existence. I don't
know if that's possible, or if maybe they were movin' too
quick to see."

Durand narrowed his eyes at Blunt, pressing his finger-tips together while he considered what to reveal to their would-be ally.

"It's possible," he said, "though *upyr* as young as Frank and Li-Hua shouldn't have that power. You mentioned another witness saw the box at the first robbery."

"Chicago," Blunt confirmed. "Two dead in that one, and six injured. A female teller saw the one you call Li-Hua tossin' the box like a toy. Li-Hua dropped it when the shootin' started, and it landed on the floor next to the witness. She described the same dragon engravin' as Pen, though she didn't mention it lightin' up. She's probably lucky she didn't try to touch it, or the bitch would have killed her, too.

"Sorry," he added in an aside to Pen for his language. When Pen demurred any necessity for that, Blunt fingered the edge of the tabletop. His hands were beaten up but graceful, the sort that could probably load his six-shooter pretty fast. One finger sported a gold signet ring. "I have to say, Mr. Durand, you don't seem too surprised to hear about this thing. You have some idea what it is?"

"A myth," Durand said, his dark eyes distant.

Blunt snorted. "Not anymore."

Again, Durand paused before speaking. In spite of his mixed feelings for the mercenary, Graham found himself pricking up his ears.

"Our kind have been around a long time," Durand said. "So long that the first of us seem like fairy tales to the rest. One of those first was rumored to have created a special casket as a gift for a favorite child, to allow the younger vampire to become her equal in an abbreviated amount of time."

"Because your kind don't become masters until they've lived a few centuries."

"If they become them at all," Durand unbent enough to answer.

Blunt seemed to appreciate his concession, though he was wily enough not to say thank you. He took a piece of half-eaten corn bread in his long, worn fingers and began crumbling it. "So . . . why hasn't this casket contraption been givin' lots of baby vampires a leg up?"

"According to the story, the master's favorite tried to betray her. Heartbroken and enraged, she buried the box somewhere in the Orient where, I suppose, someone who believed in fairy tales must have dug it up. And before you ask, I can't tell you how the casket works. That sort of magic has been lost. I can't even tell if it's truly steal- ing souls. Energy, certainly, which is pushing Frank and Li-Hua past limits I never thought they'd develop."

"Seems to be makin' 'em nuts as well," Blunt observed.

"It does," Durand said. "Minds like theirs weren't meant to assimilate so much power so quickly. I do not disagree that they're becoming quite dangerous."

Blunt had reduced the square of corn bread to a hill of crumbs. He looked at it, then up at Durand. "You don't believe in souls?"

Perhaps it was a trick of the candlelight, but for just a moment something softened in the mercenary's cold, hard face. "I do not believe there is any way to prove their exis- tence. Or if they survive death."

"And you'd know," Blunt pressed.

"No more than any other. For my kind, the afterlife—if there is one—must be as much a matter of faith as it is for yours."

Blunt nodded, but Graham couldn't tell if this answer had satisfied. Seeming to come to a decision, Pen's old mentor braced flattened hands on the tablecloth and leaned forward. "All right, where do we start on catchin' these jokers?"

"*We* don't start anywhere. Not unless you agree to let me bite and thrall you."

Durand had leaned forward like the other man, the posi- tion of his hands and body mimicking Blunt's. Even across the length of the dining table, his movement caused the Texan to draw back as if he'd been crowded. When Durand bared his fangs in an insincere snow-white smile, the sharp teeth glistened. To Graham's surprise, Blunt looked ner- vous but not cowed.

"Is that really necessary?" Pen asked.

"It is," Durand said, his voice insidiously gentle. "Though thralling your friend is probably not an option, even with his permission."

"What do you mean?" Pen turned from Durand to Blunt. "Roy, what is he talking about?"

"Why don't you show them?" Durand suggested, just as soft as before. "It's on your chest, isn't it?"

Now that all eyes were on him, Blunt exhaled a resigned sigh and began unsnapping his shirt. Beneath the faded blue cotton, his chest was hard and tanned but not particularly muscular. A tattoo of an elaborate Celtic cross stretched across most of it. If Graham blurred his vision, he could see the lines and swirls of it shining, very subtly, within Blunt's skin.

"Got this in Edinburgh," Blunt said. "Artist swore his family used to be druids. I thought it was a bunch of hooey until I met you."

"It's a younger magic than the one that made the box," Durand said. "But if you really thought it was 'hooey,' I suspect it wouldn't have worked."

"You're only sayin' that so I won't have all my men get one."

"Maybe," Durand said with one of his small, hooked smiles. "Though it is nice to know they don't have one yet."

"Well, shoot," Blunt said, realizing too late what he'd let slip.

Durand's smile fell away, his face returning to its more usual icy mask. "You may leave now. We have business to discuss without you."

"My men and I can help," Blunt objected as he rose. "We're on the same side."

"We are today," Durand said. "I prefer to plan for tomorrow."

As soon as Blunt was gone, Pen began to speak.

"Wait," Durand said, one palm lifting.

Graham bristled at his peremptory gesture, but Pen touched his arm to calm him. The older vampire's eyes were closed, and his chest was lifting on a slow, deep breath—far slower than a human would have used to fill his lungs. Graham had the odd impression that the air in the room was thickening. The feeling disappeared a heart-beat later, leaving his ears popping.

"What was that?" Ben asked.

"You felt my spell?" Durand opened his eyes, the focus in them acute.

"I felt something," Ben said, drawing back nervously.

"Hm," Durand said before seeming to dismiss him. He shifted his gaze to Graham. "Blunt has ears all over this property. I've woven a cloak of silence to prevent his men from eavesdropping."

"Are you certain we won't need their help?" Pen asked.

"I'm certain we can't afford it." Durand considered Pen, an attention she didn't quail under. Graham supposed if you were Arnold Anderson's daughter, it took a lot to make you shake in your shoes.

"I am agreeable to your participation," Durand said at last. "I can read you if I need to, and you don't seem prone to hysteria. Your combat training may come in handy for protecting Mrs. Fitz Clare and her . . ." He waved his hand distastefully.

"Baby?" Sally prompted, her lips curving. Ben squeezed her shoulders, but Graham could tell his little sister was more amused than insulted.

"That's very good of you," Pen said, her own amuse-ment better hidden than Sally's. "Though I do feel Roy and his men ought to be given sufficient information to defend themselves, should Frank and Li-Hua cross their paths again. I know Roy. He won't stop tracking them just because you refuse to take him into your confidence."

"I agree," Graham said. "They saved Pen's life. They deserve to know the basics."

"And if one day they turn those 'basics' against you and yours? What will you think they deserve then?" Durand's tone was dry, his eyebrows climbing his forehead in dark, arched wings.

"It isn't as simple as us against the humans," Graham

said. "We wouldn't be here if we didn't have enemies among our own race."

Durand erased his expression with a single, unnerving blink. "Very well. But *I* shall explain the minimum they need. *You* are not to share more."

Graham knew this was the best compromise they would get. In truth, he wasn't sure he wanted better. Roy Blunt's eyes were sharp, his interest in Graham's and Durand's nature intense enough to approach obsession—if it hadn't already slid into that. He nodded his agreement at Durand, for once in accord with the other man.

"So," Ben said. "Where *do* we start looking? Blunt didn't seem to have any better idea than we do where Frank and Li-Hua are. If they've killed twenty people, waiting until they rob another bank doesn't seem the most responsible approach."

"We might not have a choice," Durand said. "On the other hand, they might decide to lie low. They haven't lost all their self-control. Chances are, they'll guess Pen contacted you."

"We could ring Estelle," Sally said, turning a heavy silver bread knife in her hands. "See if she can dreamwalk them like she did Daddy."

"We could," Durand conceded. "In the meantime, however, I suggest we head for Chicago."

"Where the first bank was robbed," Ben said.

"And where the first reports of the box showed up. Perhaps we'll find whoever Frank and Li-Hua obtained it from. Perhaps they left clues to their endgame."

At his mention of an endgame, sparks of red kindled in Durand's irises—either because he thought his old employers were a menace, or because he relished a good, hard fight. Had Graham still been human, he would have shivered at the uncanny hellish light. As it was, he experienced a similar quickening. Graham had to admit he was a predator now himself.

"Well," Sally said, breaking the taut moment. "I guess going to Chicago is better than trying to search the whole country!"

* * *

Their discussions for the night concluded, Graham was left restless. Blunt would have been dismayed at how easily he avoided the patrols while gliding silently down the overgrown paths behind the plantation house. This area had been a formal garden, but the swamp was reclaiming it, black fingers of water creeping in from the edges. Graham stopped when he reached the river. Spanish moss hung in a shredded curtain from the big oak trees. Behind that veil an old landing listed, half in, half out of the slow current. A low reptilian shape crawled off as Graham arrived, disappearing into the river with a heavy splash.

From the way his cat quivered with excitement, Graham concluded he'd encountered his first gator.

His cat wasn't the only one who'd been given food for thought tonight. Graham realized he'd only seen one side of Pen's history. Her father had raised her as a princess, as beloved as she was spoiled. Her mother had treated her like Cinderella before the ball. That Pen wasn't more mixed up was a marvel. That she was amazingly strong and independent—in spite of both her parents—struck Graham as a miracle.

"Peahen," he whispered to the wavelets lapping at the submerged dock. The back of his eyes pricked for the gawky girl-child Pen must have been. If it had been up to him, he'd have made that dreaded nickname her badge of honor.

The guards Pen had erected suddenly made sense. Of course she was bossy, and of course she was prickly, too. Why would she give herself a chance to fall in love? Her heart had betrayed her quite sufficiently as a girl.

For good or ill, no such fear hampered Graham. Though he'd lost his birth parents, Edmund and Ben and Sally had given him a whole new family to care about. Graham's heart might not be the most courageous of the Fitz Clares, but it was courageous enough.

I love her, he thought, chills chasing across his skin. *I love Pen Anderson.*

The revelation filled him with a resolve that wasn't altogether optimistic. In all probability, he'd loved Pen for a while, maybe before Switzerland even. From the start, she'd gotten under his skin, treating him like he was her father's reliable but somewhat boring pet protégé.

Whatever else she felt, at least Pen didn't think he was boring now.

Graham thrust his hands into his trouser pockets, rocking back slightly on his heels. His groin was heavy, edging closer to arousal. He wanted Pen—would always want her, he expected—but that didn't mean he could win her thorny heart in bed. Her body, yes, but not the rest of her.

Aware that he wouldn't be satisfied with less, he turned his steps toward the house. Now that he knew to look for it, her scent led him to the small dormer window that opened out from her childhood room. One light leap took him to the attic's roof. Pen wasn't in the room yet, so he slipped inside. The space was every bit as parsimonious as he'd supposed: mere servant's quarters with a sagging bed and a bare plank floor. Pen's expensive clothes looked funny hanging from the pegs on the walls.

Cinderella, indeed, he thought.

He grinned at the iron poker she'd left leaning beside the bed. That wasn't going to be her sole protection this evening. He removed his clothes and left them, folded neatly, on a slatted kitchen chair. Being here, surrounded by her scent, had him hard and aching, but Graham ignored the fierce arousal. He couldn't get rid of it, but he knew one way to make it wait.

He shifted into his cat form with a brisk shake of his limbs and a silent order to relax. Once he'd explored the garret to his furry self's satisfaction, he jumped onto her bed to wait.

Pen had said he was easier to talk to when he couldn't talk back. If that was what it took for her to trust him, Graham was perfectly willing to be sneaky.

Bridesmere

⸎

Estelle didn't like losing track of Edmund. Either she was with him or—now that Percy had returned from flying the others across the pond—his nephew was. If Edmund wandered off without one of them to anchor him, bad things tended to happen. Predicting the nature of the trouble was impossible. Edmund's powers seemed able to flare in myriad directions, turning Estelle into a childminder for her own fiancé.

She bit her lip as she replaced the parlor's telephone in its cradle. This was one of Bridesmere's more modern rooms, with pale gold walls and delicate Art Nouveau furniture. A hand-knotted William Morris carpet warmed the cold stone floor. Estelle curled her bare toes into it but still felt chilled.

She hadn't wanted to tell Sally the chances of her dream-walking anyone were slim. Lately, Estelle was lucky to get a solid hour of sleep at a time, and she'd never used her gift without first connecting to Edmund. That truly wasn't going to happen. Edmund was as careful of meeting her eyes these days as if she were the vampire—a caution she was beginning to admit the wisdom of.

The inside of Edmund's head wasn't a place sane humans wanted to be.

Estelle pushed up from the armchair where she'd sat in her pajamas to answer Sally's late night call. Edmund had been hunting earlier. In his wolf form, he was less prone to unexpected accidents. He'd returned in human guise not long after midnight to make furious love to her. Estelle couldn't deny she'd enjoyed it. While being taken by him was one of the few times she forgot her worries. Now, however, she had no idea where he'd gone.

Relax, she told herself as she closed her eyes. She still knew how to sense his presence if she let herself be peaceful. She doubted any amount of estrangement could break that bond.

Tugged by a faint awareness, she padded through the dimly lit corridors of the ground-floor level until she reached the tower Durand had chosen for his quarters. Though the door opened without creaking, a gust of icy air rushed out. Spring arrived in northern England late. Estelle stuck her head into the stairwell and thought she heard voices. Her funny ear didn't kick in to make them clearer, but one voice sounded like Edmund's.

Fighting a shiver and wishing she'd grabbed a dressing gown, Estelle climbed the cold granite treads. Bare incandescent bulbs lit her way, so unadorned their wires were strung along the stone.

She was almost to the top when Edmund's voice snapped to perfect clarity. If it hadn't, she might not have believed it belonged to him. The scorn that dripped from his words was like nothing she'd ever heard from him.

"For the love of heaven, Claris," he was saying. "You couldn't spare two minutes from your *ladies* to speak to our sons today?"

"They have their nurse," a woman answered. "But, prithee, dearest husband, how much time have *you* spent with them this month?"

Estelle's backbone shuddered as if a strong hand were shaking it. Claris had been Edmund's wife when he was human. Since *she* hadn't been made a vampire, she was dead as mutton. A second wave of fear rolled through her when she noticed the light in the stairwell was flickering. Percy's jerry-built electric bulbs were gone. In their place, torches burned in iron brackets.

"Edmund!" she called, hurrying up the final steps.

Edmund spun as she burst in, the motion causing the hem of his long black silk robe to lift. Ironically, the garment wouldn't have been out of fashion when he was human.

Estelle glanced all around, but he was alone in the tower room.

"Sorry," he said, sounding embarrassed. "Just thinking aloud."

He was lying. He knew he'd been lost in the past. He simply didn't realize he'd been so lost he'd brought its old vibrations alive for her. Estelle knew she'd heard Claris speaking, knew she'd seen and smelled those pitch-soaked torches crackling on the stairs.

She struggled to get her pulse in order as she walked to him. His nerves were sufficiently wound up that when she laid her hands on his shoulders, the muscles that composed them flinched.

"Maybe we should leave here," she said. "Go stay with Robin in London. I think this old castle is haunting you."

"Don't be silly." He gathered her hands together and squeezed gently. "Sometimes a man has to . . . think things through."

"Edmund—"

"No." He dropped his hold on her and turned away, bracing his arms on either side of the arrow-slit window. "I don't want you calling Robin or Aimery. It's bad enough I'm not helping catch Frank and Claris. I won't take Robin and my brother away from important work."

"Frank and Li-Hua," she said softly.

Edmund twisted his head to look uncomprehendingly back at her.

"You said you're not helping catch Frank and *Claris*."

Shock slapped across his face. He tried to hide it behind a frown, but not before Estelle saw his terror.

"It's nothing," he said. "A slip of the tongue. This used to be Claris's room."

Estelle hadn't needed Edmund to tell her that.

"Come to bed," she said. "There's an hour or so till dawn."

"I'm keeping watch," he said, and turned his back on her.

Why don't you watch this? Estelle thought, restraining

herself with an effort from flipping him a rude gesture. If she'd honestly believed her anger would help, she would have cast caution to the winds. The problem was, she didn't know what would work. She'd tried everything she could think of, short of defying Edmund to call his brother. She'd have tried that, too, if Percy hadn't been positive it would stir up more trouble.

Our Council leader is a lovely fellow, Edmund's nephew had said. *As fair and honest as the night is long. Saint Aimery is also the last person anyone who fears he's cocking up his life would want to turn to.*

Fine, then, Estelle snarled to herself, spinning away to stomp down the stairs. She wouldn't call Aimery or Robin or box Edmund's ears the way her strong right fist wanted to. She still had an ace up her sleeve. As long as she didn't ask permission, no one could forbid her from playing it.

She felt less confident after she'd dug the requisite scrap of paper from the bottom of her stocking drawer. Estelle had been surprised to be given the number, and more than a little wary of putting it to use. Edmund wouldn't like it, but the person this dialing code belonged to might really know something. Nim Wei was considerably older than Aimery, and no one would dream of calling her a saint. Most importantly, there was a *sympathy*—for lack of a better term—between Edmund and London's queen. His former lover made peace with the darkness he dreaded finding in himself.

Muttering a brief prayer for courage, Estelle pulled the green parlor's 'phone back into her lap.

The line rang ten times before it was picked up. Estelle expected to reach a secretary, but the laughing man who answered didn't sound like one.

"The queen is sitting on her throne," he teased, the throaty hitch in his breath suggesting what sort of throne it was. "If this isn't deathly important, you had best ring off."

Estelle swallowed but decided to press forward. She'd already interrupted, and Edmund wasn't getting any better as time went on. "This is Estelle Berenger, Edmund Fitz Clare's fiancée."

The man uttered a sound of protest as a mattress creaked.

"Give me that," someone hissed, and then Nim Wei's voice came on.

"Estelle?" the vampire queen of London said. "Has something happened to Edmund?"

The use of her Christian name surprised Estelle, but she could only be glad for the quickness of the queen's concern. She needed Edmund to be important to Nim Wei right now.

"Edmund is . . . troubled," she replied cautiously. "His control over his new powers isn't improving the way it should. He's convinced his brother, Aimery, won't have been through what he's experiencing, but I hoped you might know something that would help."

The pause that stretched from the other end was dead silent.

"Do you fear for your safety?" Nim Wei asked finally.

Estelle gripped the 'phone tighter. This was a question she hadn't wanted to face. "Not at this moment, but matters may be headed in that direction. I don't like to say it, but I'm not sure Percy would be strong enough to stop Edmund if he truly forgot himself. I'm not sure even Robin could."

Something tapped against the telephone—a manicured fingernail, was Estelle's guess. "You're at Bridesmere."

Estelle had little choice but to trust Nim Wei with the truth. "Yes."

"I'll be there as soon as I'm able after sunset tomorrow."

An involuntary sound broke in Estelle's throat, but it was too late to protest. The buzz of the dialing tone indicated Nim Wei had rung off.

Estelle put the handset back where it belonged, staring without seeing at the unlit coal in the parlor's cold fireplace. She'd done what she thought she had to, and the die was cast. London's queen was coming here. Would Edmund welcome his old lover—perhaps more than Estelle was ready to have him do? Normally, the thought wouldn't have crossed her mind, but Edmund was scarcely normal now.

If he hadn't feared Nim Wei's ruthless nature would taint his own, she could have been the one to change him.

Estelle wondered what Nim Wei had made of Claris. Had the vampiress thought twice about luring Edmund to cheat on her?

A delicate shiver ran across her shoulders as she recalled Claris's voice. It had been sweet as treacle but uncaring at the same time. *A liar's voice*, Estelle thought, one who wouldn't hesitate to poison her own husband.

Then, as though the memory were an explosive with a delayed fuse, Estelle recalled what Edmund had said: *You couldn't spare two minutes to speak to our sons today?*

Sons—in the plural.

Estelle had thought Robin was Edmund's only son by blood.

She stood so quickly the telephone tumbled from her lap with a clang. What else didn't she know about her beloved?

Route 75

Shortly after sunset, the American contingent congregated at the end of Peachtree's crushed-oyster-shell drive. Thanks to Ben's refusal to ride in one more train, they were now the proud owners of a 1933 Chrysler DeSoto four-door sedan, bought from a dealer known around Charleston as "Uncle Bob."

"Hm," Sally said, stepping onto the running board to peer into the shiny dark blue auto's interior. "I like that it has a radio."

Pen thought the way Sally's husband watched her bottom as she did this was pretty sweet, though clearly, Ben's concern over his wife's reaction to his purchase overrode his continuing captivation with her anatomy.

"It's roomy enough for all of us," he said, his arms crossed defensively. "And reliable. And we can travel on our own schedule."

"And *you* wanted to drive," Sally said, ducking out again with a laugh.

"Be glad I didn't buy the Airflow," Ben retorted. "Now that is an ugly car."

"This is fine," Sally said, flinging her arms around him in an exuberant embrace. "I bet 'Uncle Bob' was shocked at how good a deal you got."

"He was wincing a bit," Ben conceded, his cheek pressed so tenderly to her hair that Pen had to look away. She needed no reminder that she would never be loved like that. "I expect my accent made him think he could fiddle us."

Durand had finished making a slow orbit around the car. Pen noticed his boots didn't crunch on the drive at all. Vampire magic, she supposed.

He faced Ben imperiously. "You will show me how to operate this vehicle."

"Er," Ben said, still holding Sally. "Have you ever driven a car before?"

"It does not matter. I am physically coordinated and have an excellent memory."

"That's all right," Graham broke in, seeing his brother's dawning horror. "I can spell Ben with the driving, and so can Miss Anderson."

Pen smiled at her shoes. Graham had been calling her Miss Anderson whenever Durand was around, probably in an attempt to break the mercenary of addressing her by her Christian name. Pen found his protectiveness silly but endearing—almost as endearing as him curling up on her feet last night as his cat. She'd expected him to seduce her, had been looking forward to it, to tell the truth. At the least, she'd thought she could count on him wanting her. But while her body had been disappointed, she couldn't deny she'd been comforted by his company. She'd slept better than she had since the attack—even if Graham's cat was big enough to hog half the bed.

"You can watch us drive," Pen said to Durand. "Pick up the rules of the road before you have a go yourself."

Durand's lips thinned with disapproval. Sensing an argument that might disturb their team's fragile camaraderie, Pen decided it was time to distract him.

"Shall I show you what *I* bought at Uncle Bob's?"

Ben's gaze snapped to hers. "You bought something?"

Pen smiled and popped the DeSoto's trunk. Four freshly cleaned Winchester Model 12 shotguns lay in the well, one for her and each of the men. She took one out and worked the pump action. "Uncle Bob sells these from his back room. They haven't got much range, but you can count on their stopping power. Plus, we have some flexibility as to what we load in the cartridges. I was thinking iron buckshot would be good."

Durand took the gun from her, squinted down the barrel, and tested the trigger. Pen could see he wouldn't have any trouble operating it.

He handed it back to her and nodded. "This was well thought out of you."

He might have been impressed by her foresight. With his usual lack of expression, it was hard to tell.

"I knew we couldn't take them on empty-handed," Pen replied.

"There's none for me," Sally pouted, coming around to look.

"I have this for you." Pen pulled out a little pearl-handled derringer. "It's small enough for you to handle, but it only holds two shots, so it's strictly for close up and as a last resort—*not* for running into the thick of things."

"Oh, it's darling!" Sally cooed, precisely as Pen expected. She'd known better than to get Sally a weapon that wasn't cute. "Thank you ever so much!"

Pen hadn't expected Sally to hug her, or that the girl's big blue eyes would well up. Generally speaking, Pen wasn't demonstrative. Squeezed breathless and feeling awkward, she looked over Sally's curls at Graham. Being hugged by his sister was a bit like being squished by a peach in a flowered dress.

"Don't look at me," Graham said, his grin impossible to miss. "I could have warned you she liked presents."

"Wonderful presents!" Sally sniffled ominously into Pen's shoulder. "The baby is very, *very* happy with you right now."

"Um." Pen patted her back haphazardly. Sally's talk about the baby's feelings made her nervous.

"If we're all armed now," Durand cut in, his voice as cool and arid as dry ice, "perhaps we could stow our luggage and be off."

"Oh, sorry, sorry!" Sally cried, releasing Pen—but only to scamper back toward the house. "One more trip to the WC, and I'll be ready."

Durand neither said a word nor twitched a facial muscle.

Nonetheless, Pen knew the vampire was thinking this would be a long journey.

Pen had been on driving trips before with her college friends, but she'd never been on one quite like this. As promised, the DeSoto was sturdy, reliable, and covered twenty-two miles per gallon of gasoline. Sally required rather more fuel and maintenance stops than the car, the baby being extra fond of small snacks. Watching Durand lure waitresses behind greasy roadside diners added new meaning to the term *quick bite*. Graham ate human food, but only in his cat form. Ben was happy as long as Sally was—at least until Durand declared that he was ready to drive.

He did passably well, Pen thought—a little jerky but not too bad. Certainly not as bad as Ben's white-knuckled grip on the chrome door handle would indicate. For his part, the mercenary obviously hadn't expected Sally would remain up front with him, a position she insisted kept her from getting queasy. Durand tolerated her presence, but categorically refused to let her tune the radio to *Amos and Andy*. The comic show was such a national craze that shopkeepers would turn it on to keep their customers in the store. It was Sally's bad luck that the centuries-old vampire hadn't fallen for its charms.

"You will listen to classical music," he intoned. "Chopin is good for babies who need their naps. Touch it, and I'll thrall you," he added when she reached for the dial again. "And neither your husband nor your brother is quick enough to stop me."

"You're lucky I'm *not* napping," Sally huffed. "That turn you wanted to take was going to Pittsburgh."

"You're lucky you're not an empty husk lying in a ditch," Durand muttered.

"Oh, really?" Sally crossed her arms beneath her eye-catching pregnant breasts. "Is that how they teach you to talk to humans in icy-faced vampire school?"

Pen was in the middle of the backseat. She watched, fascinated, as a muscle ticked hard in Durand's jaw. The light from the dash's instruments was dim, but she could see his teeth were so tightly gritted his slightly swarthy skin had gone white. Control was important to this man. With her special powers of annoyance, Sally seemed well on her way to destroying it. Concerned that the vampire was about to burst, Pen leaned forward.

"Would you like me to drive?" she offered.

"No," Durand growled. "I am perfectly capable of ignoring this young, gestating human."

They were lucky Ben was dozing, or his tone would have caused trouble. Seated beside her, Graham slid his hand up Pen's spine. His palm was just barely warm, his fingers infinitely gentle. As they rubbed her nape underneath her hair, something in Pen melted, something she had no intention of basing decisions on. She did, however, settle back and look at him. Graham wagged his brows toward Durand.

Icy-faced vampire school, he mouthed, grinning.

"I heard that," Durand snapped, causing Graham and Pen to snicker like schoolchildren.

The warmth that blossomed inside her as they shared the joke brought back every scrap of her nervousness. She stopped laughing as abruptly as a vampire would have. Graham had been different since that stupid dinner with her aunts. He'd been softer. Kinder. And she didn't trust it one bit.

Even now, as she turned away from him, he tucked a wave of hair behind her ear, probably feeling sorry for her, probably preparing to let her down easy. Why else wouldn't he have slept with her? It wasn't like she'd made bedding her a challenge. Meeting her mother's side of the family must have convinced him she was too twisted up for intimacy.

"You should sleep," he said, the slow petting of his hand around her skull tempting her to cuddle into him. Pen ignored the urge ruthlessly.

"I will," she said.

She closed her eyes to do it, pressing her head into the seat and not his broad shoulder.

Chicago

~~~~~~~~~~~~

They reached the Drake Hotel in Chicago at two in the morning, pulling up beneath the broad front awning approximately five hours later than Pen had estimated it would take. Ben had driven the last leg of the journey. Groaning, he shoved the car door open, unfolded his long body from behind the wheel, and stretched with both his arms up. It was a measure of his exhaustion that he handed the DeSoto's keys to the valet without a single extra instruction.

"God," he said, yawning until his jaw cracked. "What I wouldn't give for a few hours in a real bed."

Sally giggled as she joined him, which surprised no one.

"How is it," Durand asked, offering his hand to help Pen swing out, "that you've known her for months, and you haven't killed her yet?"

The question required no answer, so Pen just smiled. The mercenary seemed to view Pen as his lone ally in his complaints against Sally. On Pen's other side, Graham let out a grunt that could have been irritation or agreement. His mood had darkened as soon as Durand joined them in the backseat, a territorial issue, perhaps—though Pen had been careful to place herself between the two vampires. Both the men's legs were long, but it was Graham's knee that continually bumped hers—as if he had to prove how much space he needed compared to Durand. For the final miles, the tension had grown so thick she'd almost felt her skin prickle. Interestingly, the more Graham fumed, the nicer Durand treated her.

It was as if the older male thought of Graham as a

rival he should tease. Pen refrained from telling him this couldn't be farther from the mark.

"Don't carry everything," Pen cautioned as Graham began unloading their luggage. He *could* carry everything, of course. The car as well, for all she knew, though this would draw attention. "Let the staff earn their tips."

"I know," Graham said a trifle sharply, then visibly released his breath. "Sorry. Long trip. I don't mean to take my temper out on you."

He touched Pen's face so gently her jaw dropped into his palm. After all that brooding, who'd have thought he'd do this? She found she couldn't look away from his rich brown eyes. Their depths were glowing, just a little, as if he did still want her. Caught in their spell, her body warmed helplessly.

"I . . . I'll go in and check our reservations," she stammered.

Sally and Ben were already waiting in the lobby as she climbed the stairs. The Drake was a handsome establishment, grand and dark, with fancy stone decorations around the doorways and glossy paneling on the walls. Pen could have saved quite a few pennies by booking them elsewhere, but she knew the amount of privacy wealth could buy. Given her purpose and considering the hour, she was taken aback by the number of people—in evening dress, no less—who milled around beneath the huge chandeliers.

"What's going on?" she asked a passing bellboy. "Why is it so crowded?"

"Century of Progress Exposition," he said. "Lots of visitors in town. And we opened a new bar to celebrate being able to drink again." He rolled his eyes as if he, like Durand, considered her an ally. "Everyone who's anyone is making us their watering hole."

Pen rubbed a finger across her lips as the busy bellboy went on his way. She'd forgotten the World's Fair was here this year. She hoped the crowds wouldn't complicate their search. As for the new bar, well, they'd give that a wide berth. Pen had no desire to see everyone who was anyone right now.

As if the thought were a jinx, someone called her name.

"Pen!" the woman cried, waving as Pen turned reluctantly.

"Binky," Pen said weakly.

Binky hurried across the Drake's plush carpet on heels that would have given Pen vertigo. She looked wonderful in her slinky pink evening gown, slimmer than when Pen had last seen her, and sporting a stylish caramel bob that flattered her long, interesting face. With a cry of pleasure, she kissed the air on either side of Pen's cheeks.

"Darling," she cooed. "I knew that had to be you. No one else's shoulders look quite like yours from behind—or no woman's. But why didn't you tell me you were in town? Rudy and I would have thrown a do with the gang."

Rudy was Binky's husband, a nice but phlegmatic banker who served as foil to Binky's quick glitter. That and his money explained why Binky had married him.

"I'm here on business," Pen said, though she doubted this would put Binky off. It especially wouldn't put her off after Durand stepped beside her. Binky's eyes went big as the tall, dark mercenary slung his arm around Pen.

"She's here on *my* business," he said, pulling out his European suavity. "I was hoping to keep her to myself. You understand, I'm sure."

Quite possibly, he was exerting the power of his gaze. Pen's old friend looked mesmerized enough to be thralled. Sadly, this appearance was misleading. Had Durand asked, Pen would have warned him no vampire magic could overcome a woman like Binky's curiosity. Indeed, she was already tucking her elbow through Pen's to tug her away.

"I'll have her back in no time," she promised as Durand gaped. "Just long enough for a quick, gossipy drink in the Coq d'Or."

When Pen glanced over her shoulder, not knowing how to stop this wrench in their plans, she spied Ben restraining Graham by both arms. Strangely—or maybe not—it wasn't Pen he seemed to want to pursue. Illogical though it was, Graham's flame-shooting fury targeted Durand.

* * *

Oh, my God," Binky breathed once the cocktails arrived at their little table in the back of the smoky bar. "That was one smooth piece of man you had draped on you. Your father must loathe him."

"Daddy hasn't met him," Pen said unsurely. For no good reason, she felt uncomfortable letting Binky believe Durand was her lover.

"Even better!" Binky exclaimed. "Secret affairs are the best. And I am sorry to have dragged you away, but I have the most horrifying story to share with you."

Binky looked more titillated than horrified. Despite Pen's disinclination to be there, she reminded herself that having horrifying gossip imparted to her was better than being pumped for it.

"Do tell," she said with an archness Binky would find familiar.

"Well—" Binky leaned over the tabletop. Her diamond-encrusted bracelet hit the wood with a clank. "Do you remember that funny fellow, Jack Vandertote? The one who liked to show up at parties he hadn't quite been invited to?"

Pen sipped some of her fruity drink up its straw. "He ran a charity, didn't he? Save the Soiled Doves, or something like that."

"Precisely. Always busy collecting money, and somehow never paying it out." Binky sniffed down her longish nose. "Rudy pegged him for a flimflam artist the night they met."

"I gather something happened to him."

"He disappeared, which isn't horrifying in and of itself, but he was last seen in that shantytown over on Canal. Hideous place. They ought to bulldoze it, if you ask me." Binky shuddered and then went on. "Now here's the horrifying bit. The same night Vandertote went missing, they found a murdered girl there, beneath the tracks of the 'L.' Young, long, curly hair, just the sort he used to sniff around. Her body, what the rats hadn't nibbled on, was drained of blood—every drop of it, gone. One of Rudy's friends bribed a copy of the crime scene photographs from the police. You simply can't imagine how revolting it was. Poor girl looked like Snow White had been deflated. Some people are actually saying it must have been vampires."

If Pen hadn't been wearing a jacket, Binky would have seen the gooseflesh that swept her arms. Though she regretted the final violation of the nameless girl by Rudy and his friends, she knew she had to ask her next question. "I don't suppose Rudy kept a set of the prints?"

"God, no." Binky tossed back the rest of her cocktail and signaled for a refill. "One look was enough for us. That isn't the end of the story, though. You remember Douglas Whitford, right?"

"The Idiot," Pen said unthinkingly. Her flush of shame came a breath too late. Did she and Binky really regard so many of their circle so scornfully? As if a lash had struck her, she recalled Graham once saying she didn't know how to be nice.

Binky, of course, didn't bat an eye at the slur.

"That's the one," she said. "As you may know, the Idiot suffered a few unfortunate financial losses after the Crash, but that didn't stop Vandertote from cozening contributions out of his wife. When Whitford heard he'd disappeared, he thought he'd mosey up to his penthouse, see if he could get those contributions back—pawn Vandertote's silver, or some such thing."

"Daring," Pen said, her ears practically vibrating with eagerness.

"Well, they don't call him the Idiot for nothing. Anyway, he went to that place Vandertote has on Lake Shore Drive, the tall one, you know? Up the elevator the Idiot goes, and what should he hear when he gets out, but a damn piano concerto."

"Someone was in the apartment." Pen's goose bumps were chasing each other now. Li-Hua played the piano, as she recollected. Could the culmination of their search really be this close?

Luckily, Binky was too intent on her story to notice Pen's tension.

"Yes," she said, "someone was inside, but the Idiot was three sheets to the wind, so he goes ahead and bangs on the door. Some man—a tall blond god, according to Whitford—strolls out in nothing but a towel. Tells Whitford he and his wife are Vandertote's cousins. Says Vandertote's gone on a long vacation, and they'll be taking care of the place."

"Sounds fishy," Pen observed.

"That's what I say!" Binky crowed. "But the Idiot swore he believed him. Made us promise not to call the police."

Pen knew exactly what could make a man—even one who wasn't an idiot—swallow a tale like that. She also knew how dangerous *dis*believing it could be, especially if the cause was what she surmised.

"It might not be bad advice to stay out of it," she told Binky carefully. "I mean, who knows what shady business Vandertote was mixed up in?"

"Oh, you know Rudy." Binky waved cigarette smoke from her face. "Never thinks twice when he can think three times. I doubt he'll say anything to anyone. What a story, though. Honestly. I couldn't have made it up if I tried."

Her throaty laugh reminded Pen why they liked each other. It was more than knowing the same people, more than having been to the same parties for years and years. It wasn't even because Binky had dropped this miraculous answer into her lap. Binky wasn't perfect, but she seized life and enjoyed it as best she could. That, more than any other reason, made her a kindred soul.

Never mind Binky wouldn't dream of risking her safety for someone else. The whole world couldn't run around acting like Fitz Clares. What mattered was that if anything happened to Binky, Pen would never forgive herself. Before *she* could think twice, she reached across the table and squeezed her hands.

"Binky," she said, "you are a dear, dear friend."

To her amazement, Binky's eyes filled with tears—which made her the second woman in a week whom Pen had caused to well up.

"Oh, Pen," Binky said, blinking hard as she cleared her

throat. "That . . . that means a lot, coming from you. To tell the truth, we, all of us, think of you as the best apple in our crowd. Truly, it's a wonder any of us can stand you!"

Pen laughed as was expected and kissed her friend's cheek.

"And now I need a favor," she said, "and I need you not to ask why."

"Anything," Binky swore.

Pen knew her too well to accept that at face value. People she knew had already brushed too close to Frank and Li-Hua. If word somehow got back to the renegade vampires that Pen and the others were in Chicago, they might lose their best chance to catch them. Worse, someone Pen cared about could get hurt.

"I mean it, Binky. I need you not to tell anyone you spoke to me tonight, not even Rudy—no matter how tempting gossiping is."

"Are you worried your father will hear about that delicious man?"

"Binky," Pen said, her laugh now exasperated.

"Right. No questions. You aren't in trouble, though? You know Rudy and I would help if we could. Both of us adore you."

They did adore her, after their fashion. Because of that, Pen wasn't going to endanger them.

"I'm not in trouble," she said, wishing she had a vampire's power to persuade. "And if you help me by keeping quiet, I'm certain I'll stay that way."

Graham strode back and forth across Pen's spacious hotel room. He told himself he wasn't pacing, simply stretching his legs. Christ, though, nothing had gotten easier since he realized he loved her. Maybe this was what being in love meant—these knots in his belly, this itching under the skin. If so, he was doing it up in spades. He'd wanted to kill Durand when he'd pretended to lay claim to Pen earlier, despite the older vampire's thrall being light-years ahead of Graham's. Pen was *his*. Graham knew that in his bones.

Only Ben had prevented him from tearing Durand's arm off Pen. As to that, Graham would have been delighted to tear it off *Durand*.

Sighing, he rubbed his face. His fangs were half down with anger, an extra hardness behind his lips. With a growl he tried to muffle, he forced them back into their sockets.

And then he stilled, every cell alert and excited. Pen's light, sure strides were approaching the door. His fangs ran straight out again as her key slid into the lock. That lapse was joined a second later by the vicious hardening of his cock.

"Graham," Pen said, obviously surprised to see him. Her face looked strange, as though she were struggling to absorb a shock.

"Are you all right?" He stepped to her without a thought, their closeness immediately making his body sing. "I saw Durand didn't manage to prevent your friend from dragging you off."

Pen pulled her hands from his, which obliged him to notice he'd taken them. Seeming oddly numb, she lowered herself to the edge of a nearby chair. Had he misstepped by deciding to woo her somewhere other than in bed, or was she merely off balance? Graham was relatively certain he'd been right to change strategies. His previous pattern hadn't been getting good results. Well, good carnal results, maybe, but not romantic ones.

"Pen?" he said as she sat there staring at the floor.

"I'm fine," she said. "I just—" She shook herself and looked up at him. "Your fangs are out. Are you hungry?"

His prick twanged as if she'd tugged it. "I came to see how you were."

This would have been more convincing if his voice hadn't come out husky.

Pen jumped up and went to the telephone. "I'll call room service. Unless—" She stopped. Hesitated. Graham's groin tightened. "Are you tired of eating as your cat? I know you . . . like blood the most. I could— I mean, I don't mind helping you out."

Graham's throat closed in. He *had* misstepped if she

could regard him that unsurely. He moved to her in a twinkling, lifting her hand to press a kiss to the pulse beating in her wrist.

"I like *your* blood the most," he grated.

She flushed and cut her gaze away.

"Pen," he said. He meant it as a scold but ended up sounding more like he was groaning. Pen heard it that way, too. Her nipples budded beneath her blouse, the little peaks pushing out the taupe satin. Lord, she was killing him.

"I don't mind," she repeated, and held out the wrist he'd kissed.

It was a lovely wrist, but she was insane if she thought he was going to bite her there. Instead, he trailed his fingertips up the inside of her arm. Her tiny shiver made his own spine tingle. Taking her shoulders, he pushed her gently onto the bed.

"Sit," he said, his voice still an octave lower than normal.

"You don't want to feed from me?" she asked, now rather breathless herself.

He knelt before her, unable to resist drawing her index finger into his mouth. She gasped—a wonderful catch of sound—as he sucked it the way he wanted to be sucking other parts of her: licking it, flicking it, curling his tongue around it until the heat that rolled off her body felt like an open fire. In moments, Graham was burning as hot as she was. He knew if he wasn't careful, he—and they—were going to end up exactly where they'd been before.

"I want to feed from you," he said, too aroused to lie. "Your wrist is simply too slender for me to bite."

"Oh," she said, delightfully pink. "I— You—"

She wore a narrow tweed skirt tonight, and under that, a cream-colored, lacy-edged slip that had to be real silk. It invited his hands beneath it, up her stockings, and onto the bare, warm skin of her upper thighs—thighs he now knew were taut and strong because of Roy Blunt's training. Graham took his time stroking them: retreating, advancing, teasing her flesh with what he wanted to do to her. Pen was trembling before he finished. She was used to him domi-

nating her, and in some ways he was still doing that. In
others, he felt like her acolyte, ready and eager to worship
everything she was. He drank in her wide-eyed expression
as he rubbed a gentle line where a tendon ran toward her
mound. Her lips had fallen open for quickened breaths.
The scent of her arousal, of her surging blood, was unbelievably appealing. No one else smelled like Pen did. Not
in the entire world.

He was probably more addicted to that scent than he
ought to be. If it turned out he needed her the way Sally
needed Ben, he could be in big trouble.

"This spot," he said, touching the smooth inner curve
where her thigh was strongest. "If you let me, I'll bite you
here."

Beneath her silk undergarments, her labia twitched.
Unable to stop himself, Graham feathered a touch across
the dampening fabric, brushing the harder bump that was
her clitoris. Blood washed Pen's cheeks in a scarlet tide,
causing her scent to rise. Convinced he was about to go
crazy, Graham shoved her skirt up and mouthed her thigh.
His jaw ached with his urge to widen it.

"Here," he growled like an animal. "Just a bite and no
more."

When her fingers tangled in his hair and clutched him,
he suspected he'd chosen the right approach. When she
moaned, low and quavering, at the gentle drag of his fangs,
he couldn't have any doubt.

He set the tips against her muscle, his tongue curling out
between them to taste her skin. Since he'd said he was only
going to bite her, it seemed wrong to shove his hand under
her panties. He pressed the length of his thumb over them
instead, pushing her labia and clitoris hard back against her
bone. The sound and feel of her increasing wetness ren-
dered it impossible not to drive his teeth into her.

She came the instant he drank. His bite was inherently
orgasmic, and—like any woman—she was capable of more
than one climax. What he didn't expect was that his cock
would jerk at her cries, responding flagrantly to her pleasure,
to her hot blood running down his throat, to the infinitely

right sweetness of making her a part of him. The strafe of his swollen glans against his tightened trousers was nearly enough to trigger an orgasm. Sweat popped out on his brow in a sudden wave. With balls that ached from the torture of holding back, he tore his teeth from her thigh a millisecond before his seed could burst free.

His thumb, apparently, had a mind of its own. Its pad was rolling over and over her swollen bud, as if he simply couldn't get enough of her coming.

"Graham," Pen gasped, her head thrown back. "My God, you're good at that."

He drew his hand from her. Because his legs wouldn't hold him in his condition, he sat on his heels, his fists balled on his thighs, his muscles shaking violently. His cock felt like a separate creature, so distended from watching her find fulfillment that it was strangling. His undergarments were wet with pre-come, and the telltale fluid hadn't stopped flowing yet. He swept away the two beads of red he'd left on her leg. Sucking them off his thumb, he tried to pull himself together.

This wasn't easy with the dizzying buzz of her blood in him.

"Tell me now," he said, ignoring how far from rational he sounded. "Tell me what your friend from the lobby said to put that look on your face, like you'd had the wind knocked from you."

Pen touched his hair. The strands were stirring subtly as his aura untousled it. Though he was determined to show her she meant more to him than sex, part of him wished she'd notice he remained erect, that she'd insist he find release inside her velvety tight pussy. This, however, wasn't uppermost in Pen's mind.

"I can hardly believe it," she said, the absentminded combing of her fingers doing devilish things to his spine, "but I think I know where Frank and Li-Hua are . . ."

Lake Shore Drive

With sixteen stories of apartments, Jack Vandertote's building on Lake Shore Drive resembled an unnaturally tall French château. Beginning on its uppermost levels, the highest of which was their goal, three completely useless fairytale-style towers sprouted up toward a mansard roof. To Durand's eyes, the structure looked ludicrous, a cacophony of old and new he could not care for. Americans were strange, he thought, perpetually torn between leaping into the modern world and toadying up to the past.

Durand liked things to be one or the other.

"Pull in here," he said to Ben, having decided to let the human operate the car. He was better at it than Durand, though Durand knew he would improve with practice—preferably without the Fitz Clare girl chattering next to him. Sometimes Durand thought humans needed instruction in being quiet.

Ben stopped the car beneath a row of newly budding trees. He hadn't parked directly in front of the building entrance, but Durand could see the door from their position across the street. To their right, a well-groomed park formed a greensward between the road and the huge body of water that was Lake Michigan. This aspect of the city Durand approved of. Though sadly bereft of mountains, it reminded him of Lake Geneva in his homeland. His memories of that were pleasant, but he pushed them away from him.

"Turn off the headlamps," he said.

Ben did so, leaving the interior of the auto lit only by streetlights.

"What now?" Sally asked from her princess throne.

"Now we wait," Durand said, knowing he had to answer. However silly Sally was, the others wouldn't tolerate him disrespecting her. "The fair is open after dark, and its grounds are an easy walk from here. With such a feast spread before them, the odds are slim that Frank and Li-Hua won't be hunting there tonight. Once we see them leave, we can set up in their penthouse."

"Like an ambush." Sally twisted in her seat to face Durand. Ben turned at the same time, as if the pair were connected by invisible strings. Pen, Durand noticed, had the presence of mind to maintain her watch on their enemies' front door. When Sally's little brow furrowed, he half expected Ben to echo the expression.

"Yes?" Durand prompted, figuring he might as well get Sally's next question over with.

"Won't they kill someone if they hunt?"

"Not necessarily," Durand said. "But they may."

"So while we're sitting here waiting in our ambush . . ."

"Yes," he confirmed. "An innocent human may be dying."

Sally sucked in a breath of dismay.

"We can't follow them to the fair," Graham said before his sister could object. "They'd have no trouble disappearing into the crowds, and we'd risk tipping them off that we're on the trail. Besides which, the fight would be very public. This might not be a perfect plan, but it's the best we have."

Sally twisted her lips into a shape no *upyr* mouth would have formed. To Durand's astonishment, she didn't voice her protest, just jerked her head in grudging acceptance and looked away.

"You have the building plans?" Pen asked, a change of topic he was inexplicably grateful for.

"I do," he said, having thralled them from the residence's manager. He handed the sheets to her. Together, she and Graham unrolled them across their laps, taking quiet note of the exits and the various means of moving from floor to floor.

Durand saw he'd made a better choice than he'd known

by allowing Pen to join this mission. Graham was strong for a young vampire and had more self-control than most, but it was Pen's strictly human professionalism that helped settle the others. As long as she followed Durand's lead, he suspected they would as well. Even Graham was calmer in her presence, seeming to forget the territorial anger Durand should have known better than to stir up. Then and there, Durand swore he wouldn't do it again. Too much lay at stake for him to be . . . entertaining himself in that childish way.

He didn't have long to berate himself. He spied Frank and Li-Hua exiting the building a moment before Sally stiffened in the front seat.

"There they are," she whispered.

Durand's old employers were dressed like Americans—Li-Hua in a dress and jacket and hat, and Frank in a single-breasted, three-piece suit. They looked happy, sprightly, holding hands like any couple might as they proceeded briskly down the smooth sidewalk. As Durand watched, Frank bent to kiss Li-Hua's cheek.

Durand wasn't prepared for the wave of intense dislike that rolled over him. He hardly subscribed to the world at large's morals. He hadn't in life, and he wasn't going to in death. Those two, though, had led him down a path that besmirched his own concept of honor. There were reasons he'd acted as he had when he worked for them, but he absolutely did not appreciate the stain it left—no more than he appreciated Frank and Li-Hua's reckless behavior putting all their race's heads on the chopping block. As far as Durand was concerned, the best aspect of modern times was that humans *didn't* believe in them. If Frank and Li-Hua changed that before he could stop them, he wasn't sure his unlife would be worth living.

"They *are* heading toward the fair," Graham murmured, pulling Durand from his reverie. He moved to open the car door, but Durand reached across Pen's body to catch his arm.

As he did, he realized his oath not to tease Graham might be irrelevant. Graham had bitten Pen recently. The pair's scents were mingling. He couldn't question that they were forming a bond.

"Wait," Durand said, returning to the task at hand. "We don't know how sharp our enemies' senses have become. They'll be focused on prey now, anticipating the hunt. I don't want to do anything to draw their attention away from that."

Graham released his grip on the door handle.

"Ten minutes?" Pen suggested, showing Durand the time on her watch.

Durand sank back against the seat. "Ten minutes should work," he said.

Durand led his makeshift team into the building by snapping the lock on a rear entry. Frank and his lover would have to be crazier than he thought not to bite and bespell the doorman. Luckily, the lift wasn't difficult to take without being spotted, and far easier on human legs than the stairs.

Durand ordered them to stay inside while he checked the small foyer on the sixteenth floor. The marble-lined space was empty; Frank and Li-Hua hadn't posted a guard. Entrances to the two penthouse apartments led off from either side. When Durand laid his hands on the paneled wood of the doors, neither betrayed signs that living beings were inside. One, however, hummed with the energy vampires left behind when they resided anywhere for long.

"This one," he said as Graham stepped forward cautiously. Durand was gratified to see Graham had his shotgun out.

"Let Ben pick the lock," Pen said before Durand could twist the knob. "They'll know something's wrong if it's broken."

Bemused, Durand stepped aside to watch her hand Ben a set of tools from the pack she carried across her back. The younger Fitz Clare crouched down in front of the lock, making those distorted faces mortals were so fond of as he probed the mechanism with the picks. He seemed familiar with the process. Less than a minute passed before the door clicked open.

"Hurrah!" Sally whispered, her exuberance at her husband's illicit skills causing one side of Durand's mouth to lift.

The hint of a smile dropped from him as he stepped inside. He was in a gallery hung with dozens of portraits of nearly identical black-haired girls—Vandertote's selections, he imagined. The gallery was lit by skylights, through which the unavoidable glow of the electrified city fell. To his left, a stately living room with a fireplace overlooked Lake Shore Drive. To his right was a twist and then a corridor. It was up this corridor that a faint charnel-house scent wafted. Graham gasped softly as he recognized what it was.

"Take Sally to the living room," Durand said to Ben. "Find her a hiding place. If you think you hear Frank and Li-Hua coming, rap twice lightly on the floor. Either Graham or I will hear you."

"Am I with them or you?" Pen asked.

Durand took in her quiet calm, knowing their enemies weren't likely to show up soon. "With me," he said. "We're going to search the back of the apartment."

They found the bodies in what was probably a maid's room, stacked up like cords of wood on the bed. Three were dressed in the garb of servants, most likely Vandertote's. The other two Durand identified by their smell as belonging to the neighboring penthouse. Durand judged the oldest bodies were a few weeks' dead, prevented from outright rotting by the dryness of the artificially heated air and their dearth of blood. Fortunately, spring didn't arrive early in Chicago, and as a result, the corpses were partially mummified. All their necks had been savaged.

"Lordy," Pen said, the back of her forearm pressed to her nose. "Who are these people?"

"Staff," Durand said. "And the neighbors, whom I suppose we now don't have to worry about disturbing."

"Pardon my ignorance," Graham said, his voice slightly rough with shock, "but isn't it unusual for our kind to keep their victims around?"

"Highly," Durand said. "No vampire in his right mind would want a decaying body anywhere near his lair."

"So they aren't in their right minds."

"No," Durand confirmed, meeting Graham's jerky stare. "And I cannot predict whether that will work for or against us."

Graham's eyes steadied as he squared his village strong-man's shoulders. "Can we get Sally out of here?"

"Not without losing Ben as well, and—with all the power our enemies have amassed—I foresee us needing every shooter we have."

Durand let Graham absorb this, not surprised to see his gaze return to the horror on the narrow bed. Pen watched Graham's face instead, and Durand knew she'd already reached the conclusion Graham was working on. Graham had been trained as a spy and not a soldier. There was a difference.

"They'll kill again," Graham said slowly. "They won't stop until we stop them, and maybe one of us is going to die in the fight."

Pen put her hand on Graham's shoulder. She didn't say a word, but Durand could sense her touch bolstering him. Perhaps it worked the other way as well. Perhaps Pen was being brave so Graham wouldn't have to steady her. Once Durand had known all about such bonds. He didn't think he wanted to anymore.

"Very well," Graham said, the sigh that carried the words almost inaudible. "Where do you want us positioned?"

The press had dubbed this World's Fair the "Rainbow City" in honor of the dazzling array of colors that blazed from its many modernistic exhibition halls. All the struc-tures were new, all the starkest possible contrast to the gray, Depression-gripped metropolis outside the sprawling grounds. Most were cheaply built of prestressed concrete and sheet metal, but in the dark, beneath the dramatic light-ing that bathed them, none appeared less than palaces.

Loving the display and—even more—its effect on the

gawking crowds, Li-Hua threw back her head and laughed.
She and Frank stood at the end of the reflecting pool that
graced the Travel and Transport Building, a crazy, angular
bulk that looked a bit like a crown.

"*Your* crown," Frank murmured hotly next to her ear.
"Shall we select some new subjects to sacrifice their souls
to their queen?"

Li-Hua squeezed his hand in delight. There were plenty
of subjects to choose from: countless beating hearts, endless oceans of blood pumping. Farmers and corporate
moguls, socialites and secretaries, all came to wander the
fair. Who would even miss them if they didn't walk out
again? Everyone knew things happened in a place like
this. For all the exposition's glamour, violence could lurk
anywhere.

The presence of so many potential victims made Li-Hua
giddy. She spun in a circle and laughed again, adoring how
sharp her awareness had become. This was what she'd
always been meant to be. She could hear conversations a
mile away—children whining over dropped ice cream,
couples ducking into shadows to steal a kiss.

Pick me, each soul seemed to cry to her. *No, no, pick me.*

And then another awareness, like icy rainwater down
her neck, caused her spine to snap straight.

"What is it, love?" Frank asked.

Li-Hua whirled around to view the wide, tree-lined
avenue they'd come up. Easily a thousand humans rib-
boned along its length, like blood cells jostling through
an artery. She couldn't see their home from here, but she
could feel it.

"Someone's been sleeping in my bed," she said softly.

"Someone broke into the penthouse?"

Li-Hua nodded reluctantly, licking her sharpened fangs.
She wanted to enjoy herself, not fight to defend their lair.

"We can't allow that," Frank said, chafing her gently
from neck to shoulder. "What if it's that cowboy who's
been chasing us?"

Li-Hua snarled at that idea, which caused a passing

father of three to shoot her a startled look. Frank's glare turned the man's nervous gaze away.

"If Blunt is the intruder," Li-Hua said, her little hands clenched to fists, "we can make him my next subject."

Durand never got to position Graham strategically, nor did Ben have time to rap out a warning. The front door simply exploded in a hail of splinters as Frank and Li-Hua came home.

"Shoot as soon as you see them," Durand ordered his current companions, reduced to necessities. "Head or heart. Don't stop until you're out of bullets."

Then he and Graham were racing up the dark corridor, too swiftly for Pen to keep up. They could hear—and soon see—Ben firing from the living room. The width of its entrance allowed him to take cover behind the wall and still hit Frank, who was silhouetted at the end of Vander-tote's gallery. Frank wasn't facing Ben. The pellets jerked his body forward, toward Durand and Graham, but didn't seem to inconvenience him otherwise.

Durand took half a second to admire Ben's willingness to shoot a man in the back.

That done, he yanked his favorite iron knife from his boot and leaped in Frank's direction.

"*You*," Frank said as Durand's face flashed into visibility beneath the skylight. His surprise gave Durand the opening he wanted to grapple hand to hand. If he could plunge his knife directly into Frank's heart, it might do some good. It was an old blade that had soaked up a lot of power. Unfortunately, the alarming increase in Frank's strength didn't make stabbing him easy.

"Head," Durand barked to Graham, hoping the boy could avoid winging him. Durand suspected iron shot would do him more damage than it did Frank, a theory he didn't really want to test out. The air above him whizzed with projectiles, so Graham must have understood what he meant.

Graham was hitting Frank, but the bullets sank into his flesh as if it were water, as if he had the power to simply absorb them. The wounds weren't even bleeding, though Frank did falter slightly at each impact.

"Fool," Frank growled, slamming Durand down to the floor. "You never should have betrayed me and my pear blossom."

On his knees straddling Durand's waist, Frank punctuated his words by boxing Durand's head. Frank might have been strong, but he wasn't careful, and Durand was the more skillful fighter by a few centuries. He was definitely motivated. Though his brain felt like it was rattling, he shoved his knife into Frank's breastbone.

The blade wasn't long, and no blood welled around it, but Durand knew from personal experience that the tip had nicked his enemy's heart muscle. Desperate to increase his advantage, Durand put all his strength behind thrusting it deeper. This, at last, had some effect. Frank reared up from him and roared, fighting with Durand for control of the antique hilt.

The change in position enabled Ben to join Graham in pumping shot into Frank's ostensibly indestructible skull.

Durand had a fragment of time to wonder where Li-Hua was before he saw her leap like a monkey onto Ben's back. She had odd red lumps scattered on her face, as if the shotgun pellets were lodged just beneath her skin. Ben must have alternated between shooting her and Frank. More lumps formed as Pen skidded into the gallery and took aim at the vampiress.

The American was a hell of a shot, breaking open the gun and reloading faster than the majority of her race could have done. All the same, Durand knew her arrival was too little, too late. Li-Hua's delicate hands were crossing around Ben's head—one to his chin, the other to his temple.

Shit, Durand thought as she snapped Ben's neck with a sound as sharp as a gun's report. Ben crumpled to his knees underneath her weight.

"No," Graham bellowed, letting his finger off the trigger.

Pen stopped shooting, too, then resumed a heartbeat later. She had shifted her bead to Frank, judging—as Durand did—that he was closer to actually dying. Frank's head wobbled back and forth at the new barrage.

With a scream of rage, Li-Hua rushed forward and caught Frank's arm. In one continuous blur of motion, she pulled him onto his feet, wrenched Durand's knife from his sternum, and backhanded Pen hard enough that her rangy body cracked the paint on the gallery's wall. The human female slid down it, still conscious but just barely. Seeing his mate in danger, Graham flung himself at Li-Hua.

"Bitch," she spat at Pen, kicking back Graham's attack without turning to look at him.

"You're the bitch," said a voice none of them expected to hear.

Sally had emerged from the Chinese cabinet where she'd been hiding. Durand hardly recognized her. Her skin was dead white, her rosebud mouth pressed into a grim, thin line. Furious as she was, her eyes were more flame than sky. She held the pearl-handled derringer in both hands.

"Are you going to shoot me, little girl?" Li-Hua cooed, clearly not viewing Sally or her gun as a threat. Beside her, Frank swayed but didn't fall over. "Are you upset because I broke your pretty brother's neck?"

Graham choked out a noise like a tormented animal, but Sally simply tightened her grip. She'd stepped right up to the smirking vampiress, the muzzle of her gun nudged flat against Li-Hua's heart.

Li-Hua opened her mouth to mock her when Sally squeezed off her first shot. To Durand's amazement, considering how easily she and Frank had shrugged off the other hits, a brief gush of blood fountained from the hole in her chest.

"Ow," Li-Hua said, pressing her palm to it.

"I have another bullet," Sally said. "Want to see if that one tickles?"

She didn't get a chance to compress the trigger, though Durand was already up and moving to help her. Before he could, sanity—or maybe self-preservation—seized Li-Hua.

Grabbing Frank, who continued to look woozy, she streaked down the back corridor. Cursing, Durand followed. The pair was heading for the fire escape, running so fast it sounded like the air was tearing. The speed he was forced to attain to try to match theirs was dizzying. Glass crashed as the couple burst together out a small window. Apparently, wounded or not, they were ignoring the ladder. Durand grabbed the sill and leaned out, wishing he could believe they wouldn't survive a sixteen-story drop.

When he spotted them with his sharpened vision, his overexerted heart nearly stopped beating.

Frank and Li-Hua weren't falling. They were soaring through the chill night air, their bodies black and birdlike against the clouds. The thought was crazy, but it looked as if they were flying. Durand had heard rumors that the most powerful elders could do this, but he'd never credited them. When Frank and Li-Hua's tiny figures landed on the roof of an office building, at least two miles distant, Durand still wasn't sure what he'd seen. All he knew was that he could no longer pursue them.

With shock ringing in his ears, he drew his head back inside the window. His hands were bloody from the broken glass, but they healed quickly. He heard Sally sobbing at the opposite end of the long penthouse.

He swore in the guttural *Schwyzerdütsch* of his youth, the fit of temper short but hot, hating this evidence that he'd failed to lead his team to their objective. As he staggered to join them, he retrieved his family knife from where it had tumbled. The practical part of his mind noted the blade was clean. When he returned to the gallery—somewhat calmer—a thankfully less horrifying shock awaited him.

Ben Fitz Clare was cradled across Sally and Graham's laps. Pen stood near but apart from them, her arms wrapped impotently around her waist. To the casual observer, Ben was as dead as dead could be: no heartbeat, no respiration, eyes staring and unresponsive. Durand, however, was no casual observer, and Durand could read energy much more precisely than Ben's brother.

"Lay him back on the floor," he said. "*Gently.* You don't want to jostle him."

Graham turned his head toward Durand, his expression very close to desolate. Though he wasn't making a sound, his face was as tear-washed as his sister's.

"He's dead," he said angrily.

"Not quite," Durand responded. "Your father strengthened his energy. His life force is still inside him. If we move quickly, we might be able to bring him back."

Saying one of them might die wasn't remotely the same as having it happen. Graham's throat was raw with grief, though—unlike Sally—he hadn't let out a single sob. In his present state, Durand's offer of hope was almost as cruel as losing Ben again.

"Don't you think I tried to heal him?" he demanded.

Durand's eyes didn't flicker at the accusation. "I only know what I sense."

"Maybe it's true," Sally interrupted, a little hesitant, her voice ragged from crying. Graham jerked his head around to stare at her. With a grimace, she pressed both palms to the slight curve of her belly. "Maybe Ben isn't dead. The baby still feels all right."

"Stretch your brother out on his back," Durand said calmly. "Let's see what we can do for him together. Sally, sit on that couch for a minute. It isn't human energy Ben needs right now."

Graham couldn't disobey the older vampire; he was too sure of himself. Dimly, he was aware of Pen sitting next to Sally to clutch her hand.

"Hold his knees," Durand instructed as he knelt above Ben's head. "I want you to keep his body braced while I pull."

So gently he could have been a human, Durand wrapped his long white fingers around the back of Ben's skull. Vertebrae began to scrape and crunch as he tugged.

"Steady," Durand said when an involuntary protest broke in Graham's chest. "There. I think his spine is aligned."

"What should I do now?" Graham asked hoarsely.

"Spread your hands around his navel, against the skin. Take deep, slow breaths and let whatever energy wants to flow out of you."

The flesh of Ben's stomach was already cooling. Graham tried not to wince as he followed Durand's instructions. Durand's eyes were closed, his hold cradling Ben's head. With every breath the older vampire took, lines Graham hadn't realized were on his face smoothed out. Durand looked as cool and peaceful as a statue, which Graham struggled not to resent.

"*Now*," Durand said, the word coming out strangely slow and dark.

Graham's palms buzzed as energy began to be drawn from them. Suddenly, Durand's aura was visible: a soft white gold light that emanated most strongly around his hands. Sally's gasp told him she could see it, too. The glow pulsed in time to the slow beat of Durand's heart, gradually entraining Graham's to the same rhythm.

As soon as their hearts were in synch, Graham could tell his energy was flowing into Ben's body. He could sense it moving inside his brother, could see it with something other than his eyes. Still Ben wasn't breathing. Still his heart did not beat. His skin was warmer, though, pinker, and Graham's rib cage tightened with desperate hope.

"Come on," Sally whispered from the couch. "Come on, Ben. Don't let that stupid fangster get the best of you."

A muscle in Ben's leg twitched.

"He moved!" Graham said.

And then Ben did more than move. He sucked a harsh gasp for air and blinked his eyes rapidly.

"Christ," he said, a weak, ghostly sound. "What the bloody hell happened?"

Sally dropped to the carpet beside him, laughing and crying and petting his wildly disordered hair. "My God, Daddy really did make you different!"

Durand eased away from Ben, letting Sally hold him instead. He rose gracefully but slowly to his feet. The healing didn't seem to have drained him, though Graham wouldn't have said he looked a hundred percent himself. Something about tonight had shaken their leader.

"You hurt Li-Hua," Durand said to Sally. "You made her bleed when none of us could. I'd say that means *you're* different, too."

The Drake Hotel

Someone knocked on the door to Sally and Ben's hotel room. Since Ben was sitting in bed with the covers up, Sally went to answer it . . . after a precautionary peep through the peephole.

"Ugh," she said, and pulled it open.

Even for one of the undead, Durand looked stiff. Sally knew he'd heard her reaction from the thinning of his already thin lips.

"I came to commend you on your bravery," he said, somehow managing to sound disapproving. "Your actions tonight may have preserved all our lives."

"Sticks in your craw, doesn't it, dead boy?"

Ramrod straight to begin with, Durand pulled himself at least an inch taller. "If my manner led you to believe that—"

"Oh, forget it," Sally said, too tired to play with him. She trudged to the bed and sat on it. "You brought my husband back from the dead. In my book, we're even."

"He wasn't dead." Durand followed her in as warily as if their room might contain a bomb. He seemed relieved to find Ben propped against a stack of pillows and dressed in pajamas. Presumably because he found her spouse less irritating, Durand addressed him. "You weren't dead. Just close to it."

Ben twined his fingers with Sally's. "I like the part of the story where my wife 'preserved all our lives.' I only wish I'd seen it."

Sally pinkened under his admiration. No matter what

Durand thought of her high opinion of herself, she knew she was no hero.

"I was angry," she said, her shoulders pulling up in a shrug. "I wanted to make Li-Hua pay for hurting you."

"I am thinking on what you did," Durand said gravely. "There may be something more important than the obvious in it."

Sally didn't know what he meant by this. Before she could come up with a way to ask, the mercenary spoke to Ben.

"Evidently, when your father blended his energy with yours, he gave you more physical resilience than most humans. You can rely on that to continue, but if I were you, I'd avoid pushing the issue so far again."

This was all Durand had to say. He nodded curtly to both of them and strode for the door.

"Durand," Ben said, his hand suddenly twice as tight on Sally's. Durand stopped and turned on his heel, which seemed to necessitate Sally's husband clearing his throat. Sally blinked at Ben in surprise. He was so nervous, his palm was wet.

"Yes?" Durand said.

"Do you—" Ben swallowed. "Can you tell if I'm going to remain human?"

Durand's face went blanker than usual. "No."

"Oh." Ben shifted on the bed. "Well. Thank you for answering."

Durand made a quicker job of his exit than he had the last time, almost blurring back into the corridor. The force with which he shut the door sent a sheaf of hotel stationery fluttering to the floor. Ignoring the mess, Sally scooted around on the covers to face the dearest man she knew.

"You're worried about that?" she asked him in disbelief. "About . . . tipping over into being a vampire?"

Anger tightened Ben's face, heightening the vivid green of his eyes.

"Of course I'm worried. You should be, too. You know how fond I've become of—" he lowered his voice as if someone else might hear "—of biting you when we have

sex. What if I turn into a vampire and could really do it?
What if I wanted to bite our daughter?"

"You wouldn't!" She knew he wouldn't. Ben had saved
her at the orphanage—before their father or Graham
showed up. No more than a boy, he'd nearly starved himself making sure she would not. That he believed he could
hurt anyone he loved offended her.

Clearly suffering from exactly this stupidity, Ben took
her shoulders between his hands. "We don't know I wouldn't
hurt her. From what I've seen, *upyr* urges are very strong.
Graham almost killed the first human he fed from."

"Oh, pooh," Sally said. "Graham didn't kill that woman.
He just was afraid he would." She crossed her arms at
Ben's continued resistant look. "Have you forgotten who
raised us? Daddy was a vampire. He never bit any of his
children. In fact, he was a better father than most people
could dream of."

"The professor is an old vampire, with centuries of self-
discipline. I'd be new, Sally. I'd be dangerous."

"Ben!"

His hands moved to her face, gently stroking her features as if he meant to memorize the feel of each one. When
his thumb brushed across her sensitive lower lip, neither of
them could help shivering.

"You'd be harder to kill," Sally said softly, her fingertips
at rest on his lean, hard chest. "I confess I wouldn't mind
that."

"I would," he murmured back. "I want to live as long as
you do, and not a day longer."

Sally's eyes burned with emotion as his gaze held hers.
The depth of his love for her humbled her. Everything had
happened so fast tonight she hadn't had time to consider
what she'd do without him. In the sincerest prayer she'd
ever sent to heaven, she hoped she'd never find out. Ben
was her better half—her sweeter, braver, infinitely more
responsible better half.

"As long as our daughter," she whispered in correction.
"Even if I died, I'd want you to stay alive to watch over
her."

He smiled at her, a single, beautiful tear rolling down his cheek.

"Agreed," he said, and silenced any more conversation with a tender kiss.

Pen piled the two bulging cardboard boxes atop each other and carried them across the hall to Graham's room. She told herself this was business, not her being afraid to be alone because she couldn't forget the sight of Frank and Li-Hua just *taking* those shotgun blasts.

Arms full, she used the toe of her shoe to knock on his door.

Graham opened it with vampire swiftness, widened his eyes, and took the load from her. His room was large and handsomely appointed, decorated in cream and green. Like hers, it was only a bed and bath. An empty meal tray with lick marks indicated he'd eaten—something she tried not to be crestfallen about.

Graham was within his rights to avoid a repeat of last night. No doubt it had been more momentous for her. He wasn't the one who'd had the vast majority of his orgasms with her as his partner.

"What are these?" he asked as he set the boxes on the long, low dresser that ran along one wall.

"Papers from the desk in Vandertote's library. It looks like Frank and Li-Hua used it for storage, too. Durand gathered up everything he could find so we could go through the lot at our leisure here."

"Where is Durand?"

"Skulking in the park across from their building in case they come back. He doesn't think they will," she added as Graham's mouth opened. "He's hoping we can find a clue in here to where they'll go next."

She pulled a face at the piled-up disarray in the two boxes. Organization hadn't been any of the vampires' specialty.

"Vampires don't really skulk," Graham said. "We're simply extremely quiet."

When Pen looked up, Graham wasn't wearing his glamour, just a small, boyish smile. His true appearance dazzled
her: the ivory smoothness of his skin, the unexpected
affection in his jewel-bright eyes. The old Graham was in
there, too, the man she'd once thought so easy to dismiss.
She'd been wrong about that. All along, his decency and
determination had been making their case to her. *I'm out
of the ordinary*, they'd been saying. *I'm trustworthy, and
I'm strong, and any woman with half a brain would want
to hang on to me.*

"Are you all right?" Graham asked.

She knew he meant was she all right because she was
staring at him like a fool. That, however, wasn't a question
she was going to answer.

"If you call jumping every time I hear a noise *all right*,
then I'm fine."

Graham laughed at her acerbity. "Sometimes I forget how much more you're risking than Durand or I. You
always seem to take everything in stride."

"Roy trained me right," Pen said wryly. "Somebody has
to step in and do what needs doing. Anyway, from what I
saw tonight, Frank and his pear blossom could kill you and
Durand just as dead as they could me."

Graham ran his palm around one side of her hair,
obliging her to fight the will-stealing urge to lean into the
caress.

"Sorry, Pen," he said, the gentleness of his voice yet
another peril. "You can't convince me you're not brave."

"Well, we don't need bravery now. We need patience and
sharp eyes." Forcing herself to crispness, she lifted one of
the boxes and shoved it into Graham's arms. "Pull out your
old secretarial skills. We're searching for anything that
might suggest where the dastardly duo is headed next."

"Aye, aye," Graham said, and dumped the carton upside
down on his bed. When Pen gasped at his rashness, he
grinned at her. "Want to bet I'll get through mine faster
than you get through yours?"

"No," she said, surprised by his playfulness and leery
of joining in. She began to sort through her box more

carefully, pulling short stacks out and setting them on the long dresser. Most were obviously Vandertote's nonsense regarding his "charity," and she paid them less mind. She was standing with her back to Graham, but every so often she felt a spot of heat on the vertebrae in her neck, as if he'd turned his gaze to her. She liked the sensation more than she ought. Hell, she liked the sound of his quickly flipping through the papers. It was companionable—comforting, an effect she found very welcome after the night they'd had. When he stopped without warning, she was so attuned to him a strong, hot flush tingled down her spine.

"Your father should have come with you," he said, out of the blue. "No matter how many irons he had in the fire, he shouldn't have let you face your mother's funeral alone, much less your aunts. When it comes to being there for people you love, the rest of the world can go hang."

Pen looked at him, her throat abruptly and uncomfortably tight. "You don't mean that."

"Don't I?"

Graham was a naturally serious person, but she'd never seen his expression quite so decided as it was now. Spindles of gold gleamed in his eyes, like embers sunk in cognac. His jaw was set, his lips firm and smooth. Pen struggled not to lick hers at the memory of kissing them.

She hadn't tasted him since Charleston.

"I was glad you came," some shred of honesty forced her to admit.

"I'd come whenever you wanted," he said.

Pen's face blazed in response. He couldn't mean that, or maybe he meant it in some way she hadn't thought of, one that wasn't so loverlike—as in: he'd come help any poor soul who needed it. Completely flustered, she dropped her gaze to the document in her hand. After a blink or two, her vision made sense of it. It was a purchase agreement for a property in Texas. One of the flourishing signatures at the bottom was F. Hauptmann.

"Oh," she said, her heart contracting sharply for a new reason. "I wonder if this is what we've been looking for!"

* * *

For as long as Durand waited, Frank and Li-Hua didn't try to reclaim their Chicago lair. Satisfied they wouldn't, he returned from his surveillance shortly before dawn. He pulled the draperies shut in his room, but he wasn't sleepy. Ignoring the bed, he stood looking through a strip of sheer curtain liner, watching this New World city turn from black to gray.

The contrast to the cities of his past was substantial. Nim Wei had made him a vampire in the 1400s, when he'd been handsome enough to attract the queen's attention. There weren't many master vampires among her get; a deliberate act, some thought, to eliminate potential rivals from being born. Durand hadn't cared about that—or wouldn't have, if he'd known what it meant. When the time came that he might have resented the limits her particular gift imposed, he'd been a creature of grief and rage. All he'd wanted was sufficient time to revenge himself on his enemies.

That revenge was long since accomplished, whole branches of human family trees lopped off for what they'd done to him and his brothers. He'd been lucky enough to live in Geneva, a city Nim Wei ruled by representative—which meant less oversight and more freedom for her offspring. In time, he'd shaken even that thin chain off, because why should he answer to *upyr* who weren't as frightening as him? He lived in death as he had in life, selling his sword to whomever would meet his astronomical asking price. He'd soldiered for kings and popes, for captains of industry and captains of clipper ships. His inner chill had grown too pronounced to consider whether he was gradually growing tired of immortality.

And then Frank and Li-Hua had found him in a ramshackle tavern on the coast of Greece, wondering which commission he should take next. They'd offered him the one thing he discovered he still desired: the ability to create others in his own image.

The rebels had tried to steal the secret of changing humans from Edmund Fitz Clare. They'd failed in part because his family had rescued him. Despite this earlier disappointment, they might have succeeded in their goal when they captured Vandertote's Chinese box. Durand had never fought *upyr* as powerful as them. If it were possible to transform a human with brute force, he thought the pair had enough of that for the job.

Durand understood the change now, and had understood it ever since he saw what Edmund did to Ben in Castle Lohengrin's dungeon. The change was meant to be an act of mutual trust between vampire and mortal, built of acceptance and perhaps caring. Durand didn't remember his own change. Like most elders, Nim Wei had erased his memory afterward. Now he wondered if he'd have refused Frank and Li-Hua back in that tavern if the casket's sanity-stealing magic was what they'd been hawking.

He caressed the leather-covered hilt of the knife he'd laid carefully on the windowsill, the stamp of his family crest a familiar texture under his fingertips. He hadn't performed his nightly ritual, where he honored his fallen brothers by reawakening the pain he'd felt after losing them. The scars on his chest would disappear if he didn't cut them open soon. Though he knew this, he left the blade where it was.

His hands were remembering reviving Ben Fitz Clare.

He'd healed a human tonight, or an almost human. He couldn't deny Ben had earned his aid. So had Sally, for that matter. They'd been better soldiers this evening than any Frank and Li-Hua had found for him: brave to the best of their abilities, following orders to the extent that was reasonable, and showing initiative when those orders could not cover shifts in events. Over the centuries, Durand had commanded many who didn't perform as well.

He curled his fingers into his palms to stop their buzzing.

He'd healed a human tonight.

Some cultures would say he was responsible for Ben's life now.

Durand snapped his teeth on a curse. These Fitz Clares were insidious, with their stupid hand-holding and their laughter and their unexpected willingness to die for each other. They made other people feel things when they were around them, longings they'd much rather have left behind.

Without a doubt, Durand could lay at their doorstep the unaccustomed soul-searching he'd been sucked into tonight.

Bridesmere

Edmund paused to gather himself outside Bridesmere's library. Estelle was expecting him to handle this, to behave as if his faculties truly were intact. Never mind he could have throttled her when he heard what she'd done. Her decision had been based on wanting to help him.

"I won't bite," Nim Wei said through the open door. She hadn't raised her voice, so Edmund knew she spoke to him.

Unable to put it off any longer—for pride's sake, if nothing else—he forced himself to step inside the large book-lined room.

London's queen stood before the crackling hearth with her back to him, her long straight hair hanging to her waist, her all-black, all-velvet tunic and trousers limned by the flames. Her tiny size perpetually startled him. Given the strength of her personality, she should have dwarfed every room she was in. This room dwarfed her, making her appear as slight as a child—though the four-inch heels of her musketeer boots tried damned hard to counter the impression.

She turned to confront him only after he'd come within arm's reach. Her face was narrow and delicate, her dark eyes shining like onyx. Both she and Li-Hua were beautiful, but Nim Wei was also *more*: more subtle, more seductive—more dangerous, he supposed. When she pursed her pouting pomegranate mouth, it was difficult to look anywhere else.

"So," she said, her tone amused. "I hear you're being an ass. As I recall, you were an ass once or twice with me."

"We weren't together that long," he reminded her.

Nim Wei ran her tongue around her lips and smiled. "I suppose that means you make a habit of being one."

His anger didn't rise to the bait, and he realized Estelle *had* done him a favor. She'd called the one person to help him whom he felt no need to be nice to.

"If you don't like it, you can leave," he said.

Nim Wei's amusement intensified. She had but a step between her and the deep leather chair nearest to the fire, but she managed to saunter there. She sat, crossed her slender, booted legs, and placed both her dainty hands on her topmost knee. The exaggerated femininity of her movements would have left most males with their heart racing. Edmund counted himself fortunate he wasn't one of them.

"Why don't you sit?" she said. "I know a little story you should hear."

Edmund sat somewhat less gracefully than she had. Nim Wei's eyes followed the way he hitched up his trouser legs.

"You imitate them better than I do," she said.

He hadn't been trying to act human, but he let her think he was. "I'm waiting," he observed.

Nim Wei picked up a goblet of wine she must have set on the lamp table earlier. She didn't drink, but ran one fingernail around the gold-dipped rim. "Very well, Edmund. Since you insist on foregoing the niceties. Once upon a time, I appointed a master vampire named Raoul as my nest proxy in Madrid. He took as his mate a woman named Rebeca. The two were a love match, not unlike you and Estelle—though that love expressed itself a bit more bloodthirstily than yours. They were quite the couple, deadlier than Frank and Li-Hua, but much more self-disciplined. They'd step right up to the line of what I'd tolerate and never edge an inch over."

Nim Wei shook her head in remembrance, allowing herself the indulgence of a wistful sigh. Rather than respond to her dramatics, Edmund turned his gaze to the fire where flames were licking up a huge black log. In the wavering light, the big fleur-de-lis on the stone surround—symbol of his family's Norman origins—looked like they were dancing. Somewhere inside him, his wolf groaned with exhaustion. He was tired of being like this: angry, guilty, helpless to help those he loved. When Nim Wei leaned forward, probably to recapture his attention, the hissing sweep of her hair registered as if in a dream.

"Given Raoul and Rebeca's penchant for violence," she continued, "it's no wonder they had enemies, especially among the recently reconquered Moors. One of them decided to punish Raoul by catching Rebeca alone on horseback and separating her from her head. Naturally, the injury killed her. Not so naturally, Raoul went completely mad. He didn't simply grieve, he set things on fire with his eyes. Set *people* on fire if they looked at him the wrong way. He began to have hallucinations, to imagine he was talking to people who were long dead. I didn't hear if he started translocating accidentally, but that's an upper-master-level gift. Very rare, as it happens. I wouldn't mind having it myself."

As if his neck were on a turntable, Edmund shifted his gaze to her. Nim Wei sat back in her chair, satisfied to have drawn his focus again. She lifted one slim eyebrow. "I take it this sounds familiar."

"What happened to Raoul?" he asked hoarsely.

"His people tried to put him down, but he was too powerful. Dozens died in the attempt. In the end, I had to kill him myself. I didn't enjoy it, either. That Madrid nest was never so well run again."

Her words were flippant, but her face was sober. Edmund's lungs stopped going in and out. His eyes felt locked to Nim Wei's.

"Rebeca was Raoul's balancer," she said. "They chose to tie their energy together so that each could benefit from the other's strength. When those bonds were severed . . ." Nim Wei spread her hands, palms up. "Raoul lost his balance, and he couldn't get it back. I think a similar thing is happening to you, though your Estelle isn't dead. For whatever reason, you've built a wall between you two where you used to connect. You need to tear it down or else cut your ties more cleanly. Trust me, we'd both rather no one asked me to help kill you."

He could see she meant it. She didn't want to kill him, however much hostility might linger between them. Maybe she even still loved him a tiny bit.

"I can't leave Estelle," he said. "She's the other half of my soul."

Nim Wei's expression flickered and then smoothed out. "Then your choice is simple. Put your fear or whatever the hell your problem is behind you and let your mate back into your head."

"Just like that."

"No one said *simple* was the same as *easy*." She pushed to her feet and looked down at him. "If you need any more incentive, allow me to inform you that I'll be staying here, in your old castle, until I'm sure it's safe to let you continue existing."

"You shouldn't be so sure you could stop me," he tossed out, his anger flaring—briefly—like an old friend. The library's one remaining lightbulb cracked softly and went out. Nim Wei smiled at his subtle flinch of embarrassment.

"I'd find a way," she said. "I didn't get where I am without being resourceful."

Highway 55

Graham was taking the wheel for their journey south. Pen resigned herself to sitting in the back with Ben and Durand, but when the valet returned the car to the Drake's front awning, Graham wrapped his fingers around Pen's elbow.

"Wait," he said and turned to Sally. His manner toward his sister was firm but calm. "You're sitting in the back tonight. Ben will keep the baby from making you queasy."

Sally narrowed her eyes at him, opened her mouth, then shut it as if thinking better of what she planned to say. Graham must have used some special older brother power on her. As far as Pen could tell, he wasn't thralling her.

"Fine," Sally said and reached stiffly for the rear door handle.

Durand helped her with it, throwing Graham a look as if he'd pulled a two-headed rabbit out of his sleeve. Graham's mouth curved as he turned away, obviously pleased—and amused—to have impressed the vampire.

Thus, Pen found herself sitting next to Graham with a clear view through the front window. As they left the city that had both piqued and delayed their hopes, a cloudy, lavender-tinted sky darkened over tall gray buildings. Traffic was thick, the tightly packed headlights like earthbound moons. No one spoke as rain began to sprinkle the windshield. Graham turned the wipers on.

Maybe it was her imagination, but Pen thought she could feel his heat stretching to her across the width of the

car. That wasn't supposed to happen. Vampires stayed cool
unless they were angry or aroused.

"I can drive, too," Pen said, tucking one leg up to turn
slightly in the seat.

Graham glanced at her. The road was public, and his
glamour was in place, but the impact of his gold-kindled
gaze still felt like lightning sizzling to her core.

"You can take over when I'm done."

Sally made a noise, probably regarding the seating
arrangements. Graham didn't give her a chance to voice
her request.

"No," he said. "Ben is still recuperating. He can't drive,
and that means you should be sticking close to him."

Ben laughed and hugged Sally with both arms, whispering something mollifying in her ear.

"Wow," Pen murmured, watching Sally settle back cuddled to Ben's chest. "A week with you, and my aunts would
be mincemeat."

Graham reached out to squeeze her knee. "You can
mince them yourself, if you decide that's what you want
to do."

His expression of faith was nice, but she hardly noticed
it. His palm was hot, the sheer male size of it swallowing
her knee. He left it where it was, his fingers kneading, his
thumb fanning a muscle on the side of her thigh. Clearly,
their brief abstinence—at least regarding intercourse—had
affected her. Sensation streaked unstoppably up her leg,
coiling into a throbbing ball in her sex. That ball seemed
to fill her, swell her, pressing nerves his thumb had no
way to reach. To her dismay, slick, warm fluid squeezed
from her folds, causing her to blush as Graham's nostrils
flared. His big chest jerked as he took a breath. Pen tensed
in response.

It occurred to her that he wasn't the only supernatural
being in this car who could smell her response.

Just when she feared she'd moan, Graham took his hand
away. Her knee felt twice as cold by comparison.

Pen gritted her teeth together, turning her eyes deter-
minedly to watch the wipers chase the light but steady rain

across the windshield. Had Graham meant to excite her, or was it an accident? Did he regret it? Was he fighting his own reaction to touching her? His weight shifted on the seat, so maybe he was.

Rather than succumb to the lure of seeking evidence in his lap, Pen twisted her head even farther away from him. She barely saw the landmarks they were passing. Fantasies seemed to be slamming into her brain. Dragging her hand up his heavily muscled thigh. Cupping him between the legs. Opening his trousers and sucking the great silky crest of him into her mouth. His balls would be tight and hot, his veins distended rivers her tongue could trace up his long, stiff shaft. Her palm seemed to remember the exact heft and shape of his testicles . . .

With a strangled sound, Graham pulled her gaze to him.

His face was a very nonvampiric red, the skin of his knuckles stretched by his grip on the steering wheel. Before she could stop herself, her eyes dropped to the hump that lifted his zipper. Her mouth went dry at the size of the throbbing mountain. She could actually see the slow, hard beat of his cock pounding.

Amazed, she looked at his tense profile. Graham had heard her thoughts? Graham had reacted to them this way? Pen had been under the impression that he wasn't much of a mind reader.

As if his erection were a magnet, her gaze slid to it again. The material of his trousers was stretched even tighter than it had been a second ago, the creases seeming to struggle to contain his enormity. What she wouldn't have given to be riding that monster, to feel that thick, velvet friction pumping inside of her. Her sex clenched hard just imagining it, its growing wetness clamoring to be rubbed on him. Graham made another small, pained sound and began to reach his hand toward her.

"If you two don't stop," Durand said, "I'm going to dump you out at the nearest inn."

"Stop what?" Sally asked as Pen and Graham both jumped guiltily.

"Nothing," Graham said firmly. "Why don't you take a nap?"

Perhaps it was stupid, but Pen couldn't help searching his now stony face for answers.

Durand chose the roadside restaurant they pulled up to, pointing his arm out the window and saying, "There." What qualities had drawn him to the place Graham couldn't guess. Perhaps the waitresses smelled especially tasty here.

Ben hung back to see to the DeSoto while the rest of them went in through the jingling door.

The rain they'd seen in Chicago had become a memory many miles back. Seeming unaffected by its absence, the restaurant was a large structure, more or less clean and—despite it being the middle of the night—lorry drivers occupied all the round, red-cushioned stools at its counter. Durand disappeared as soon as they crossed the threshold, probably tracking some female who'd gone out the back on her break. Graham found himself uncomfortably preoccupied with what the other *upyr* was doing. Durand wouldn't be hampered by considerations for his victim's feelings, nor was the woman—or women, as had happened—likely to want the mercenary to restrict himself to a bite. Thralled or clearheaded, females flocked to Durand. He was the dangerous character their mothers warned them about.

Graham tried to push this from his imagination as the hostess led them to a clean table. Thinking about Durand's escapades wasn't helping him squelch the effects of that unexpected moment in the car, when Pen's sexual fantasies had bombarded him. He'd had to button his jacket as soon as he got out, because certain very visible parts of him remained oversensitized.

"Here you go," said the matronly hostess. "This booth is all ready."

The booth was in a corner, complete with its own garish coin-slot phonograph. Sally loved the automated machines, playing them wherever they stopped, but Graham didn't think he could listen to "I Get a Kick Out of You" even one more time. It reminded him too much of the "kick" he got out of Pen.

"Please," Graham said when Sally opened her change purse to dig inside. "My ears are all worn out."

Sally cocked her head at him. "*You* look all worn out, Graham. I thought that wasn't supposed to happen now that you're . . . you know."

"I'm worried," he said, which he probably shouldn't have admitted.

Pen finished sliding after him onto the bench. Her leg bumped his in a fashion that seemed intended to be comradely. Graham appreciated that, though it also sent a surge of quite unneeded excitement through his partial erection.

"We'll do better next time," Pen said, "now that we know what we're up against."

Graham's fists balled with frustration on the tabletop. What they were *up against* was too much to handle. He nearly jumped when Pen slipped her silky hand over his. With her beside him, *partial* arousal wasn't going to remain so long.

"We need better weapons," he said glumly.

"I have contacts in Texas. We can put together an arsenal—even leaving Roy out of it like Durand wants."

"We almost killed Frank," Sally added, her little nose wrinkling as she said the name. "I'm sure we would have gotten him with a smidge more time."

It sounded to Graham like Durand hadn't shared his theory that Frank and Li-Hua could fly, an example Graham might do well to follow—team morale, and all that.

"You're right," he said, sitting straighter. "Next time we'll do better."

"What about 'Smoke Gets in Your Eyes'?" Sally asked hopefully, plainly done with fretting about his mood. "I've hardly played that at all."

Graham laughed and gave in to her, closing his eyes as the song's sultry opening began. The notes were crackly but clear enough. When they proved too evocative, he tuned his vampire hearing in elsewhere. Over at the counter, a driver was telling a story about a recent trip through Oklahoma, how he kept passing old pickups with what looked like whole houses heaped in their backs.

"They had piles of mattresses," he was saying. "Trunks and lamps and—I swear to God—kitchen stoves. Those Okies are hightailing it out of that dust bowl fast as they can. Lord knows what the Californians will do with them when they're there."

The story didn't fill Graham with the pity that it might have. He knew the situation could be worse. After all, the people of California weren't liable to want their souls.

These Americans are innocents, he thought. *They've no idea how much more trouble they could be in.*

He hoped they never found out. He understood how sometimes one more straw was too much to stand.

Ben startled Graham's eyes open by plopping into the seat next to Sally. Ben was a good sport to have gone along with Graham's claim that he was recovering. The energy with which he moved said he was perfectly all right.

"We're all fueled up," he said. "I checked the oil, and the tire pressure is fine."

"Good," Graham said. "Thank you."

Sally did him one better by kissing Ben on the cheek. "My husband is a genius," she cooed.

"Don't overdo it." Ben laughed.

Though he squirmed away from Sally's rain of kisses, their happiness spilled from them like a shining light. Graham couldn't even be jealous. It was too right for them to be happy, too sweet in the face of what they'd come so close to losing last night. Graham never wanted anything bad to touch either one of them.

When he shot a look at Pen—almost involuntarily—she was staring hard at her menu. Her wavy auburn hair had fallen forward across one sharp cheekbone. His hand lifted before he could stop it, threading the locks behind her elegant ear. Touching even that much of her sent a zing up his finger. She smiled at him nervously.

You deserve to be just as happy, he thought to her from his heart. *I wish you knew that as surely as I do.*

Per usual, his thoughts went nowhere.

"I think I'll have a hamburger," she said.

Having extricated himself from Sally, at least temporarily, Ben planted his forearms on the table. "There's one
thing I don't understand. What's so special about Texas?
From what I hear, there's nothing there but poor people and
bad weather."

"Don't forget the starving cows," Pen said. "And the
tumbleweeds."

"Right," Ben agreed. "So why would Frank and Li-Hua
want to go there? They can't rob banks if the majority of
the local ones have failed."

"I don't know," Pen said, "but until Estelle can dreamwalk for something better, that property they bought outside of Amarillo is our best lead."

Durand never did join them in the restaurant. As they
walked out to the mostly dark parking lot, Pen spotted him
lounging back against the midnight blue DeSoto with his
elbows braced on the hood and his ankles crossed. His
fedora was slanted forward to shade his eyes, his slightly
dated suit jacket fallen open to reveal a very flat stomach.

Something about this uncharacteristically relaxed posture caused Graham's stride to stiffen next to hers.

"You didn't eat," Durand observed to him when they
were close enough for a human to have heard. "Please do
so before you force me to ride in that auto with you again."

"Here, Graham," Sally said, holding out a sack with a half
dozen leftover hamburgers. "Your kitty cat can eat these."

Graham's glare was bright enough to light up his face—
and to prompt his little sister to fall back a step. Realizing
what he'd done, he smoothed his features.

"Thank you," he said a little too politely as he accepted
the greasy sack. "Pen, why don't you come with me and
watch my back while I change?"

Pen saw how this was working: Durand gave him an
order, which he resented but had to obey, so he turned
his officiousness on her. He didn't even glance over his

shoulder to see if she was following him. That didn't matter, though, because Pen knew how to control her temper for the sake of the team.

She didn't run after him; that would have been too compliant, but she did walk quickly.

"I say, Durand," Pen heard Sally pipe up as they left. "Is that a lipstick smear on your crotch?"

"I believe it's two," Ben returned. "One is more carmine than the other."

Then both broke into snickers.

Pen had to chuckle at the pair's one-two delivery. She knew Durand hated being the butt of jokes. Rather than share her amusement, Graham let a growl circle in his throat. Pen supposed he didn't appreciate the mercenary's needs being satisfied when his were not.

"Graham," Pen called, beginning to get breathless. "You're walking too fast for me."

They'd reached the straggly pine and oak woods that surrounded the restaurant's parking area. During the day, the trees wouldn't have provided much cover. At night, with only the stars to light them, they offered better concealment.

Graham waited for her to catch up, then—still not turning around—reached blindly back to catch her wrist in his hand. She realized he wasn't carrying the hamburger sack anymore. He must have tossed it somewhere along the way.

"I'm sorry," he said, his thumb feathering over the spot where both her nerves and her pulse had begun to jump. "I wanted to treat you differently than this."

Pen wasn't certain a translation of this cryptic statement would add to her happiness. She stepped around Graham to look into his face. They were a foot apart, his heat emanating from him noticeably. His eyes seemed worried as they searched hers. Pen suppressed an urge to clear her throat.

"You could be seen here," she pointed. "We should move farther in."

"Yes," Graham agreed, and suddenly sealed his mouth over hers.

The kiss was deep and hungry, his fangs sliding down even as his tongue stabbed in to battle hers. The feel of both moving together was unbelievably arousing. Pen couldn't fight the waves of need that rolled through her, her temperature rising swiftly as she kissed him back. Groaning loudly, Graham lifted her beneath the ass. Without a moment's hesitation, her arms slid behind his neck to help hold herself.

Thanks to her skirt, her legs were easy to wrap around him. Thinking clearer than she was, Graham pulled off her shoes and shoved them into his coat pockets.

"Fuck turning into my cat," he said.

And then he was running at vampire speed with her clinging close to him. Leaves and branches whizzed by them along a path only he could see. His hand covered her bottom to crush her against his groin. That pressure was delicious. Pen's skirt was bunched around her waist, and he was grinding her into him even as he ran, the knob of his cockhead nudging her clitoris with every stride. Pen was soon dizzy from more than being carried fast. Only her panties and his trousers separated them. Graham was throbbing right against the seam of her pussy's lips, so hard, so thick, she wasn't certain she could hold off coming.

By the time he thudded her spine against a tree trunk, she was quivering on the verge of climax and soaking wet. His continued, hungry kiss was all that saved her sanity.

She didn't know how far he'd run, just that they were deep in the forest now. She'd never made love outdoors before. It tweaked something in her psyche, making her feel both vulnerable and insanely bold. Dying to touch him, she thrust one hand into the back of his trousers. He actually shivered when she pushed her palm over his buttocks. Burrowing beneath his shirt, she found two dimples beside his tailbone, the little depressions smooth as cream beneath her circling fingertips.

"God," he groaned, tearing free from their mutually ravenous oral exploration. "Please pull off your panties before I rip them."

He helped her drag them down her legs, too impatient

to wait for her fumbling hands. The scrap of ivory silk and cotton disappeared like her shoes had into his coat pocket. He almost purred as he ran his grip up her stockinged legs, after which he hiked her back onto him. Before she could fit them together the way she wanted, he curled his left hand between them over her mound, two long, strong fingers sliding between her folds and into her creamy sheath. The way they moved was hard to complain about, especially when his dextrous thumb found the aching swell of her clitoris and worked its hood firmly over it. Delight spangled like fireworks through the nerves of her sex. She couldn't have stopped her body's reaction for anything.

"Pen," he growled as liquid heat ran into his palm.

His mouth crashed down on hers, eating her again. Pen squirmed like an eel gone mad, caught between his hands front and back. He was stroking her inside and out, pushing her too fast and well. As nice as what he was doing felt, she wanted to come around something better, something more *personal*, than a pair of fingers. She knew Graham wanted that, too. He was grunting with eagerness, the ridge of his immense arousal rubbing at her hip. Forced to get his attention somehow, she grabbed two fistfuls of his hair and pulled.

"Graham," she said, gratified to hear him panting like a freight train. "Shove your cock in me now."

"Pen—"

"Do it," she insisted.

His eyes blazed from gold to white. He yanked his zipper down so fast it whined. His heavy erection fell through the gap but not far. Like an addict hungry for her fix, Pen reached for it, caressing the velvet smoothness, tugging the flaring rim. An image flicked into her mind: herself on her knees before him, the edge of her teeth pressing into his stiff penis. The idea was sexy, but it felt strangely like it wasn't hers. Without thinking, her hold on him tightened.

"Keep that up," Graham grated, his hips moving helplessly in her fist, "and you risk not getting what you're asking for."

She wasn't sure she believed him, but she let go, her

fingertips slipping up him reluctantly. Their eyes seemed locked together, the fire in his as strong as a chain. She felt him shove his trousers past his hip bones, felt him steady his jerking shaft in his hand. With the smallest wince, he ran the fat, sleek head up and down her slit, the wideness of it spreading her labia. The sensation of silky flesh meeting silky flesh caused both of them to moan. He probably would have kept it up, but the closeness of the home she had for him was too tempting. He fit the head against her gate, shuddered, and then he was driving in, his neck flexing back with pleasure as her pussy surrounded him. She almost came from that first long thrust, from the way his breath rushed out and his fingers clenched like pincers on her bare bottom.

Her own grip mimicked them on the muscles of his shoulder and his thick, strong neck. Not that her fingers could dig in like his. His body was hot, coiled steel, his erection more of the same. He was so full inside her, so hot and pulsing and excited. The edge of pain his size inspired was exactly what she'd been craving.

Please, she thought, her body desperate for release, her pride just strong enough to keep the words inside. *Please, Graham, fuck me hard.*

As if he'd heard, his cock bucked within her flesh, the sound that rumbled in his chest as desperate as she felt.

"Christ," he said, shocked and raspy. "I don't know how careful I can be."

Pen wasn't afraid. Graham always took care with her. He took care with everyone. She was happy, even relieved, when he let loose with a thrust so forceful it reverberated up to her skull. The spot only he seemed able to reach inside her gave a warning throb, as if his blunt, bulging tip had knocked on a magic door. Pen cried out as her orgasm broke, the rippling contractions making his cock seem bigger.

He went wild at that: vocal, violent, his arms iron bands between her and the rough tree trunk. He cried her name as if it hurt his throat, driving his slick, hard pole into her. No spike had ever been hammered harder, not to save someone's life. Graham had to hold her so he wouldn't bounce her off of him, every sleek percussion causing the ache inside her to soar higher. His thighs were tireless, but he widened the spread of his feet to sling himself in harder. Dry pine twigs snapped under his shoes, a rare amount of noise for one of his kind to make. His grunts and snarls were driving her crazy, sweat dampening the back of his neck where her hand wrapped it.

Though his ball sac was tight, it slapped the skin of her sex like a soft spanking. His chest heaved as he dragged in air.

"Yes," she urged, wanting more and more of precisely this. "Graham!"

He ejaculated with a roar, a burst of seed so hot and strong it would have been impossible to miss.

"*Yes*," he ground out, echoing her, his voice pulled tight by the way his head had flung back with ecstasy. Pen's body clenched helplessly.

"Jesus," he gasped, struggling to push through her increased snugness.

She knew there was more to come. Graham wasn't relaxing—the opposite, in fact. She could feel his muscles gathering with an unbearable tension. His arms tightened around her as his lips nuzzled a longing moan into her neck. He sucked her, licked her, his tongue soft and wet as his mouth watered. The pistoning of his hips picked up. As it did, his shirt jerked smooth and fast against her aching nipples, his chest hard as stone and hot. Pen clutched the back of his head, using the strength of her legs to pull her pussy tighter into his groin.

With a groan that said he couldn't wait a second longer, his fangs slid into her vein.

The instant he drank, they climaxed together, as though their entire bodies were being squeezed—every muscle, every cell overwhelmed by rapture. Colors flashed inside her head as she writhed wildly. Pen heard herself making noises like an animal, and Graham's were just as primal. How much she needed this abandonment, how much she *adored* it, frightened her. She was lost in Graham. In that blinding, shuddering moment, she knew she'd give more than her life for him. Her soul was his, as easily as if he'd whipped out Frank and Li-Hua's dangerous brass box.

When he released her neck to kiss her, deeply, wetly, her own blood buzzing from his tongue to hers, it didn't once occur to her to fight.

Still, he wasn't finished. His thrusting slowed to a soothing beat of loin to loin, the hand he'd wrapped around her bottom kneading gently now. Pen moaned and rolled her hips over his motions, greedy for even this soft pleasure. Graham liked what she was doing. He came one more time, a brief, gasping burst that was followed by throaty sigh. However little this act meant to him, Pen loved that she'd unraveled him so much. He pulled gently from their kiss but not her body, his hips still pinning her to the tree, his forehead resting sweaty and hard on hers. Insects resumed their chirping in the sudden quiet.

The forest around them smelled of pine and sex.

Pen bit her lower lip and tried not to lean too obviously into him. She knew she couldn't relax her legs yet. They, like her, didn't want this to be over.

"You okay?" Graham whispered.

Pen nodded wordlessly, enjoying him stroking her tangled hair back a bit too much. Tenderness like his could keep a world of troubled thoughts at bay.

"I'm sorry," he said. "I didn't intend to do that again. You mean more to me than"—he paused to search for a word—"than a bonk and a meal."

Pen's thighs fell from his waist as if they'd been pushed, her stockinged feet thumping to the bracken-prickled earth. This sounded suspiciously like Graham's version of "maybe we can be friends."

Pen didn't like hearing it any more than her discarded beaus had enjoyed hearing it from her.

The Dust Bowl

They were somewhere in Kansas when Pen first realized she wasn't prepared for what lay ahead. Oklahoma didn't change her mind, and neither did crossing the border to Texas. She'd read accounts of the drought, had seen footage in newsreels, but the reality that surrounded their current journey was a far cry from those two-dimensional images.

The landscape was dark, the country road flat and straight and lit only by the cones of their car's headlights. The sky was clear and star-filled, the horizon broken occasionally by low hills. The sense of utter emptiness was what made Pen shiver—and the odd sandy dunes that spilled across the asphalt for long stretches. This was no beach, and the dunes weren't sand but very dry topsoil that had eroded and blown away. The car's tires skidded unpredictably when she hit it, forcing her to fight to control the wheel.

They hadn't passed another vehicle for hours.

"*Scheisse*," Durand said, a soft hiss of a curse. He was in front with her, his profile turned to the side window. Pen concluded he could see what stretched beyond it better than she could.

"Just keep going," he said when she looked at him. "Let me know if you have trouble following the road."

He had his hands on the dash and door, palms flattened, skin glowing as if his fingers were sticks of fire. When the engine faltered and then steadied, she knew he was feeding energy into it, supporting the gears and pistons with his *upyr* gifts. A glance in the rearview mirror revealed Graham doing the same. The look on his face was as grim as Durand's. It made her glad Sally and Ben were sleeping.

Despite the vampires' magic, the car gave out thirty minutes later. Pen tried to restart it with shaking fingers, but all she earned was a sick rattle.

"I'll get out," Durand said.

Sally woke up, coughing, at the hollow thunk of the door shutting. This was when Pen noticed everything inside the car—herself included—was covered by a film of gray brown grit. Since the windows had been rolled up, this was unnerving.

"Manifold sounds clogged," Ben said, and slipped out to join Durand.

Graham found some water for Sally to drink, while Ben walked around the car and popped the hood. He and Durand leaned inside. Five minutes later, they closed it up and got back into the car. Both of them were wheezing, though Durand was less than Ben. The vampire being affected at all tightened Pen's throat with dread.

"Dust," Ben said, coughing harshly against the back of his sleeve. "A beastly lot of it. I think I can clean it out and get it working, but not here. The wind's picking up and blowing this stuff around."

"We passed an abandoned farmhouse a few miles back," Graham said. "You could fix the car in the barn."

Pen hadn't seen hide nor hair of these buildings, but Durand nodded.

"You and I can propel the auto," he said to Graham. "The others best stay inside."

"How far are we from Amarillo?" Sally asked hoarsely.

"Too far," Pen said, though she wasn't sure exactly. She looked at her watch. "We've got about an hour until sunrise."

"So we'll rest." Ben pulled Sally gently to his side. "And go on tomorrow night."

Pen disliked the idea of waiting only a little more than she disliked the thought of going on. Though she wanted to get the coming confrontation—if there was going to be

one—over with, she also knew the impulse to hurry wasn't
wise.

Graham's gaze met hers as he and Durand got out to
push the car. She didn't know what his eyes were saying,
just that they steadied her.

Graham had never seen anything like this fine sandy dust.
He and Durand put their backs into pushing the DeSoto
through it, but it felt like they were wading in sifted flour. It
took a full ten minutes to backtrack to the dark farmhouse.

The barn seemed sound enough when they reached it,
though here, too, dust drifted against hay bales. The stalls
were empty, the animals and their keepers gone.

"Tomorrow," Ben said, giving the DeSoto a tired pat.

A long hemp cord, frayed but not broken, stretched
between the barn door's iron handle and the front railing
of the house. Pen stopped to run her hand along it, her brow
furrowed.

"My God," she said, looking to the house and back as
comprehension dawned. "They must have needed this to
find their way when the dust blew up."

"Like an old London fog," Ben said, pausing beside her.
Sally shuddered in the curve of his arm. That she didn't say
a word troubled Graham.

"The house is clear," Durand said, back from checking
it. "You can go inside."

Graham didn't expect much, and he didn't get it. The
farmhouse consisted of a bedroom, a living area with
bare plank floors, and a rudimentary dugout kitchen. The
water pump didn't work—assuming there was water to run
through it—nor did the crudely wired electricity. Presumably, the outhouse had a similar cord arrangement to the
barn. Matches being absent, Durand lit two lanterns with
sparks from his energy. Their glow illuminated a motley
and sagging assortment of furniture—whatever the former residents hadn't wanted to take with them. Flowered
wallpaper had once dressed up the walls. Now gray brown

streaks ran down it, as if the ceiling were weeping dust. Ben and Sally and Pen stirred up piles of it with each step.

It rather amazed Graham that modern human beings lived like this.

"Well," Sally said, her voice rough and shaky, her hands crossed protectively over her stomach. "At least there's nothing to attract rats."

She made a sound as if she were trying to laugh and couldn't manage it, then rubbed her eyes like a sleepy child. Durand blurred to her so swiftly everyone gasped.

"Don't," he said, easing her fists away. "I know your eyes itch, but you'll scratch your corneas if you rub. If you'd permit me . . ."

He held up his hands with the palms shining. Sally glanced at Ben and then nodded, letting Durand use his power to clear the grit from her eyes. When she was better, he did the same for Ben and Pen.

"Thank you," Pen said.

Durand jerked his head in answer and turned toward the one bedroom. The single window was covered with a double layer of bedsheets, its cracks also stuffed with rags. The efficacy of the barriers was questionable—against the dust anyway. The cloths were as stiff as if they'd been soaked in the dust. On the plus side, Graham thought the encrusted sheets would block the sun nicely.

Pen trailed after Durand when he stepped inside. "You and Graham will be safe in here?"

"Yes." Durand dropped his duffel on a mended cane chair. Aside from an ancient mattress, this was the room's only furnishing. "Do you know how to administer an injection?"

Pen nodded that she did.

"Good," Durand said. "Graham and I should rest up tomorrow, but if anything happens, the cocaine in my kit is the surest way to rouse me."

Graham watched the pair from the door. There could be no doubt that Durand trusted Pen. What surprised Graham was that his eyes were almost soft as he regarded her.

In truth, Graham wondered if the mercenary was aware of
this.

"This is getting too much for Sally," Durand said quietly. "She's held up well for a human, but after what Li-Hua
almost did to Ben, she's losing her nerve."

"You can't blame her," Graham said, his voice as low as
Durand's. Neither Sally nor Ben needed to hear this.

"Blaming her isn't what I'm doing," Durand said.

Sensing there was more, Graham stepped inside and
closed the door behind him. Durand let his glamour fall,
probably so Pen could see in the darkened room.

"I think we need her," he said.

"*Need her*—" Graham and Pen spoke in unison.

"Yes," Durand said, seeming unsurprised by their chorus.
"Li-Hua wasn't the first *upyr* Sally injured unexpectedly.
She . . . poked the eye of one of my men back in Switzer-
land. The injury never healed properly."

"You think she has some sort of gift," Graham said.

"She's been living with your father since she was a
child. Even before he became a master vampire, his aura
must have been powerful. I'm sure you all noticed you were
healthier than most mortals."

"Yes, but—" Graham stopped abruptly, seeing no point
in arguing. If Ben had an unnatural affinity for mechanics,
why shouldn't Sally have extra power to harm vampires?

Durand spoke into his silence. "We need to keep her
from breaking down. If we don't get the chance to stock up
on artillery, she may be our best advantage."

Graham gawked at him in disbelief, though—actually—
this little speech was more in line with what he expected of
the Swiss soldier. His kindness in healing Sally suddenly
made sense. After all, what use could Durand have for
a—how had he put it?—a *gestating human* apart from her
potential as a weapon?

Pen exchanged an eye roll with Graham, then scrubbed
one hand across her forehead. "I'll make sure I don't put
her under stress tomorrow. Ben has to fix the car anyway.
I'll go out on my own to search for supplies and leave him
to coddle her."

"On your own?" Graham exclaimed in dismay.

"Pen can reach me mind to mind if she's in trouble," Durand said. "If she truly concentrates."

Graham didn't want to let on how much he resented that. He should have been the one Pen turned to, the one who helped her when she needed it. Then again, knowing Pen, she probably believed it ought to be the other way around.

He couldn't wonder Pen had clashed with her mother and her aunts. They would not have fathomed a woman who naturally thought herself anyone's equal—be they famous Southern beauties or centuries-old vampires. Pen would be civil, more or less, but she would not bow. *She* would help save her country. *She* would help save the world. No limitations of gender or nature would convince her she should not try. Graham wasn't going to change her mind. He wasn't sure he wanted to. Even now, his admiration for her flooded up inside him.

Nothing stopped him from loving her, including her cussedness.

Pen came to him at the small, acid laugh that broke in his throat. Hesitantly her hands touched his, her fingertips soft points of warmth on his palms. Though Durand's glow was behind her, Graham had no trouble reading her concern.

"I know it isn't nice to talk of using Sally. If we're lucky, we won't have to. There's something else, though, something that's been troubling me." Pen's fingers tangled with Graham's and tightened, and it seemed just possible she was taking comfort from him. "West Texas is where Roy Blunt grew up. These are his stomping grounds. If we caught wind of that property Frank and Li-Hua bought, it seems likely that he has, too."

"You think he'll go after them?"

Durand had taken a step closer. At his question, Pen threw a look at him over her shoulder. "I'm convinced he will. More to the point, I'm convinced he doesn't have a snowball's chance in hell of keeping any of his men alive."

"His men aren't our priority," Durand reminded her.

"I don't know," Pen said. "If stealing their souls is going to make our enemy stronger, maybe they matter, too."

As soon as it was light, Pen followed the road to the nearest town. A perversely pleasant breeze stirred miniature dust tornadoes up to knee level. She'd taken the precaution of tying her best silk scarf around her mouth and nose, but she was grateful the distance she had to travel wasn't more than four miles. She was grateful for her trousers, too, dirty though they were. They'd be useful if she needed to run. Running wasn't far from her thoughts right now. The silty moonscape that stretched around her had her neck prickling, and it wasn't only because she felt exposed.

If Frank and Li-Hua were holed up in their Amarillo property, Pen didn't think she was close enough for them to register her approach—even assuming the vampires were awake. What had her nerves coiled like wires was the transformation nature itself had wrought. Land that had once rippled gold with wheat now blew tumbleweeds. Farm buildings sat half buried, stranded in the drifting sea that had been topsoil. Pen spotted a little forest of horns sticking out of one dry gray pile and jerked her gaze away.

She didn't want to know the pain those cattle had died in.

Amazingly, signs of life remained. She was passed by a clanking pickup whose driver turned wide eyes to her. His mouth and nose were covered by a red bandana, the dust turning everyone into *bandidos*. Pen suspected if he'd recognized her as a local, she'd have been offered a ride. As it was, she didn't mind walking. This place, this situation, gave her plenty to think about.

She had a feeling her father knew how bad things were here, and that this—rather than any lack of caring—explained why he hadn't accompanied her to Charleston. Each job was precious, each scrap of hope. To her mind, Arnold Anderson was every bit the hero she aspired to be.

The creaking rise and fall of a pump jack beside of the road suggested why this area hadn't gone completely ghost.

There was still a bit of "gold" here, just not the sort you could eat. The oil derrick also might account for the care people were taking not to let the town succumb. Actual grass, mostly green, carpeted the little square in front of the small courthouse. As Pen halted, staring in surprise, two tiny, bent old women swept off the dust with brooms. They weren't the last she saw, either. The farther she walked, the more human beings she passed. Had they not all been wearing masks, the morning almost would have seemed normal.

When she entered the North Fork General Store and Farm Supply, she joined a dozen customers. A wiry, middle-aged clerk came to help her without delay. Pen was happy for the man's assistance. She needed food, water, maybe something clean to wear for her and Sally.

"Passing through?" he asked as they were settling the bill.

Pen nodded, watching him count her money out carefully. There wasn't much cash in the register. She guessed the townsfolk did a lot of business through barter. Between the drought and the Depression, this part of the country had reverted to frontier habits. Pen hadn't paid much for what she'd gotten—the advantage, she supposed, to being one of few with hard currency.

"Someone will give you a ride," said the clerk, gesturing to her parcels. "Especially if you can pay. You can ask anyone outside."

Pen's breath caught in her throat. She bet she could get lots of things if she could pay: labor, goods, perhaps even loyalty. Maybe Frank and Li-Hua weren't completely crazy. Maybe they'd picked their future base of operations perfectly. Shivers swept up her nape as the metaphoric lightbulb clicked.

Who had a more renewable stash of wealth than a pair of bank robbers? Where were they likelier to escape the eye of law and order than in a place whose inhabitants had long since learned to distrust the government? Dillinger was a hero to people bankers had foreclosed on. Frank and his pear blossom must have thought they could live like gods.

Thanks to Graham's father, they'd lost their hoped-for kingdom in Switzerland. Maybe Texas was where they were trying next.

"Tell me," she said, striving to keep her tone conversational. "Things seem better here than in some places. Have you gotten New Deal funds, or is there some other reason?"

The clerk's laugh turned into a gut-wrenching cough. When he recovered, he smiled at her as if he were used to hacking out his lungs. "The Red Cross blows through, now and then. Leaves us a pile of masks. We've got our own angel, though. Some German fellow up in Amarillo. He's buying businesses, right and left. Says he wants to be ready to turn this area around when the rains come back. Heck, he bought himself a ranch and hired a whole bunch of hands."

"You ever meet him?" Pen asked.

"Saw him once," the clerk answered with a shrug. "Looked like a slick one, dressed up in his New York duds. Had a wife who was Chinee. Not that it matters. His money spends fine. Most of us would rather not run to California to pick fruit. I mean, we can't feed our cows, and Roosevelt pays us pennies on the dollar to slaughter and dump 'em. What sort of 'New Deal' is that when folks are starving?"

Pen knew it was a form of supply and demand adjustment, but kept the words to herself.

"These are some tough times," she said instead sympathetically.

"Don't I know it!" the clerk agreed.

Probably due to the microscopic particles in the air, the sunset was as beautiful as any Pen had witnessed in the Caribbean: breathtaking oranges and reds that melted like candy into a wash of intense purple. Because Sally was reluctant to leave the house, and Ben would not leave her, Pen admired it from the porch alone.

Graham and Durand were awake when she came back in, both sitting on the broken-down couch rubbing their faces. They looked sleepy but good, each man strong in his way, neither likely to back down during a fight. It amused her to imagine them sharing the ancient mattress, maybe squabbling over who took which side. Nothing of the sort seemed to have happened. She had to admit they made a good team, with Durand supplying the ruthlessness Graham lacked. Pen wasn't sure when she'd begun trusting Durand, but she knew they were lucky he was on their side.

She tugged her scarf down from her mouth and shared what she'd found out.

Graham grasped its significance quickly. "If the area does recover, Frank and Li-Hua will own most of it. Including the locals' gratitude."

"It makes sense," Durand agreed, "though they're gambling on weather patterns turning around. Were you able to get details on the ranch they bought?"

Pen sat on the arm of the sofa next to Graham. She reached across him to hand Durand the sketch she'd made. "This won't be completely accurate. I didn't want to ask too many questions and raise red flags. I do think we can assume the couple dozen hands they hired are acting as their army."

"At a minimum, they'll have bitten and thralled them," Durand said. "But they may have changed some as well."

"Can they do that?" Ben's voice came from the doorway of the crude kitchen. Sally had both arms around his waist, her face pressed to his shoulder. Pen had the impression they'd been discussing something upsetting. "I thought changing humans was a special ability."

"It is, but they're so bloated from the souls they've stolen, they may be able to accomplish it with brute force."

"Great," Ben said bitterly. "Something else to worry about."

"You're going to have to shove your worries aside," Durand warned. "If we delay going after them, they'll only get stronger, and that's not something we can afford."

"Why does Ben have to go?" Sally asked, hugging him

tighter. "You and Graham are much more powerful than he is."

"We need Ben to keep the auto running long enough to get us there. It's forty miles from here to Amarillo. If Graham and I travel in the open, in this dust, we won't be at the strength we need when we arrive." Durand had risen to his feet as he spoke. Now he walked to Sally, human slow but with vampire grace. Though he betrayed no signs of impatience, his face was very serious. "Once we reach Frank and Li-Hua's base, if Ben chooses, I won't ask him to take part in the fighting."

Pen and Graham's jaws dropped at this concession—not what they expected from their highly practical leader.

"You'll need me," Ben said, his protest uncertain.

Durand kept his eyes on Sally. "I know you can't come with us. I've heard you coughing. I know this dust isn't safe for you and your baby."

"What about—" Graham hesitated. "What about Sally's power?"

"I believe I know a way to take it with us and leave her here."

"You're looking for a trade." Sally stared up at Durand like a mouse held mesmerized by a rattler. Pen couldn't help but notice the circles under her eyes. They were all that subdued Pen's urge to smack her. Well, that and knowing she didn't understand what it was to worry for an unborn child. Pushed to her limit, Sally wadded Durand's pristine shirt in her fist, then just as quickly released it. She shook her finger at him instead. "You want something from me in return for letting Ben stay out of danger. But he'll fight anyway if he's there. Graham is his brother."

"I'd do my best to keep him safe," Durand swore.

"What do you want from her?" Ben asked.

"A few ounces of her blood. No." Durand lifted his hand to forestall Ben's outrage. "I don't want it for myself. I want it for our ammunition. I believe an iron bullet dipped in her blood will cause a wound our enemies won't be able to heal."

"You *believe*," Ben said.

Durand's thin mouth twisted with one of his rare flashes of humor. "Truthfully, I believe it so strongly I'd rather not test the theory out on myself."

Sally pushed away from Ben's side and straightened, keeping her hold only on his hand. "I'll do it on one condition: You go and leave Ben with me."

"That bargain I cannot make," Durand said softly.

"Sally—" Ben burst out, unable to remain silent.

"No, Ben," Sally said, her expression as stubborn as Pen had ever seen it—and that was saying something. "I can't lose you again. I *won't*."

"Could you lose Graham?" Ben demanded.

"Could you lose our daughter?" she returned. Her lips were trembling, her eyes glittering on the verge of tears. Ben's face was red as he drew breath.

"Miss Anderson will stay with Sally," Durand intervened.

"What?" Pen gasped, horror flooding her. "No!"

"You're the best choice." Durand's level black gaze shifted to her, his strength of will palpable. "Once Sally and Ben are separated, she may need medical care. You know enough to provide that."

Pen knew basic first aid; Roy's training had ensured that—a fact Durand must have read from her mind. "You and Graham can't face all those men alone."

"I believe we can with Sally's blood to help us."

Ben turned to her as well. "Please," he said. "I'd agree to let Durand have what he wants from Sally if I knew you would stay with her."

His voice was husky. Even as Pen glared at him, one shining tear rolled down his left cheek. She decided then and there that handsome men should not be allowed to cry. Sally she could have resisted. Ben made her heart squeeze so tight it ached.

"She's everything to me," he pleaded. "You know I'll fight no matter what Durand promises. You know I'll treat Graham as if *he* were everything to *you*."

"Damn it." Pen's eyes were burning, and she had to spin away from the rest of them. She wiped her own wet face angrily. Blasted Fitz Clares turned everyone weepy. And how dare Ben act like he knew what Graham meant to her? When Graham's big hands settled on her shoulders, she bit her lip hard enough to hurt.

"Thank you," he said, the very worst words he could have chosen. "We all know she'll be safe with you."

Pen made a sound that was too close to a growl. Annoyed with herself, she blew out her breath. She'd been given an assignment, and she couldn't deny it was logical. She had too much pride to do any job halfway. She covered one of Graham's hands with hers. Then, because touching him threatened to re-agitate her emotions, she stepped away from him.

"Come on," she said to Sally. "I'll draw your blood. If we leave it to dead boy here, he'll just enjoy it too much."

Sally's chin was quivering too badly for her smile to convince, though she made a good try of it.

"Righto," she said, her eyes evading Pen's. "I'm sure none of us want that."

Amarillo

Graham had left the farmhouse with a nagging feeling of important things undone. He wished he'd had a moment alone with Pen. He wouldn't have minded sharing more than a hug goodbye. Maybe he'd even have confessed he loved her. People did that before they went into battle. They didn't always mean it as much as he did, but this could have been one of his better chances to have her accept the words.

But they'd been caught up in the business of preparation: treating the bullets, taping the cracks in the car. The latter had worked like a charm. Ironically, the drive to Amarillo turned out to be easier than any of them foresaw.

Now Durand, Graham, and Ben lay flat on their bellies behind a wire and post cattle fence, in as good a shape as they were going to be. Inside the pasture, a little herd of unhappy longhorns huddled among the surviving clumps of buffalo grass. The wind was blowing up with an eerie hiss, the air so dry it felt stuffed with electricity. The vampires had discovered they shouldn't touch Ben, because the sparks that crackled out at the contact were substantial enough to knock him over.

Graham began to feel as if Texas was a different planet, where normal expectations went arse over teakettle. What this would mean for the coming conflict, he hadn't the foggiest. Even leaving the weather and the dust aside, the flatness of the landscape and the sheer distances between things weren't what he was at home with.

Thankfully, Pen had bought two pair of field glasses

at the general store. Graham and Durand each had a set to their eyes. The lenses magnified their vision to the extent that Durand had grunted with approval when he first peered through them.

Graham had enjoyed that. Pen was helping them even from afar.

"They should have put the cows away," Ben said.

Durand didn't shush him. He'd erected the same cloak of silence he'd used all those nights ago in Pen's Charleston dining room. He lowered his binoculars and passed them to Ben. "I don't think these ranch hands are concerned with cows anymore."

Frank and Li-Hua's guards were patrolling their low-slung Spanish-style adobe house. They were armed and undoubtedly used to guns, but they didn't strike Graham as soldierlike. Their movements were stiff, their eyes roving but empty. When a coral snake slithered across the ground ten feet away from one, the man never noticed it.

From a strategic standpoint, it disturbed Graham that every guard they saw had been changed. From a personal one, their odd behavior was more unsettling. Graham hadn't been like that when he was a new vampire.

"What's wrong with them?" he asked.

Durand narrowed his eyes. "If I had to hazard a guess, I'd say they were revenants."

"Revenants?"

"Zombies," Ben offered, his jaw clenched so tightly Graham thought his teeth must be in danger of chattering. It occurred to him that being separated from Sally was hard on his brother, too. He'd been looking out for her all his life.

"They've been changed," Durand said, either unaware of or ignoring Ben's unease. "You can tell by the way they glow. I suspect, however, that they were transformed so violently, so unwillingly, that it killed too big a piece of their humanity. They're just mindless followers now. With luck, their patrols make Frank and Li-Hua feel safe enough to let down their guard, but I don't think they'll present too great an obstacle to us."

"There are a lot of them," Ben said, the small human squirm of his body betraying his discomfort with their numbers.

"Yes," Durand agreed. "It would be better if we didn't have to waste our special cartridges killing them. My biggest concern, though, is one of them spotting us and warning their makers."

"I could change shape," Graham offered. "Sneak in as my cat from the other side of the house. They're not paying attention to the wildlife. If you wrapped your cloak of silence around you and Ben, we might all slip right by them. You could tie a shotgun to my back so I'd still be armed."

"Ammo, too," Ben reminded.

Durand looked into Ben's eyes and then into Graham's. Graham didn't think he'd ever seen anyone so calm. The mercenary's thoughts seemed to tick as mechanically as a clock as he judged their readiness.

His coolness heightened Graham's awareness of the bead of sweat rolling down his spine. The reaction was part nerves, part the fact that the southern part of this country was much warmer than the north.

"Very well," Durand said. "I suppose that's a plan."

Graham's mood usually improved when he changed form. His feline side had far less convoluted emotions. Tonight, the skin beneath his fur quivered. His cat didn't fancy this weather even a bit. The thick, static-laden air made it want to scramble away and hide, especially when it noticed clouds piling up on the horizon. They resembled storm clouds, but Graham sincerely doubted they carried rain. Electricity flickered inside them: queer green flashes rather than lightning bolts.

Ben had to scratch him between the ears to keep him still enough for Durand to tie the shotgun and ammo on.

Sorry, he tried to say, but naturally all that came out was a muffled *rrow*.

"Any time you're ready," Durand said.

Graham wriggled at the unfamiliar weight on his back.
The harness Durand had rigged was uncomfortable but
secure—and tight enough that it didn't slide. Knowing
there wasn't much point in waiting, he flicked his ears at
the others and flattened his body to crawl under the barbed
wire fence.

Being gray was helpful in this landscape. Despite his
greater than normal size, Graham's cat had no trouble
evading the guards, even when it came to jumping on window ledges to search for who was inside. He didn't find
Frank and Li-Hua, but there was a casement with a broken
latch that he could slip through. His heart beat faster as he
landed in the empty room. The house smelled musty, and
it was very quiet, the rising whistle of the wind muted by
thick walls. Deciding his cat's nose was an advantage, Graham didn't change back to human form. He smelled spoiled
food in the kitchen and a body decomposing in a cabinet.
Both were best ignored, so he went on. The terra-cotta floor
was cool beneath his toe pads as he trotted silently down a
corridor. When he reached a turning, the slow, soft thump
of immortal heartbeats warned him to freeze.

Whiskers twitching, one curled paw hanging in the air,
he poked his head around the corner.

Two big guards sat at a folding table at the end of a passageway, handguns holstered under their beefy arms. Both
had the bulk that came from a lifetime of hard labor. Instead
of uniforms, they wore faded blue jeans and button-down
plaid shirts. Graham saw at once that they were different
from the rest of the new *upyr*, in part because they were
engaged in an apparently heated game of poker, something
they could not have done if they were mindless. Frank and
Li-Hua's technique must have been improving, or perhaps
these two had volunteered to be changed. In any case, they
were alert and individual seeming. They glanced up but
didn't seem alarmed when moans of pain floated through
the door behind them.

Graham had no doubt the vampires causing those
moans were his ultimate targets. Maybe this was how they
obtained their victims' consent to be changed. Maybe the

body in the cabinet had been an earlier misfire. Then again, maybe torturing people was their idea of fun.

He pivoted his ears to search for signs of Durand and Ben. Ben's mortal limitations would have slowed Durand down, but they should have arrived in the house by now.

We're here, he heard Durand say quietly. *Try to relax, and I'll read your situation from your mind.*

Graham sat on his haunches, doing his best not to fight the other's intrusion. Though he couldn't control what Durand saw, he knew this was easier than trying to send thoughts himself. He ran his memory over everything he'd seen, ending with the two guards and the nondescript brown door. When a foreign flare of satisfaction spread through his mind, he knew Durand had read what he intended.

Good, the mercenary said. *Those two are the only vampires besides Frank and Li-Hua who I can feel in the house. If you could lure them away from their post, without raising an alarm, I'll have a clear path to our enemies. I'm sensing they're underground with whoever they're torturing. If we're lucky, the entrance these men are guarding is the only way in or out.*

This wouldn't be an advantage unless Durand killed Frank and Li-Hua fast enough. Otherwise, they'd simply barrel over him. Since Durand probably knew this, Graham didn't bother emphasizing the thought.

If you show these men your cat, Durand suggested, *that might be sufficient distraction.*

Marvelous, Graham thought, wondering if the guards had iron bullets. Frank and Li-Hua hadn't armed their men with them before, but at that point, they also hadn't been attacked by *upyr.* He'd have to chance it, he supposed. Taking care to move slowly enough to be noticed, he darted across the *T*-shaped intersection of the passageways.

"Shit," said one of the guards. "What was that?"

Graham heard two safeties being clicked off the guards' pistols. One of their chairs scraped back, but neither of them stood up. Hoping for a better reaction, Graham padded to the center of the intersection and meowed at them. To his disappointment, only the shorter of them rose.

"That ain't no pussy cat," said the taller, his gun drawn but resting on his thigh. "That's a damned cougar."

"Cougars ain't that furry, Cleve," said the other, "and they ain't gray."

Cleve set down the hand he'd been playing. He'd been muscular as a human, and he was no less so as a vampire. His shoulders looked like they would split his shirt when he leaned forward in his chair. "What the hell is that on its back?"

Graham's cat shook itself in annoyance. Little though he wanted to be attacked, if those two were just going to sit there, debating what he was, he wouldn't accomplish what Durand needed.

"You think we should call the boss?" the shorter guard asked.

This was the last thing Graham wanted, but then a burst of inspiration struck. The guards had been playing each other for money, which was a possible motivation for them joining Frank and Li-Hua in the first place. Before they could gather themselves to stop him, he darted forward, grabbed the "pot" in his teeth, and ran away again.

"Hey!" both guards protested, with Cleve adding, "I had a full house!"

Graham hadn't fully integrated his vampire strengths into his cat form. The guards were faster than he was, so he had to rely on feline agility to stay ahead of them. *Path's clear*, he broadcast as well as he could, praying Durand was tuned in.

His mind wasn't calm enough to listen for answers. A bullet slammed the cowhide couch he'd just leaped over. From the burned rust smell coming from the hole, he could tell the slug was iron.

Hell, he thought, wondering if he could change and run at the same time. The shotgun Durand had tied to his back was banging into him, slowing him even more. He doubled back, charging right between the two vampires, causing both to stumble in surprise. Despite the ploy, their next shot winged his shoulder. With an inner lurch, he realized if they actually sank a bullet in him, he'd lose his ability to shift form; the iron would dampen that power—which would mean he couldn't return their fire any more than he could outrun them.

Cursing, he streaked toward the room with the open window. He had to calm himself, had to think clearly enough to regain his human form. A floor tile exploded inches from his hind legs. His heart was galloping so hard it threatened to burst his ribs. He needed a second without this panic, but his pursuers weren't giving him one.

Think, he ordered himself. *Be a bloody man, damn you.*

His anger undid the handicap of his fear. He changed so fast he barely dematerialized. He hit the floor and rolled, his hands stretching for the shotgun as it flew from him. Luckily, it hadn't poofed along with its harness. Graham was naked, but he had a weapon, and his reflexes were at full *upyr* speed. He got off two shots before the guards stopped skidding.

To his amazement, he aimed well enough that the contents of both cartridges hit bodies.

"Fuck," said the man whose leg he'd sprayed. The injury wasn't bad enough to stop him. Angry but not particularly debilitated, he sighted down the barrel of his black .45, too close to miss Graham's heart in a million years. Graham's perceptions slowed as though time itself had turned to cold tar.

Graham was instants from losing everything he cared about.

Then the other man, Cleve, dropped to his knees on the terra-cotta, one hand clutched to his shredded chest. He gasped, eyes round with shock, after which he just disappeared. There was no burst of light like most vampires died with; he simply flicked out of existence.

Evidently, despite their delay in acting, Sally's blood-dipped iron pellets packed quite a punch.

"Wha—" the other had long enough to say before he vanished the same way.

Graham would have escaped scot-free, if the shorter man's pistol hadn't gone off when it hit the floor.

* * *

Ben and Durand ran through the moonlit house, guns out
and bodies low to the ground. Since Durand made no noise
at all, Ben had no trouble hearing the guards chasing his
brother.

Stay on your toes, Durand said straight into his mind.
Whatever happens is going to happen fast.

Durand flipped the folding card table on its side in front
of the cellar door, then gestured for Ben to take up position
on one knee a few feet from it. The flimsy table was no barrier, but it might trip someone.

If anyone comes up those steps, you shoot them, Durand
instructed. *Head or heart, no hesitation, just like Pen
taught you. Believe me, I'll warn you if it's me.*

He didn't give Ben an opportunity to ask questions, just
opened the door and slipped like a shadow behind it. Ben
braced the shotgun stock on his shoulder, aiming for the
blackened strip of the opening. Sweat trickled down his
temples as he pictured Durand creeping down the stairs,
trying to take creatures with supernatural hearing by surprise. The person Frank and Li-Hua were torturing had
stopped moaning. In the quiet, Ben hardly dared draw
breath.

Nerve wrenching though it was, the silence didn't last
long enough. Ben's body jerked as gunfire rang out, not
from the cellar but from the ranch's ground level.

Christ, he thought, instincts screaming for him to run
toward the sound. If Graham had been shot . . .

Graham was more than his brother. Ever since their
days in the orphanage, Graham had been Ben's hero.

But Ben had to stay, because shots suddenly exploded
nearer to him. The roar of Durand's shotgun was followed
by the ear-splitting crash and bang of vampires fighting in
an enclosed space. The floorboards bucked, forcing Ben to
brace his back on the wall or be shaken off his foot and
knee. Someone shrieked in agony—a man, he thought,
though he couldn't tell if it was Durand. Ben tightened
his finger on the trigger a second before a dark shape sped

through the door with a rush of sound like a speeding train.

Cheap wood flew as the shape tore through the folding table. Ben didn't realize he'd depressed the trigger until he saw the flashes from the end of his gun's muzzle.

If he hit the figure, it didn't show.

The vampire hissed and lashed out at him. Ben's head smacked into the wall, the claw marks on his cheek spurting blood. He caught a surreal glimpse of Li-Hua's glowing, maddened face before she was gone. He blinked in astonishment at the trail she'd left. She'd been moving so fast, she scoured a trough in the red floor tiles. He thought— He closed his eyes to bring back the image. He wasn't certain, but he thought she'd been carrying a body beneath one arm.

He wondered if it had been Frank. If it were, he hoped the bastard was dying.

"Ben!" Durand called, sounding strained. "Get your ass down here!"

Ben pulled himself together to descend the cracked wooden stairs. The cellar was stone-lined with a bare dirt floor, now in shambles from the vampires' brief but mono- lithic fight. Ben stepped over heaps of broken glass and canned vegetables to reach a small, lantern-lit storeroom. There he found a battered-looking Durand crouched over Frank, both hands throttling his muscled neck. Frank was deathly pale and not shining, the pool of blood beneath him explained—at least partially—by the eye-widening absence of his right leg. That half of his trousers was also gone, the stump at his hip raw but sealed. Despite the injury, the vampire was still strong enough to try to throw Durand off.

Between gasps for air, he cursed in German and gnashed his fangs.

"Him I shot," Durand panted. "But I could use some help controlling him."

"Happy to," Ben said, lifting the shotgun back to his shoulder.

"No!" Durand's voice was hoarse. "Don't kill him. He's our bargaining chip to get Li-Hua back."

"If my brother's dead, so is he."

Ben meant every word, without compunction. When Frank's pale blue eyes turned to him, all he wanted was to snuff out the light behind them.

"Your brother isn't dead," Durand said. "Just wounded. And the quicker we take care of this, the quicker we get to him. Grab those chains from the wall and help me wrap this one up."

The chains had been restraining someone recently, perhaps the mystery body Li-Hua had carried out. Blood dripped wet from the links. Too numb to be sickened, Ben lifted their weight off the hooks. Durand heaved Frank's upper body off the floor, clearly preferring that Ben handle the iron.

The shift in position must have heightened the pain of Frank's missing leg. For a moment, his eyes rolled white. He shook himself conscious with obvious difficulty.

"I won't help you," he swore as Ben bound his struggling arms behind him. "My pear blossom will drink your souls before you use me to get to her. Never will I turn against my beloved."

Durand pushed to his feet and looked down at him. The mercenary's face was gory from the fight, his fangs slowly retracting. Bones crackled in his cheek and arm as various injuries healed themselves. Ben could actually see his right cheekbone unflatten. His once-white shirt was in scarlet shreds.

"Never's a long time," Durand said. "I expect we can break you a good deal sooner than that."

Li-Hua crouched behind a wind-blasted juniper, watching the enemy pick off her men one by one. Thanks to the approaching storm, the ground swirled with dust as high as her waist. Each time one of her soldiers fell, the cloud of gray swallowed them. Had they known how to use their brains, the obscuring haze would have made excellent cover.

As it was, Li-Hua didn't mind their loss too much. She and Frank could create more children: more and better. Without her or Frank to lead them, their first batch of *upyr* were useless—neither organized nor intelligent. No, it was the principle of the thing that galled her.

Durand and his little crew were on the roof of *her* home, with *her* beloved lying helpless in a cocoon of chains. The disappearance of his leg when Durand shot it had been a breath-stealing shock. For a second, she'd thought Frank's whole body would vaporize. Li-Hua couldn't imagine how the invaders had accomplished it. A fluke, most likely, or some secret weapon she'd be all too glad to turn back on them.

Of her enemies, only Graham Fitz Clare showed a hint of an injury, his shoulder bleeding sluggishly from an iron shot. He was naked, his hugeness all the more apparent because of his lack of clothes. She licked her lips as she remembered how much she'd enjoyed tricking him when he was mortal. He'd been as grateful as a virgin for her least favor. Durand she should have seduced when she'd had the chance. She was certain their former captain wouldn't have dreamed of switching sides if he'd known the glories of her body.

"You should surrender," rasped the man whose wrist she was holding cuffed. She was so strong now that trapping him was effortless. "Your men don't stand a chance against theirs."

"You should shut up," she said, pushing the words into his sky blue eyes.

His mouth snapped closed satisfyingly. He was like Cleve and Harris had been after they were changed. He obeyed direct orders as though he were thralled, but he could also think for himself. Unlike Cleve and Harris— whose loss she did regret a bit—he had no interest in her and Frank achieving their goals.

Fortunately for him, he was of use to her. If Durand took a hostage, Li-Hua would take two. Whether this idiot liked it or not, he was the key to that. He had a connection to some people she was angry at, people who thoroughly deserved the comeuppance she had in store.

Li-Hua took his chin in her hand and held it steady.

"I have a job for you," she said, putting her superior will into the order, "and you're not going to dream of mucking it up."

North Fork

The more the wind kicked up outside the farmhouse, the tighter Sally curled into a ball on the aged couch. Though comforting people wasn't Pen's strong suit, it didn't take long to conclude she couldn't just stand by watching a pregnant eighteen-year-old hug her shins and shiver.

"Are you sure you're—"

"Please." Sally cut her off with her teeth gritted. "Don't ask if I'm all right."

Pen moved from her post at the window to sit by her. Sally had a blanket clutched around her as though the night were much cooler.

"You could tell me if you weren't," Pen said, her leg bumping Sally's tightly curled bare toes. "I promise I wouldn't think less of you."

"Wouldn't you?" Sally pressed her face closer to her knees. "*You* wouldn't have asked Durand to spare your husband. *You'd* rather be fighting with the men."

"Sally." The tenderness that welled up in Pen was utterly unexpected. Sally had said nothing Pen hadn't thought, but that didn't seem to matter to her emotions. As much to regain her composure as to soothe her companion, she laid her hand on Sally's trembling back. "You were brave when we needed you to be. You're the one who gave us the ability to harm Li-Hua."

Sally sniffled and then flung her arms around Pen. "I don't feel safe without him! When he leaves, it's as if the world is filled with horrible dangers."

"Oh, honey," Pen crooned into Sally's baby-fine blonde

curls. She hugged Sally back, wishing she could tell her the world held nothing but kittens and lollipops. "Maybe you'd feel better if we found a shirt of Ben's for you to wear."

Sally mumbled something Pen couldn't hear.

"What did you say, honey?"

The two lanterns Durand had lit were dim, but when Sally lifted her head, Pen saw tears swam in her big blue eyes. "You *are* good enough for Graham. I'm so sorry I thought you weren't."

Pen laughed, because Sally had as funny a knack with compliments as she did with smart-ass remarks. "I wouldn't worry about that," she said dryly. "Graham's interest in me isn't permanent."

Sally opened her mouth to answer when a rolling boom of thunder caused both women to jump.

"You'd think it was going to rain," Sally said breathlessly.

"Come on." Pen rose, tugging Sally gently to her feet. "Let's see what's happening out there."

As in the other rooms, a doubled bedsheet draped the single front window. Behind it, Pen had rubbed a clearer circle in the dust-coated glass. She squinted through it, her eyes refusing to make sense of what they perceived.

A mammoth wall of clouds was moving toward them, stretching over the horizon as far as she could see and boiling up perhaps ten thousand feet in the air—nature's own skyscraper. The wall was black, its depths lit up by the jagged veins of thin lightning bolts. It was hard to judge, but Pen thought the monster wasn't more than a few miles off.

A few miles would make the storm closer than the town. North Fork would have been swallowed. Not that safety waited for them there.

"What *is* that?" Sally asked.

Pen's heart was drumming in her throat, requiring her to swallow before she spoke. "I'm pretty sure it's what people here call a black blizzard—a bad dust storm. Sally, I think we'd better go to the root cellar."

She hadn't wanted to frighten Sally, but to her dismay, Graham's sister rubbed the clear spot bigger and put her nose to the glass. "Pen, someone is out there. They're walking up the road toward us."

She gave Pen room to look for herself. There was someone: a man in a cowboy hat whom the intermittent snakes of lightning were outlining. His leanness and his stride looked familiar. When he reached up with one hand to press his Stetson down more firmly, she knew for sure.

"My God," she breathed. "That's Roy."

She caught Sally's arm before she dashed to the door. "Think, Sally. How does he know we're here?"

Sally tugged at her hold. "He must have run across our men. They must have sent him back to us."

"Maybe," Pen said. "But let's wait and see what he has to say."

The semiautomatic Durand had insisted she keep on her person was tucked into her waistband. She didn't draw the pistol, but she did click the safety off.

Sally stared at her accusingly. "I'm sure he just needs shelter."

Pen nodded, but didn't budge.

"Stay behind me," she warned as his boots clumped onto the wooden porch.

"His footsteps are making noise," Sally hissed. "Graham's and Durand's are silent. *And* he's not glowing."

Pen didn't have time to remind her this might be something he could fake. Roy pounded on the door.

"Pen," he said. "Open up! I've got news about Graham and the others."

Pen drew the gun, aimed it where she thought Roy was, and jerked her head for Sally to move back farther. "Tell me what it is from there."

"Chrissake," Roy said. "I've got half a pound of dust in my lungs by now."

It was the cough that broke Sally's self-control. It was wet and hacking and—apparently—human. She scooted past Pen to unbar the door. As she yanked it open, their first sight of Roy was his fist dropping from his mouth.

"Thank you kindly, miss," he said.

He sounded like the Roy that Pen knew, looked like

him, stood like him—forthright and straight. Nonetheless, she cocked the hammer of her gunn.

The noise brought Roy's eyes to her. The sadness she found there made her fear spike dramatically. If the news about Graham was bad . . . If she'd lost her chance to discover what could grow between them . . .

Her own stupidity astonished her. She'd been so busy trying not to let Graham matter, trying to keep her heart safe from being hurt, that she might have let a treasure slip through her fingers. Graham already mattered. He had for a long, long time. The pain of that realization—the intense *regret*—felt like talons ripping her soul in two.

"Pen," Roy said. "I'm sorry."

She wasn't thinking quite fast enough. She didn't notice the sudden intentness in Roy's muscles. His hand shot out to circle her throat, and the shake he gave her was so violent the pistol flew from her hold to skate across the floor.

Pen had to give Sally credit. She didn't freeze or shriek, but tried to run for the lost weapon. Roy caught her by the back of her collar before she'd gone two feet. Horrified, Pen watched fangs shoot out from Roy's gums. The glow he'd been damping burst out with hunger. He was panting . . . but not from exertion. Gripping both of them at once didn't seem hard for him at all.

The way he licked his teeth at Sally's struggles made Pen's skin crawl.

"Please, Roy," she begged, praying her old mentor was in there. "Don't hurt Sally."

"I won't," he growled, his burning gaze shifting back to her. His facial muscles tightened with what might have been anger. "I *can't*. My mistress ordered me to track your essence and bring you to her unharmed."

Amarillo

Once any threat from Frank and Li-Hua's soldiers had been dispatched, Durand tossed Frank off the roof to Graham. Graham caught him, then carried him into the ranch's beam-ceilinged living room. The wind had long since blown out the electricity. Lacking Durand's skill with sparks, Graham used a match to light the logs in the beehive-shaped kiva fireplace.

"You're dead," Frank said as Graham propped him in a chair. The iron he was trussed in had drained his strength enough to turn his white skin gray—or perhaps that was the result of the pain from his missing leg. He wasn't struggling anymore, his remaining energy expended by his threats. "All of you are dead."

Graham didn't respond, turning to watch Durand help Ben into the house. The storm held furious sway outside, and Ben was affected the worst of them. Though Durand had done what he could, dust caked Ben from head to toe. A harsh, hacking cough bent him at the waist.

"*He's* dead at least," Frank laughed. "Second time's the charm, I guess."

Graham clenched his jaw, but Durand sat Ben on the cowhide couch and strode as coolly to their prisoner as if he'd said nothing.

"You can die easy, or you can die hard," Durand said, "and the same goes for your lover. If you'd prefer not to see her suffer, you'll tell us where her bolt-hole is."

Frank curled his upper lip at him. "My pear blossom is more powerful than a lowly hireling like you can dream."

"And yet, she ran," Durand said pleasantly. "She ran from this lowly hireling while you were screaming like a baby and crawling across the floor with your leg blown off."

"It will grow back," Frank averred.

"Nice to think so, I'm sure."

"She will figure out how you hurt me. She will turn your trick back on you."

Durand braced his hands on either side of Frank's chair, leaning close enough to insult. "Your pear blossom is so far off her rocker she couldn't figure out where the sun comes up."

Frank spat into Durand's face.

"As you like," Durand said. Straightening, he pulled a shiny silver pistol from the small of his back, chambering a round and pulling the trigger in almost the same motion.

Frank's right foot exploded, causing him to shriek and arch as if the high-backed chair were electrocuting him. Threads of blue light danced upward along his calf, the crackle of their progress eerie to hear. When Frank settled, moaning and bright with sweat, his other leg and its trouser were missing up to the knee. Frank looked down at this new loss in horror.

With neat, calm movements, Durand tucked the gun away, then wiped Frank's spittle from his cheek with a handkerchief. "Handy thing about you and Li-Hua being so powerful. You certainly can survive a lot of damage."

"Jesus," Ben murmured from the couch.

The muscles of Graham's throat convulsed, and he hoped that, as a vampire, he wasn't capable of throwing up. He reminded himself that catching Frank and not Li-Hua would leave their mission worse than half finished. Li-Hua had always had strong barriers to being read, barriers she'd been able to loan to Frank. If they didn't convince him to talk, she'd be wreaking havoc for who knew how long.

"Shoot me all you want," Frank panted, though his eyes showed white all around. "I would die for Li-Hua. *Die* for her."

"Really?" Durand cocked his head at him. "How about

if I offered to shoot off something more personal? You
want to gamble on your stones growing back?"

Graham and Ben exchanged wary glances, so caught up
in this standoff that they weren't watching Durand's back
as well as they should. Durand, too, must have been more
involved than he appeared. The voice that interrupted from
the doorway took them all by surprise.

"I wouldn't damage Frank anymore," it said. "Not if you
want your women back in one piece."

Sally had started to cry when Pen wrapped one of Durand's
white dress shirts around her head. Their leader had two
outfits that Pen had seen, and given the frequency with
which he wore them, she assumed his power had sunk into
them. Durand had healed Sally once before. With luck, this
aura-imbued cloth would protect her out in the storm.

"This smells like *him*," Sally complained.

"Shush," Pen said, aware of Roy waiting not very
patiently by the farmhouse door. The only reason he'd
let her do this was because two dust-suffocated hostages
would enrage his mistress. "I know you'd rather have Ben's
shirt, but it wouldn't help as much."

Pen tied her own scarf around her face and turned to the
man she'd once looked up to with all her heart. By concealing his real motivation for recruiting her, her former mentor
had shaken—but not destroyed—that admiration. Whether
she should let it be destroyed now, she wasn't sure. Roy
looked back at her, his pupils huge, his fangs run out dis-
concertingly. His face was almost his own—younger and
less weathered, but still recognizable. Then he swallowed
as if his mouth had filled with saliva.

How newly made was Roy? Had Frank and Li-Hua let
him feed even once? If they hadn't, Pen hoped Li-Hua's
influence was ironclad.

"We're ready," she said.

Roy moved too quickly for her to prepare herself, grabbing her and Sally under his arms as if they were carpet
rolls. He kicked the front door off its hinges, causing it to

fly past the barn. Then he ran, with a speed most sports cars couldn't muster, the world turning to streaks of different shades of gray. The moment he crossed into the storm wall, Pen lost all sense of direction.

Apart from the green white sparks of electricity, she couldn't see a thing—not the flat Texas landscape, not the tip of her nose. It wasn't even worthwhile to try, considering how the dust scratched her eyes. Roy must have been using something other than sight to guide him. Inside the storm, the wind was screaming like a banshee, gusts of it forcing Pen and Sally's legs to flap behind them. Roy was stronger than the wind and fast enough to keep the frequent forks of lightning from catching them. Depending on their attacker for their safety was very strange. Pen's skin buzzed from all the energy in the air, the intensity of the sensation extremely uncomfortable.

Then Roy stopped without warning.

The hair on Pen's scalp prickled for a new reason. Someone she couldn't see had joined them in this gray netherworld.

"I'll take this one," said Li-Hua's disembodied voice. "Carry the other to the ranch and share my demands."

"Pen!" Sally cried, apparently the one Li-Hua was taking. Pen didn't have time to comfort her.

"Yes, mistress," Roy concurred and took off.

Pen wanted to struggle, but it seemed pointless. She had no weapon, no plan, and Roy was speeding through the storm again, his arm tight and immovable around her waist. She cursed to herself, then decided that was no use, either. An opening to act would come. She just had to wait and be alert for it. Ironically, Roy had taught her that himself.

Entering the ranch house and escaping the battering wind was a shock. Her eyes teared wildly, but once they finished, she could see again. As Roy set her on her feet, she gaped at the sight of Frank and his missing legs. Had their side's men done this? Was this what their treated bullets accomplished? The men ranged around Frank in his high-backed chair: Ben and Durand and Graham. The tallest of them, Graham wore only a film of dust, the power of his body obvious from behind. It was hardly the time to notice, but Graham's bottom was so tight it was actually cute. Probably, this had a more potent effect than normal due to Pen being glad to see him alive.

She found her throat was too tight to speak as Roy announced himself.

"I wouldn't damage Frank anymore," he drawled. "Not if you want your women back in one piece."

The men spun to face them. It hadn't been long since she'd seen Graham, but the golden flare of his eyes hit her like a punch. His mouth fell open as he registered her situation. He seemed more alarmed by it than she was.

"Pen," he said, soft as breath.

"Drop it," Roy barked, because Durand had drawn a pistol.

Roy's left arm had been around Pen's neck since they entered, a choke hold he could have used to snap her head off at any time. Considering this, it really was overkill to add the bowie knife at her jaw.

"Drop it, or I slit her throat," he advised.

Durand lifted his hands with the gun still in one. "What are you doing, Blunt? I thought this woman was your friend."

"I can't help it," Roy snarled. "When that vampiress turned me into what she was, she stole my will."

Durand took a cautious half step closer. "That's not strictly true. If part of you hadn't consented to become immortal, you wouldn't be yourself now. You'd be a revenant like the others. You wouldn't be a sharp enough tool for Li-Hua to use."

Roy's anger came out as a growl, the knife pressing dangerously harder into Pen's skin.

"Don't," Durand said, setting his pistol down on a small table.

His compliance surprised Pen. He hadn't seemed the sort to give in to threats. And maybe that wasn't what he was doing. His eyes were fastened on Roy's like he was trying to use his thrall. Pen wondered if it were possible for him to succeed.

"You don't want to cut her," the mercenary said softly. "You'd only make things harder on yourself. I can tell her blood calls to you."

Pen felt Roy's Adam's apple bob. "They wouldn't let me feed."

"I'd let you feed." Durand's voice was cool black velvet. "Off me, if that's what you'd like. All you have to do is fight to win back your will."

"I tried!" Roy roared, the volume of his protest inducing her heart to skip. "I tried for days while they tortured me."

"Stop pushing him," Graham said to Durand in an undertone. "We don't want him to snap."

Roy began to laugh, the arm that trapped Pen's neck trembling. "I loved her. Almost like a daughter. And now I want to sink my teeth into her throat. That's what's going to happen if you break Li-Hua's hold on me."

The arousal that pressed into Pen's back wasn't fatherly, but she supposed Roy had a lot of hungers Frank and Li-Hua had not allowed him to sate. Sensing an opening, Frank chose then to rectify that.

"You can have the female," he said, speaking to Roy for the first time. "Do what Li-Hua wants, and you can choose your reward."

"Gag him," Durand said without looking back.

As Graham moved to do it, Ben stepped forward. His fists were clenched white-knuckled at his sides. If the others hadn't been there, Pen suspected he would have attacked her old mentor.

"Where's Sally?" he demanded in a shaking, furious tone. "What have you done with my wife?"

The vampiress had taken Sally to an abandoned mine. Sally bet Pen would have known where it was. Given her predilection for being prepared, Graham's girlfriend had probably memorized every hiding place in the area. Sally didn't have the faintest notion where she'd been carried, apart from guessing they were deep in one of the shafts.

Storm sounds echoed along the rough, excavated walls, occasionally resonating in the creosote timbers.

Li-Hua's glow was the only light Sally could see by.

Though dust stiffened her long black hair, Sally's abductor was as beautiful as an ivory doll, her lips painted pomegranate, her lashes drawn by a fine quill pen. Beautiful or not, the vampiress was behaving strangely, even for an uncanny being. She sat on the ground with her legs bent up in her baggy trousers, her gaze fixed on an object cupped in her hand. It looked to Sally like a man's signet ring, the sort a father leaves to his son. Li-Hua's eyes moved back and forth as she watched it, as if she were having a waking dream.

"Whose ring is that?" Sally mustered the nerve to ask.

Li-Hua curled her fingers over it, her head turning in the birdlike way *upyr* sometimes had.

"I remember you," she said. "I healed what your little gun did to me. You won't take me by surprise again."

Sally had pulled Durand's shirt on top of her own, but gooseflesh still broke across her arms. Had there been a chance Li-Hua *wouldn't* remember someone who'd shot her? Just how weak in the rafters was this woman?

"I won't try to," Sally promised. "I was simply wondering what you're doing."

"Using my eyes," she said. "He's too new to keep me from borrowing them."

"Ah," Sally said. Did Li-Hua mean Pen's friend, Roy? Was she watching what was happening to the others through her link to him? She wanted to ask how they were in the worst way, but for once in her life she didn't dare speak up. Instead, she pressed one hand to her belly, uneasily aware that her separation from Ben was beginning to take a toll. The baby wasn't happy to be here and was letting her know she'd better do something.

"Your friends shot Frank," Li-Hua said, her dark gaze cooling in a manner Sally couldn't like. "Blew his leg and foot straight off."

Sally licked her lips nervously. "Maybe he'll heal."

"Maybe," Li-Hua agreed. "And maybe I should shoot you like they did him."

It occurred to Sally that the blood Durand had taken from her might be the reason shooting Frank had injured him this time. If Sally bled, would Li-Hua drink from her? And if she drank, would she die? Perhaps Sally should cut herself. Lure the vampiress into feeding. The danger would be worth it if this killed her. Unfortunately, if Li-Hua only sickened and then figured out what Durand had done, Sally would have handed their best advantage to the enemy.

Indecision gripped her, all the more frustrating because she suspected Pen would not have been paralyzed.

I'd rather you didn't shoot me, she began to say when she realized her stomach had made up its mind about her quandary. She had time to run ten yards before everything she'd eaten that evening came up again.

"That's quite disgusting," said the vampiress. "If you don't want me to kill you, I'd advise you not to do it again."

Bridesmere

When Estelle woke from her light slumber, Edmund was curled around her back. His hold was gentle, his fingers playing lightly on her forearm. It was night; not time yet for him to rest. He'd simply laid down to keep her company. Maybe being close seemed easier when she was sleeping. He smelled of the woods behind the castle, his smooth skin in a pleasant state between warm and cool. She moved her hand to tuck his against her breasts.

"Sorry," he whispered. "I didn't mean to wake you."

Estelle wished he had. She didn't know how to reconcile his sweetness with his refusal to let her in. At least when they made love, she could pretend they were intimate. She knew Nim Wei's arrival had changed something. Ever since Edmund's private conversation with her, he'd been quiet. Whether the vampire queen had helped, Estelle wasn't sure. If she hadn't, Estelle was at a loss what to try.

She wriggled around beneath the covers, wanting to be face-to-face—which was when she noticed she and Edmund weren't alone in the tower bedroom.

Two boys stood solemnly hand in hand at the foot of the bed. One looked about fifteen. The other was three or four. The younger boy had hair as pale and fuzzy as a baby chick's. The elder's dark gold waves were very much like Edmund's.

"I'm Thomas," he said.

"I was John," chimed the other.

Estelle sat up with the covers clutched to her pajama top. Her heart was knocking her ribs.

"Don't talk to them," Edmund warned. "You'll only give them more power."

Thus spoke the voice of experience, though Estelle didn't see how what she did could matter. The boys weren't ghostlike in the least. To her eyes, they were solid, real, down to the peach fuzz glinting on their cheeks in the banked firelight.

"Father killed us," the elder said.

Edmund made a sound: pain catching in his throat. He turned away and closed his eyes, one fist pressed to his mouth. Estelle couldn't stand to see him like that, not for a second more.

"Killed you, did he?" she said, returning her attention to the boys. "Where's your bloody stab wound? Or the evidence that he snapped your neck?"

"Estelle." Edmund laid a cautioning hand on her arm.

"No, Edmund. I want to hear how you think you killed these two boys—the sons you didn't want me to know about, I presume."

"How I *think* I killed them." Edmund's face was a study of astonishment. "Estelle, my guilt can't be argued. They've come here to testify."

"To testify to what *you* put inside them. You've been calling up these ghosts. They replay the memories and pronounce the sentences you want them to. They're your modern-day version of a hair shirt."

"He killed us," the younger lisped, his insistence an impressive re-creation of three-year-old stubbornness. "He could have saved us, and he let us die."

"Fine." Estelle crossed her arms and glared at the toddler. "Tell me how you died."

"Fever," he said. "He let me visit my mother in the convent, and I fell ill. He should have known she wouldn't take care of me."

"And you?" she asked the elder.

"Riding accident. Snapped my spine. He could have called Lucius to change me. I could have had the same immortal life as my brother, Robin. I could have watched my children grow up."

"Your *children*?" Estelle flung off the covers and left the bed, her bare feet slapping the antique carpet. "How old were you when you died?"

As if she'd made a thrust they couldn't parry, the specters flickered like candle flames and blew out.

"How old was he?" she demanded of Edmund instead. Her fiancé looked uncomfortable.

"Thomas died when he was forty-two. But I never tried to interest him in the mystical world. I never let him see that side of life the way I did Robin."

"Did Thomas act as if he wanted you to?"

Edmund was sitting tailor-fashion on the bed, facing her. His chest was bare, his muscles carved marble. He looked down to where his hands gripped his ankles. "I didn't give him a chance. Thomas always seemed . . . more literal-minded than Robin, not as imaginative. I feared he would think me mad."

"Maybe he would have."

"Fear is no excuse!" Edmund's voice was rough with old guilt and pain. "He was my son as much as Robin. He should have had a choice to live or die."

Estelle sat back down next to him. "Edmund, love, I'd be willing to bet my funny arm he did have a choice. There must have been signs that something strange was happening in your household, to your family. *Upyr* hide well but not perfectly. Every time your brother and his wife visited, Thomas could have seen. If he'd wanted to know the truth, you wouldn't have been able to keep it from him. This—" She waved her hands to encompass the vanished ghosts. "This guilt you're carrying is no more than lingering sorrow at having children die before you. I'm sure most parents who experience it feel the same. If only they'd done this or that. If only they'd loved their children better when they were alive. I'd say the past can't be rewritten, except you nearly have. You rewrote it with Graham and Sally and Ben. You proved the love you're capable of."

Edmund wagged his head, his breathing uneven. "John was so hard to lose. After—" He rubbed his face, then left his hands covering his eyes. "After we discovered Claris had tried to kill me, I knew I'd have to send her away. She was pregnant, though, so we watched her like a hawk until the babe was born."

"You thought she might harm it?"

"I knew she might. John was my son, and she'd wanted Aimery's. My younger brother obsessed her since the day they met. He was the warrior-hero. I was only the heir." Edmund dropped his hands and looked at her, a film like melted diamonds sparkling on the piercing blue of his eyes. "We received reports that Claris was settling in at the convent, that she'd become genuinely devout. When she wrote to request to see John, he was old enough to ask about her, to want to know who his mother was. I thought the nurse and the guards I sent with him would keep him safe. I should have gone myself. I shouldn't have let him out of my sight."

Estelle pulled him into her arms, his hold on her back suddenly, desperately tight. "John could have succumbed to a fever even if you were there. Those were different times, and you weren't an *upyr* yet. You couldn't have healed him any better than the nuns."

"I never got a chance to say goodbye," he whispered, then pushed back and wiped his tears. "My own son. All I could do was bury him. His body was so little."

His haunted expression said he was seeing that body now. Feeling for him more than she could say, Estelle cupped his cheek. His skin was warm, sure sign of the emotions roiling inside him. Her own voice shook when she spoke. "How could you believe any of this would make me think less of you?"

"I failed them."

"You didn't. Damn it, Edmund. Even when you were rewriting history with your new family, you made many of the same decisions. You never forced your children to know the truth. You protected them as well as you could and let them live their own lives. I know you won't pressure them to become immortal, no matter how much you want to hold on to them. You were furious when you thought Graham made that choice too young."

"He made that choice to save me. Because my mistakes put countless lives at risk."

"Edmund." Estelle threw her hands up in frustration. "Graham likes being a vampire. And he has as much right as you to want to save those he loves."

Edmund looked down, his fingers plucking peaks into the silvery gold coverlet. It was richer than anything she was used to, probably woven hundreds of years ago. "That isn't all I'm ashamed of."

"Then tell the rest. Let me decide for myself how horrible you are. That's what this is about, isn't it? You've been hiding from me, because you think if I see who you really are, I won't love you anymore."

Edmund's expression tightened. "Losing your love isn't something I could bear."

"Well, too bad," Estelle said impetuously. "If there's truly a reason I ought to hate you, I deserve to know what it is."

She was sorry she'd said the words as soon as they were out, but perhaps she should not have been. The air in the bedroom changed, prickling with the rise of Edmund's energy. She'd made him angry, but she'd also brought him out of his doldrums. He was engaged with her, connecting in spite of himself. Though she couldn't hear his thoughts, his emotions brushed her like gathering clouds.

"You want to count my sins?" he snarled.

"You said it yourself. Fear is no excuse. This distance between you and me is keeping us from helping your children. Maybe letting me in won't solve all the problems you've been having, but I know, Edmund, I *know* your love for them is strong enough to try."

"And if I fail? If I let them down like I did my sons?"

His questions held as much plea as anger, both emotions painfully strong. She didn't know how to convince him the past was dead, not when it was so clearly alive for him. Nor could she promise this would fix everything. He must have known she couldn't. The lines of his face twisted, too many feelings at war in him. She was a little frightened when they all smoothed.

"So be it," he said.

He clapped his hands on her head and kissed her, his lips forcing hers apart, his tongue spearing against hers aggressively. Estelle gasped at the rough intrusion, but rather than hesitate, Edmund twisted off the bed so he could push her body back and down without mercy. He had one foot on the carpet, one knee on the bed frame, and his thighs were spreading hers apart. By the time his groin met hers, his erection bulged full and hot against the silken front of his pajama bottoms. Her own sleep trousers began to rip from the hem upward, though both his palms remained on her ears.

The ability to shred garments without touching them was a master power she hadn't known about.

It thrilled her, as so many things about him did, in spite—or perhaps because—of how terrifying his abilities could be. She warmed inside and grew liquid, her hips squirming helplessly under his. He grunted, and the sound of ripping cloth multiplied.

Delicious shivers swept Estelle's skin. He was using his new power to undress himself. Magically freed, his cock spilled from his clothes and touched her, the skin of its head as smooth as satin at the apex of her labia. His size was, as always, formidable: the most basic form of masculine dominance. He must have felt her pleasure bud pulsing. He yanked her bottom closer to the edge of the bed, then rolled his hips to make his shaft and head slide over the tender swell.

The slippery friction drew a moan from her.

"Is this what you want?" he asked.

He was panting, firelight glinting off the tips of his fangs. Estelle pulled her hair away from her neck. "Only part of it."

As invisibly as a thought, her pajama top was ripped from her breasts, the material parting like it had been clawed. Though he'd done the deed himself, a muscle in his jaw ticked when he looked down. She could feel her nipples tightening beneath his gaze. His cock surged longer, fuller, as if it also possessed powers. A forward rocking of his pelvis pressed it lengthwise between her folds. The texture of his distended veins drew her attention to how they throbbed. Good as this felt, his shaft was a thickness she'd rather have had inside her. She tightened her grip on the muscles that framed his waist.

"Edmund," she said huskily. "Do you want me to think you aren't brave enough for this?"

His eyes shot sparks at her, but her challenge steadied him. His hips shifted angles, putting the broad, smooth tip of him at her gate. As soon as he was there, he shoved without preamble, both of them sucking in sharp breaths. She was ready for him, but she was tight, and his circumference was large. The first hard push only drove him in halfway.

Overcome by the sensation of partial penetration, his fingers punched through the sheets and into the mattress.

"The rest," she urged, arching her neck to the side for him.

He licked his sharpened eyeteeth as if he couldn't help himself. This was what he'd resisted, no matter how furiously they'd made love. She felt his pulse accelerate inside her, heard his respiration break with need. She knew he loved biting her, and he hadn't done it in far too long. Estelle wanted to give herself to him in every way possible, to have them be one at last. Determined to coax him, she slid her hands up the flexing planes of his back.

With a rumbling groan that reverberated through all her nerves, he struck her neck with his fangs.

Pleasure catapulted her into an instant orgasm, clenching her sheath in spasms around him. She went as wet as if she'd flooded, the sudden increase in lubrication allowing him to drive his hardness to the end of her. He groaned again, his arms wrapping her so tightly that the hard beads of his nipples dug into her breasts. She loved that he was bending over her, that every immortal muscle in his legs could be brought to bear on plunging into her. Their bodies were sealed together—by strength, by sweat, by a desire so overmastering it made her ache even with him throbbing inside her. Wanting to get closer still, he yanked one of her legs higher up his ribs, folding it calf to thigh.

The combination of grips he had on her knee and under her back made her feel simultaneously trapped and safe. She moaned when he took a second hungry pull from her vein.

Even that wrenching pleasure wasn't enough for her. She climbed him with her other leg, ecstasy blurring her thoughts as he began to thrust vigorously in and out. His motions weren't smooth like they usually were. He was jerking, huffing, moving roughly to rub whatever spots on his body were begging to be pressed to hers. He spilled into her with each bite—brief, strong spurts that suggested his release was too massive for a single explosion. The sounds he made were wild and unself-conscious, calling matching cries from her. In truth, Estelle found his loss of control almost too exciting.

She didn't know what would happen when the barriers between them fell.

Before she could consider slowing down, those barriers tumbled. One moment their separate bodies writhed together, and the next she was in his head, the images so clear she lost her real surroundings.

She saw herself on the Orient Express to Zurich, in the pretty burgundy compartment. She was on Graham's lap, and he was biting her neck.

They'd had no choice except to do this. Graham had been a very new vampire. Feeding on humans who weren't as strong as she was seemed dangerous. Even with Estelle's unusual resilience, Graham had felt the need for a guard. Ben had watched them, his back pressed uncomfortably to the compartment door. It was his memories Edmund had seen this through, memories he must have read when Ben gave his blood to save him.

Though they'd done nothing sexual, it was evident from Estelle's movements that Graham's bite had aroused her.

She'd known this scene would hurt Edmund if he saw it. Hoping to spare him, she'd prayed he wouldn't read it from her. *Upyr* were territorial, and the experience of feeding was one of intense closeness. Edmund's kind could hardly prevent their bite from being climactic. What Estelle hadn't realized was that Edmund would feel so guilty for his fury against his son. That he knew Graham had once been attracted to Estelle made it worse. Her unavoidable response to being bitten felt like an actual threat. From the point of view of Edmund's wolf, Graham had been attempting to steal his mate.

The man in Edmund had fought the wolf's reaction, inadvertently compounding it. If he'd simply acknowledged his violent feelings and let them go, they might have passed without doing harm. But he loved his son and hated himself for wanting, even briefly, to rip him into small bits. When he'd pushed Estelle away to stop her from seeing, their estrangement had increased his difficulty controlling his powers. From that all the rest had sprung, including the specters who haunted him.

Why focus on only one reason to feel guilty when you could dredge up dozens from the past?

Estelle returned to the present with a shuddering gasp.

Edmund had collapsed on top of her, emptied but not relaxed. When she stroked her hands around his head to his sweating neck, every tendon she touched was coiled.

"I'm sorry," she said, hugging him gently. "I shouldn't have hidden what Graham and I did from you. It made it seem more important than it was."

"*You're* sorry." His head lifted far enough to meet her gaze. His skin was unusually flushed. "I'm the one who hasn't conquered those old demons. I was as jealous of Graham as I've ever been of my brother, and with far less cause. I *knew* that I could trust you."

"We're meant to trust each other. We're both stronger when we do."

He searched her eyes, his features slowly softening with wonder. "You still love me, despite what you saw."

She touched his beautiful lower lip, reddened from kissing her. "You still love me, so that works out well."

"*Jesu.*" Tension ran out of his muscles in one big wave. "I'm an idiot."

"Don't start that again," Estelle said.

The scold lacked much of an edge. He was still inside her, and her body felt like caramel set in the sun—so warm, so safe, so peaceful now that their auras hummed together again as one. Edmund's faults, what he had of them, seemed unimportant to her. He might be a vampire, but surely he was allowed to be human. *She* had no intention of trying to be perfect after all.

Estelle, he murmured into her mind, amused and tender and probably more thankful for her forgiveness than he needed to be. *You are perfect.*

Estelle smiled and let her eyelids drop. She could sleep, she thought—nice and soundly, as she hadn't in a long while.

They slept, but there was no "perchance" about the dream. The moment Edmund saw Frank, he knew the vision was real. In all his nightmares, he'd never imagined his enemy without legs. Had this been an ordinary dream, it might have pleased him. In this one, all he felt was a tightening dread. Pen was hostage to a former ally, Ben was wheezing like an old man, and Sally was God knew where. Ben was Edmund's touchstone, but Edmund couldn't do more than brush his thoughts. They were too agonized to hold on to.

"Holy hell," Estelle gasped, bolting up from the bed in synchrony with him. Her hand was pressed to her trembling breasts as if to keep her heart from escaping. "I didn't know that reestablishing our bond would make us dreamwalk this fast."

"Could you tell where they were?"

Estelle nodded jerkily. "Texas. Someplace called Amarillo. I thought I caught a glimpse of Sally in a cave with Li-Hua, but that could have been Ben's fears."

"You saw more than I did." Edmund was pacing beside the bed, though he could not recall leaving it. Distracted, he pushed his hand through his hair. "We have to get to America. Li-Hua will be desperate now that Frank's been caught. And she's the more dangerous of the pair. From what Sally told you in her calls, she's stolen a lot of power. I don't think all of them together can handle her."

"I'll start packing, but—" Estelle took one of his hands in hers. "Even with Percy as our pilot, traveling to America will take days."

"I can take us." Edmund's head was cold, his voice not quite familiar.

"You?" Estelle didn't seem to doubt him, just to be surprised. "How?"

"Nim Wei says I've gained the ability to translocate, to move instantaneously from place to place. You saw me do it once."

"On the ramparts. When you thought I wasn't safe up there by myself." Estelle looked up at him and bit her lip. "Edmund, not to throw cold water, but crossing the ocean seems a good bit harder than popping up a wall."

"I know." He rubbed his face in frustration. "I shouldn't have said I'd take us. It would be better for me to make the attempt alone."

"If—" Estelle hesitated, drawing his gaze back to her. "If Nim Wei knows about this power, perhaps she can help you use it. Perhaps she could go, too."

"You wouldn't mind?"

"Edmund."

He laughed at her soft rebuke. "Very well. You're better at trusting than I am. It would be good to bring another master into the fight. Durand's close to that level, but he isn't in Li-Hua's league. I'm not certain I am myself."

"Together you would be." Estelle's confidence took his breath. She rose and pulled on a dressing gown, her gorgeous naked body momentarily robbing him of thought. He had to blink before he could focus on her eyes again.

"I'd want to come," she added as she tied the belt. "Assuming Nim Wei thinks this plan is viable. I believe we've established that you're stronger when I'm with you. Or steadier anyway."

Wistful, he smoothed her hair behind her ear and shoulder. "Are *you* stronger with me?"

Estelle laughed outright, the sound so sweet it caused his eyes to burn. "Are you having me on? When you're beside me, I feel like an Amazon!"

* * *

Nim Wei had taken over Graham's cellar rooms. She found them cozy with the brown velvet curtains to warm the walls. The suite was masculine, it was true, but its red-and-cream patterned rugs weren't so different from what she had in her fortress beneath London. If she had to remain here for the duration of her good deed, she preferred to be comfortable.

That good deed might be completed sooner than she'd thought. The moment Edmund and Estelle appeared at her door, she could see they'd reestablished their connection. Edmund looked like he'd shed a century overnight, and Estelle simply glowed. In Nim Wei's experience, only humans could radiate pure happiness like that.

"So," she said, leaning against the door frame with her arms crossed beneath her breasts. "Come to tell me I can go home?"

The lovebirds exchanged wary looks.

"Er," Edmund hemmed. "We are, of course, very grateful for your assistance. Coming here to help Estelle control me was above and beyond the call."

"But?"

"But I could use your advice about something else."

Nim Wei was startled to discover that this pleased her. To hide her reaction, she turned and went into the room. She poured wine for the three of them, having found Bridesmere's supply of reds to her taste.

"It's not spiked," she said when Estelle hesitated to take hers. "With anyone."

"I'm here about my ability to translocate," Edmund said, handily masking his beloved's embarrassment. "Since I only did it the first time by accident, I'm hoping you could explain more fully how it works."

Nim Wei sat in a chair, crossed her legs, and sipped. "I'm not certain I can help you. Translocating is your skill, not mine—peeved though I am to acknowledge that. I've only heard about the gift secondhand."

"The thing is—" Clearly thinking better of remaining on his feet, Edmund took the chair across from hers, leaning forward as Estelle moved behind its back. Estelle's hand slid to his shoulder as if no better home for it existed. "We have a need to get to America very quickly, and I don't know if I can cover that distance."

"With a passenger, I take it?" Nim Wei drew her thumb around the rim of her goblet. "I've heard such feats are possible, but I think you'd need a bit more . . . wattage, as electricians say."

Surprisingly, the lovebirds had the self-control to zip their mouths while Nim Wei considered how much further she wished to involve herself. On the one hand, helping Edmund might be dangerous. On the other, the idea of one of her oldest detractors being in her debt was delectable.

"You're going after Frank and Li-Hua?" she asked.

"Frank has been captured," Edmund informed her. "Li-Hua remains at large. I think the others will need help handling her when she inevitably comes to Frank's rescue."

Nim Wei set down her glass and turned her upper foot in a circle. "I'd enjoy being part of that." More than *enjoy*, actually. It was *her* rule Frank and Li-Hua had rebelled against. Squashing them would be satisfying in the extreme—not that Edmund needed to know that. "I'll do it. I'll share my power with you. Coupled with yours, it ought to be enough to get you anywhere in the world."

The manner in which Edmund's jaw dropped was comical.

"We can take a few practice runs," she added. "You and me at first, and then you and me and Estelle. Maybe start with a hop across the Channel to Paris."

"London," Estelle suggested faintly. "There isn't as much to drown in between here and there."

Nim Wei laughed, the warmth of the sound as pleasant to her throat as wine. "We won't be crossing water. We'll be folding the very fabric of the universe."

"You're sure?" Edmund said, having recovered his power of speech. "You'd share your energy with me?"

Nim Wei's laugh settled to a grin. The urge to tease him

was as irresistible as it was new. She wasn't used to feeling gently fond of him. "It's a funny thing, Edmund, how everyone seems to trust you more than you trust yourself."

Her onetime lover had enough of Estelle's blood in him that he blushed.

They survived experimental hops to London, Edinburgh, and finally Paris with Estelle. The City of Lights was beautiful at night. Edmund reveled in Estelle's sharp intake of breath at the illuminated Arc de Triomphe. As to that, Nim Wei might have been impressed herself, despite her power being the petrol that was revving his engine. Auriclus had indeed given him a present when his death pushed Edmund into elder status. It had been too long since he'd felt this in command of himself.

"How do you know what to do?" Estelle marveled when they reappeared in the dark courtyard at Bridesmere.

Edmund had his arms around her, and she was looking up, just a little, into his eyes. Their closeness in height felt more satisfying than ever. "I'm not sure I can explain it. It's as if there are rooms in my head where I stashed the gifts Auriclus gave me. When I'm ready to open the door, I have access to a whole new clockwork. I look at the gears, I understand more or less what they do, but—truthfully—they turn themselves."

"*Very* specific," Nim Wei said, a roll of eyes in her tone. She stood beside them on the grass, her delicate hand wrapped firmly but not tightly around his elbow. "Though I do thank you for getting our clothes there and back this time."

To leave her current outfit to the Frogs would have been a crime. Nim Wei's trousers and vest were of skintight leather dyed a red so deep it reminded him of fresh blood. A coal black Chinese dragon reared up the back of her sleeveless vest, which bared the smoothly muscled arms of a swordswoman. Her boot heels, also black, were sharp enough to stab hearts. Compared to her, Edmund and Estelle appeared dowdy. They were wearing regular street clothes.

Edmund dropped the arm Nim Wei was using as her anchor from Estelle's waist. He suspected she didn't relish being so much shorter than the two of them.

"Thank you," he said. "Your power was quite helpful."

The hint of annoyance smoothed from Nim Wei's face. With hooded eyes, she smiled at him. "Please," she said, cool as cream. "You've only seen a fraction of the force I possess."

She was right. He hadn't imagined the whole of it. She put her hand in his this time, pressing their skin together, palm to cool palm. Edmund felt a buzz penetrate his fingers a second before the door to her full resources blew open.

He couldn't contain his gasp at the scope of it. He and Nim Wei's strength might be similar, but her power was amazingly orderly. More than her many centuries explained this. It was her nature, he saw, to make a place for everything and put everything in it. She controlled herself—body, thoughts, feelings—and had been doing so since before she became *upyr*. Even her mysticism was a form of control, a means of allowing herself to bend with the flow of the universe. To her, magic wasn't magic; it was a pattern behind a pattern that sufficient contemplation allowed her to exploit.

Ruthless she might be, and dangerous, without a doubt. She was not, however, the soulless monster he'd sometimes thought.

Edmund was almost certain he owed her an apology.

"Enough," she said, her energy slapping him back a step. "I didn't give you leave to read me."

"Forgive me," he said, adding a polite bow. When Nim Wei nodded, he turned his gaze to Estelle. "Are you ready, love?"

Her lovely gray eyes were wide. She must have caught a wisp of what he'd seen in Nim Wei. Shaking herself, she slid her arm around his waist. Edmund did the same to her, so that they held each other securely. Her closeness by his side felt so right he couldn't fathom how he'd ever pushed her away.

"I'm ready," she said.

Rocking L Ranch

Graham could see they weren't going to get anywhere soon with Frank, not after Roy arrived with Pen. Legs or no legs, the fact that Frank's pear blossom was collecting hostages heartened him.

"I need clothes," Graham announced, and slipped off to the ranch's back bedrooms to search for some. Neither Ben nor Roy liked him leaving, but that was too bad. Graham wasn't going to do anything that might get Pen or Sally killed. He simply didn't care to stand about in his altogether while they worked to break this impasse.

The jeans and shirt he found most likely belonged to the taller of the two guards he'd killed. Because they were all that fit, Graham couldn't worry that this was macabre.

"Get back here now!" he heard Roy shout as he buttoned the worn blue shirt.

Graham wondered if strolling back slowly might be a good idea. Maybe the high-strung new *upyr* would take a misstep if he was rattled. Wondering was all he had time for before he stiffened. A low but powerful rumble was vibrating through the atmosphere. Though the sound was barely audible, it was foreboding, making his nerves squirm beneath his skin. Was the storm worsening, or had Li-Hua changed her strategy and come here? Did vampires who could fly sound like rocket trails?

He sped back to the room where Frank was. Here, the basso growl deepened, so intense that Graham's vision of the others rippled like a heat mirage. Pen and his brother seemed oblivious to the effect, but Durand had his head up to scent the air.

What in blazes? Graham thought, his fists clenching instinctively at the strong creeping sensation. It ceased with a pop in his ears like a lift going up too fast. He had to blink at what he saw then.

Three more people stood in the firelit room: Edmund— looking much better than when they'd left him—Estelle, and the vampire queen of London. Realizing his mouth hung open, Graham forced it shut.

As Pen's old mentor might have said, it appeared the cavalry was here.

From the traveler's perspective, the transition from one location to another was instantaneous. Prepared for it, Nim Wei took in the situation with a single sweep of her gaze: Frank in the chair, Graham's confusion, the brand-new *upyr* with his hostage. Li-Hua's mark was very strongly on him, but more than that, he seemed to be harboring an active link to her. Rather than try to break it, Nim Wei filed this information away for possible later use. She passed a quick, silent message for Edmund to do the same. Though he was more concerned than she was for the unknown girl's safety, he complied grudgingly. Nim Wei's eyelids slitted when her attention lit on Durand. Those sloe black irises and shoulder-length raven hair were hard to forget. "I remember you," she said. "After I made you, I left you under Maurice's rule in Geneva."

"You did," he conceded, offering her a smooth, crisp bow.

Maurice's rule appeared not to have taken. As a blood-drinker and her get, Durand should have smelled like she did: a hint of books and ink and building stone. Disturbingly, his scent was more like a river running through a city than the city itself. His aura reeked of independence . . . and of power. Nim Wei frowned to herself. She really was careful not to create hordes of potential masters, but now and then a few did crop up.

"Do you wish to debate my fealty now?" he asked
blandly.

A snort escaped her control. Durand already knew the
answer to that. With the subtlest of smiles, he ripped off
the tape that gagged her former bodyguard.

"You're free to speak," he said.

Frank sneered at him, his handsome face haggard. "I'll
only tell them what I told you. Nothing will make me sell
out my beloved."

Edmund's patience broke. He stepped forward, his fury
throbbing through him like the strange storm outside.
Frank and Li-Hua had threatened his family, his existence,
and his most basic integrity. Nim Wei subscribed to different morals, but she understood what his meant to him. The
pair had come so close to breaking him, part of him still
wondered if they would have. That alone was motivation
for a large serving of vengeance.

Wait, she said through their connection. *Let me handle
him.*

Edmund stared at her in disbelief. They hadn't brought
man-made weapons. Edmund's gift wouldn't work if they
carried iron. Instead, his power was a weapon, and every
drop of his energy tensed to refuse her.

I know Frank, she said. *He guarded me for two hundred
years. The things he wants, the things he fears—they're all
an open book to me.*

He tried to destroy my family! Edmund's mind lashed
back. *I deserve my pound of flesh from him.*

*You deserve to have this finished. Let me do that for
you. Let me use the darkness you've always feared. Trust
me, I won't let either of them off easy.*

Edmund barred her from his thoughts like a door slamming. She saw the struggle inside him only in his eyes.
They flamed so bright they'd stopped glittering.

"Very well," he said, stepping stiffly back to clear a path
for her.

Nim Wei smiled at the telltale catch in Frank's breathing, sure sign that an *upyr*'s nerve was strained. He didn't
struggle in his chains, but his eyes were abruptly whiter

around the rims. No idiot, he didn't want to be left to her sweet mercies.

"Ah, Frank," she said, her lips curving up enough to show fangs. "There may be less of you to love tonight, but I have missed playing with you . . ."

Li-Hua sat on her heels in the dirt of the silver mine, fighting to throw off the irritation that distracted her. She should have taken the other woman hostage. The little blonde was getting on her nerves.

Happily, the chit had only cast up her accounts once, but ever since she'd been huddled in the shadows by the wall, shivering like a rabbit while sneaking frightened looks at the lump in Li-Hua's pants pocket. She was thinking it was the correct shape to be their soul-sucking box, then wondering if she ought to work up the courage to snatch it.

"I should kill you for considering it," Li-Hua finally snapped.

The girl shrank back with a low whimper. Her thoughts were still buzzing, though, so Li-Hua tuned them out, drawing in and letting out a breath to return her focus to the link between her and her new child. Roy's signet ring glinted within the lambency of her palm, rolling back and forth, back and forth, until her vision shifted and she saw the ranch through his eyes again.

Her body stiffened when she recognized who'd come. Their queen was there—their *former* queen, she corrected. Nim Wei was nothing compared to Li-Hua's current magnificence. An ant beneath her shoe. A smudge ground into concrete.

But Nim Wei didn't know this yet. She sauntered across the room in her snug red leather and her high-heeled boots, acting for all the world as if she still had some right to Frank. Li-Hua wet her lips as she watched Frank's gaze slip up and down the queen's tight body. *He's just looking*, Li-Hua told herself. No male could help doing that when the bitch queen flaunted herself.

"Remembering?" Nim Wei suggested, hands braced on

either arm of Frank's chair. "All the things I did to you in bed? All the times I made it hurt so good?"

"Whore," Frank accused hoarsely.

Nim Wei leaned close enough to drag her nose up his neck. "You're the one who was getting paid. I'd say that makes you the person that term applies to."

She did something with her hand that made Frank cry out—dug her scarlet talons into his stump, Li-Hua thought. When she nipped his earlobe, drawing a bead of blood, Frank shivered involuntarily.

"I always knew, didn't I? Where the pain would be the most exquisite? I remember how you'd beg for me." Her voice changed to an uncanny mimicry of Frank's. " 'Please, mistress. Please, my queen, let me come.' Sometimes you were even chained up like this."

"I outgrew that," Frank said, his noble features glistening with sweat. "When I found a real woman to give my heart."

"A real woman." Nim Wei's derisive chuckle made Li-Hua burn. The queen's glowing white hands slithered down Frank's chest. "That would explain why your cock is about to burst what's left of your trousers. Tell me where she is, Frank, and I won't make you beg too long."

Frank jumped as her hands closed around his crotch, his inhalation loud enough to echo off the adobe walls.

"Ah," she said, suddenly sliding one set of fingers into Frank's pocket. "What have we here?"

"*No*," Li-Hua growled, her teeth grinding together. The bitch had found Frank's silver pocket watch, the one Li-Hua had used to hide a trio of iron nuggets soaked in her blood. Keeping the timepiece on his person had allowed her beloved to share her barriers to being read. Without it, even with his recent huge gains in power, Nim Wei might be able to ram her way through Frank's walls.

It was too much to hope that she wouldn't understand what she'd discovered.

"Catch," Nim Wei said, tossing the watch to Edmund Fitz Clare, their once-upon-a-time captive.

"Frank won't give in," Li-Hua muttered. "It's me he

loves. We're stronger than she is now, and he did all of this
for me."

She shuddered when Nim Wei gripped Frank's jaw
and forced him to accept her kiss. She was cutting him
deliberately with her fangs, drinking him in through the
little wounds as her tongue worked his. Frank began to
struggle in earnest as he fought the pleasure her bite could
bring.

"Let me in," Nim Wei ordered. "Let me in, and I'll make
you come the way you used to when you were with me."

"Never," he swore, straining against his chains. "*Never.*"

Li-Hua gripped the signet ring so tightly its edge sliced
her. She could feel what Frank was feeling, how his sex
was big and throbbing, how he yearned to succumb to Nim
Wei's dark ecstasy. The intensity of their interaction caused
it to bleed to the awareness of the others. Roy Blunt could
read Frank now, and consequently so could she.

She'd thought she knew every corner of Frank's mind,
thought his love for her was the sort the ages would sing
about. All this time, he'd been harboring a secret. Though
he'd tried to make Li-Hua his everything, in his deepest
heart she was nothing but the bitch queen's shadow, an imi-
tation that never rose to the original. From her looks to her
clothes to the lacquer on her fingernails, she was not quite
as beautiful, not quite as clever, not quite as nuanced an
artist in cruelty. Even as he swore eternal love to Li-Hua,
Frank knew in his soul he'd always be enslaved to their
queen.

Li-Hua went cold from head to toe in shock. It couldn't
be true. Simply couldn't. She was Nim Wei's superior. *She*
was the one who was born to rule. The destiny Frank had
promised her was no lie.

Then Nim Wei drove her teeth into Frank's neck.

His tortured body burst its bounds with pleasure, his
aura flaring, his personal world quaking violently. Seed
shot from his balls in long, fiery rushes, dragged from
some reservoir only the queen could plumb. On and on the
orgasm stretched until he finally sagged in complete surrender against the chair. The front of what remained of his

pants was black as he rolled his hips one last time with sensual languor.

His moan was unmistakable for anything but profound relief.

At last, he thought dreamily. *At last, she's claimed me again.*

Nim Wei drew back from him and licked his blood from her lips, her head rotating to catch Roy's eyes directly. Somehow, the queen knew Li-Hua was watching.

"Thank you, Frank," she said, her smugness too terrible to be borne. "I believe you've given me everything we need."

Sally truly could not cringe any harder than she was. When the vampiress leaped to her feet and screamed with fury, all Sally's body managed was an exhausted twitch.

"No," Li-Hua shrieked, her hands balled tight, the glare of her skin white-hot.

To Sally's amazement, Li-Hua rammed the wall of the mine, not with her fists but her skull, pounding into the rock-hard surface with no apparent fear for her brain. Boulder-size chunks fell into the shaft as this continued, followed by one of the supporting timbers from the ceiling.

Stop, Sally tried to say, fearing she'd bury them. A muffled squeak was the only sound that pushed from her throat. Thankfully, Li-Hua ceased her banging a moment later. She stood poker straight in the center of her own glow, her body unnaturally motionless.

"They're dead," she announced, though Sally doubted she was meant to hear. "Both of them die tonight."

Both of whom? Sally wondered, but then she noticed the vampiress was levitating, her short black boots hovering half a foot from the floor. Li-Hua's eyes met hers, their surface jittering insanely. Whatever consciousness dwelled behind them, it was very much not human. Faced with that alien gaze, Sally's heart faltered. She was going to die. She and her baby.

Then, as if Li-Hua's body were more board than flesh,

the vampiress tipped forward and flew up the shaft past her.

She flew, Sally thought, her heart starting up again violently. *She flew like a blinking missile right through the air.*

She'd also left Sally alone in a pitch-black mine.

Shaking like she had a palsy, Sally clutched the wall and struggled to her feet. Dirt and pebbles rattled to the floor, but she tried her best not to flinch. This was her chance to get out of here—preferably before the crazy fangster returned.

Nim Wei didn't know if the others realized what was coming, but she had a fair idea. Li-Hua's psyche was no more a mystery to her than Frank's.

Edmund was quick enough on the uptake to use the fledgling's split attention against him. One leaping, pinpoint kick to his shoulder separated Roy—and his knife—from his hostage.

"Leave that," Nim Wei ordered when Durand reached for the gun Roy had forced him to set on a table earlier. Durand's black eyes widened, but he obeyed. Then she noticed Graham had a double-barreled shotgun braced to his chest.

"No," she said. "Keep that hidden by your leg until I say. You don't want Li-Hua to change her mind about which target to shoot first."

"She wouldn't." Frank's horrified understanding erased the last of his lassitude.

Nim Wei grinned ferally. "Want to bet, lover boy?"

"Stay down," she added to the three humans.

They had just time to duck behind the cowhide couch when Li-Hua burst through the wall beside the fireplace, not unlike a human-shaped wrecking ball. Bits of pulverized adobe scattered as Nim Wei threw a beam of her aura far enough to highlight the abandoned gun. True to her expectations, Li-Hua grabbed it up as soon as she spotted it. Also no surprise was her turning the thing on Frank.

"Bastard," she hissed, aiming with both hands.

"No," Frank pleaded. "Beloved, I'm so—"

She depressed the trigger before *sorry* could come out. To Nim Wei's pleasure, Li-Hua was an excellent shot. The roaring iron bullet left a heart-size tunnel through Frank's chest. They could actually see the chair's upholstery behind him. Li-Hua seemed taken aback by the damage, and by the threads of electricity that crackled out from the maw she'd made.

Evidently, she'd been too caught up in her fury to realize the hit would be fatal.

She moaned in dismay, tottering back from her lover, the hand that held the pistol sagging to her side.

"Now," Nim Wei said to Graham.

"No!" Li-Hua screamed as Frank disappeared and the iron chains that had held him dropped.

Even as the links clattered to the floor, Graham's gun exploded twice in quick succession, the spray of pellets knocking Li-Hua back in jerks. More blue lightning danced from the many spots where the iron had hit. Li-Hua lost her grip on the pistol and clutched her breast.

"Damn you," she snarled at Nim Wei. "I'll see you roast—"

She was falling to her knees when she vaporized as well.

And then something absolutely unexpected happened. Dozens upon dozens of translucent rainbow bubbles materialized in the spaces where the couple's bodies used to be. Nim Wei's eyes went round at the sight. Edmund gasped and—interestingly—Estelle did as well. These apparitions must have been the souls Frank and Li-Hua stole. For a moment, they simply bobbed in the air as though confused. Nim Wei tried to sense them more clearly, but if they had thoughts, their language was too foreign. They began to make the faintest ringing sound, like the chiming of fine crystal. Then, one by one, in a fashion so orderly she would have sworn it was rational, each glowing sphere whizzed up the chimney.

Nim Wei found this intriguing but no reason for paralysis. She strode to the spot where Li-Hua had been standing and crouched down. The shotgun pellets hadn't disappeared with her body. Nim Wei picked one up and sniffed it, grimacing only slightly at the burn of the iron on her fingertips. One more fallen item merited retrieval, after which she rose and turned to Graham.

His big, broad chest was going up and down like a human's.

"You held back," she said, more curious than angry. "You didn't shoot Li-Hua until she knew she'd killed Frank."

Graham let out one last exhalation. "It seemed right. For her and us."

Nim Wei supposed this was true, though his delay could have given Li-Hua the opportunity to turn that deadly gun on her.

"Is it over?" Edmund's younger son, Ben, asked.

"Yes," Nim Wei said, immense satisfaction in the word. She couldn't remember when she'd last experienced a fight this rewarding.

"Good," Ben responded, pushing to his feet. "Maybe we could get Sally now."

"I can do that," Graham and his lover said in unison.

Amarillo

Nim Wei left the room in Graham and Pen's company, presumably to share what she'd gleaned from Frank concerning Sally's whereabouts. The silence they left behind them underscored the ringing in Edmund's ears. It was over. Frank and Li-Hua were dead. That accomplishment felt so monumental, he hardly knew how to take it in.

Regardless of whether he could, there were still matters to see to. The first thing he did when his sense returned was assist Ben onto the long sofa. Durand leaned against the opposite wall with the attitude of a man who'd seen an amusing play. What his opinion on all this was, Edmund neither knew nor cared.

Weakened as Ben was by the peculiar weather, he didn't refuse Edmund's help sinking down. As he took a place beside him, Edmund's heart ached for the ordeal the boy had endured. Estelle sat on Ben's other side, closer than Edmund. Though a mere twenty-two years old, Ben was a man by mortal standards, and soon to have a child himself. All the same, Edmund sensed his son took comfort in him and Estelle supporting him from both sides. Despite her youth, Estelle had such a steady, loving way about her, she couldn't help but be a motherly figure.

"Graham and Pen will bring Sally back," she said, chafing his arm up and down. "As quick and safe as can be."

Ben nodded, then was jerked forward by a coughing spasm.

Edmund held his shoulders. "Let me heal you," he said.

"No," Ben choked out, his eyes tearing helplessly. Unable to speak, he put his hand on Edmund's chest to hold him off.

Edmund didn't understand, but he stopped moving.

"Sorry," Ben said when he finally could. Collapsing back, he blinked and met Edmund's eyes. "I'm sorry, Dad. I don't want to hurt your feelings, but I'd rather not become what you are. I'm different from Graham. The changes you've already made are enough for me."

"Oh," Edmund said, blinking a bit himself. Ben's admission stung, but not as much as he might have thought.

"Please try to understand," Ben went on. "You were, *are*, a wonderful father to all of us—even more wonderful than I realized when I thought you were human. I'll never be anything but grateful you adopted us."

"But?"

"But I don't want to have to worry about hurting my daughter. I'd be such a young *upyr* if you finished transforming me."

Edmund found himself smiling as he touched his son's earnest face. He must have done something right to raise boys this sweet. "Ben, what happened in Switzerland was an accident, because I hadn't yet learned to master my new powers. What I do now will only heal you. I'd never change you against your will."

Ben nodded wordlessly, his lips pressed together, his eyes welling up for reasons other than the dust. Feeling something raw ease inside himself, Edmund held Ben's head to press a kiss to his brow. Though he couldn't bring his dead sons back, he could love the ones he had.

"It's all right," he murmured as a tremor Ben could not control ran across his shoulders. "You've been through a lot, and you stayed strong for Sally. Now you can relax a little. Now you can let me look out for you."

Ben's arms came around him and held him tight, for a moment just a boy again. Estelle rubbed his back and smiled at Edmund, her beautiful gray eyes shining with a love for both of them that didn't require words.

* * *

When Graham and Pen stepped outside the house, the stillness was so unexpected it dizzied her.

"The storm," she said. "It's over."

The ranch looked as if it had been hit by a gray blizzard, though the balmy temperature made that impression a bit surreal. The little old sweeping ladies in North Fork would have their work cut out for them tomorrow.

"Look at the stars," Graham said, moving close enough to brush her side.

The stars were lovely, bright as diamonds, but when Graham's big hand curled around hers, she no longer had the concentration to admire them.

"Pen," he said in that serious, soft voice of his.

She closed her eyes. Their big adventure was almost over. Soon he'd have no reason to be here. He'd return to England with his family, and she'd try not to crumble into the pit of missing him. She suspected avoiding that would be even harder than the last time.

"We should get Sally," she said.

He turned her by the shoulders to face him. "Just one thing before we go. I think it's waited long enough."

This was it then. His thank-you-for-your-help and let's-stay-friends speech. Determined not to be a coward, Pen gritted her teeth and met his gaze. Graham looked surprisingly good in his borrowed cowboy garb—tall and capable and at home. Clearly as reluctant to hurt her as she was to be hurt, he drew a steadying breath.

"I'm in love with you," he said.

Pen's thoughts momentarily refused to form. "You're in love with me."

She supposed disbelief wasn't the response he'd hoped for. A muscle bunched in his jaw, giving him the stubborn look he shared with his sister.

Somehow unable to prevent herself, Pen set her hands on her waist. "Is that why you stopped having sex with me? Because if it is, maybe you could love me a little less."

Graham's eyes darkened angrily. "That's all you have to say to me—that maybe I could *love you a little less*?"

Pen started to make a smart retort, then stopped. Truth was, she didn't know what to say. She'd been so braced for him to reject her, she wasn't sure what she felt. Something, that was certain. Something fizzy and excited that was far too dangerous to trust. She thought she'd been brave to admit to herself she loved him. This, though, this idea that they were in love with each other, that they might try to be together for more than sex or mild affection, demanded more courage than she had.

If they tried and failed at *that*, the damage would be bigger than a simple broken heart.

"Pen?" he asked more gently.

Her eyes were burning, probably awash with mortifying tears. "Could we, maybe, discuss this later?"

Her voice was as rough as if she'd spent the last hour screaming. Graham's expression softened, his anger running out all at once.

"Yes," he said. "Of course we could."

Pen wasn't certain why, but his understanding increased her wariness. Maybe he sensed this, because his face split into a grin that creased it more widely, more boyishly than she'd seen it do when he was human.

"Hold on," he said, and swung her into his arms.

She squeaked when he began running at vampire speed and clutched his neck in spite of herself. His hands held her securely, but no one made her feel more feminine than Graham, nor could she doubt he was showing off. What he was doing was an obvious display of power. His fangs had run out with enjoyment, which added a unique dimension to his grin.

The whole business excited her more than seeing Nim Wei trick the truth out of their enemy.

This was not a reminder she was easy with. The things London's queen had done might have been a means to an important end, but they were also awful. Watching her cruelty arouse Frank, seeing him jerk in those chains as he climaxed explosively, shouldn't have made Pen wet. She was lucky Graham had been her partner in her erotic experiments. He'd never hurt her more than she wanted.

Then again, he wouldn't hurt her, period, if she let herself lose him.

Glum and rattled, she was relieved when they reached the old silver mine Nim Wei had described. Pen remembered spotting it on a survey map of the area. A heap of tumbleweeds blocked the blackness of the entrance, the skeletal bushes anchored by a tall drift of dust. The place seemed so forsaken it wasn't pleasant to imagine Sally being held hostage here.

Slowing to a halt, Graham set Pen carefully on her feet, his arm squeezing her shoulders as if he couldn't not touch her.

"Do you hear that?" he asked.

She heard something, faint and scrabbling. "Turn on your glow."

Graham dropped his glamour and moved closer to the mine. "Sally? Sally, if that's you, stay where you are, and we'll rescue you."

The scrabbling stopped.

"Wait," came Sally's raspy voice. "I see your light. I'm almost there."

Pen laid her hand on Graham's sleeve to stop him from rushing in. "Let her. If she wants to get herself out, let her."

She didn't know how to explain that Sally would feel better later if she did this now. Graham stared at her, hopefully not thinking she was being unfeeling. Then he touched the side of her face, very lightly, and nodded.

"Help me clear the opening," he said.

Pen helped, though he hardly needed her assistance. It wasn't more than a minute before Sally stumbled through the opening they'd made. Though shaky and covered in dust, she appeared to be in one piece.

The instant she could reach him, she fell into Graham's arms and began to weep.

"Are you all right?" he asked, rocking her with his face

pressed into her curls. "Ben's fine. And Father's come. And Frank and Li-Hua are dead."

"Good," Sally said—to all of it, apparently.

The sight of tears dripping silently down Graham's cheeks tugged at Pen deep inside. Part of what she'd fallen in love with was his capacity to give his heart to his family without reserve. Even if she'd hated his little sister—which she didn't—she'd have been able to care for Sally for Graham's sake. It was true what people said, she guessed. The more you loved, the more love you had to give.

A bit uncomfortable with that, and knowing someone had to be practical, she dug her scarf from her trouser pocket and shook the worst of the dust from it.

"Pen!" Sally exclaimed, finally seeing her there.

Pen's offer of the scarf inspired another cry, this one of gratitude. With a happy sigh, Sally blew her nose into it.

When she finished, it was Pen's turn to be engulfed in her tight embrace. Somewhat at a loss, she tried to pat Sally soothingly.

"Pen," Sally said, laughing and crying at the same time. "You'd better stop helping us like this. If you don't, Ben and I might have to name our baby Penelope!"

Trusting the others to remain occupied with their reunions, Nim Wei drifted away to look for the man called Roy. He was a loose end, and she wasn't fond of them. She found him in the shambles of the cellar, in what smelled like a closet for onions. He'd been tortured down here, she saw, which made this an odd place to seek refuge.

"You should have run farther if you didn't want to be caught," she said.

Then she opened the door on him and the vegetables.

He was sitting backed into the corner of the narrow space, on the verge of cringing but managing to refrain. She noticed his blue eyes crinkled when he squinted into her glow. He was one of those mortals whose greatest beauty doesn't come in the flush of youth. As an *upyr*, he appeared around forty—seasoned but not old. Though his

fangs were extended, they didn't look threatening. Probably he was too hungry to pull them up. The newly made
had strong appetites.

She sensed him trying to steady himself.

"I know you've got to kill me," he said in his strange,
broad drawl. "They turned me into a monster."

Nim Wei's mouth slanted as she crouched down to his
level. The scent of potatoes joined the stronger one of
onions. "Since I'm a *monster* myself, that might not be the
most diplomatic term."

"You're not like me. No one makes you do things against
your will. No one makes you want to hurt your friends. I
still want to drink from 'em, even now that those two are
dead. I'm too weak to be one of you."

He said this with an ironic dignity. Nim Wei let her
hands dangle from her knees. "It's true few humans are
really suited to being changed, though you weren't as weak
as some Frank and Li-Hua chose."

"They tainted me."

She liked that word even less than *monster.*

"Perhaps." She sorted through the memories she'd
appropriated from Graham's lover. Reading minds had
always been a strong gift for her. "Where are your men?"

"Some are dead. Some got away when I was captured.
They'll be waitin' on me to get back."

He dragged his tongue around his fangs, thinking—
reluctantly—that the strapping male humans in his care
would be very vulnerable to him.

Nim Wei cocked her head at him. "Didn't they let you
feed?"

Blunt rolled his lips together and shook his head.

"Do you want to?"

"Chrissake, ma'am," he said. "Stop playin' with me and
finish this."

"Answer the question: Do you want to feed? And I'm
not asking what your body wishes you would do. I'm asking what you want as a man."

"No." He pushed himself straighter on the sacks of vegetables. "I don't reckon I have the strength to hold off much

longer, but if I had my druthers, I'd go back to bein' a mortal man."

"Well, then, Captain Blunt, I guess this is your lucky night." From her pocket she pulled out the dragon box, which she'd gathered up from the floor where Li-Hua had disappeared.

The fledgling jumped to his feet in horror, shrinking back against the closet's boards. "You want my soul?"

"No," Nim Wei said, surprised to discover how true this was. She wasn't at all tempted to go down the road Frank and Li-Hua had. "I prefer to cultivate my powers naturally. This little trinket, however, has more tricks than that up its sleeve. With your permission, I can use it to reverse what was done to you."

"You can change me back?" Blunt breathed.

"I may be the only *upyr* alive who knows how, considering I was acquainted with the vampire who made the box. Naturally, I'd trust you to remember I did this favor, and not put me on your associates' list of 'bad' vampires."

She liked that he didn't answer at once, but took a moment to weigh the deal. He knew she could kill him if she wanted, that she made this offer because she believed he'd have some value as an ally.

"I'm a man who honors his debts," he said.

Satisfied, she flipped the metal box open one-handed.

Ben was the one who noticed Nim Wei hadn't come back from her discussion with Graham and Pen. Breathing easier now, and preferring not to sit on his thumbs while Graham rescued Sally, he told his father he'd look for the queen.

"Be careful," Edmund warned. "Nim Wei helped us, but she isn't a tame tiger."

Ben nodded, though he was almost too numb for caution. Now that the worst danger was defeated, the rest of his worries seemed to have free rein to race around his head.

He wasn't certain why, but his feet led him to the cellar door Li-Hua's earlier escape had turned to kindling. The steps behind were usable, the rosy luminescence at their bottom informing him he'd found something.

The sight of Nim Wei crouched over Pen's old boss made his stomach drop. The queen wasn't the only person they'd lost track of.

Roy was stretched on his back on the bare dirt floor, his eyes closed and sunken, while Nim Wei pressed the infamous dragon box to the center of his brow. Rays of crimson light sheared out from its jagged edges, making her slim white fingers look like they were on fire.

"Sh," she said without looking away from Roy. "He asked for this. I'm not hurting him."

"Losing his soul won't *hurt him*?" The queen was too intimidating to shout at, but Ben imagined she heard his horror.

"I'm turning back the change," she said. "He wants to be human again."

Roy groaned and stirred. "Jesus," he said. "That's about the worst hangover I ever felt."

He sat up with Nim Wei's help, propping his back on a half-broken set of shelves. Ben stepped closer nervously. Roy still looked younger than before, but that he was mortal was obvious. His color was a combination of flushed and green, his eyes too weary to keep open.

"Thank you," he said, closing them. "I don't think I've ever been so happy to feel like somethin' the cat dragged in."

Smiling faintly, Nim Wei rose smoothly to her feet. Ben braced himself as she turned to him. Roy was in no state to help him confront her. He was out like a light. Left to his own resources, Ben gestured to the box she was snapping shut.

"We thought that poofed along with Li-Hua."

The curve of her mouth deepened. "Magic this old is hard to destroy."

"Maybe you should give it to my father. For safe-keeping."

Nim Wei's teeth flashed white with her quiet laugh. "Maybe your father should have warned me your sister's blood kills vampires."

Ben's eyebrows drew together at this apparent change of topic.

"Yes," Nim Wei murmured. "Imagine the target she'd be if that news got out, though odds would be even as to whether my kind would want to kill her or just keep her as a pet."

Ben's breath rushed out of him. "You wouldn't do that to her."

"I probably wouldn't," she corrected. "I don't want a pet myself, and—frankly—your father is more comfortable as a friend than an enemy. On the other hand, this puts you and I in the position to work a trade."

"A trade."

"Silence for silence."

Ben hesitated. Could he really leave that awful artifact in her hands, even to keep Sally safe?

Nim Wei lifted the box on the flattened palm of her hand. The dragon's ruby eyes were gleaming, but only in the reflection of the vampiress's glow.

"Take it," she said.

Ben eyed the thing like he would a snake. "Why?"

Nim Wei laughed again. "Because it will keep you from turning. No matter how powerful your father grows, no matter how long you stay with him, you'll never tip any farther over the edge."

It was everything he'd wanted wrapped in a bow, which made him twice as suspicious. "Why would you do that for me? That's a lot of power to give away."

"None at all," the queen dismissed. "I'll know where to find you if I want it back."

When Ben continued not to accept her gift, she took his hand and pressed the thing into it. Disturbingly, the tarnished brass was warmer than her skin.

"The casket is safe with you," she said. "You can't use it except in this one small way, and if everyone thinks it was destroyed, no one's going to look for it." She tilted her head at the sleeping man. "I'll erase this one's memory of me using it."

Something about her insistence gave Ben pause. Not

being able to read minds didn't mean he couldn't read people.

"You could destroy it," he said slowly. "If anyone knows how, it's you. You want me to have this because you care about my father, and I'm important to him. You have no intention of telling anyone about Sally's gift."

Nim Wei's dark brows winged up her white forehead, her expression wry enough to convince more confident men than Ben that their ideas were cracked.

"Please," she said. "I'm the bitch queen of London. My heart is as black as soot. Does my doing something for nothing really sound plausible?"

It was too close to dawn for Edmund to attempt to ferry all of them back to England—even supposing this wouldn't have exhausted him and Nim Wei. Luckily, they found a boardinghouse in North Fork where they could stay for the day.

Though Graham was nearly dead on his feet, he escorted Pen to her bedroom door.

His eyes were sleepy but calm as he stroked her hair from her face. Pen wished they could stand like this forever. Always on the same side. Never bickering.

"Tomorrow night," he said. "You and I will talk."

She pulled his hand down and held it. "Tomorrow night I'll be in Charleston."

"Charleston! Pen . . ."

"You need to be with your family, Graham. At least for now."

"I want—" He bent down from his greater height to catch her gaze. "Pen, I hope you understand I want *you* to be a part of my family."

Her throat tightened. Did she want that? She knew she wanted him, but his family was so much to him—maybe everything. Though her father loved her, she'd grown up playing second fiddle to his business. Was she prepared to take that kind of role with Graham? Did she even understand the level of devotion the Fitz Clares felt for each other? To be a part of that was alluring. She simply wasn't sure their circle could expand to include her.

"I have my own family matters to take care of," she said.

This was true, and it rang in her voice that way. With worry in his eyes, Graham ran his thumb across the back of her knuckles. He spoke with the thoughtful deliberation she couldn't believe she'd once thought was dull.

"I know it would be a mistake to push you. I know you have your own life, and that's been the case for some time. It isn't my intent to crowd you. It won't ever be."

She thought there must be a "but" coming after this. Instead, he carried her hand upward, pressing it to the slow and steady beat of his heart.

"I'll see you," he said, holding her eyes with his. "I won't let it be too long."

Then, down the faded and dusty carpet that lined the hall, he walked away without kissing her.

He left Pen consternated by her own inevitable conclusion: Graham Fitz Clare might just be the most perfect match for her in the world.

Peachtree Plantation

The columned house seemed different as Graham walked up the crushed-shell drive. The grounds remained lush, the Spanish moss still draping the spreading oaks. What was missing was the sense of neglect. Strings of tea lights lit the veranda against the dark. In the dappled light, he saw the grass had been clipped, creating stretches of actual lawn within the jungle of greenery.

Graham's inner tomcat wrinkled his nose at these signs of domestication, then decided it made no mind. Beyond the reach of the emerald lawn, the swamp was there as before. His cat would have plenty of exotic creatures to test its prowling skills on.

At the moment, Graham's cat was not his priority. It had been two weeks since he'd last seen Pen, almost more than his patience could tolerate. He'd caught hints from Pen's thoughts that he was headed in the right direction, but hints weren't guarantees. He was nervous and excited, and his cock had been hard as granite from the moment Percy's plane touched down. Percy's willingness to bring him was fortunate. Graham's vampire cousin had been quite provoked at being excluded from the fight in America. The only reason Percy had relented was because they seemed to have rooted out the last of Frank and Li-Hua's European cohorts.

Well, that and the fact that the trip let him tease Graham mercilessly.

But Graham could take a bit of chaffing—so long as Pen was happy to see him. He stepped up to the door and knocked, noting the fresh white paint on the house's exterior.

A smiling female servant let him into the entryway.

"Mr. Fitz Clare," she said, taking his hat from him. "We were hoping you'd come tonight."

Once inside, the house was warm in more than temperature. Everything was cleaned and polished—from the sparkling chandelier to the marble floor. The old water-stained wallpaper had been replaced with paint in soft pastel shades. The furnishings were the same antiques as before, but they, too, looked like they'd been cared for.

As Graham gazed around in wonder, he noticed two scents were gone.

"Pen's aunts have left," he said.

The servant turned back from the foot of the stairs, her grin wide and mischievous. "Oh, yes. Miss Pen sent them packing soon as she came back. You've never heard such whistling and singing as we had those first few days. Now, you wait here, you hear? I'll tell Miss Pen you've arrived."

Graham nodded, helpless to disobey, as the cheerfully efficient woman skipped up the sweeping steps. He would have liked to go up and greet Pen in private, but he supposed this was for the best—at least until he knew what kind of welcome he'd get.

"Graham," came Pen's voice from the landing.

He looked up and instantly knew why people said hearts could sing. Pen looked so utterly herself—slim and quick and stylish in a vaguely pajama-ish silk outfit. The matching tunic and trousers were a pale mint green embroidered with butterflies. Her wavy auburn bob was brushed to a gleam, and the sultry Southern heat had brought a becoming color into her skin. She could have been about to throw a smart cocktail party. Instead, this amazing woman was greeting him. His mouth stretched with a smile he could not hold in.

"You look *wonderful*," he said.

The blush in her cheeks deepened, which set him humming down to his bones.

"Stay there," he said, already bounding up to her. "I'll save you the trouble of the trip down."

She gasped, because he'd come up a bit too fast. Caught by surprise, her hands fluttered to his shoulders as his lightly clasped her waist.

"That's considerate of you," she drawled.

"I've been told my manners are impeccable."

She laughed, a soft and intimate sound. His body pounded in reaction, his hold on her tightening. He stretched his fingers to fan lower on her rear.

"You smell wonderful, too," he growled.

He gave her a tiny tug, impelling her hips closer. The moment they hit the solid length of his erection, her heat rose a few degrees. The evidence that she wanted him was a torment and a delight. His fangs were cutting into his lower lip, their hardness hankering for her softness just as his cockstand was.

"Don't kiss me here," she warned, her palms shoving ineffectually at his chest. Knowing what he did about her, he suspected she didn't mind him not moving. "Some of the servants are peeking around the doors."

He sensed them, too, more clearly than usual. Some had known Pen since she was a child. Others were dazzled by her New York glamour. None gave off a vibration of being unhappy that she was in charge.

"Just tell me where you want me," he said, "and I'll lay myself out as privately as you like."

That made her laugh as well. Grabbing his hand, she tugged him after her down the hall. Her eagerness had him giddy. When she stopped, he saw she'd kept the pretty blue bedroom for herself, the one he'd stayed in when they first came here.

The covers on the big, soft bed were turned down.

"Pen," he said, the breath he needed for her name stolen by the sudden slamming of his arousal.

"Before we . . . start," she said, her implication yet another kick to lust. "I want to ask . . . to be sure really . . ."

He wrenched his gaze from the bed to her. "To be sure of what?"

She wet her lips nervously. "I've been having the strangest dreams. Erotic dreams, about you." She cleared her throat as he began to grin. "Before I assume something that isn't true, I thought you might tell me how much of you was in them."

She lifted an item from the sheets that he hadn't noticed: a long white silk scarf, such as she often wore. It could have been the twin to the one he'd pinched and kept in his night table. That scarf had become his friend again while they were apart. He hadn't begrudged the waiting, but his hungers were too strong to do without release at all.

It was his turn to blush as she pulled the length of sheer material through her hand. "In my dreams, you used a scarf like this to pleasure yourself. You pretended it was me when you came."

His mouth was gaping, but he needed it open for extra air. "Yes," he said, a trifle hoarsely. "It's true I was doing that. I took a scarf of yours on the train back from Switzerland."

"*Switzerland*. I thought it was the one I gave Sally in Texas."

"No." He found himself smiling. "You've been under my skin for longer than you realize."

She bit her lip in a manner that made his blood throb between his legs. "So have you," she said in a rush.

Her confession warmed him from the inside out, until the love that welled up inside him was as strong as the desire. He wanted to swear he'd never disappoint her, that she'd never need to be afraid of admitting she cared again. Her next words drove the ability to speak lucidly from his brain.

"I want to make your dream come true," she said. "I want to use this scarf on you. I want *you* to be my prisoner."

"You—" His voice broke and then nothing else would come out.

"Take off your clothes," she said, the tremor beneath the order increasing his excitement. "Get on the bed. I'm going to hurt you a little. I know you've dreamed about your lover being rough."

"I've dreamed about *you*. You're the one whose mercy I want to be at."

Pen swallowed, and nodded, and watched his hands move with human slowness down the buttons of his shirt. His muscles were beautiful, precisely what she thought a man's chest should be. Considering how long it had been since she'd touched him, she couldn't resist helping him undress.

He closed his eyes as she eased off his sleeves, as she ran her hands down his strong, lovely arms. His nerves were very sensitive to her touch, responding with little shivers under his ivory skin. She loved her power over him, but even more, she loved his power over her. The shape of him, the way he narrowed from chest to hip, would have caused weaker women to swoon. His belt clanked as she drew it out from the loops that held it. The sight of the giant bulge beneath his waistband shoved yet more heat through her.

At some point, he'd shifted his shaft around until the crest pointed up. Imagining his hand in there, on himself, was more than her heart could stand.

She was on her knees before she knew it, the belt wrapped around her hand. Adoring his ungiving hardness, she turned her face like a cat across his cloth-covered erection. It was a short step from that to dragging her open mouth over him.

With a soft, pained sound, Graham's fingers tangled in her hair.

"Jesus," he said. "Pen."

She pulled his zipper down carefully. His cock pushed against it and then swung free. Even its weight could not pull the thing horizontal, a fact that made her fingers curl with longing. It took all her self-control not to touch him. He was so substantial, so thick and pulsing and hard. A bead of moisture gleamed on the slit in the tight-skinned head. She looked up and found him staring down at her with golden fire smoldering in his eyes. He wasn't trying to hide his fangs.

"Belt or scarf?" she asked.

The faintest flush stained his cheeks. "Belt," he burst out.

She wound the leather around his shaft until its jerking length was completely wrapped—exactly as he'd done with her stolen scarf in his dreams. Though she hadn't constricted the belt, his crown grew redder, wetter, that clear moisture trickling out as if the thought of what was coming was simply too exciting.

"Move back against the footboard." The order was so husky she was glad he had good hearing. "Grab the posts. If you let go or break them, I'll be angry."

He gripped the rice-carved mahogany, the position spreading and stretching the huge muscles of his chest. He must have liked obeying her. His diaphragm was moving faster with his breathing.

Breathing faster herself, Pen drew the scarf from where she'd dropped it on the mattress. His eyes followed its slow swing. "I can tie your wrist with this, or I can bind it around your balls."

He flinched at the second choice, but his cock jumped at the same time, rattling the dangling belt buckle. An image sprang full-blown into her mind, its clarity making her skin prickle. Heated fluid overran her sex. She knew what he wanted.

"Balls it is," she rasped.

She wrapped him tightly where his scrotum joined his body, around and around, until only enough silk remained for her to tie the ends. When they were secure, his balls stood out from the tourniquet, flushed and firm with high arousal. Accepting the invitation they presented, she bent forward and sucked one. Graham's reaction was almost all she'd hoped for. His legs began to tremble, his palms slapping the posts as he shifted them. Determined to affect him more, she turned her head and drew the other side of him into her mouth. His skin was silkier than a human's, the structures inside harder. Though she wasn't shy, her strongest suction could not pull him farther onto the cradle of her tongue.

"Pen," Graham groaned, his body writhing as helplessly as if she'd cuffed him.

"Can you come?" she asked against the pulse that was beating wildly inside his thigh. "Can you ejaculate when you're bound up like this?"

"I don't know," he gasped. "Probably. The constriction might make it easier to hold back."

"Do hold back," she said. "I don't want you coming anywhere but inside me."

"My climax might tear the scarf."

Any other man would have been bragging. Knowing he wasn't, Pen gave his balls a sharp admonitory tap with her nails. "Be sure that doesn't happen."

He squirmed around his enjoyment of the little sting. "I want to come inside you already. I didn't . . . pleasure myself as much as *upyr* my age need to."

He wasn't playing a role. He meant the warning in honesty. A delighted laugh bubbled up in her. "My God, Graham! You're too much fun to be true!"

He frowned, and she loved that, too.

"Graham," she purred into the musky scent of his groin. "I swear I'll make holding back worth your while."

Before he could argue, she fisted him around the leather, pumping him up and down as if he were bare. The little sounds he made were delicious. Pain. Hunger. Pleasure at the tight pressure on his cock. When she put her mouth on his crest and suckled, he cried out hoarsely. He tasted like heaven against the greedy swipes of her tongue. Getting him wet, feeling him heat and stiffen, was absolutely her pleasure.

He took what he gave her, begging with his body and not his words. He seemed not to want to interfere with her preferences. Even her name did not escape his throat, just half-strangled cries and moans. He grew tenser, and tighter, until his thigh muscles felt like knots. The harder she worked him, the more forcefully he shook. When she released him and looked up, he'd nicked his lower lip with his fangs. Because he was what he was, he licked it off. His face strained with the intensity of his longing to ravish her.

She knew that wasn't all he wanted, knew because she'd seen what his version of her always did in his fantasies. With a quiver of anticipation, she pulled the opposing ends of the leather belt.

His body was too strong for the force she used to harm him, even on this sensitive part of him. It did hurt, though, enough for him to fling his head back sensually. He growled when she yanked harder. To her amazement, he didn't break the bedposts.

"Pen," he warned, his voice barely intelligible. "I can't control my reactions when you do that."

She wanted to push him, wanted to push herself. She drove her mouth down over his cock again, taking him farther, getting him wetter, letting her teeth edge between the tight leather strips. He shuddered, the sound he made an animal grunt.

This was his fantasy. This was the act he craved.

Please, she heard him say in her head. *Please, Pen, bite me.*

She bit him and he screamed, but not because of the pain. He screamed because it felt so good, because it was the perfect match to his dark desires. He even screamed because it was her doing this to him. She was accepting every side of his nature. More, she was sharing them. His ecstasy danced through her, rising, peaking, breaking through the clawhold he had on it. She heard cloth rip— the scarf, she thought—and the taste of semen flooded her mouth.

It was one hard gush, hot and irrepressible. Graham groaned like this moment was the truest torture, every muscle in his body clenching with the struggle it was undergoing. A second, shorter gush hit her throat . . .

And then his climax just stopped.

She pulled back from him in shock.

"You stopped," she said shakily. "You were in the middle of coming, and you cut it off."

Graham panted twice before he could talk. "Don't remind me," he said.

"Stay there," she said, rising to her feet and stepping

back from him. She tore her clothes off in record time, her body burning everywhere his blazing eyes touched it. For once, she didn't worry that she was too sharp or boyish. His every twitch said she was beautiful to him. His gaze fastened on her nipples as if he were kissing them. They tightened and heated until they were hard as stones.

"Pen," he warned in a tone that brooked no denial, "the second you're naked, I'm taking charge."

Graham knew he wouldn't be able to stop himself. His nature was what it was. In the battle of the sexes—or the races—he had to rule. Though he loved what Pen had done to him, she'd always suit him best as erotic prey.

Surely enough, the moment her green silk panties fell to the floor, he tore off the belt that wrapped him and grabbed her by the waist. He meant to throw her willowy body onto the bed, but the second he touched her, he couldn't bring himself to let go. Her skin, her heat, her human vulnerability, demanded he pierce her without delay. He caught her firm little bottom as her sleek, long legs came around his hips. With a groan that echoed off the walls, he thrust his aching prick into her.

Pleasure nearly drove him to his knees. Her bite had pulled him close to coming, and her creamy heat swallowed him in bliss. She was so eager she was dripping. Grunting for the control it took, he bent his legs, tensed his muscles, and hopped them both onto the mattress.

He turned in the air to put himself on the bottom, but Pen still gasped as she bounced on him. Though he'd braced her, the fall drove him all the way into her. She undulated with pleasure as she sat up, her inner muscles rippling and clutching him.

"My God," she moaned as he ran his palms to her hard-tipped breasts. "How is it I always forget how damn big you are?"

She was as lovely as a flame, trying to wriggle her pussy over his "damn bigness." He rolled her under him all the same. He knew she relished being trapped by his weight. A sudden, extra gush of wetness told him this hadn't changed.

"I can't wait," he said, already moving inside her. "I need to bite you now."

Far from objecting, she grabbed his head and pulled him down to her neck. He nuzzled her throat and moaned, taking in her fragrance, her softness, holding off another second . . . two . . . until he had to plunge his fangs in or else go mad. They peaked together as her blood flowed across his tongue. He felt her body from inside her head, how he overwhelmed her, how she wished this would never end.

Wanting to give her everything she wanted, he wrapped her close and tried to stop his orgasm from bursting out in one go.

He couldn't at first; he'd been waiting too long, and coming at the same time as her felt incredible. At last, though, he cut it off.

"Graham," she moaned, clutching at his back.

He released her neck and gazed down at her. Both of them were sweating, both of them flushed with need. Set amidst all that hectic color, Pen's slanting whiskey eyes looked like pools of fire.

"I'm going to be moving fast," he said raggedly. "I don't think I can help myself. I'll make it last as long as I can, and I'll try not to be too rough."

She bit her lip until the plump flesh paled.

"I know," he said. "You don't want it *too* gentle."

"I love you," she whispered, her hands sliding upward to frame his face.

He kissed her, and nicked her, and then—as she moaned at the spike of pleasure—he did precisely what he'd promised.

He made her come until she swore she couldn't do it again. Knowing better, he turned them on their sides and spanked her small bottom. That drove her even wilder, the smacking sting of his palm flipping some switch she didn't have control over. Graham paddled her until her skin flamed pink, locking his mouth to hers for deep, tongue-tangling kisses he couldn't have survived without. His power over her was heady, her response to him a thief of sanity. His ejaculation broke from his hold twice more, though he was able—through a rather loud and sweat-popping effort—to wrestle it back each time. With each suppression, his need for full release surged higher.

"Let go," she pleaded as her body strove against his. "Graham, let go."

He was snarling as he thrust now, maddened by delight and lust. Pen's fingers found his pointed right nipple and twisted hard. The little pain streaked through him like a whip. He choked on a cry, almost, almost going.

"Now," she insisted, her other hand working down between them. "With me this time."

He shoved her uppermost thigh higher, opening her for the acceleration of his need-crazed strokes. He was trying to be gentle even as he worked to go deep. Fast but easy was what he aimed for. Fast and easy and as bloody far as there was. He knocked the end of her passage as if his cock were an oiled piston. She was wet enough for him to do it. Soft enough. Relaxed enough.

But maybe not patient.

His breath whined in his throat as her hips flung urgently back at him, the drumbeats on his sensitive cock-head intensifying. He wasn't certain he could hold back again. He wanted desperately to let loose, to sear her with the stored-up jet of his seed.

"I love you," he gasped.

And then her hand closed on his testicles.

She squeezed him hard enough to inflame the tenderness he'd caused himself by curtailing his climaxes. That was all it took. His fuses blew like hers had when he'd spanked her. His ejaculation was volcanic, his release so intense, so consuming, that it blotted out his thoughts. He heard himself shouting from a distance, felt his hips grinding into hers. It wasn't too much force, because she was spasming, too. That was the cherry on his ecstasy. He came in fiery spangles that seemed to draw sparks of joy from his fingertips. Every vein was coming, every eyelash.

The final contracting gush wrenched a groan from him. "Pen," he sighed. "Pen."

He'd rolled back when he collapsed, and she lay—panting but content—on top of him. His cock had slipped from her when they turned. To his exhausted pleasure, her hand found and cradled it, her thumb caressing its laxness.

"You should be wetter," she murmured. "You came so much."

He twitched at the reminder of that sweet relief. "It's something to do with being *upyr*. Our seed evaporates."

"Hm," she said and pressed a sleepy kiss to his chest.

"Don't," he said. "Stay awake awhile longer."

Slower to recover than he was, Pen groaned as he slid out from under her.

"Five minutes," he promised, loving the way she looked limp and naked against the sheets. "It's barely midnight. If I don't give this to you now and get it over with, there's no chance that I'll fall asleep."

Pen propped herself higher by pulling a feather pillow beneath her breasts. The position tempted him to paddle her arse again. "Give me what?"

He turned around and found his trousers, the little red leather box a square lump in one pocket.

"Here," he said, willing his hand not to shake as he held it out.

Pen was sitting up now, her legs folded to one side and her eyes gone big. "You got me a present?"

"It's a bit more than a present," he conceded.

His heart thumped faster as he waited for her to open it. He told himself this was the right move to make. It wasn't too soon. Pen loved him, and reassuring her early and often that he felt the same could only be to the good. Her fingers fumbled a little as she pushed the box's tight hinge up. Inside, tucked into a black velvet cushion, the perfect one-carat diamond sparkled with rainbow fire.

"Oh," she said, her voice soft and feminine. Her hand fluttered to the pulse beating at the base of her throat. "*Graham.*"

"Don't answer now," he said. "That ring is for you to keep, to think about until you're ready to put it on. When I see it on your finger, I'll know you'll marry me."

"Graham." Tears trembled on her lower lashes as she looked at him.

He sat back down on the bed. "When you're ready," he repeated. "I can be patient. As you may have noticed, I have all the time in the world."

She tried to smile but didn't quite succeed. Still open, the leather box was cradled in her hands, resting on one thigh. When she spoke, her voice was very serious. "You said something to me once: that I didn't know how to be nice."

"Pen, that was before I knew you. Before I saw what was in your heart."

She shook her head, her expression wry. "You weren't completely wrong—or not so my aunts could tell."

He laid his hand on her knee. "I wish I'd been here to help you with them."

"I know." She lowered her head and smiled. "Knowing you would have held my hand made me want to take care of them myself. I couldn't have Graham Fitz Clare thinking I was weak."

"Never," he said. "Never."

She lifted her smile to him. Its curve was wistful, wanting to believe but not yet daring. "My point is, I can be a selfish woman. When it comes to you, I don't want to come second to anyone."

He knew why this was, knew why she'd fear what had happened with her father would repeat itself with him. He tried in every way he knew to show he meant what he said next. "You won't ever take second place with me. I love my family, but you're the woman I want beside me. We can be partners, Pen. We're different, but we fit—maybe even more than we've discovered yet."

She laughed and rubbed at her rosy cheeks. "Only you could make being *partners* sound romantic."

"So you'll think about my offer."

She leaned into him and hugged him, simply holding

him tight. After a minute, she pushed back reluctantly. "I have responsibilities to fulfill here. Trying to start a business, for one, so the plantation can support itself. Now that Prohibition is over, we're thinking of resurrecting a historic pecan liqueur recipe. The old cook's daughter thinks she remembers the ingredients."

"I'm sure you'll make a success of it. I'm also sure we could work out a compromise regarding where and how we live." He had a few in mind himself, though he suspected she'd like them better if he let her come up with them.

"I'm not saying 'no,'" she added, the haste in her voice tugging at his lips.

"I'm not hearing 'no,'" he said.

Though she pushed his shoulder like a boy would, the gleam in her eyes was all woman. She flopped back onto the bed laughing.

"I need a nap," she announced. "Your aura mustn't have started rubbing off on me. Wake me when you're tired of listening to me snore."

He gave her no empty reassurances on that score, just tucked her against his body and petted her hair. That his inner cat was the one who purred, she didn't have to know right then.

Bridesmere: July 1, 1934

❦

That color!" Sally exclaimed, stepping back from the free-standing mirror in which Estelle was reflected. "It's positively smashing with your eyes."

That color was the soft slate blue of Estelle's wedding gown. She smoothed her hands self-consciously down the front. The dress was heavy Italian silk with overlong pointed sleeves. The plunging scoop neck curved snugly around her breasts, after which the cloth fell in a gleaming, pearl-encrusted column to puddle around her shoes. The ivory underkirtle was a linen so soft it felt like a cloud. With her wavy hair down around her shoulders and the bit of makeup Sally had dusted on, Estelle looked like a beauty from a pre-Raphaelite painting.

She told herself it wasn't overly vain to think so. The dress had been a wedding present from Edmund's sister-in-law, the apparently powerful wife of the *Upyr* Council's head. If it flattered more than expected, that was likely due to Gillian's centuries of experience with such things. Perhaps Estelle was mistaken, but the old rayed scar around her right eye actually seemed fainter than usual.

"I wonder how she knew your size," Sally marveled, adjusting the perfectly straight fall of one of Estelle's sleeves. "People say she's extra gifted at reading minds. If she ever comes here in person, I'd best stay away from her."

Estelle ducked her head to conceal her smile, but Sally still saw it.

"I know," she said. "Everything comes out of my mouth anyway. I shouldn't bother trying to hide."

Grinning and obviously unrepentant, she folded her hands on the now impressive prow of her belly. At seven months along, she managed to appear both maternal and adorably young. "Too bad Gillian didn't send a dress to make me look magically thin."

"You look wonderful. Radiant."

"Not as radiant as you!" Sally crowed.

Estelle blushed a little, then turned at a soft but decisive knocking at her candlelit chamber door.

"I'll get it!" Sally cried, still light enough on her feet to run.

At first, Estelle thought it was Graham whom Sally was admitting. The *upyr* at the threshold possessed a similar height and build, even a similar posture. The impression faded as he stepped inside. This vampire's hair was longer, his eyes a smoky gray flecked with gold. Though he wore a human-style morning coat and gray-striped trousers, she suspected the muscles beneath were those of a warrior. His face was absolutely stunning, with dramatic, slanting cheekbones and a cleft in his chin.

"Wow," Sally murmured, gaping up at him.

The man's smile was very gentle as he dropped his huge hand to her small shoulder. "I'm Aimery, your uncle—and *your* soon-to-be brother-in-law."

His eyes softened even more as they met Estelle's. The brotherly resemblance she'd missed on her initial glimpse grew clearer—especially around his beautifully cut mouth. The biggest difference lay in the half brothers' auras. Edmund's energy was concentrated and intense, a blade to pierce the heart with joy. Aimery's was like an ocean that had relinquished its need to storm. Percy had called him *saintly*, and in that moment, the term didn't seem too strong. The compassion Edmund's younger brother emanated was like a gentle spice in the air.

"Do you suppose," he said to Sally, giving her shoulder another pat, "that you could give your father's bride and me a little time alone?"

Sally shut her mouth and blinked. "Certainly," she said. "I'll just—" She looked at the door. "I'll just check on the veil."

Aimery's grin at her departure turned him into something less saintly and more human. "What a little kitten! I hope she and her husband won't be disappointed when they find she's having a boy."

"My wife told me," he explained. "Sometimes Gillian gets snoopy."

"Oh," Estelle said, realizing the supplier of her wedding dress must be here. "I . . . I'm certain we're very glad you've both come."

"Didn't expect us?" Aimery teased archly.

His eyes were twinkling with amusement, but Estelle still felt uncomfortable answering. "Edmund mentioned you might be busy with Council work."

Aimery moved to her cluttered dressing table, his blunt-tipped fingers skating across the edge. Estelle's funny ear could almost hear him gathering his thoughts. He glanced at her sideways through thick lashes.

"Edmund came to us in Rome last week, using his new power. We knew he was marrying, of course. Hence, the wedding gift."

"He loves you," Estelle said, wanting there to be no mistake. "If he didn't invite you sooner—"

"I know," Aimery said. "My brother's heart is less of a mystery to me than it is to him—which would annoy him to know, I'm sure." His smile was crooked and endearing. Then and there, Estelle knew she would love him.

"As it happens," he added. "Edmund did more than invite us. He asked me to officiate. I wanted to make certain that was all right with you. If you'd rather have a priest or a minister . . ."

"No." Estelle's hands were clutched at her waist, her sudden upsurge of sentiment tightening them. If Edmund was making peace with his feelings about his brother, she could only be happy. "I'm sure we're honored you're marrying us."

"Good." He looked into her eyes. Though she didn't

sense him reading her, she knew he was. She also knew when he finished, because he crossed the distance between them and took her face in his hands. His hold was as careful as if she were spun sugar. "If I'd chosen someone to love him, I couldn't have done better."

An unexpected laugh caught in Estelle's throat. "He'd never have let you choose, so it's just as well he took care of it."

Aimery laughed and then let her go. As he reached the door, he lobbed one last revelation over his shoulder. "I'm afraid your guest list has expanded. When the British packs heard that Edmund was marrying, they decided to come as well."

"What?" Estelle gasped. "How many new guests is that?"

"Don't worry," Aimery soothed. "Graham and Percy are handling it."

He disappeared too fast for her to ask the million questions that had sprung up.

"Oh, my God," she breathed, her throat gone tight with the prenuptial panic she'd been lucky enough to avoid till then. Graham and Percy had better be handling it. They only had—*good Lord*—fifteen minutes until midnight.

"Are you all right?" Sally asked, returning with her tea rose–decorated veil.

Butterflies flitted through Estelle's stomach at the unmistakable symbol of what she was about to do. Her lower lip began to tremble, and her eyes filled with tears. She knew she wasn't frightened, simply overwhelmed with feeling. Finally, astoundingly, she was going to marry the man she'd loved since she was fifteen.

"Oh, boy," Sally said, clearly misinterpreting her condition. She laid the veil on the back of the nearest chair. "You stay here. I'll go get Daddy."

Edmund arrived so quickly she thought he must have used his new power. He caught her hands to his pale gray waistcoat, his tenderness at odds with his thunderous expression.

"Did my brother upset you?" he demanded. "Did Gillian? I *knew* you wanted to wear the gown you picked out yourself!"

"I'm fine." Estelle laughed, kissing the knuckles that clutched hers. "Sally misunderstood. It just came over me all at once: that I'm marrying the love of my life at last."

"I made you wait too long," Edmund said darkly.

She clasped his golden head to stop it from wagging. "Now is the perfect time, and tonight is the perfect night." She bit her lower lip as she grinned. "I heard some of your wolfy friends have arrived."

"I'm sorry about that, love. We won't fit in Bridesmere's chapel anymore. Graham and Percy are moving everything to a clearing in the woods."

"That sounds lovely. You and I, joining our lives together beneath the stars."

"There *are* stars," he admitted, his hands sliding down her back. "It's clear tonight, and not so warm that our human guests will sweat." His fingers drew circles on the upper curve of her bottom, causing a pleasant shiver to skip down her spine. Seeing it, Edmund's flame blue gaze steadied on her own. "You really *are* happy about this."

"I'd be happier if you kissed me."

"Sally painted your lips."

"Kiss me where no one will see."

She shrugged out of the shoulder of her slate blue gown, exposing the swell of one generous breast. Edmund's attention was immediately caught. He stroked her collarbone with his fingertips, his gentleness leaving no doubt as to her preciousness to him. His eyes glowed hot when they rose.

"Estelle," he said, his voice gone husky. "If I kiss you the way you're thinking, you truly will be a blushing bride."

Estelle's grin widened.

"Very well," he said, smiling a bit himself. He dipped her back across his arm as if they were dancing, his hold so firm she knew she would never fall—though the move did hasten her breath. Her giddiness increased as he drew his silken mouth across the curve of her breasts, whispering warm, soft praises while his fangs gradually lengthened behind his lips. Aroused by this evidence of his interest, she tightened her grasp on his neck. Her knees had begun to tremble uncontrollably.

This was exactly the sort of response Edmund loved. With a muffled groan of longing, he pushed her fitted bodice under her breast, the cloth supporting it like a sling. His tongue ran around the bead of her nipple, then sucked it, then pulled the whole areola between the wet satin of his cheeks. The suction and the press of fangs felt so lovely, she scarcely needed the added pleasure of his thumb circling her other breast's budded peak.

"My love," he murmured, and bit her in slow motion.

She came the same way, languorous, aching pulses that started between her legs and ran thick as honey out through her veins. Edmund dropped the barriers between them, allowing her to feel how much he wanted to go with her. His body was taut, his erection jerking and hard. He was saving his climax for later, for when they were man and wife.

His restraint made her orgasm spike so dramatically she cried out.

When he set her back on her feet, she was wobbling more than a little. His lips curved upward as he tucked her breast back into her dress. He hadn't healed her completely. Beneath the cloud-soft linen, the mark of ownership throbbed like a second heart.

"There," he said, the satisfaction in his eyes all male. "*Now* you look perfect."

"You look randy," she teased, gazing pointedly at his swollen groin. "And buttoning your tailcoat isn't going to cover that."

"I find I can't mind," he said airily. "If people conclude I'm mad for my bride, it will be too true to dispute."

Graham couldn't recall being this satisfied with life before. Looking around the pretty flower-bedecked clearing, watching his father and Estelle exchange vows, he experienced the most incredible sensation that all was

well. However irregular the setting, everyone was enjoying the midnight ceremony. In the relocated pew across
the mossy aisle from him, Percy and Robin sat with Nim
Wei. London's queen was smiling faintly, while Percy and
Robin beamed. Seated beside Graham, Sally was sniffling
happily into Ben's chest. Ben held her with an expression
of supreme contentment, the prospect of being a father no
longer seeming to frighten him.

Graham could think of few things better than seeing
everyone he cared about flourishing.

Even Christian Durand, who sat far off in the back, bore
a shadow of joviality. His arms were folded, but his eyes
were warm—as if he were amused by his pleasure in the
proceedings.

The invasion of *upyr* canines intrigued Graham's cat,
who thought it might try hunting with them later. If the tom
could dream of chasing alligators, why not running with
wolves? Graham's human side was not alone in gaining
confidence in its powers.

In a way, the British packs were also family, since their
line sprang from the same progenitor as Graham's. Their
presence at his father's wedding made him feel part of
something bigger than himself. No doubt their characters
varied, but he was looking forward to meeting them.

All in all, he had no regrets, not even that Pen was sitting rows back with her father. She would come to him
when she was ready. He'd read enough from her mind to
know that was just a matter of time.

His ears caught her whispering to her father, telling him
she'd catch up with him later. Graham forced himself not
to turn as he heard her slipping along the pews.

"Scoot over," she murmured to Sally, inspiring a soft
giggle.

Though he tried to act nonchalant, he couldn't keep his
gratified sigh inside as she slid into the seat next to him.
Her elbow nudged his warmly.

"Here's the good part," she said.

Edmund and Estelle were kissing—rather more deeply
than the average newlyweds. Graham smirked to himself,

knowing his father had to be working to hide his fangs. Finally, the couple broke their embrace, and everywhere around the clearing, people jumped up and clapped. Held within the curve of her husband's arm, Estelle blushed furiously. Graham's father wasn't much more contained. He looked so happy, his vampire glow seemed a hair's breadth from breaking free.

"The bride and groom!" Edmund's brother, Aimery, called—which inspired a round of true wolf whistles.

Typical to her tomboy streak, Pen's might have been the loudest. She grabbed Graham's arm and squeezed, then slid her hand down his sleeve to weave their fingers together excitedly.

Graham's body jerked the instant he felt the ring. Thumbing the diamond, his heart pounded so hard he thought it would burst with joy.

"Yes," she said, grinning up at him. "Any time *you're* ready."

2:22 a.m.

The three men—or almost men—met within a tall ring of evergreens a judicious distance from the festivities. Now that the meat of their discussion had been completed, the slightly stocky American was puffing on a cigar.

"So," he said, tipping back his head to blow a silvery smoke ring. "We're agreed. X Section continues . . . internationally."

The ink-haired Swiss merely nodded, but the third man spoke. "In times like these, it seems foolish not to keep an ear to the ground."

"And Robin Fitz Clare?"

"Has proven he understands the need for discretion."

Another fragrant smoke ring rose through the pine branches. When it disappeared from sight, the American dropped his cigar and ground it beneath his heel. "Agreed."

The Swiss made a movement so small the only thing

that shifted was the reflection of the starlight on the surface of his eyes. "The queen shouldn't be brought into this. She likes to rule whatever she touches."

"You're pretty new to this circle to be making demands."

The Swiss smiled faintly at the American industrialist. "Edmund doesn't think I'm wrong."

The American frowned but didn't argue. "I don't want my daughter knowing about our association. She needs to be protected."

"If your daughter spends much more time with Graham, she's not going to have normal weaknesses anyway. The Fitz Clares have a habit of . . . rubbing off on people they're close to." The dark-haired man sounded strangely merry when he said this, as if he very much enjoyed the irony.

Before the American could respond, his British counterpart turned his gaze to the celebration. Someone had carried a piano from the castle into the forest, and it was playing a bouncy waltz. With the sense that they were seeing something rare and fine, the Englishman's companions watched his handsome alabaster face soften.

"Excuse me, gentlemen," he said, lightly touching both their shoulders. "If we're done here, I'd really love to dance with my brand-new wife . . ."

Turn the page for a preview of the first book
in the Mindhunters trilogy by Kylie Brant

WAKING NIGHTMARE

Available September 2009 from Berkley Sensation!

Summer gripped Savannah by the throat and strangled it with a slow vicious squeeze. Most faulted the heat and cursed the humidity, but Ryne knew the weather wasn't totally to blame for the suffocating pall. Evil had settled over the city, a cloying, sweaty blanket, insidiously spreading its tentacles of misery like a silent cancer taking hold in an unsuspecting body.

But people weren't going to remain unsuspecting for much longer. This latest victim was likely to change that, and then all hell was going to break loose.

Compared to Savannah, he figured hell had to be a dry heat.

The door to the conference room opened, and the task force members began filing in. Most held cups of steaming coffee that would only make the outdoor temperature seem more brutal. Ryne didn't bother pointing that out. He was hardly in the position to lecture others about their addictions.

Their voices hadn't yet subsided when he reached out to flip on the digital projector. "We've got another vic."

A close-up picture was projected on the screen. There was a muttered "*Jesus*" from one of the detectives. After spending the last two hours going through the photos, Ryne could appreciate the sentiment.

"Barbara Billings. Age thirty-four. Divorced. Lives alone. She was raped two days ago in her home when she got off work." He switched to the next set of pictures, those detailing her injuries. "He was inside her house, but we don't know yet if he'd been hiding there or if he gained access after she arrived. She got home at six, and said it was shortly after that he grabbed her. She's hazy on details, but the assault lasted hours."

"Where'd he dump her, the sewer?" Even McElroy sounded a little squeamish. And considering that his muscle-bound body housed an unusually tactless mouth, that was saying something.

Ryne clicked the computer mouse. The screen showed a photo of a pier, partially dismantled, with the glint of metal beneath it. "A cage had been wired to the moorings beneath this dock on St. Andrew's Sound. That's where he transported her to afterward."

"Looks like the kennel I put my Lab in," observed Wayne Cantrell.

Ryne flicked him a glance. As usual, the detective was sitting slouched in his seat, arms folded across his chest, his features showing only the impassive stoicism of his Choctaw heritage. "It is a dog kennel," Ryne affirmed. The next picture showed a close-up of it. "Sturdy enough to hold a one hundred thirty–pound woman. The medical exam shows she was injected twice. It'll be at least a week before we get the tox report back, but from her description of the tingling in her lips, heightened sensation, and foggy memory, this sounds like our guy."

"Shit."

Ryne heartily concurred with Cantrell's quiet assessment. It also summed up what they had so far on the bastard responsible for the rapes.

The rest of the photos were shown in silence. When he got to the end of them, he crossed to the door and switched on the overhead lights. "Marine Patrol wasn't able to get much information from her when they found her, so they processed the secondary scene. Her preliminary statement was taken at the hospital, before the case got tossed to us."

"Where's she at now?" This was from Isaac Holmes, the most seasoned detective on the case. With his droopy jowls and long narrow face, he bore an uncanny resemblance to the old hound seen on reruns of *The Beverly Hillbillies*. But he had an enviable cleared-case percentage, a factor that had weighed heavily when Ryne had requested him for the task force.

"She was treated and released from St. Joseph/Candler. She's staying with her mother. The address is in the file."

"Where the hell is that other investigator Dixon promised?"

McElroy's truculent question struck a chord with Ryne. He made sure it didn't show. "Commander Dixon has assured me that he's carefully looking at possible candidates to assign to the task force." He ignored the muttered responses in the room. If another member weren't assigned to the group by the end of the day, he would have it out with Dixon himself. Again.

"We need to process the primary scene and interview the victim. Cantrell, I want you and . . ." His words stopped as the door opened, and a slight young woman with short dark hair entered. Despite the double whammy of Savannah's heat and humidity, she wore a long-sleeved white shirt over her black pants. He hadn't seen her around before, but given the photo ID badge clipped to the pocket of her shirt and the thick folder she carried, he figured her for a clerical temp. And if that file contained copies of the complete Marine Patrol report, it was about damn time.

"I'm looking for Detective Robel." She scanned the occupants in the room before shifting her focus to him.

"You found him." He gestured to a table near the door. "Just set the folder there and close the door on your way out."

Her attention snapped back to him, a hint of amusement showing in her expression. "I'm Abbie Phillips, your newest task force member."

"Does the department get a cut rate on pocket-sized police officers?" There was an answering ripple of laughter in the room, quickly muffled. Ryne shot a warning look at McElroy, who shrugged and ran a hand through his already disheveled brown hair. "C'mon, Robel, what is she, all of fourteen?"

"Welcome to the team, Phillips." Ryne kept his voice

neutral. "We can use a woman to help us interview the victims. We've been borrowing female officers from other units."

"I hope to give you more assistance than that." She handed him the file folder. "A summary of my background."

The folder was too thick for a rookie, but it also wasn't a SCMPD personnel file. He flicked a gaze over her again. No shield. No weapon. Tension knotted his gut as he took the folder she offered. He gestured to the primaries in the room in turn. "Detectives Cantrell, McElroy, and Holmes. We had another rape reported last night and I was just catching everyone up." To the group he said, "I'll need all detectives and uniforms to the scene. Holmes, until I get there, you oversee the canvass. I'll meet you later."

There was a scraping of chairs as the officers rose and made their way to the door. Abbie turned, as if to follow them. His voice halted her. "Phillips, I'd like to talk to you first."

She looked up at him. At her height, she'd look up to most men. She couldn't be much more than five foot two. And her smoky gray eyes were as guileless as a ten-year-old's.

"We could talk in the car. I'm anxious to get a look at the scene."

"Later." He went to the projector and shut it off. Pulling out two chairs beside it, he gestured toward one.

She came over, sat down. He sank into the other seat, set her file on the table in front of him, and flipped it open. He read only a few moments before disbelief flared, followed closely by anger.

"You're not a cop."

Abbie's gaze was steady. "Independent consultant. Our agency contracts with law enforcement on problematic cases. If you're worried about my qualifications, the file lists my experience. Commander Dixon seemed satisfied."

Dixon. That backstabbing SOB. "I think there's been a misunderstanding." Ryne delivered the understatement in a steady tone. "What our task force needs, what I requested from Commander Dixon, was another investigator. Preferably two. What we definitely do not need is a shrink."

There was a flicker in those calm gray eyes that might have been temper. "I have a doctorate in forensic psychology—"

"We need a *doctor* even less."

She ignored his interruption. "And since joining Raiker Forensics, I've been involved in nearly three dozen high-profile cases."

"Shit." He was capable of more finesse, but at the moment diplomacy eluded him. "Do you realize what kind of case we're working here? I've got a serial rapist on the loose, and with this latest victim, the media is going to be crawling up my ass. I need another experienced investigator, not someone who'll shrink the skell's mind once we get him."

She never flinched. "You'll have to catch him first, won't you? And I can help with that. I consulted on the Romeo rapist case last year in Houston. The perp is currently doing a twenty-five-year stretch at Allred. Of the cases I've worked, well over half involved serial rapists. I'm exactly what you need on this case, Detective Robel. You just don't realize it yet."

The mention of the Houston case rang a bell, but he didn't bother to pursue the memory. "If we have need of a psych consult, we can always get one from a department psychologist."

"And how many of them—how many of your department's *investigators*—have been trained by Adam Raiker?"

Ryne paused, studying her through narrowed eyes. He had no trouble recalling that name; few in law enforcement circles would. The former FBI profiler had achieved near legendary status until he'd disappeared from the radar several years earlier. "Raiker? I thought he was—"

"Dead?"

Maybe. "Retired."

Her smile was enigmatic. "He'd object to either term."

He was wasting his time. The one he needed to be leveling these objections against was upstairs, where the administrative offices were housed, playing political handball.

His chair scraped the floor as he rose. "Wait here." He left the room and strode through the squad room. But halfway up the stairs leading to the administrative offices, he met the man he was seeking, followed by his usual entourage.

He shouldered his way through the throng surrounding Dixon. Raising his voice over the din, he said, "Commander, could I have a word with you?"

Dixon held up a hand that could have meant anything. In this case, it apparently meant to wait until he'd finished the joke he was telling to a couple suits who seemed engrossed in his every word.

Derek Dixon had barely changed in the nearly dozen years since Ryne had first met him. The observation wasn't a compliment. He had pretty boy blond looks and the manner of a chameleon. Jovial and charming one moment. Sober and businesslike the next. He was the ultimate public relations tool, because he was damn good at being all things to all people. Ryne happened to know that his habit of trying to be *one* thing to all women had nearly destroyed his marriage.

But being a womanizing narcissistic prick hadn't slowed the rise of his career. In Boston he'd been the department's special attaché to the mayor. He'd come to Savannah three years ago as commander of the Investigative Division. The fact that his wife was the chief's niece might have had something to do with his procuring the job, but Ryne was hardly in a position to judge. When he'd accepted Dixon's surprising offer of a job here a year ago, he'd hitched his career to the other man's.

It was a troubling memory, but not the one that kept him awake nights.

There was a loud burst of laughter as the suits expressed their appreciation of Dixon's humor, which, Ryne had reason to know, could be politically incorrect and crudely clever.

"Excuse me for a moment." Dixon clapped the two closest men on the shoulders. "I need to speak to one of my detectives." The crowd on the stairwell parted for him like a sea before a prophet.

"Detective Robel." He flashed his pearly caps. "Here to thank me?"

"I appreciate the extra person assigned to the task force." Whatever their past, whatever had gone between them, Ryne always maintained a scrupulously professional relationship with the man in public. "But I'm not sure bringing in an outsider is going to be as much use to us as another department investigator would be."

Annoyance flickered in the man's eyes. "Didn't you read her qualifications? Phillips has background unmatched by anyone on the force. You've heard of Raiker Forensics, haven't you? They're better known as The Mindhunters, because of Adam Raiker's years in the fed's behavioral science unit. The training in his agency is top-notch. With the addition of Phillips, we're getting a profiler and an investigator, for the price of one."

"Price." They descended the stairs in tandem. "Resources are limited, the last inner-department memo said. Seems odd to spend them on an outside 'consultant' when we have cops already on the payroll who could do the same work at no additional cost."

Although he'd tried to maintain a neutral tone, Dixon's expression warned him that he hadn't been entirely successful. The man glanced around as if to see who was within hearing distance and lowered his voice, all the while keeping a genial smile pasted on his face. "You don't have to worry about the finances of this department, Detective, that's my job. Yours is to track down and nail this scumbag raping women in our city. If you'd accomplished that by now, I wouldn't have had to bring someone else in, would I?"

The barb found its mark. "We've made steady progress . . ."

"Don't forget that my ass in on the line right along with yours. Mayor Richards has had me on speed dial since the second rape."

Already knowing it was futile, Ryne said, "Okay, how about adding another person to the task force in addition to Phillips? Marlowe out of the fourth precinct would be a good man, and he's got fifteen years experience."

They came to the base of the steps and stopped. The

suits were standing a little ways off, and judging by the looks they kept throwing them, were growing impatient.

Dixon's words reflected the same emotion. "You wanted another person assigned, you got her. Work with the task force you've got, Detective. I need results to report to the chief. Get me something to take to him." His gaze moved to the men waiting for him. "Have you verified the connection between this latest assault and the others?" Ryne had updated Dixon and Captain Brown before the briefing this morning.

"I've got CSU at the scene. My men are on their way over."

"Good." It was clear he'd lost Dixon's attention. "Let me know when you get something solid."

Ryne made sure none of the anger churning in his gut showed on his face as the commander walked away. Keeping the mayor happy would have been the driving motivation behind Dixon's hiring an outside consultant. The second victim had been the mayor's granddaughter, a college student snatched on her way to work and driven to her grandparents' beach home, where the attack had taken place. The man had an understandable thirst for results, and Dixon's hiring of Phillips was only the latest offering. Assigning another department investigator to the case wasn't as dazzling as putting a profiler to work on it, especially one affiliated with Adam Raiker, a man practically martyred for the Bureau some years back.

At least he hoped he'd read Dixon's intentions correctly. Ryne turned and headed back to the conference room. He sincerely hoped the man was just playing his usually style of suck-up politics and not engaged in a cover-your-ass strategy, designed to leave his image untarnished if this case went bad.

Because if that were the situation, Ryne knew exactly who'd be left twisting in the wind.

When Detective Robel reentered the room, Abbie could tell that his mood had taken a turn for the worse. It wasn't evident from his expression. But temper had his spine straight, his movements taut with tension. "Let's go," he said abruptly.

Without a word, she got up and followed him out the door. He made no effort to check the length of his strides. She almost had to run to keep up with him, a fact that didn't endear him to her. He stopped at one cubicle and dropped the folder containing her personnel information on the desk, then picked up a fat accordion file sitting on its corner.

"Here." He shoved it at Abbie. "You can catch up on the case on the way."

On the way where? To the scene? To the victim? She decided she wasn't going to ask. His disposition had gone from guardedly polite to truculent, and it didn't take much perception to recognize that she was the cause for the change. His attitude wasn't totally unprecedented. He wouldn't be the first detective to resent her presence on his team, at least initially. In her experience, cops were notoriously territorial.

Rather than trotting at his heels like a well-trained dog, Abbie kept the detective in sight as she followed him out of the building and down the wide stone steps. Almost immediately, her temples dampened. Though barely noon and partly overcast, the humidity index had to be hovering close to ninety percent, making her question how the majority of her assignments just happened to be located in walking saunas like Savannah. Houston. Miami.

The answer, of course, was the job. Everything she did was dictated by it. If there was room in her life for little else, that was a conscious choice. And one she'd yet to regret.

Robel paused at the bottom of the steps as if just remembering she was accompanying him and threw an impatient look over his shoulder. Unhurriedly, she caught up, and they headed toward the police parking lot.

"Do you have any experience with victim interviews?" he asked tersely. "I want to talk to Billings before I stop by the scene."

"Yes."

"Follow my lead when we get there. We've developed a survey of questions I'll lead her through. If you have anything to add afterward, feel free."

He led her to an unmarked navy Crown Vic, unlocked it. She slid in the passenger side while he continued around the vehicle to the other door. Before following her into the car, he shrugged out of his muted plaid suit coat, revealing a light blue short-sleeved shirt crisscrossed by a shoulder harness. He laid the suit jacket over the seat between them as he got in.

"I'm never going to get used to this weather." He slid her a glance as he backed the car out of the slot. "How do you stand wearing long sleeves like that in the middle of summer?"

"Superior genes." Ignoring his snort, she spilled the contents from the file he'd given her onto her lap. Flipping through the neatly arranged photos and reports, she noted they were sorted chronologically beginning with the first incident reported, three months earlier.

She looked at the detective. "So if this latest victim turns out to be related to the others, she'll be the . . . what? Fourth?"

Ryne pulled to a stop at a stoplight. "That's right. And she's almost certainly related. He's injecting them with something prior to the attacks, and they all describe the same effects—initial tingling of the lips and extreme muscle weakness. It turns the victims' memories to mush, which means they haven't been able to give us squat when it comes to details about the attacker. From the descriptions they give, it also does something to intensify sensation."

"Maybe to increase the pain from the torture," she murmured, struck by a thought. If that were the actual intent, rather than just hazing the memory or incapacitating the victim, it would be in keeping with a sadistic rapist.

The hair on the nape of her neck suddenly prickled, and it wasn't due to the tepid air blasting from the air-conditioning vents. The atmosphere in the vehicle had gone charged. She slanted a look at Robel, noted the muscle working in his jaw.

"What do you know about the torture?"

Feeling like she was stepping on quicksand, she said, "Commander Dixon told me a little about the cases when we discussed my joining the task force."

"This morning?"

"On the phone yesterday afternoon."

The smile that crossed his lips then was chilly and completely devoid of humor. He reached for a pair of sunglasses secured to the visor, flipped them open, and settled them on his nose.

Irritation coursed through her. "Something about that amuses you?"

"Yeah, it does. Considering the fact that the last time I asked Dixon for another *investigator*"—she didn't miss the inflection he gave the last word—"was yesterday morning, I guess you could say it's funny as hell."

Abbie stifled the retort that rose to her lips. She was more familiar than she'd like with the ego massage necessary in these situations, though she'd never develop a fondness for the need. "Look, let's cut through the unpleasantries. I have no intention of muscling in on your case. Since I was hired by Dixon, I have to provide him with whatever information he requests of me. But my role is first and foremost to assist you."

His silence, she supposed, was a response of sorts. Just not the one she wanted. Her annoyance deepened. According to Commander Dixon, Robel was some sort of hotshot detective, some very big deal from—Philadelphia? New York? Some place north anyway. But as far as she could tell, he was just another macho jerk, of a type she was all too familiar with. Law enforcement was full of them. Departments could mandate so-called sensitivity training, but it didn't necessarily change chauvinistic attitudes. It just drove them deeper below the surface.

Abbie studied his chiseled profile. No doubt she was supposed to crumple in the face of his displeasure. He'd be the sort of man to appeal to most women, she supposed, if they liked the lean, lethal, surly type. His short-cropped hair was brown, his eyes behind the glasses an Arctic shade of blue. His jaw was hard, as if braced for a punch. Given his personality, she'd be willing to bet he'd caught more than his share of them. He wasn't particularly tall, maybe five foot ten, but he radiated authority. He was probably used to turning his commanding presence on women and melting them into subservience.

One corner of her mouth pulled up wryly as she turned back to the file in her lap. There had been a time when it would have produced just that result with her. Fortunately, that time was in the very remote past.

Ignoring him for the moment, she pored over the police reports, skipping over the complainants' names to the blocks of texts that detailed the location, offense, MO, victim, and suspect information. "I assume you're using a state crime lab. What have the tox screens shown?" she asked, without looking up.

At first she thought he wasn't going to answer. Finally he said, "GBI's Coastal Regional Crime Lab is here in Savannah. The toxicologist hasn't found anything definitive, and he's tested for nearly two dozen of the more common substances. Reports on the first three victims showed trace amounts of Ecstasy in their blood. All victims deny being users, and the toxicologist suspects that it was mixed in controlled amounts to make a new compound."

She did look up then, her interest piqued. Use of an unfamiliar narcotic agent in the assaults might be their best lead in the case. Even without a sample, it told them something about the unknown subject. "Have you established any commonalities so far besides the drug?"

"Their hands are always bound with electrical cord, same position. Never their legs. At least not yet. He stalks them first, learns their routine. For most he gets into the house somehow, different entry techniques, so he's adaptable. But one victim he grabbed off the street and drove thirty miles to her grandparents' empty beach house for the attack."

"Same torture methods?"

He shook his head. "The first victim he covered with a plastic bag and repeatedly suffocated and revived. The next he carved up pretty bad. Looked like he was trying to cut her face off. Another he worked over with pliers and a hammer."

"What about trace evidence?"

"Nothing yet." And all the tension she'd sensed from Robel since she'd met him was pent up in the words. "He's smart and he's lucky. A bad combination for us. After the second rape I entered the case into the Violent Criminal Apprehension Program, mentioning the drug as a common element. Only got a few hits. After the third one I resubmitted, thinking the drug might be a new addition for this perp. I don't have those results back yet, but I'm guessing we're going to get a lot more hits focusing only on the electrical cord as a common element."

"It's unusual to switch routines like that," Abbie mused. "Some rapists might experiment at first, perfect their technique, but if you've got no trace evidence, it doesn't sound like this guy is a novice."

"He's not." Robel turned down a residential street. "He's been doing this a long time. Maybe he's escalating now. Maybe it takes more and more for him to get his jollies."

It was possible. For serial offenders, increasing the challenge also intensified their excitement. The last three victims of the Romeo rapist had been assaulted in their homes when there had been another family member in the house.

With that in mind, she asked, "Are there any uncleared homicides in the vicinity that share similarities to the rapes?"

He looked at her, but she couldn't guess what he was thinking with the glasses shielding his eyes. "Why?"

"He had to start somewhere." Abbie looked out the window at the row of small neat houses dotting the street. "A guy like this doesn't get to be an expert all at once." She turned back to Robel, found him still surveying her. "Maybe he went too far once and accidentally killed his victim. Or something could have gone wrong and he had to kill one who could identify him."

"Good thought." The words might have sounded like a compliment if they hadn't been uttered so grudgingly. "We checked that. Also looked at burglaries. Nothing panned out." But her remark seemed to have splintered the ice between them.

"I'm not surprised the burglary angle didn't turn up anything. This isn't an opportunity rapist. Sounds like he goes in very prepared, very organized. His intent is the rape itself, at least the ritual he's made of the act."

Ryne returned his attention to the street. "I'm still trying to figure out why he *doesn't* kill them. A guy with that much anger toward women, why keep them alive and chance leaving witnesses?" He was slowing, checking the house numbers.

She needed to familiarize herself with the file before she was close to doing a profile on the type of offender they were hunting. But she knew that wasn't what Robel was asking for. "Depends on his motivation. Apparently he doesn't need the victim's death to fulfill whatever twisted perversion he's got driving him."

"Maybe it's the difference in the punishment. Serial rapists don't face the death penalty, even in Georgia."

But Abbie shook her head. "He doesn't ever plan to get caught, so consequences don't mean much to him. He may be aware of them on some level, but not to the extent that they would deter him."

"I worked narcotics, undercover. Did a stint in burglary, a longer one in homicide." He pulled to a stop before a pale blue bungalow with an attached carport. Only one vehicle was in the drive. "I can understand the motivations of those crimes. Greed, jealousy, anger." Switching off the car, he removed the sunglasses and slid them back into their spot on the visor. "But I've never been able to wrap my mind around rapists. I know what it takes to catch them. I just don't pretend to understand why they do it."

Abbie felt herself thawing toward him a little. "Well, if we figure out what's motivating this guy, we'll be well on our way toward nailing him."

"I guess that's your job." Robel opened his door and stepped out into the street, reaching back inside the vehicle to retrieve his jacket. "You get in his head and point us in the right direction. That's what Dixon had in mind, isn't it?" He slammed the door, shrugging into his suit coat as he rounded the hood of the car.

Abbie opened her door, was immediately blasted by the midday heat. The rancor in his words had been barely discernible, but it was there. So she didn't bother telling him that getting inside the rapist's head was exactly what she planned on doing.

It was, in fact, all too familiar territory. She'd spent more years than she'd like to recall doing precisely that.

Kissing Midnight

THE FIRST BOOK IN THE FITZ CLARE CHRONICLES
BY *USA TODAY* BESTSELLING AUTHOR

EMMA HOLLY

Edmund Fitz Clare has been keeping secrets he can't afford to expose. Not to the orphans he's adopted. Not to the lovely young woman he's been yearning after for years, Estelle Berenger. He's an *upyr*—a shape-shifting vampire—desperate to redeem past misdeeds.

But deep in the heart of London a vampire war is brewing, a conflict that threatens to throw Edmund and Estelle together—and to turn his beloved human family against him...

penguin.com

M413T0209